Edward Armstrong

Elisabeth Farnes

Edward Armstrong

Elisabeth Farnes

ISBN/EAN: 9783337245719

Printed in Europe, USA, Canada, Australia, Japan

Cover: Foto ©Raphael Reischuk / pixelio.de

More available books at **www.hansebooks.com**

ELISABETH FARNESE

"THE TERMAGANT OF SPAIN"

BY

EDWARD ARMSTRONG, M.A.

FELLOW OF QUEEN'S COLLEGE, OXFORD

"Principessa di quelle doti che la rendono a tempi nostri degna di
ammirazione, ed a' posteri memorabile."
FRANCESCO VENIER.

"La reine était veritablement une folle furieuse elle a perdu
l'Espagne."
MARQUIS D'ARGENSON.

"Après tout c'est une bonne femme."
DUC DE NOAILLES.

LONDON

LONGMANS, GREEN, AND CO.

AND NEW YORK: 15 EAST 16th STREET

1892

ABBREVIATIONS. EDITIONS.

A.	Alberoni to Prince of Parma.
P. of P.	Prince of Parma to Alberoni.
C. F.	Carte Farnesiane. Archivio di Stato. Napoli.
R. O. S.	Record Office (Spain).
Brit. Mus. Add.	British Museum Additional MSS.
Alcalá.	Archivo General Central. Alcalá de Henares. Estado.
Relazioni (Bragadin and others). Relazioni. Senato III. (Secreta). Venezia.	

Villars.	Mémoires de Villars. Collection Petitot.
S. Simon.	Mémoires de S. Simon. Chéruel et Regnier. 20 vols. Paris, 1874.
	Papiers inédits. Lettres et dépêches sur l'ambassade d'Espagne. Drumont. Paris, 1880.
Montgon.	Mémoires de Montgon. 8 vols. Lausanne, 1753.
Louville.	Mémoires de Louville. 2 vols. Paris, 1818.
Noailles.	Mémoires de Noailles. Collection Petitot.
	Correspondance de Louis XV. et du Maréchal de Noailles. Rousset. 2 vols. Paris, 1865.
Richelieu.	Nouveaux Mémoires du Maréchal Duc de Richelieu. Lescure. 4 vols. Paris, 1869.
De Tessé.	Mémoires et Lettres du Maréchal de Tessé. 2 vols. Paris, 1806.
Mme. de Tessé.	Souvenirs de Frouillay de Tessé, Marquise de Crequy, 1710-1802. 7 vols. Paris, 1836.
D'Argenson.	Journal et Mémoires. Rathery. 9 vols. 1859-67.
	Le Marquis d'Argenson et le ministère des affaires étrangères du 18 Nov., 1744, au 10 Jan., 1747. Zevort. 1 vol. Paris, 1880.
	Études diplomatiques. Duc de Broglie. Revue des Deux Mondes. 1889-90.
S. Phelipe.	Comentarios de la guerra de España. 2 vols. Genova, N.D.
Campo Raso.	Memorias politicas y militares. 2 vols. Madrid, 1792.
Belando.	Historia Civil de España, 1700-33. 3 vols. Madrid, 1744.
Rel. Dip. Sav.	Bibliotheca Storica Italiana. Relazioni diplomatiche della Monarchia di Savoia. Periodo III. 2 vols. 1886-88.

Poggiali.   Memorie Storiche della città di Piacenza.   12 vols.   Piacenza, 1757-66.

Galuzzi.   Istoria del Granducato di Toscana.   9 vols.   Florence, 1781.

Carutti.   Storia della diplomazia della Corte di Savoia.   4 vols. Turin, 1875.

Von Arneth.   Prinz Eugen von Savoyen.   3 vols.   Vienna, 1869.

Baudrillart.   Philippe V. et la Cour de France.   2 vols.   Paris, 1890-91.

INTRODUCTION.

THE eighteenth century is remarkable for the number of its interesting or influential queens. If Queen Anne be taken as closing rather the previous generation, the age of the Stuarts and of Louis XIV., yet the importance of Caroline of Anspach upon English history must not be underrated. But upon the continent this peculiar feature of the century is more striking. The names of the Empress Maria Theresa, of Catherine of Russia, of Louisa of Prussia, and of Marie Antoinette, have all been deeply carved in history. Elisabeth Farnese is unquestionably less well known than the other queenly celebrities, and yet she hardly yields to them in importance. "The History so-called of Europe," wrote Carlyle, "went canting from side to side; heeling at a huge rate according to the passes and lunges these two giant figures, Imperial Majesty and the Termagant of Spain, made at one another for a twenty years or more." [1]

Elisabeth's career is indeed inferior in personal interest to that of the other four continental queens. This is due perhaps less to character than to the unsociable seclusion which her husband's eccentricity forced upon her. Her reign, moreover, falls mainly within the period which lies between the death of Anne and of Louis XIV., and the accession of Frederick

---

[1] *Frederick the Great*, v. 2.

the Great and of Maria Theresa, which is possibly the flattest level in the history of Europe. Such levels are conducive to material progress, but tiresome to the historical tourist, and good guide-books are consequently scarce. In Elisabeth the epic grandeur of Maria Theresa and Catherine of Russia, and the tragic pathos of Louisa of Prussia and Marie Antoinette, are alike wanting. The history of her married life sinks at times to monotonous Terentian comedy; it was, upon the surface, prosaically prosperous and undramatically dull. Yet her influence upon the fortunes of Europe for more than thirty years was undeniable. Within the limits assigned, she may be regarded as the leading personage; she caused at least the death of more soldiers and the drafting of more treaties than any one other potentate.

The marriage of Elisabeth Farnese to the King of Spain caused the renewal of the struggle between Bourbon and Hapsburg which the Treaties of Utrecht and Baden were meant to close. But the conflict takes a less majestic, less national, and more personal form. To win a heritage by war for the son of Elisabeth, to preserve a heritage by treaty for the daughter of Charles VI., or to combine the interests of the two children by marriage—such were the main problems of European politics.

Notwithstanding the personal aims of Elisabeth and of her chief opponent, the lack of domestic episode, and, it may be added, the mediocrity of character, renders her biography the history of a period rather than of a person; it is essentially a study in diplomacy, and the ministers are consequently often more prominent than the mistress. Yet it is a period which lends itself to biographical treatment, for in the exhaustion of national forces, and in the absence of national interests, the individual acquires unnatural importance. Europe was now as sensitive to diplomatic as she once had been to religious currents. Insulation was impossible when every nation had foreign rulers, when, in Lémontey's words,[1] in Spain was found an Italian Government, in England a German, in Poland a Russian, in Germany a Spanish, in Italy an Austrian, in Portugal an English, and in Russia everything but a Russian. Even in France under the regency the dominant ideas were English, and after the regent's death the Walpoles were believed to be more absolute across the Channel than at home.

Pure diplomacy has little attraction for Englishmen. It is natural, therefore, that no important work has been written in English upon the foreign history of the period stretching from the Treaty of Utrecht to the death of Charles VI. since Coxe published in 1813 his *Bourbon Kings of Spain*. It is just to add that from the value of this work time has detracted little. The number of documents also that has been edited in Europe in relation to the present subject is curiously small. It has been necessary, therefore, to rely mainly on unprinted sources. These are of course only too numerous. Coxe alone made a large collection of papers bearing more or less directly on the reign of Philip of Spain. The difficulty lies in selection. The warp of the present work may be said to consist in despatches written from the scene of action, from the Spanish Court. Into this have been woven threads from other

---

[1] *Histoire de la Regence*, i. 101.

contemporary documents, memoirs, or histories. The appearance of the first volume of M. Baudrillart's *Philippe V. et la Cour de France* led to the abandonment of a design to utilise the despatches of the French ambassadors at Madrid. These are of peculiar value, owing to the intimate relations of the writers to the Court in their quality of *ministres de famille*. On the other hand, at the close of Philip's reign Noailles confesses that not one had taken the trouble to make himself acquainted with the Spanish character and interests. This criticism cannot be applied to the more important of the English envoys, Methuen, Bubb, Colonel Stanhope, Schaub, Keene, and Lord Bristol, whose letters form the foundation of this work. Their despatches may be read in the Record Office, and are supplemented by their instructions from the home Government, and by the documents which they forward from the foreign office at Madrid, and by other information which they collect. The consuls' letters are also replete with interest of a more local and special character.

Two of the English ministers deserve a special mention. Colonel Stanhope, afterwards Lord Harrington, had an intimate knowledge of Spain, where he was appreciated both by Court and people. S. Simon and other foreign ambassadors speak of him with respect amounting to awe. He had the art of talking much and saying little. S. Simon describes him as inimitable at " pumping ". The Portuguese ambassador wondered at his patience in never interrupting his interlocutor. Reserved by nature, and taking his pleasures solemnly, he went into society from a sense of duty. He reduced the system of secret intelligence to a science ; monks and friars, says the Abbé Montgon, were among his favourite *employés* in this department. His embassy extended from October, 1717, to November, 1718, and from June, 1720, to March, 1727. In the absence of an English minister, caused by the siege of Gibraltar, the *lacuna* is supplied by the despatches of the Dutch envoy, Vandermeer, who acted for both the English and French Governments.

Benjamin Keene is an authority of no ordinary value, owing to his long residence in Spain before he was appointed envoy, and to the unusual number of years during which he held his appointment. He was of a good middle-class family, resident at King's Lynn, and was thus a constituent of Sir R. Walpole, to whom he owed his subsequent promotion.[1] He lived in Spain as tutor in a gentleman's family, then as South Sea agent and Consul General. Leaving Spain at the outbreak of hostilities in 1727, he returned in September of the same year, to receive shortly afterwards his appointment as minister. He incurred much unpopularity with the opposition in England by his signature of the Convention of 1739, but after the peace of Aix-la-Chapelle was again appointed to the embassy of Madrid, and remained there until his death in 1758.[2] He died at his post, vainly imploring his

---

[1] Keene's brother was the Bishop of Chester and of Ely, on whom Walpole conferred a benefice, that he might make a suitable husband for his own natural daughter. The new incumbent, however, kept the living but jilted the lady.

[2] "I cannot quit this chapter," wrote Horace Walpole, "without lamenting Keene. My father had the highest opinion of his abilities; . . . he had great wit, agreeableness, and an indolent good-humour that was very pleasing."—Letters iii. 122. Elsewhere Horace Walpole speaks of him as one of the best kind of agreeable men he ever saw, quite fat and easy, with universal knowledge.

careless Government to recall him, that he might die
in the country to which his eyes were always turned.
At once humorous and pathetic are his utterances on
the exile to which he was condemned; his letter to
M. Delafaye of May 30, 1732, may serve as an example.[1] "Do not mention Kensington, nor walks, nor
gardens, nor canals, to one whose eyes have been dried
up with staring upon a brown, parched country all his
life, or the very best part of it.   I shall fall sick like
the Swiss *de la maladie du Pais*, and want to be amongst
you.   The satisfaction, however, of being a little serviceable will always make me content to stay where
you think proper, though one who serves in Andalusia
may in several respects be lookt on as a burnt-offring."

Keene, like Stanhope, was most successful in the
department of secret intelligence, and was no doubt
assisted by his knowledge of Spanish character, and his
power of adapting himself to his company.   The Abbé
Montgon, who visited Gibraltar in his company, said
that he was made by nature to make friends, and admired the readiness with which at the garrison mess he
went through the list of toasts which was too long for
the abbé's idea of temperance.   With the Spanish
minister Patiño Keene lived always on the most friendly
terms, and the stolid Dutchman, Vandermeer, expressed
delight at his appointment.[2] The English sympathies of
the Spanish Court after the peace of Aix-la-Chapelle were
mainly due to Keene's endeavours.   Few public servants

[1] Keene had much regard for M. Delafaye, the secretary of the
Duke of Newcastle.   His confidential letters to him are perhaps even
more interesting than his despatches.

[2] "I have a real esteem for him, and am delighted that he has been
sent."—Vandermeer to Newcastle, Sept. 29, 1727. *R. O. S.*, 161.

have better deserved the knighthood, which was the tardy and sole reward for unremitting toil, an impaired fortune, and broken health.[1]

For the story of Elisabeth's marriage and for the first five years of her reign the correspondence of Alberoni and the Duke of Parma is of supreme importance, and yet it has hitherto not been utilised.[2] It exists in the Carteggio Farnesiano in the Archivio di Stato at Naples, whither the Farnese documents were taken by Don Carlos on his transference from Parma to the Two Sicilies. The value of these letters is due not only to the character of Alberoni, but to his unique position as being at once envoy of the Duke of Parma, and practically first minister of Spain. To realise the situation we may imagine Walpole as adding to his actual position the post of envoy to the Court of Anspach, and as describing in his despatches the results of his own ministry and the character of his queen and her surroundings. Alberoni's correspondence clears up much that has been a mystery, especially with regard to the marriage of Elisabeth, the expulsion of Madame des Ursins, and the real responsibility for the Sardinian and Sicilian expeditions. These letters are supplemented and continued by those of the Marquis Scotti, another Parmesan agent, which have some importance from his confidential relations to the queen. By both these envoys numerous documents relating to the Court and country were forwarded, which are frequently of value or interest.

[1] Keene's graceful monument, with its excellent medallion portrait, may be seen in S. Nicholas Church at Lynn.

[2] Signor A. Professione is now engaged in writing, mainly from this source, a sketch of the career of Alberoni.

The intrinsic value of these papers and the peculiar interest which attaches to the earlier period of Elisabeth's reign have induced me to give to it a somewhat disproportionate space. These first years are in fact decisive for the reign ; they exhibit the formation of Elisabeth's character, the direction of her aims, and the difficulties which their fulfilment encountered. Subsequent ministers were in great measure trained in Alberoni's school, and continued his methods.

The prejudice with which English and French ambassadors were apt to regard Elisabeth is best corrected by a knowledge of the Italian view of her aims and character. Mr. Horatio Brown has most kindly supplied me with copies of such portions of the *Relazioni* of the Venetian Ambassadors as bear more directly upon the subject. These comprise the complete *Relazione* of Bragadin, 1725, and parts of those of Erizzo, 1730 ; Da Lezze, 1733 ; Venier, 1735 ; Capello, 1738 ; Correr, 1742 ; Morosini, 1747 ; and Ruzini, 1754. These, though not entering into diplomatic details, are of interest as summing up at intervals the condition of the Spanish Court and Government, and as giving portraits of the royal family at different stages of their life.

M. Baudrillart has done excellent service by his report upon the treasures relating to this period which exist in the archives at Alcalá de Henares.[1] Mr. F. D. Swift generously interrupted his studies upon King James the Conqueror, and sacrificed the comparative comfort of Madrid to make researches at Alcalá in my behalf. He furnished me, among other material, with the letters proving Alberoni's renewed relations with

[1] *Archives des Misssions Scientifiques et Litteraires*, 1889, vol. cxv.

the Court of Madrid in 1726-27, and above all, with information relating to the secret treaty of Vienna of 1725. Señor Don F. Garcia has most kindly forwarded to me copies of documents relating to this treaty and to the Family Compact of 1733.

Among contemporary authorities which are to be found in print the Spanish writers are somewhat disappointing. The Marquis of S. Phelipe, a Sardinian by origin, was chiefly engaged in diplomatic missions away from home, and had not an accurate knowledge of Court life. He died in 1726, but his work was continued by Campo Raso up to 1742; part, however, of this continuation has been lost. More important, perhaps, is the *Historia Civil* of the Franciscan Belando, a rare book, for it was impounded by the Inquisition. It is dedicated to Elisabeth Farnese, and is written, except where the Jesuits are concerned, with moderation and sense, expressing, perhaps, the view of the average Spaniard, disliking foreigners, but not ill-disposed to the Government. It concludes in 1733. *The Life of Isabella Farnesio*, purporting to be written by an exiled adherent of the Prince of Asturias, is little more than a violent diatribe on the queen.

Within the last year has been published volume xciii. of the *Coleccion de Documentos Ineditos para la historia de España*, containing the diary of the Duke of Liria during his mission to Russia from 1727 to 1731, the object of which had not been previously clearly ascertained.[1]

It is much to be regretted that the MSS. Memoirs of Macanaz on the reign of Philip V. have not yet been

---

[1] For an account of this mission see *Quarterly Review*, January, 1892.

published by the Real Academia de la Historia, in whose possession they appear at present to be. The name of this great jurist is still honourably known in Spanish history, for R. Maldonado y Macanaz has contributed to the *Revista de España* valuable studies on Alberoni, and on "The Relation of France to Spain in the Eighteenth Century".

The connection of the two countries was so close even after the fall of Mme. des Ursins that the French memoirs of the period naturally dwell much on Spanish affairs, and interesting passages relating to Elisabeth's career may be found in almost all those which fall within this period, such as those of Barbier, Louville, the Duke of Richelieu, Marshal de Tessé, Madame de Tessé. Far more important, however, are those of S. Simon, Villars, Montgon, and D'Argenson. Of the merits of S. Simon it is scarcely necessary to speak. To the historian he is at times a dangerous guide, but his marvellous art of "seeing and making others see" gives him a supreme value in the eyes of a biographer. Apart from the period of his embassy to Spain he always treats Spanish affairs at considerable length and had a thorough knowledge of the Court.[1] The memoirs were composed from his papers in later life, and I have preferred to use, where possible, the letters and despatches written from Spain, published by E. Drumont, which give a yet more vivid and probably a more accurate picture of events.

---

[1] " Il faut avouer qu'il est remarquablement informé sur l'Espagne et qu'il s'est livré à des études aussi sérieuses qu' étendues sur les personnages, et institutions de ce pays. Les documents espagnols serviraient mieux que la plupart des documents Français sa reputation d'historien."—Baudrillart, *Philippe V.*, i. 31.

The memoirs of Montgon have been unduly depreciated on the ground that they were written from memory after the embargo laid on his papers by Fleury, and highly coloured by vanity and prejudice. M. Baudrillart, however, has found his accuracy confirmed during his researches at Alcalá, and I have independently arrived at the same conclusion from a perusal of Stanhope's and Keene's despatches in the Record Office, where several of his own letters are also to be found. Montgon was on terms of such close intimacy with the royal family that his information, granting his accuracy, is of peculiar value.

Large use has been made of the memoirs of Villars. The marshal had a special interest in the Court of Spain, with which he was at times in correspondence. Apart from the interest of his opinions on the relations of France and Spain, he embodies in his notes of the meetings of Council a short *précis* of the despatches from Madrid. The admirable edition of the Marquis of Vogüé has unfortunately not advanced sufficiently far to be available for this period. On the other hand, Anquetil, from whom the editions of Petitot and Michaud Poujoulat are drawn, became tired of his mutilations before the year 1723, after which date the memoirs are, for historical purposes, substantially unaffected.

The racy doctrinairism of the Marquis d'Argenson adds to the interest, if it sometimes detracts from the historical value of his memoirs. This very quality, however, became an important political factor between November, 1744, and January, 1747, during which he was Minister for Foreign Affairs. Owing to the want of Spanish authorities for this period, and the withdrawal of the

English embassy from Madrid, D'Argenson becomes our chief authority. His memoirs receive valuable illustration from his correspondence with Vauréal, French minister at Madrid, published by Zevort, and from a series of articles from the pen of the Duc de Broglie in the *Revue des Deux Mondes* for 1889 and 1890. It must be borne in mind that both D'Argenson and Vauréal were avowedly hostile to Elisabeth Farnese and her system. The so-called memoirs and correspondence of Marshal Noailles serve as a corrective to this prejudice.

Inasmuch as Elisabeth's reign affected Italy as closely as it did Spain, Italian authorities are of importance. The early part of the reign is illustrated by the correspondence of the Savoyard ambassadors at Paris,[1] and by the *Relazione* of Del Maro, Savoyard minister at Madrid, published by Carutti.[2] Foscarini in his *Storia Arcana* gives a vivid picture of Italy under Imperial rule previous to 1733. Buonamici's work upon the later Italian war is well-nigh a classic, and has been translated into English. Poggiali, the historian of Piacenza, was contemporary with the queen, and Galuzzi, the historian of the Grand Duchy of Tuscany, was but little later. The reign of Don Carlos has been described at length by Beccatini. Among the modern authors to whom I am indebted, several have already been mentioned. The letters given by Von Arneth in his *Prinz Eugen* are of high importance for the episodes of the Imperial alliance, the mission of

---

[1] Biblioteca Storica Italiana. *Relazioni diplomatiche della Corte di Savoia.* Francia Periodo III., vols. i. ii., 1886-88.

[2] *R. Accad. delle scienze di Torino.* Serie II., vol. ix.

Königsegg, and the widening breach leading to the war of 1733. An admirable monograph on the Quadruple Alliance was published by O. Weber in 1887. Carutti has lavished the documentary treasures at his disposal upon his *Storia della diplomazia della Corte di Savoia*, which is indispensable for an undertaking of the important relations between the Courts of Madrid and Turin. The first volume of Baudrillart's *Philippe V. et la cour de France* has appeared within the last year.[1] It deals at present with but one year of Elisabeth's reign, but it is doubtless destined to be the standard authority upon Philip V. Had it appeared earlier, I should have hesitated to undertake the present task ; it is perhaps equally difficult to precede or to follow such a work. It is almost unnecessary to state that the eloquent and readable general history of Spain, by Lafuente, has been a constant companion.

I have thought it hardly necessary to enumerate all English authors who are of utility for this period, though it may be worth while to point to the running commentary furnished by the *Annual Register* and the *Gentleman's Magazine*, both which sprang into existence within its first few years. The harvest stored by Coxe in his *Kings of Spain*, and in his memoirs of Lord Walpole and Sir R. Walpole, is at once to be admired and grudged by a gleaner in the same field.

It was originally intended that this volume should be accompanied by a history of Maria Theresa from another hand. Apart, therefore, from the failure of the English ambassadors' reports, the years succeeding the death of the Emperor Charles VI. have been intention-

---

[1] The second volume appeared in 1891, since the MS. left my hands. I have therefore been able to make but slight use of it.

ally treated on a slighter scale, inasmuch as the empress queen becomes the more prominent figure in European history.   My efforts have accordingly been chiefly limited to pointing out the diversity of the views of the Spanish queen and the French minister with regard to the future of Italy.   I must express my sincere gratitude to Miss F. Armstrong, my industrious fellow-worker in the Record Office and at Naples, to Mr. H. Brown and Mr. F. D. Swift for the services already mentioned, to Count Ugo Balzani for much valuable information and advice, and to the Commendatore Capasso for unceasing kindness during researches in the Archivio di Stato at Naples, over which he presides with so much ability.   The officials of the Literary Search Room in the Record Office must be weary of hearing that, in attention to their visitors' needs, they set up a model of all that a Public Office should be.

November 1, 1890.

TABLE OF CONTENTS.

PAGE

Introduction, ... vii.-xx.

CHAPTER I., 1692-1714.

Elisabeth's Ancestry—Childhood, Early Letters and Education—
Parma during the War of Succession—Prospects and Suitors, . 1-7

CHAPTER II., 1714.

Character of Philip V.—Influence of Mme. des Ursins—Proposals
for the King's Re-marriage—Alberoni suggests the Princess of
Parma—He Wins Mme. des Ursins—Elisabeth becomes Queen
of Spain—Alberoni's advice as to her Future Conduct—Growing
Jealousy of Mme. des Ursins—Elisabeth's Journey to Spain—
Her Meeting with Alberoni—The Chaplain Maggiali—The In-
terview with Mme. des Ursins—Elisabeth Meets her Husband
—Mme. des Ursins is Expelled from Spain, ... 8-33

CHAPTER III., 1715.

Effects of the War of Succession upon Spain—Possibilities of Reorganisation—Elisabeth's Mastery over her Husband—Alberoni's
Criticisms upon Elisabeth—The Love Affair of Maggiali—Arrival
of Laura Pescatori—Elisabeth's Character and Daily Life—Relations of Spain to France and to Italy—Changes in the Government—The French Court and Alberoni—Philip and the French
Succession—Prospects of War with England—Death of Louis
XIV., ... 34-57

CHAPTER IV., 1715-16.

Philip and the French Regency—Rising Power of Alberoni—Influence
of the Duke of Parma—Elisabeth's Italian Ambitions—Condition
of Italy—Hostility of Spain to the Emperor—Prospects of
Spanish Intervention in Italy—A Spanish Squadron at Corfu—
Louville's Mission to Madrid—Commercial Treaty with England
—Treaty of Westminster—Reconciliation of Spain and the
Papacy, ... 58-83

CHAPTER V., 1717-18.

PAGE

Arrest of Molines—Conquest of Sardinia—Its Value to Spain—Policy
of Lord Stanhope—The Triple Alliance—Attempts at Mediation
—Policy of the Regent and of the King of Sicily—Alberoni's
Reforms—His Relations with Russia, Sweden, and Turkey—The
King's Illness, ...   84-109

CHAPTER VI., 1718-19.

Invasion of Sicily—Battle of Cape Passaro—Rupture with England,
France and the Papacy—French Invasion of Spain—The Fall
of Alberoni, ...   110-125

CHAPTER VII., 1720-23.

Ilicultics of Peace—Proposed Cession of Gibraltar—Treaties with
England and France—The French Marriages—French Influence
at Madrid—Philip's Abdication, ...   126-137

CHAPTER VIII., 1720-23.

Increased Influence of Elisabeth—S. Simon's Mission to Spain—His
Description of the Court—Daily Life of the King and Queen—
Elisabeth's Character—Her Unpopularity—The Italian Party at
Madrid—The Spanish Adherents of the Queen, ...   138-158

CHAPTER IX., 1724.

Reasons of Philip's Abdication—The Royal Retreat at S. Ildefonso—
Government of King Luis—Character of the Young King and
Queen—Death of Luis—Philip and Elisabeth Resume the
Government, ...   159-168

CHAPTER X., 1724-26.

Rumours of Alberoni's Recall—Elisabeth Leans towards an Imperial
Alliance—Rise of Ripperdá—His Mission to Vienna—The In-
fanta's Betrothal Annulled—Breach with France—Treaty of
Vienna—Hostility to France and England—Alliance of Hanover
—The Secret Articles of Vienna—Return of Ripperdá—Intrigues
with the Pretender—Alliance with Russia—Administration of
Ripperdá—His Disgrace, ...   169-199

CHAPTER XI., 1726-28.

sabeth and her Ministers—Ascendancy of Königsegg—The King's
Confessors—Rupture with England—Blockade of Porto Bello and
Siege of Gibraltar—The Spanish Party in France—Mission of
Montgon to Paris—The Preliminaries of Vienna—Elisabeth's
Hostility to England—Convention of the Pardo, ...   200-221

CHAPTER XII., 1728-29.

PAGE

Congress of Soissons—Proposals for Cession of Gibraltar—Elisabeth's Disappointment with regard to the Imperial Marriages—Her Coolness towards the Court of Vienna—Negotiations with France and England—Rise of Patiño—Treaty of Seville, . 222-239

CHAPTER XIII., 1729-31.

Recall of Königsegg—Delay in the Execution of the Treaty of Seville —Differences between France and England—Spain Hampers English Commerce and Threatens Gibraltar—Death of the Duke of Parma—Don Carlos' Succession to the Italian Duchies—The Second Treaty of Vienna—Don Carlos Sails to Italy—Elisabeth's Success, ... 240-258

CHAPTER XIV., 1726-31.

Philip's Illness—Danger of his Abdication—The Portuguese Marriages —The Court in the South of Spain, ... 259-270

CHAPTER XV., 1732.

Don Carlos in Italy—Threatened Rupture with the Emperor—The Expedition to Oran—Diplomatic Struggle between England and France—Prospects of Alliance between Spain and France—Commercial Disputes with England—The Commission of Claims —Philip's Malady, ... 271-294

CHAPTER XVI., 1733-34.

The Polish Succession—Imperial Administration in Italy—Alliance of Spain and France—Treaty of the Escurial—Alliance of France and Sardinia—Treaty of Turin—Ill-feeling between Spain and Sardinia—Conquest of Naples and Sicily by Don Carlos—Siege of Mantua—The Preliminaries of Vienna, ... 295-306

CHAPTER XVII., 1733-35.

Diplomacy during the War—Separate Negotiations of Spain with the Emperor—Preliminaries of Vienna between the Emperor and France—Indignation of the Spanish Court—Rupture with the Pope and with Portugal—Autocracy of Elisabeth—Administration of Patiño, ... 307-326

CHAPTER XVIII., 1736-37.

Spain Assents to the Preliminaries of Vienna—Death of Patiño—Ministry of La Quadra—Advances towards England—The Court at S. Ildefonso—Arrival of Farinelli—Betrothal of Don Carlos to Maria Amelia of Saxony, ... 327-344

CHAPTER XIX., 1738-39.

PAGE

Commercial Relations with England—Colonial Activity of Spain—Agitation in England—The Right of Search—The Convention respecting Claims—Its Rejection by the Opposition in England—Declaration of War—The Spanish-French Marriages—Aversion of Spaniards to the Rupture with England—Events of the War—The Policy of Fleury and the Opinions of D'Argenson, . . 345-360

CHAPTER XX., 1740-46.

Death of the Emperor Charles VI.—Claims of Philip and Elisabeth—War of Austrian Succession—The Spaniards in Italy—Effects of Fleury's Death upon the War—Treaty of Worms—Family Compact of Fontainebleau—Gallo-Spanish Campaigns in Italy—Disaccord between French and Spanish Courts—Vauréal's Embassy to Madrid—His Character of Elisabeth—D'Argenson's Policy in Italy—Separate Convention between France and Sardinia—Indignation in Spain—Mission of Noailles—Death of Philip V., ... 361-387

CHAPTER XXI., 1746-66.

Accession of Ferdinand VI.—Treaty of Aix-la-Chapelle—Parma and Piacenza are awarded to Don Philip—Elisabeth's Retirement at S. Ildefonso—Her Intrigues at the French and Spanish Courts—Death of Ferdinand VI.—Elisabeth's Regency—Arrival of Charles III. in Spain—Final Withdrawal of Elisabeth from Court—Her Death, ... 388-396

CONCLUSION.

Estimate of the Historical Importance of Elisabeth's Career, . . 397-399

ELISABETH FARNESE.

CHAPTER I.

1692-1714.

ELISABETH'S ANCESTRY—CHILDHOOD, EARLY LETTERS AND
EDUCATION—PARMA DURING THE WAR OF SUCCESSION
—PROSPECTS AND SUITORS.

ILLUSTRIOUS blood flowed in the veins of Elisabeth Farnese,
for Europe's highest dignitaries, both spiritual and temporal,
had contributed to her existence. She was the descendant
of the last European emperor and the last Renaissance pope.
But the fount heads of the race were not unpolluted. The
Farnesi owed their fortunes to the marriage of a bastard
daughter of Charles V. to a son of the bastard of Paul III.
Their territory of Parma and Piacenza had been in its origin,
and had again latterly become, a buffer state between Papacy
and Empire. It was indeed recognised as a Papal fief, but it
had been detached from that group of municipalities, which
had been crystallised into a state under the rule of the Dukes
of Milan. It was therefore always liable to the revival of
imperial claims.

Alexander of Parma had alone, perhaps, personally added
lustre to the family. The race had been chiefly remarkable
for its domestic tragedies; and in later days for its abnormal
fatness and its peculiar marriages. Elisabeth's grandfather
had married two sister princesses of Modena; her mother

. B

wedded two brother princes of Parma. The arguments for marriage with a deceased wife's sister were equally applicable to union with a dead husband's brother.

The future Queen of Spain was the child of the first of these two husbands, Odoardo, eldest son of Duke Ranuccio II. Her mother was Dorothea Sophia, daughter of Philip William, Elector Palatine, and sister of the widowed queen of Charles II. of Spain, and of the mother of the Emperors Joseph and Charles.

The child was born on October 25, 1692, and was christened Elisabetta. In the following year her little brother was buried from his cradle, and within a short space she also lost her father. "He ceased to live," writes Poggiali, the historian of Piacenza, "on the morning of September 6, stifled so to speak by his own weight, and suffocated by his extraordinary fatness. He was bewailed by all and especially by his wife, who loved him with a depth and tenderness uncommon in any class, and certainly not easily to be found in princely married life." S. Simon's description of his daughter's more pleasing traits recalls the father's character as related to Poggiali by one who knew him intimately. He possessed gifts which were in the highest degree calculated to win hearts. Among these were a peculiar friendliness in general intercourse, and a ready wit. He was marvellously sprightly in his jokes and repartees.

Little as is known of Elisabeth's early life, the short accounts of the Court of Parma throw light upon her future character. She seems to have combined some of the characteristics of all her near relatives. The great Duke Ranuccio died when she was two years old, but his name must have been a household word throughout her girlhood. He too was bright and fond of amusement, devoted to music and the theatre, never weary of welcome to actors and musicians. Yet he was untainted by the irreligion and impropriety of his age. No word that was immodest or profane was heard upon the boards at Parma. It may have been from him that his grand-daughter inherited her boasted

propriety, her passion for building, her interest in manufactures, and her patronage of religious orders. Ranuccio
was regarded as the ideal *Padre di Famiglia.* His son
Francesco on his succession was barely seventeen, but was
serious and old for his age. In 1696 he married his brother's
widow, who was eight years his senior. The wedding was
naturally quiet. It was thought a pity that Dorothea, with
her influential relations and her substantial dowry, should
leave the family. It was hoped that she would give an heir
to the Farnesi ; but, notwithstanding the aid of the baths of
S. Maurizio, she lived with her husband thirty years and
was childless. The duchess was a lady of religious tendencies
and serious tastes. The duke was eager to propitiate her ;
for she shared with her sister of Spain an unrivalled and untiring capacity for nagging. Her temper, moreover, was not
reliable ; and in later years, during the stormy negotiations
for succession to the duchy, Benjamin Keene speaks of her
as proving herself to be the genuine mother of her daughter.
Strained relations between girls and their mothers are not
peculiar to the last quarter of the nineteenth century. Elisabeth entertained for the duchess, at most, a decorous regard.
During her early years in Spain, the Duke of Parma constantly entreated Alberoni, his envoy at Madrid, to induce
the queen to write more often to her mother and to resist
the temptation of what schoolboys call a score. For her
step-father Elisabeth had a constant and unbounded affection, which was not without its influence upon European
politics. Alberoni more than once says that he was the only
living person for whom she cared. She would ask him to
show her a miniature of the duke which he possessed, and
her eyes would fill with tears. It was he that received
and preserved the little girl's childish letters, from which
the sand still falls which she had sprinkled. Her first
literary effort is dated December 12, 1698, when she was
six years old. A heroine's first letter is perhaps always
worth transcribing, even if the composition be not quite
original.

" My Most Serene Lord and most respected uncle,

" I cannot better employ the first fruits of my pen than in wishing your Highness happiness at the Holy Christmas-tide. May it please your Highness to accept my duty and to give me the proof of it by presenting me with many opportunities of serving you, professing myself to be your Highness'

" Most affectionate niece and servant,

" ELISABETTA FARNESE.

" Parma, December 12, 1698." [1]

It is gratifying to find that such Christmas letters were more substantially acknowledged by the tender-hearted uncle. Two years later the child's style is more natural, and it is she that has a gift to offer to her uncle.

" My Most Serene Lord and most respected uncle,

" To give your Highness a proof of my respect, I present your Highness with one of my teeth, as being the dearest part of myself, begging your Highness to give in exchange for the gift the favour of your commands, and to believe me your Highness'

" Most affectionate niece and servant,

" ELISABETTA FARNESE.

" Parma, July 6, 1700." [2]

Elisabeth's handwriting in early youth was peculiarly clear and legible, but deteriorated in after-life. The question of her intellectual attainments is somewhat difficult. Poggiali eulogises the sprightliness of her intellect and the extraordinary directness of her thought. She could speak and write Latin, French, and German. After studying grammar, rhetoric, philosophy, and the use of the globes, she would spend many hours a day over her books, religious, historical or biographical. Her step-father speaks of her great abilities

[1] *Arch. Nap.*, C. F. 361.   [2] *Ibid.*

in his confidential letters to Alberoni. It is possible, how--
ever, that she was over-educated, for the latter complains of
her indolence and lack of interests. S. Simon's evidence on
this point is perhaps conclusive. Her education he represents as being that of a *pensionnaire* from an inferior *pension;*
she possessed no intellectual tastes and never acquired them.
She resembled the schoolboy who knew nothing and never
wanted to know more. Her reading in after-life was limited
to religious books. Her total ignorance of politics was of
great disadvantage to her throughout her career, and she
lacked the industry to acquire a knowledge of the details of
government. Great pains, however, had been bestowed
upon accomplishments. She had been most fortunate in her
dancing master, a Frenchman; she had been taught paint-
ing by Pierantonio Avanzini. Music was always a delight
to her; but her favourite employment was embroidery.

The girl was strictly brought up, confined, says S. Simon,
to an attic in the palace of Parma. It would be pleasant to
connect her early years with the villa in the sleepy, old-
fashioned garden across the river, dear to the tourist tired
with Correggio and Toschi. The enlargement of this villa
into a palace was due to a later date, and the Court seems
more often to have resided at Piacenza, in the great, square,
red palace just beyond the town,—now redolent with bar-
rack smells and strident with neophyte buglers, its stately
gardens trampled into dust by the goose-step of generations
of recruits. In Italy a "military centre" is the monotonous modern fate of the great royal and religious houses of
the past.

With the accession of Francesco and the outbreak of the
War of Spanish Succession, Court life became less gay if more
eventful. The musicians and buffoons were discharged, the
ducal revenues, or such as were left after imperial exactions,
were lavished on blue uniforms for the Irish Horse Guards
and on visits of ceremony to the princes and generals who
were brought by the war to Italy. Among these was
Elisabeth's future husband, who, in April, 1702, invited her
step-father to half-an-hour at cards. Shortly before her

marriage she must have danced with another relation of the future, Frederick Augustus of Saxony, who was entertained at a splendid ball, that being his favourite pastime. It was noticed that though still a Protestant he was accompanied by able instructors in the true faith.

The towns of Parma and Piacenza were saved from the worst horrors of war partly by the prudent hedging of their duke, partly by the protection afforded by the Papal standards. Yet the French and imperial armies were constantly marching through the territory and lived at free quarters on the inhabitants. Italy did not at first sight appreciate her modern ally, the Pomeranian grenadier. In 1711 the duchy groaned beneath 6000 Prussian soldiers, to whom quarters were assigned by the uncompromising Daun. These, writes Poggiali, were "the most turbulent, undisciplined, and bestial people that Italy had seen for a long time, loathed to the last degree by the Italians, who had fatal experience of their licentiousness and barbarism".[1]

Shortly before this event, during a quarrel between Church and Empire, the duke was ordered to receive the investiture of his dominions as an imperial fief, an appurtenance of the Duchy of Milan. A peace was patched up between the litigants, and the matter was referred to a sleeping commission, to become in after years a subject of no slight importance to Elisabeth Farnese. Notwithstanding the duke's game of cards with Philip of Anjou, he was ultimately forced to take the imperial side, and all intercourse was suspended between the Courts of Spain and Parma. Alberoni, however, represented to Philip that the duke was acting under the immediate compulsion of the German soldiery and against his will, and the Spanish *chargé d'affaires* was suffered to remain at Parma, though without official character. It was for this service that Alberoni received the title of count. The fact is of moment, as showing his belief in anti-Austrian sympathies in Italy, on which his future policy was based. The young princess also, notwithstanding her

---

[1] Poggiali, x. 264.

imperial connections, must have longed for the liberation of Italy from the barbarian, and many of her future diatribes are the echo of these early troubles.

Sickness followed in the wake of war. Elisabeth escaped the plague, but was attacked by small-pox of so virulent a type that, notwithstanding her strong constitution, she ran grave peril of death, and her face remained notably scarred. The malady which marred her beauty went nigh to mar her matrimonial prospects. But she was not void of substantial attractions, and, therefore, not without her suitors. Her uncle Antonio was developing the family fatness in celibate comfort. Steps had been taken to induce the Pope to provide for succession to the duchy in the female line, and there were prospects slightly more remote of the reversion of the Grand Duchy of Tuscany. The Prince of Piedmont and her cousin, the heir of the Duke of Modena, were said to be both negotiating for her hand. Had the former match been realised much future history might have been forestalled. A marriage seems at one time to have been actually arranged with the Prince Pio della Mirandola, a collateral descendant of the Phœnix Pico. The prince, however, might well be regarded as a detrimental, for he had been robbed of his principality by the Austrian Government, and was a mere officer in Spanish service. For him Elisabeth always entertained a warm regard, which she generously extended to his wife.

More need not be said of the early life of the young princess, before the King of Spain's unexpected proposal was disclosed to her in her twenty-second year.

CHAPTER II.

1714.

CHARACTER OF PHILIP V.—INFLUENCE OF MME. DES URSINS—PROPOSALS FOR THE KING'S RE-MARRIAGE—ALBERONI SUGGESTS THE PRINCESS OF PARMA—HE WINS MME. DES URSINS—ELISABETH BECOMES QUEEN OF SPAIN—ALBERONI'S ADVICE AS TO HER FUTURE CONDUCT—GROWING JEALOUSY OF MME. DES URSINS—ELISABETH'S JOURNEY TO SPAIN—HER MEETING WITH ALBERONI—THE CHAPLAIN MAGGIALI—THE INTERVIEW WITH MME. DES URSINS—ELISABETH MEETS HER HUSBAND—MME. DES URSINS IS EXPELLED FROM SPAIN.

PHILIP V. had won his kingdom at the cost of his brave Savoyard queen. Peace came too late to save the poor little warrior. Danger and fatigue and the exigencies of the most affectionate and least considerate of husbands had worn out a system naturally frail. She died on February 14, 1714, in her twenty-sixth year. Yet she had lived too long. Her subservience to Mme. des Ursins had cooled the enthusiasm of the Spaniards. She had spent herself for Spain, and was said to be ready to sell Spain to Savoy. She was more regretted at Paris than Madrid. The story is told that as her remains were being carried to the Escurial the procession passed near Philip and his hunt. He followed the funeral train with his eyes until it was out of sight, and then turned to pursue the chase. Well might S. Simon believe that princes are not made like other folk. The king was extremely touched, " mais un peu à la royale ".

(8)

Philip's re-marriage became at once the subject of European speculation. It occurred to no one that, as the king had three sons, the alternative of widowerhood was open to him and that an immediate marriage was neither necessary nor decent. It was accepted on all sides that a wife must be found, and that at once. On this head his doctor and his confessor were at accord with the man in the street. The subject is not savoury, but even biography must at times surrender the impressionist standard and capitulate to realism. Upon Philip's uxorious proclivities depends the story of Elisabeth Farnese and the history of Europe for many years. His contemporaries marked with wonder that the grandson of the great king could be content with nothing less than marriage. His conscience was unconvinced by his grandfather's example that the strictest principles may be mitigated by a somewhat easy practice. Philip combined with a character incredibly sensuous a conscience abnormally scrupulous. This combination was the tragedy of his life and of that of others. His first separation from his wife during his Italian campaign had caused those black vapours which modern medical men would dub hysteria, and laymen madness. It is a topic at once to be remembered and for-gotten. This much, however, may be said, that Philip's devotion to another was but a form of his self-love; he loved his queen because he was ill at ease without her. He was by nature the tyrant and the slave of woman. However many wives had died he would have married more, and would have been a model of troublesome attachment to all in turn. Of sentiment there was little, of self-sacrifice none. His affection, as his courage, has been called a mere brute instinct. Yet all honour to a tender conscience in an age of thick-skinned morals!

Philip's peculiarities being well known, the match-making parents of Europe were at once upon the alert. But *beati sunt possidentes;* Mme. des Ursins being in full possession seemed likely to be the happy woman of the king's choice. She took him to the Medina Celi Palace and occupied her-self the adjoining house. Spaniards were scandalised by seeing a corridor hastily erected on a Sunday between the two buildings. No Spaniards were allowed to see him; the gentlemen of his bed-chamber loudly complained of their exclusion. She appointed "recreators" to watch his movements and distract his mind. "I heard from the princess this morning," wrote Alberoni[1] on April 9, "that the king will not go to form the siege of Barcelona. In one word, she is not willing to lose sight of him."[2] Such a marriage seemed not impossible. Philip was the creature of habit, and he had been for years accustomed to obey the princess. In early days he had made Telemaque his ideal, and when he went to Spain the Duchess of Orleans had prophesied that he would soon find his Minerva. The princess had indeed acted as his brain. She was old, but with her back to the light she did not look her years. Her figure was well preserved, her features assisted by the resources of art. Although clever, she was also agreeable. Gossips at Paris said that the mysterious mission of Cardinal del Giudice to Paris was preliminary to the announcement of the marriages of Mme. de Maintenon and her friend to the Kings of France and Spain.[3] But Philip probably had other views. The story may be true that when his confessor told him the news from Paris of his intended marriage he replied: "No, not quite that," and turned brusquely away. As to the intentions of the princess, Alberoni was probably correct when he wrote: "This lady governs the king despotically, and will not let him marry unless she sees an absolute necessity, and if she lets him marry it will be with whom she chooses and with whom she believes that her hold on the government will be more secure".[4]

Of other candidates there was no lack.[5] The Duke of

---

[1] Alberoni, after the death of his patron Vendôme, resided at Madrid as agent for the Duke of Parma.

[2] *Arch. Nap.*, C. F. 54.

[3] Perrone to King of Sicily, July 12, 1714. *Rel. Dip. Sav.*, p. 189.

[4] *Arch. Nap.*, C. F. 54.

[5] Perrone wrote from Paris to the Duke of Savoy, on February 26, that a marriage with a French or Bavarian princess was already discussed.

Parma was early in the field. In his first letter after the queen's death, he asked his agent to tell him whether the king was inclined to marry again, and if so, what princesses were proposed and what considerations would determine the result. Alberoni replied that from the first instant of the queen's death he had been upon the watch to further with all his ability any inclinations which might seem favourable. He had already descanted on the actual charms and the probable gratitude of his young mistress, and had pressed that a small portrait might immediately be sent by post, and that a larger one should follow. His letters confirm the general truth of Poggiali's anecdote that the first mention of the Princess of Parma was made on the day of the queen's funeral. Mme. des Ursins and Alberoni were watching the procession from a window. They discussed the necessity of marrying the king at once. The princess named almost every suitable *parti* in Europe, but Alberoni, who had already made his choice, found exception to each in turn; the new queen must, he said, be quiet and docile, disinclined to interfere in government, and incapable of taking umbrage at the authority which the princess enjoyed. Asked where such a princess could be found, the existence of Elisabeth Farnese seemed suddenly to occur to him. He mentioned her name coldly and between his lips, adding that she was a good-natured Lombard girl, fattened on butter and Parmesan cheese, brought up in homely fashion, and had heard nothing talked about but trimmings, embroidery, and linen. It is to this not very refined remark that Elisabeth, perhaps, owed her fortunes; Alberoni's own had been due to a yet broader and coarser touch.[1]

The precise sequence of events is traced by Alberoni's own hand. The first conversation on the subject was certainly

[1] Filippo Bellardi, who in matters relating to Alberoni seems to have curiously detailed information, tells much the same tale, adding that the sentence to this effect was afterwards repeated by the king to his young wife in Alberoni's presence. He states that Philip's marriage was discussed on the day following the queen's death, and that on the ensuing Friday Alberoni proposed Elisabeth Farnese. *Sbozzo della vita del Card. Alberoni.* Ambrosiana MS., 178 *sup.*

considerably previous to April 9, and in the last week of July
success was assured. The removal of rival candidates was
due as much to the jealousy of Mme. des Ursins as to the
ability and insinuations of Alberoni. A princess of Portugal
was proposed, and this would have pleased the Pan-Iberian
sentiments of the Spaniards. But it was understood that
she was a young lady who had her own opinions, and it
would be moreover impossible to exclude Portuguese servants
and favourites from the Court. The daughter of the widowed Queen of Poland offered insufficient advantages, and
was debarred by her relationship to the royal house of France.
Extreme jealousy of French influence proved an obstacle to
the prospects of Mlle. de Clermont, sister of the Duke of
Bourbon. A most dangerous rival, however, was the
daughter of the Elector of Bavaria. Louis XIV. wrote to
the duke asking for a description of his daughter. He,
naturally, replied that she had a pretty complexion, a most
beautiful neck and an excellent education—a collocation of
characteristics which, *mutatis mutandis,* recalls the qualifications of an All Souls' fellow in olden days. Mme. des Ursins,
however, assured Alberoni that she was very ugly, and this
he capped by informing her, on medical authority, that she
was ill-formed and unlikely to bear children. Nevertheless,
the Bavarian ambassador, "a most solemn Tyrolese and as
sly as the devil," was in constant intercourse with Mme. des
Ursins; and the Spaniards, seeing which way the wind was
setting, paid him unremitting attention. The princess, however, assured the Parmesan agent that she could not bear the
man. Moreover, she feared that the duke might exchange
his dominions for Flanders, which would form a bar to her
ambitions.[1]

It remained to press the claims of the Princess of Parma.
Alberoni felt sure of the support of those who were in closest
contact with the king—his confessor, his doctor, his first
equerry, the Cardinal Giudice. If the matter were discussed
at Council, his ally, the Marquis of Bedmar, would carry

[1] She was at this time hoping for a principality in the Netherlands as her
reward for consenting to the general pacification.

every vote for Elisabeth Farnese. But this general favour
among the Spaniards was likely to excite the jealousy of the
princess ; and she was king and queen at once : if she could
not single-handed make a marriage, she could single-handed
mar it. On her, therefore, Alberoni lavished his attentions.
He paid constant visits to the Pardo ; her retinue, when in
Madrid, could rely upon a place at Alberoni's table, and
rarely left without a present. From the first the princess
seemed not disinclined to the choice of Elisabeth. On May
7 Alberoni wrote that she had been questioning him with
great curiosity as to the person and accomplishments of the
Princess of Parma. " She told me that she had heard that
she was red-haired. I replied that the picture which I had at
home represented her as having fair hair. She asked if she
could dance and whether she knew modern languages. I
said that she might feel sure that she possessed both accomplishments, as I knew that she had had masters from her
earliest years, and that her dancing master was a Frenchman. She asked particularly if the marks left by the small-
pox were deep or superficial, and whether they had caused
any little unsightliness. After all this talk, she repeated that
she wished to be fully informed for the sake of any emer-
gency that might occur, but that I must not draw any conclusions from it." [1] On another occasion the princess inquired as to the reversionary claims of the Princess of Parma
upon Portugal ; Alberoni replied that he believed that the
two claimants were the King of Spain and his mistress, and
that the latter was descended from the elder line. But the
essential point was to prove that Elisabeth Farnese would
serve the ambitions and bow to the authority of Mme. des
Ursins. She alone would recognise, urged Alberoni, that
she owed her throne to the princess and no other. She
alone, in accordance with the most affectionate of hearts and
the sweetest of dispositions, would cause the princess to end
her days with lustre and respect, with authority and tranquillity of mind ; she might rest assured that she would

[1] *Arch. Nap.*, C. F. 54.

come to Spain unaccompanied, and that the influence of the princess would be undivided; the Duke of Parma would consent to any conditions which she might suggest. On June 25 Alberoni was able to send satisfactory intelligence. " The lady still seems disposed to believe that the Princess of Parma is the one who is likely to suit her own convenience best, and this is the nail on which I hammered at the first and on which I ceaselessly continue to hammer; for I can assure your Highness that it is useless to introduce any other motive. I have depicted her as a good-natured Lombard girl, devoid of temper, all heart, of a character naturally sweet and manageable—just such, in fact, as she desires; and who, apart from the gratitude which she would owe, would be under the absolute necessity of abandoning herself entirely to her guidance. Your Highness must believe that, with the perfect and intimate knowledge which I possess of the lady's character, I have not neglected to win her by all the means which would gratify her sensibilities and conduce to bringing about a good result; to do the rest is in God's hands." [1]

At the very last moment Alberoni feared that his project would be wrecked by the arrival of the French envoy, d'Aubigny, who had great influence over Mme. des Ursins, and might prove a most formidable opponent to the marriage; for there was no sum big enough to buy him, nor any other means of winning him. Fortunately, the picture of the Italian girl preceded the person of the French nobleman. Yet this was subject to a mishap. The curiosity of the custom-house officials was such that they barbarously tore off the sheets of paper, which had stuck to the picture, and thus removed some of the colour, especially on the face. Such a disaster could not, indeed, alter the noble and majestic air of the physiognomy of the princess, but it marred the effect of the picture. The duke was requested to send one or two more, not through France but by way of Alicante, and the address of the Court of Parma should not appear, for it was

---

[1] *Arch. Nap.*, C. F. 54.

this that excited suspicion ; the picture might be packed in a box of eatables, for in that case the custom-house officers would just open it, receive their bribe, and go away. The princess advised butter, rather than oil, as keeping the paper wet and as being less apt to stick. Nevertheless, the "geographical outlines" were found pleasing, and this injured portrait seemed to complete the success of Alberoni's diplomacy.

Alberoni might, however, probably have spared himself the anxiety of the last month. The Prince of Chalais, nephew of Mme. des Ursins, had already been sent to Paris to consult Louis XIV., who gave a somewhat grudging consent ; and early in July a Spanish courier was sent direct from Paris to Rome, to induce Cardinal Acquaviva to expedite negotiations. The Papacy was by no means loath to regain touch with Spain. Its suzerainty of Parma and Piacenza was still threatened by the emperor ; a connection between the houses of Bourbon and Farnese would render the fief secure. The cardinal visited Parma on July 30 ; the settlements were drawn, among the clauses being a stringent provision that the queen should bring no attendant into Spain. On September 16 Cardinal Gozzadini, as *legatus a latere*, performed the marriage ceremony, and afterwards presented the queen with the golden rose. It was intended that she should come by sea to Valentia or Alicante, at one of which ports Mme. des Ursins would meet her. Philip calculated that travelling with ordinary speed she would reach Spain by the middle of October. He was burning with impatience to see his bride ; yet the jealousy of Mme. des Ursins kept him in such subjection that he dared not talk to Alberoni, as much he desired, upon a topic so agreeable. Whenever he could steal an interview, he would ask a thousand questions in undertones about his queen's personal attractions. It was in vain that Alberoni assured him that it was years since he had seen the princess, and referred him to her picture.

The correspondence between Alberoni and the Duke of Parma is of extreme interest. Here it is possible to read the riddle of the queen's short and stormy conflict with her would-be mistress, and of her permanent, deliberate domination of the king. At first the abbé is under the old spell: he is ready to cajole and deceive the princess; but, as yet, he dare not openly resist her. She had no sooner made the match than she repented. Her hand had been forced by the haunting fear that intrigues were on foot at Paris for the king's marriage. Alberoni showed her letters proving the existence of such designs, and persuaded her that delay might be fatal. But he by no means regarded her power as being shaken. "It must be laid down as a fixed point," he wrote on July 30, "that we are under an absolute necessity of resigning ourselves to the lady, for she is most indispensable to the queen in many essential matters, until she has acquired knowledge of the king's character and possession of his affections; of these, I feel sure, she will make herself the mistress very shortly. As for the rest—many things are set straight by time. . . . It will be well, therefore, at first that the queen should try to please the lady, especially in such matters as might excite her jealousy. But let her remember that *non est abbreviata manus Domini;* in a few hours she will render herself mistress of the king's heart, and then, without any stain of ingratitude, she will be able to take her fill of that of which it is both necessary and politic to deprive herself at present." The future, he continued, was with the queen. Every woman in the palace was indeed the creature of the princess, and all the ministers night and day hedged in the king: yet, let the young queen but come, and she would find men of honour who would make themselves her servants; and of these in good time the queen would have need. Let her but take good measures, and, with the character which the king possessed, she might make herself the most renowned of queens that had ever sat upon the throne of Spain. The Duke of Parma was urged that it was in the highest degree important that the queen should not allow herself to be prejudiced against the Spaniards, nor to listen to the suggestions of universal distrust which rendered the poor dead queen so ill-liked at the close of her reign. Control over the king was represented as a matter of necessity, not of choice. " The king wishes to be governed ; the queen will govern him if she will—nay, more, she must perforce govern him, otherwise, if she lets him be governed by others in the manner and on the principles actually practised, I repeat plainly that she will be the most un-happy queen that has ever been in Spain ; and your High-ness will have no credit in this Court. Bear in mind that she comes to be the step-mother of three princes, the eldest of whom is extremely high-spirited, and is, by anticipation, the idol of the Spaniard, believed to be their saviour and redeemer from the oppression in which they are held down by the French ministry."[1] On attention to the Prince of Asturias, he repeated in his next despatch, depended the queen's peace of mind ; she had every opportunity of win-ning the affection of the Spaniards ; they regarded the ex-clusion of her waiting-women as brutal and barbarous ; they complained that every lady-in-waiting was French or Irish, and that measures were already taken to reduce the queen to the condition of the Savoyard ; forgetting, however, the fact that the latter had been brought up from baby-hood by the princess, that diffidence and self-effacement had become a habit, and that she hardly suffered from the unhappy life which she led. With a queen of ripe knowledge and good understanding this would be impossible ; she had but to win her husband—the work of a few hours— and she would soon reduce the princess to a reasonable and befitting attitude. At present, however, it was necessary to swallow the bitter draught and to make a show of its being sweet and tasty, bearing in mind the maxim : " *Regnare est dissimulare* ". Patience and dissimulation must be the mainspring of the queen's conduct ; for at least a year she must show herself averse to the business of government.[2]

Gradually, however, Alberoni's tone began to alter ; he was forced to realise that even a temporary *modus vivendi* would be with difficulty attained. Mme. des Ursins was

---

[1] *Arch. Nap.*, C. F. 54, Aug. 6 and 20, 1714.

[2] *Ibid.*, Aug. 27, 1714.

busily employed in working out her own destruction. The visit of d'Aubigny had had the anticipated result; he was strongly opposed to the marriage, and had he come a month sooner it would never have taken place. The princess was in a state of painful agitation. She wished to meet the bride at the port in order to forestall other influences, but she dared not leave the king, who might slip from her control. Women seemed more dangerous than men. She carefully selected the lady who was to receive the queen. The Marquesa d'Aitona was virtuous, but of slender understanding : " an image who could not articulate two words ". It was to the astonishment of all that Alberoni was allowed to meet the queen. She apparently hoped to rule the queen through him. In her quarrels with Vendôme the abbé had contrived to retain her friendship while not surrendering his master's interests. Her irritation, however, was such that she could not control her tongue ; she satirised the princess of the petty Court of Parma, who, to be Queen of Spain, would not discard three wretched servant maids. She gave out that the queen was ugly, and that Alberoni's fair visions had little substance, for her uncle Antonio was about to marry the widow of the Cardinal Medici, and raise up seed to the Farnesi. At table she publicly announced that the king would never again inhabit the palace in which his wife had died, for his love for her was as great as ever, and that he would never have re-married had he been able to live without a wife. The meanness of the preparations made for the queen's reception at Alicante appeared to be intended as a deliberate insult, which the sensitive Spaniards keenly felt. The queen, wrote Alberoni, must console herself with the memory of the magnificence of her marriage feast at Parma. Her retinue would be obliged to bring their own *cuisine* ashore. " No queen has ever been received in a manner so unbecoming ; she will have to put up with a carriage which was used to convey the late queen in her illness from Saragossa to Madrid—the *cortège* of the princess will be very different."[1] Above all, Alberoni feared that he himself had

---

[1] *Arch. Nap.*, C. F. 54, Oct. 21, 1714.

already incurred jealousy, and that, if access to the queen were denied to him, there was none else to guide her in her difficult path. He thought it essential that she should invent a pretext for staying three or four days at Alicante, for when once the queen had joined the king confidential intercourse was at an end. This indeed would be refused even to her husband, for Mme. des Ursins had so arranged her apartments that the king and queen could not communicate without her knowledge.

In Alberoni's letter of October 21 there is every mark of genuine feeling. It was written from Alicante, whither he had gone to meet the queen, though suffering from fever and quite unfit to travel. "I foresee, as does your Highness, the stumbling-blocks and grave difficulties which the queen will encounter in her wish to provide for the king's honour and the preservation of a monarchy crushed to the ground, because governed for fourteen years past by ruinous people, whose only aim has been to plunder it and to make themselves the tools of those who would destroy it. I know also that the queen has to deal with one of the most knavish women in the world, who has little religious principle, and that all the delicate attentions that the queen may practise will avail nothing, unless she leaves her sole mistress of the government, and is content to live under her in total self-effacement and obedience. I have said on another occasion that the late poor queen did not dare, until she thought herself dying, to call a confessor in whom she could confide ; and this was, according to her own phrase, the solitary comfort which she ever had throughout her life. I know, moreover, and have told your Highness, that the remedy for troubles so great can only be applied with time, with the greatest caution and skill, and by the adoption of well-considered measures." The one consolation to which the abbé could point was that any resolute act would redound to the queen's popularity and glory. Everything depended on the view which Elisabeth might take ; if she believed that the evil could be cured by palliatives she would find that they merely aggravated the disease. She was urged to make herself clearly understood at the outset, for if he were removed she would be kept in a state of miserable ignorance, no one daring to approach her or speak a word to her. During the short stay at Alicante, Alberoni could not hope to give the queen the necessary lights; the presentation of a large amount of undigested matter would only confuse her brain and depress her spirits. His suggestion, therefore, would be made little by little as time and occasion served.

"In my first conversation I shall give her Majesty a life-like portrait of the king, who will have no will but that of his wife, or whatever other woman may be near him. I shall describe the weaknesses by which he may be caught, and I shall conclude by telling her the artifices by which the lady has contrived to be the despot, removing every one else from the king's side, and fostering in him a horrible mistrust of his vassals, maintaining herself in authority by placing the government of the whole monarchy in the hands of two men, Orri and Macanaz, without ability, without knowledge, void of law and faith and honour, looking only to their own foul interests, while rendering themselves the tools of the limitless ambitions of the lady. As for myself, I see—and that not without mature reflection—that I am sailing out into the high seas. Everywhere I see rocks ahead and the peril of shipwreck, unless I have to deal with a queen of a great heart; and even in that case I see that I shall never be free of mental and moral anxiety, and that I shall be entangled in the meshes of Court life, repugnant to my nature and to my ideal of retiring after having obtained full knowledge of its character. All my pains, however, and all my labours, I shall consider well spent if I see the possibility of their contributing to her Majesty's glory, for the situation is such that she may make herself the most glorious and most famous queen that has ever sat upon the throne of Spain." [1]

Elisabeth Farnese never came to Alicante, nor did she meet her husband in October. She left Parma on September

---

[1] *Arch. Nap.*, C. F. 54, Oct. 21, 1714.

22. The Austrian Government was known to be indignant at her marriage, and it was thought judicious to avoid imperial territory. Her step-father, her mother, and the Cardinal Acquaviva accompanied her to Monte Cento Croci, where she was joined by the Princess of Piombino and the Marquis Scotti, both of whom were to play considerable parts in her future life. Hence she crossed the mountains, and reached the sea at the Genoese port of Sestri Levante, whence she took ship to San Pier d'Arena, a suburb of Genoa. This short passage changed her plans, and possibly her fortunes. The weather was stormy, and sea-sickness is no respecter either of brides or queens. She refused to continue her journey by sea, and it was resolved to proceed by land and enter Spain by the Pyrenees. This change of purpose was attributed to deep-laid schemes, and to the suggestions of the widowed Queen of Spain. But Elisabeth Farnese was not the first nor the last whose plans have been altered by sea-sickness, and Scotti's bulletins, written from day to day, make it probable that the alleged reason was the real. At Genoa her headache was so distressing that she was sent to bed and kept there, and the doctors thought it dangerous at such a crisis of her life to subject her to further discomfort.

Elisabeth's progress along the Riviera and through Southern France was watched with the greatest interest. Here her retinue was joined by agents from France and Spain, the latter of whom were suspected not without reason to be Mme. des Ursin's spies sent to watch " her first actions and her every breath ". Different accounts, wrote Mme. de Maintenon, reached France from every halting place. The most flattering picture is that of the Prince of Monaco, which singularly confirms the later and more detailed description of S. Simon. " She is of medium height," he wrote to Torcy, " and has a good figure : the face long, rather than oval, much marked with small-pox ; there are even some scars, but all that is not disagreeably prominent. Her head is nobly set on her shoulders ; she has blue eyes, which, without being large, are as sparkling as

can be ; she can say everything with them. The mouth is
rather large, beautified by admirable teeth, which are often
disclosed by the pleasantest of smiles. Her voice is charming. Her conversation with every one is gracious, and is said
to be prompted by the heart. She is passionately fond of
music ; sings and paints very prettily ; can ride and hunt ;
Spanish is the only language which she does not know.
Lombard heart and Florentine head ; her will is extremely
strong." [1] The latter characteristic was confirmed from
other sources. The head of her household, the Marquis
de los Balbazes, could do nothing with her, and declared
that it was impossible to make her change her mind
when she had once expressed her wishes. The French
ambassador, the Duke of S. Aignan, wrote that she had
a very determined will and much pride. He believed
that it would be possible to govern her ; but, if so, it
would only be through servants for whom she might take
a fancy. [2]

The duke had met her on November 27 bringing the wedding presents of the King of France, his miniature, which
she at once put on, and, to her great delight, a mother-of-
pearl snuff-box, a gift to her at once useful and ornamental.
Two days afterwards the queen-dowager met her niece at
Pau. The widow of Charles II. lived in exile and in abject
poverty at Bayonne ; but the poor are always generous, and
she brought as an offering, or, possibly, as an investment,
pearls and diamonds and a magnificent carriage. The two
queens spent a pleasant twelve days together. They hunted
and they danced, they slept in the same room at uncomfortably close quarters ; the old queen would sing, while her
niece played the clavecin. The political situation was, no
doubt, discussed ; and the dowager is not likely to have
pressed the claims of Mme. des Ursins, who had induced
Philip to refuse his grandfather's request that she should be
allowed to return to Spain. She accompanied the queen to
S. Jean Pied-de-Port, and, according to the Duke of Parma,

[1] Baudrillart, *Philippe V.*, i. 603.   [2] *Ibid.*, i. 606.

would fain have gone further, had not her niece used some skill to break away from her.[1]

The young queen was expected to exchange her Italian for her Spanish retinue at S. Jean Pied-de-Port, but she flatly refused to do so, and continued her journey by extremely slow stages to Pamplona. It was already clear that a storm was brewing, and the Spaniards were eagerly anticipating the downfall of the French ministry. It was not only Mme. des Ursins that felt alarm at this deliberate neglect of the king's wishes. Alberoni defended the queen in public, but confided his anxieties to the Duke of Parma. He represented that the immoderate length of the visit to the queen-dowager showed little regard for a king so desirous of seeing his bride; and the friendship with a person of her character, who had shown no affection for her husband and who had always deceived him and humiliated him in his subjects' eyes, was regarded as disastrous to Philip's interests. The public were ridiculing the young queen's indolence, seeing her start on her journey at mid-day, halt for dinner two hours afterwards, and arrive at her quarters two hours before midnight, and that on bad and dangerous roads. If the king were capable of entertaining bad impressions, such reports might strike home, were the queen to continue her present mode of life, rising at mid-day, dining at 3 p.m., and going to bed at 2 a.m.; it would be a proof of unwillingness to conform to the king's tastes, for he was accustomed to dine at mid-day, then to devote himself to his favourite occupation of hunting, to sup early and retire at 10·30 p.m.,

---

[1] Elisabeth Farnese has been criticised for not allowing her aunt to return to Spain. Leave was more than once granted, and, according to the custom, certain towns were assigned as a residence. But she was never satisfied with the suggestions of others, and was one of those unhappy, middle-aged ladies whom nobody wants. Each relation would gladly foist her upon another. Between Elisabeth, her mother, and her aunt there was much acrimonious correspondence upon the subject, and the Duke of Parma is pathetic in his terror at her design of retiring to his capital. The widow of Charles II. had not borne a good name in Spain; and she seems ultimately to have consoled herself by marrying secretly a French commercial traveller. Yet she was a kindly soul and a hospitable, thoughtfully entertaining S. Simon with the fish dinners for which he had vainly craved in Spain.

in order to be able to rise early next day. The king was by nature a most affectionate husband, yet he was mistrustful, and, at times, if he got an idea into his head, extremely obstinate; he was indolent, averse to business of any kind, and, therefore, inclined to leave everything to his ministry; yet he was jealous of his authority and resented the idea that he was governed. Alberoni's anxiety reached its culminating point on his introduction to the queen. He had hoped to be at once admitted into her most intimate confidence, but she received him with extreme coldness; she had evidently conceived the strongest prejudice against him.[1] He discovered that he had been represented as the *âme damnée* of Mme. des Ursins.

The secret of the queen's extraordinary conduct was only confided to her step-father after her marriage, and has since been discreetly kept. She was naturally unwilling to exchange her Italian for her Spanish household. She would cling until the last moment to the ladies and the servants whom she had known from her childhood. But there was more than this. The journey from Genoa was responsible for the one flirtation of the queen's life; it was only natural that she should defer its termination. It is a mistake to believe that the cult of the curate is confined to Protestant circles. The young ecclesiastic has his charms whatever be his creed. One Maggiali has been attached to the queen's retinue as chaplain. He was a vain and empty-headed person, with a tendency to brag of his *bonnes fortunes*. But solidity and reticence are not the avenues to a girl's heart, whither there is little doubt that the vapid chaplain found his way. It was to this that the Princess Piombino and the Marquis de los Balbazes attributed the queen's delay. The four hours before mid-day which the queen spent in bed were occupied in "chattering" with Maggiali. The Countess Somaglia, a mutual friend, kept the door, and from time to

---

[1] Alberoni's appearance was not prepossessing, for he was short and round and had an enormous head and face. On further acquaintance it was realised that he had a noble glance, while his conversation was sparkling and there was irresistible witchery in his voice.

time the "old and stolid" Camilla was seen to pass in and
out. The consequences might be disastrous. The first
equerry, the Marquis of Santa Cruz, had observed the
intimacy, and he was a notorious gossip. Alberoni, however, was not the man to be excluded by a chaplain.
He represented to the Marquis Scotti that his reception
showed little consideration for the duke, their common
master. Alberoni well knew the soft spot in the queen's
heart—her step-father was still dearer than her chaplain,
and his reception on the following day was cordial and confidential. From this moment to his fall the queen's life is
well-nigh absorbed in that of Alberoni.

From Pamplona the queen and her new suite pressed more
rapidly forward, and at 8 p.m. on December 23 arrived at
the little township of Jadraque. Philip had remained hard
by at Guadalajara. Mme. des Ursins had left him to receive
her mistress in her capacity as chief lady-in-waiting. There
is little doubt that she intended to master the young queen
before she could influence her husband. The princess was
at supper when the queen arrived; she left the table and
their meeting took place upon the stairs. The sequel has
remained one of the mysteries of history. The queen called
in a loud voice for her captain of the guards and ordered
him to remove that mad woman. She is said even with her
own hands to have pushed the princess through the door.
As by magic a coach and an escort of horse guards appeared,
and the old princess was sent off across the winter snows
of the bleakest, most desolate uplands of Europe, in full
Court dress, without a cloak, without a change of linen,
without those creature comforts with which the humblest
traveller was provided in a country where inns could furnish
neither food nor bedding.

The princess had been for years the absolute mistress of
Spain. She had bearded and beaten the great French king
himself. Single-handed she had delayed the conclusion of the
Treaties of Utrecht and Rastadt because her private interests
were not sufficiently consulted. Her total rout at the first
encounter by an untried girl fresh from school, whom she

herself had drawn from the privacy of a petty Italian Court, was a European sensation of the first magnitude. A new actress had stepped upon the stage, the *pensionnaire* of Parma had made her first appearance in the character of the termagant of Spain. It is important, therefore, that it should be ascertained whether the queen's action was due to temper or to deliberate design, how far she acted on her own impulse, and how far she was prompted by other enemies of the princess. Every detail of the quarrel was differently described. It was not even determined whether the queen or the princess arrived first, whether the latter descended the stairs or awaited her mistress on the landing, whether the first words were cordial or the reverse, whether the offensive was taken by the older or the younger woman. Nobody in Europe believed that the untrained girl acted on her own responsibility. The rapidity, the clumsiness, the causelessness, and the efficacy of this *querelle d'allemagne* all pointed to pre-arrangement. S. Simon attributed it to the influence of the French king, offended at the princess's supposed ambition toward the throne, and by the secrecy and independence with which Philip's marriage had been arranged. It was, in fact, but the second volume to the story of Mme. des Ursins' first expulsion from Spain. Now, as then, Philip could not be trusted to be present ; he knew the scheme and · accepted the result ; he even gave such written orders as were necessary. This alone, thinks S. Simon, would explain the indifference with which he heard the event, and the imperturbable calm with which Elisabeth advanced to meet her husband. But it is certain that both French and Spanish kings were taken by surprise. Neither knew whether the other were concerned in the princess's fall, which both undoubtedly at first regretted. Louis XIV., when asked whether Philip's consent had been obtained, coldly replied : " I hope so ". In his first letter to his grandson he wrote : " I confess that, knowing the zeal of the Princess des Ursins for you and your confidence in her, I cannot but deplore her misfortune in incurring so rapidly the queen's displeasure ". Philip, on hearing the news, ordered the princess's carriage to be stopped, and wrote to her that he had heard, with as much astonishment as pain, all that had passed between the queen and herself; he begged her to have patience and to rely that he would do everything in his power to heal the breach.   She might rely entirely on his esteem and friendship.

With more reason, both in Italy and at Paris, the queen's action was ascribed to the promptings of the queen-dowager and the Cardinal Giudice.   The latter had been quite recently disgraced, and, being forbidden to return to Spain, was at this moment residing at Bayonne.   Both were personally interested in the disgrace of the princess; to both it probably implied return to Spain and to political influence. The dowager, it was believed, had persuaded her niece to make a pretext for the change of route, and it was between Pau and S. Jean Pied-de-Port that the scheme assumed shape.   It is extremely probable that the queen-dowager did indeed urge the downfall of the princess upon willing ears, and there is no question that Elisabeth arrived at Pamplona with strong feelings against her would-be ruler.   The idea that Alberoni was a creature of the princess caused, as has been seen, his cold reception.   S. Simon heard in after years from the Duchess of S. Pierre, the queen's intimate friend, that Elisabeth confessed to having gone to Jadraque with the fixed idea of dismissing the princess, but that the words to which she gave utterance were the first that came into her head.   But the prime mover in the affair was neither king nor queen nor cardinal, but the watchful agent of the Duke of Parma.   Alberoni's private letters to his master make it certain that he planned every detail of the scheme.   These letters were written immediately after the event.   He enclosed a letter from the queen which would have corrected his statements had they been false.   He had long pressed upon the duke the necessity of patience and delay; in this policy the duke had fully concurred; the letters, therefore, contained an apology for a change of plan, which he feared might not find favour.   In his first letter he briefly stated the events, and expressed a fear that his master would conceive the queen's action to be too bold and perilous, but that it was, in fact, the sole remedy for her trouble, and that he had the consolation of seeing her released from misery. When the journey was over he wrote more fully.[1] He recapitulated the offences of the princess. She had publicly described the queen as thin-necked and consumptive, had dwelt upon the king's abiding love for his late wife, and on the necessity of excluding the new queen from any share in government. She savagely criticised the slowness of the queen's journey, saying that it would serve her right if the king left her for three months at Guadalajara without seeing her. She surrounded the queen with spies. She wrote to the governors of Bearn and Languedoc asking for a schedule of the thefts of the queen's Italian retinue ; and when the Princess of Piombino's evidence was adduced she said that she had always been the protectress of bad characters. The king had been deliberately prejudiced against his bride ; he had been persuaded that the queen would blindly follow the interests of Rome. Every measure had been taken to deprive her of all succour, human and divine. Above all, Alberoni was to be excluded from the queen's presence. The secretary, Grimaldo, without the knowledge of the princess, had imparted the king's wish that the queen should join him on Christmas Eve. This arrangement Mme. des Ursins attempted to upset ; the queen, she urged, would require more time to dress herself as became her, and to rest after her fatigue. It was pre-arranged between the queen and Alberoni that the princess should be kindly and cordially received, and that every effort should be made to gain time and avoid a public rupture. Alberoni reached Jadraque three hours before the queen, and found the princess quite unable to control herself. She broke out into reproaches at the queen's resolution of proceeding to Guadalajara in her present ridiculous costume ; it was like a country wench to ride post haste to find a husband. All the queen's actions were absurd, and even her unladylike

---

[1] *Arch. Nap.*, C. F. 54, Dec. 31, 1714.

appetite showed the lightness of her character and the poverty of her intellect. Alberoni, feeling certain that the princess would forget herself in the queen's presence, then ordered two officers of the guards to be ready at the door in case the queen should have need of their services. The queen at length arrived. The princess only advanced to the middle of the stairs, but was received with the greatest distinction and kindness—with some sacrifice, indeed, as by-standers thought, of royal dignity. Scarcely had they entered the room when the princess burst into abuse, and in some measure into threats, thinking perhaps that she would do well to intimidate the young queen, who, however, was compelled to show her just resentment in defence of her own honour and that of the king outraged in her person.

Yet more conclusive, however, is Alberoni's final letter[1] on the subject, which proves that the queen's resolution was taken only shortly before the event, and that the time and manner of its execution were due entirely to his suggestion. " I fully believed," he wrote, " as does the queen, that at the first news your Highness must have been much surprised ; but, pray, do not cease to be convinced that on this one stroke depended the entire salvation of the queen. Your Highness was not wrong in supposing that the resolution was not only taken with my acquiescence but at my suggestion, as will be seen. But without the express command of your Highness and that of the queen I should never have made such a confession, being most anxious that all the good results of this measure should be attributed to her, that she should receive the glory and the applause, and that the idea should gain ground, so necessary especially at the outset, that her actions are neither suggested nor directed by any one." After dwelling on the increasing jealousy of the princess, he continued that he believed that she would forget her duty, and, intoxicated with her absolute authority over the weak mind of the king, would probably at the first meeting act with an air of insolent authority, for the express purpose of intimidating

---

[1] *Arch. Nap.*, C. F. 58, Feb. 3, 1715.

the young bride.   This would give a plausible pretext
for executing the resolution at which he had arrived
after mature reflection, and which alone, he believed, would
give security to the queen's life.   At Pamplona he had two
interviews with the queen, the second of which lasted for
nearly four hours.   From the moment of leaving Pamplona,
until the last halt before Jadraque, he was closeted for four
hours with the queen every evening.   At dinner next morning she would prettily remark that, as she could not go to
bed early, she made Alberoni the victim of her late habits.
Two consecutive evenings he went resolved to divulge his
proposal, but his courage failed him.   Finally, with God's
help, the evening before arriving at Jadraque, which they
both regarded as their last interview, he unburdened his
mind.   The queen was sitting near a little table, and he,
kneeling on one knee and leaning on the table for support,
told her his tale with his eyes filled with tears.   In their
many long interviews, he said, he had represented to her the
hell that gaped before her ; he had shown her the rocks, the
hurricanes, the inevitable shipwreck.   Remedial measures
were useless ; there was but one specific, which he had not
yet dared to propose, and she would probably regard as violent
and fraught with danger.   "All that you tell me I have seen
to be true," she replied ; " but you are quite at liberty to say
all that you please without fear that it will frighten me or
confuse my brain."   Alberoni then advised that, at the first
opening which the princess's rudeness was certain to
give, the queen should reprove her for an insolent message
delivered by her relative Count d'Albert.   Meanwhile he
would stay by the door talking on casual topics to two
officers of the guards who were his friends.   The household
of the princess should be secured, the postmaster ordered to
grant no horses, and no one allowed to pass along the road
to Guadalajara.   He then drafted the letter for the king and
the order for the captain of the guard, that the queen might
at once write it out with her own hand when the occasion
came, as indeed she subsequently did, with a dignity and
presence of mind that delighted every one.   The queen

looked the abbé straight in the eyes, and replied that his proposal was certainly bold, but that she believed her salvation to depend upon its execution. She asked how the king would take it. He replied that he expected her to raise this difficulty, but that his perfect knowledge of the king's character was the sole foundation and express motive for the proposal of such an expedient. She might rest assured that the king would approve the act when done, but not if it were previously communicated to him. To make him fail to approve it would require God's help to change his whole nature. The queen retired to bed, promising to give the matter full thought. Early in the morning before starting for Jadraque he appeared at her bedside. She roused herself, and said : " Well, now, I will tell you that I have not slept all night ; but I am unchangeably resolved to carry out all the measures upon which we agreed last night. Let us both commend ourselves to the Lord God that He may assist us in our enterprise." Her resolution was not taken lightly nor in hot haste, but with a full realisation of the difficulties and on mature reflection. In proof of this, she afterwards confessed to him that all that night and the following day she had need of all the spirit that she could command to beat down the difficulties that constantly kept occurring to her thoughts.

This recital bears every stamp of truth, and is confirmed by the first and most accurate information which reached Torcy at Paris, and which was communicated by the Duke of Savoy's agent to his master. Much sympathy has naturally been expended upon the disgraced princess in her cold and miserable drive, but some is also due to the young girl, who for a whole night and day was pondering over a step which no one in Europe had yet had the courage to take, but on which her future happiness alone depended. It was not so easy to play the termagant to a Mme. des Ursins. That victory remained with the younger woman is not marvellous. The young are more violent, wrote Machiavelli, and fortune favours violence. Young girls have not unfrequently a direct and deadly thrust which breaks down the guard of

more experienced fencers.   It is, moreover, no slight advantage to have two officers of the guards outside the door and
a troop of horse prepared to saddle in the courtyard.

Alberoni was correct in his estimate of the king's
character.   He set off in person at midnight for Alcalá, bearing a letter from the queen, and in a long and lively interview persuaded Philip that he must approve and support the
queen's action.   He even extracted a letter expressing the
royal satisfaction.   But no sooner had Alberoni left the room
than Orri and the confessor entered, and persuaded him that
it was rash to allow such independence in a queen scarcely
yet upon the throne, and orders were despatched to stop
Mme. des Ursins' carriage.   But for Alberoni's representations the princess would have been ordered to return.   On
the following day, Christmas Eve, the queen arrived at
Guadalajara towards 3 p.m.   She alighted amid loud cheers
at the palace of the Duke of Infantado.   She ran up the
steps with surprising agility, and at the door of the first room
recognised the king.   She fell on her knees and kissed his
hand.   He raised her up, and strained her tenderly to his
breast.   He then kissed her, and led her by her left hand
into the great hall, where the religious functions were celebrated by the Patriarch of the Indies.   Even at this supreme
moment of her life Elisabeth did not forget Alberoni's
lesson.   She welcomed the Prince of Asturias with all the
affection of a mother.   But the king was impatient to be
alone with his bride.   The part which she had rehearsed
with the abbé was not yet played out, and the result of this
first interview with her husband was an order that the princess should continue her journey into France.   As she
passed the mountains the Pyrenees recovered their existence,
and Spain and France were separate.

A curiously graphic account of the scene at Jadraque is given in the MS.
of Bellardi.   He is in full accord with Alberoni as to his first interview with
Elisabeth, and as to her treating him as the *anima damnata* of the princess,
adding that the widowed queen had not been sparing in her abuse of Mme.
des Ursins.   Alberoni, after suggesting that if the princess was disagreeable
the king would get rid of her, reached Jadraque three hours before the queen.

" Well ! " cried the princess, " when is the queen going to arrive? . . . She treats the king very cavalierly, making him wait like this, tramping by night like a prostitute. . . . You represented her to me as a heroine, but upon my word she is a poor creature, from her appetite downwards. I am told that she eats nothing but garlic and hard-boiled eggs." Pretending to have swollen legs, the princess stood at the top of the stairs, without descending a step. She led the queen into her room, while Alberoni listened at the door, and said : " You have treated the king, madame, very cavalierly, for you have shown little attention to his impatient desire to see you ". Then taking the queen by the waist, and turning her round like a marionette, she said : " My word, madame, you are very badly made ". Then the queen, without answering a word, cried out indignantly : " Count Alberoni, take this mad woman away ". The princess left the room in astonishment, and Alberoni, in silence, accompanied her to her chamber, and stationed sentinels there, as also over the Princess Piombino, ordering the officer not to allow any one to approach either lady. When the princess received orders to prepare to leave, she refused to do so without the king's order, whereupon it was explained that force would be used.—Ambrosiana, 173 *sup.*

CHAPTER III.

1715.

EFFECTS OF THE WAR OF SUCCESSION UPON SPAIN—POSSI-
BILITIES OF REORGANISATION—ELISABETH'S MASTERY
OVER HER HUSBAND—ALBERONI'S CRITICISMS UPON
ELISABETH—THE LOVE AFFAIR OF MAGGIALI—ARRIVAL
OF LAURA ¡PESCATORI—ELISABETH'S CHARACTER AND
DAILY LIFE—RELATIONS OF SPAIN TO FRANCE AND TO
ITALY—CHANGES IN THE GOVERNMENT—THE FRENCH
COURT AND ALBERONI—PHILIP AND THE FRENCH SUC-
CESSION—PROSPECTS OF WAR WITH ENGLAND—DEATH
OF LOUIS XIV.

ELISABETH was in after-life credited with restless energy
and unlimited ambition. The condition of Spain and of
Europe offered ample material for the enterprise of such a
character. Spain seemed to wait for the artist's hand to
mould her. Institutions, privileges, local distinctions, had
been levelled by war and by fourteen years of French bureau-
cratic absolutism. Spain, however powerful were her early
Hapsburg kings, had never before known the monarchical
centralisation which in France attracted and dispensed the
nation's material and spiritual forces. Royal action had been
everywhere checked by provincial separatism and trammelled
by administrative complexity. Etiquette had stood in the
place of a constitution ; both are, after all, but the summing
up of precedent. Whereas in France organic changes were
the work of a day and a sheet of paper, in Spain the simplest
measure had been tossed from Council to Council till it fell
flattened to the ground. The king wielded the force of the
Inquisition, but the sword had become too heavy for his

feeble arm. The nobility, bribed by title and pension to become a Court nobility, had not indeed resisted, but had controlled the Crown. A conservative respect for family and office had stifled, perhaps, the expansive powers of the nation, but had tempered the technical absolutism of the monarchy, and had proved an obstacle to the predominance of persons.

The War of Succession had shaken the official hierarchy. Men of action had thrust aside men of title ; the system was too cumbrous, too deficient in mobility for a condition of internal war, and for the changes which were its consequence. The grandees were humbled. Many had followed Austrian fortunes, and were now in exile ; their greatest, the Duke of Medina Celi, had lost liberty and life. Their lack of popularity deprived their discontent of danger. New pensions and titles tied them to the Court. Mme. des Ursins had completed the ruin of the old fabric ; Alberoni did little more than refrain from its re-creation. Opposition took the form of sullen abstention, which was, indeed, not uncommon throughout the reign.

The councils that remained were but constitutional ghosts. Membership of the Council of State had formerly been the goal of all ambition, the coping-stone of fortune. It now merely conferred the title of Excellence and the privilege of riding in a sedan chair, with a coach to follow. Of the arbiter of the monarchy, wrote Bragadin, the Venetian minister, there remained now but the name. It was superseded by the Despacho, an informal body, which met in the king's apartment, and had none of the prestige of precedent. The Council of Castile, which was the judicial court for the chief part of the monarchy, had arrogated with more success than its kindred institution, the Parliament of Paris, wide political functions, but it no longer acted as a check upon the Crown. The area of its jurisdiction was indeed increased, but it lost the strength of corporate unity. Its five chambers no longer gave their decisions in common ; distinct departments were assigned to each. Yet it still presented its weekly report to the king, and its president was an official of some importance. The presidency of the Council of Orders, which administered the estates of the great military orders absorbed by the Crown, entailed some work and bestowed some consideration, both of which were during S. Simon's visit increased by the character of its occupant, the Marquis of Bedmar, who had served with high distinction in Italy and the Netherlands, and in both the French and Spanish armies. The Councils of Marine and the Indies, of Finance, and of War were giving place to a departmental system. Since the late queen's death Mme. des Ursins had hastened the change by instituting four secretariates on the French model. The Secretaries of State, War, Marine and the Indies, and Finance, may be considered as forming a ministry. All reports, however, were usually presented to the Secretary of State, who became the chief if not the sole medium of communication with the king.[1]

The constitutions of Aragon and Valencia had ceased to exist; these provinces were governed by Castilian clerks, and held down by Castilian garrisons. Notwithstanding the remedial measures which Alberoni shortly introduced discontent was rife, and until late in the century travellers speak of the disaffection in Catalonia, where the imperial eagle was still the favourite emblem. Almost excluded from State employment and forbidden to wear arms, the Catalans turned with increased vigour to trade, and made their strip of coast land the most flourishing and civilised district of Spain.

Gallican principles were as prevalent in the Church as in the State. The resistance of the Cardinal del Giudice, while at Paris, to the fiscal claims set forth by Macanaz had led to his disgrace. The members of the Council of Castile and of the Inquisition, who opposed the royal theory, had been dismissed. Although the young queen and Alberoni professedly favoured an ultramontane reaction, Alberoni's coming breach with the Papacy was to prove that the Church was no longer a check upon the Crown.

---

[1] " These four secretaryships may be called one, for everything is referred to the Secretaryship of State, in which resided up till my departure the whole authority of the government."—Bragadin, 1725.

In France absolutism had been modified by satire and the salon, to which, since the death of Louis XIV., might be added public 'opinion, the bourse, the journal, the café, and the influence of women. The Spanish monarchy was free from any such encumbrances. In Madrid there were two journals which were practically official; there were no opposition writers to be interned or bribed. There was no political need for the monarchy to confine literature within the channel of royal institutions. The Royal Academy of History is indeed due to Philip's reign, but, unlike the French Academy, its foundation had no political significance. Spanish ladies were grossly ignorant, and the contempt with which Mme. des Ursins and Elisabeth Farnese regarded them was not wholly undeserved.[1] There was, perhaps, a well-founded belief in the lack of capable Spaniards for military, religious, and civil employ, and the fact that most important governorships and embassies were in the hands of foreigners was favourable to the absolutism of which it was partly the result.

On the other hand, there was good material for a creative genius. Under the later Hapsburgs the Spanish armies had shrunk to a handful of tattered ragamuffins, whose officers begged charity in their garrison towns. But in the War of Succession, when the French had confessed themselves beaten, native forces had succeeded and had driven English and Germans from the country. Shoes, it is true, were often wanting, and pay always, and the officers of the Catalonian

---

[1] The following description by Mme. des Ursins is confirmed by other writers. "These ladies cannot appear at the palace before five. They get up at eleven or twelve, dine at two or three, and then take their siesta. When they come into the queen's room . . . they take low seats, the wives of the grandees on cushions, and the others on the floor. If her Majesty and I do not keep up the conversation with real effort it would quite come to an end. We ask if there are none among them who dance, who sing, who play, who like to go out walking, or who are fond of cards. They answer 'No'. . . . What they really can do wonderfully well is to ask for favours for themselves, their friends, or their servants. . . . Some of them wear rosaries round their necks, agnus upon their shoulders, and hold little crosses, relics and chaplets in their hands. Their customs, madame, may have their merits, but it must be admitted they are not amusing."—Miss Bowles, *Mme. de Maintenon.*

army of occupation still owed their subsistence to the monasteries. Castelar, Minister of War, a little later clamoured for war, because the Minister of Finance would not pay the troops in time of peace.

Spain had ceased to be a rich or a commercial country. The French had exploited and ruined the American trade. French resident merchants, endowed with all privileges and freed from all liabilities, had undersold the native traders. The woollens of the northern towns had been driven from the market by French imports. French contraband had stifled the yet more flourishing silk trade of the centre and south. Seville had shrunk to a quarter of its former population. French finance had been in fashion, and its merit was gauged by the taxation which it could raise, and not by that which it could remit. When Amelot and Orri simplified finance they systematised extortion. Spain, Alberoni had said, which was not ruined by war, would be ruined by peace if Orri stayed. English and even French criticism was equally severe. Marshal Berwick believed that French financiers and contractors were more dangerous enemies than Catalonian miquelets. Methuen bore witness to the poverty to which Spain had been reduced by her French allies. The rich had been ruined by the extinction of the Juros[1] and by extraordinary taxation, which fell so heavily on the poorer sort that many sold their houses, their goods, and their very beds, and were then forced to run away and leave their families to starve. But much, he confessed, was due to Spanish indolence; their sowing and reaping was done by labourers from Languedoc and Auvergne, who took their wages across the mountains to be taxed in France.[2]

The task of financial and commercial reorganisation was

---

[1] The extinction of the Juros amounted to a measure of repudiation. They were annual charges upon the royal domains of revenues in consideration of capital advanced or services rendered.

[2] Gaspard de Saulx had early in the seventeenth century laid stress upon this weak spot in Spanish economy. Were the annual migration of 8000 or 10,000 French labourers prohibited, Spain, he writes, would be helpless. —*Mémoires,* i. 97, ed. Petitot.

therefore still before the monarchy, and it did not seem hopeless, for there was no debt, and the regular supply of precious metals gave it an advantage for immediate needs which no other Power possessed.[1] Peace and the creation of a fleet appeared to be the essential requisites of success. Such was the condition of the country which it was now Elisabeth's task to govern. Much depended on the character of her ministers, something on that of her personal surroundings. A consideration of the latter may be deferred until the Court circle has defined itself, and until it has been pictured for posterity by the magic lantern of S. Simon's observation.

The treatment of Mme. des Ursins by Elisabeth may have been brutal, but it was undeniably popular. The new queen was greeted with enthusiasm at Guadalajara. Even in Paris her spirit was admired, though its probable consequences caused alarm. Gallantry appreciated the triumph of a young and shapely queen over an old, however well-preserved, princess. Alberoni bade his master thank his Maker for the heaven-sent stroke which had secured his daughter's peace and won the applause and the affection of the Spaniards, who now saw their beloved and venerated king released from a barbarous servitude ; the heroine could hear in the public streets the acclamations, not only of the masses, but of men of rank, who greeted her as the lifter-up and restorer of the nation, as their David who had slain her ten thousands. Elisabeth seemed to be striving to please the Spaniards. In her household she was intending to replace by young ladies of family the married women, whose love affairs and tale-bearing were a public scandal. In her receptions she distinguished the grandees from the other nobility. It was rumoured that the Council of State would be restored to its former authority,

---

[1] "No monarchy has the resources which Spain enjoys," says Bragadin. He adds that these were largely increased by Alberoni's discovery of quick-silver in Andalusia, whereas this material so necessary for the Mexican mines had previously been purchased in Sweden, France, and England. The two quick-silver ships brought to the royal chest an annual revenue of 800,000 pieces of eight.

and the other councils reorganised on conservative lines.
Within a week the queen had acquired complete mastery of
her husband.   She showed no inclination to interfere in
government, persuading him that he was now absolute
master of his own will, whereas he had been the innocent
victim of the passions of others ; her only desire was to see
him powerful and glorious.   Every day the king thanked God
for his deliverance from the tyrant.   Finding himself alone
with his wife, in cosy conversation after dinner, he exclaimed : "Eh! well, my queen, if the lady had been
here we could not have enjoyed these happy moments".[1]
He added that he well knew the character of the princess,
but that he should never have dared to displease her, and
that, had she remained, there would have been hell in the
house.   He was beside himself with joy at his bride's enthusiasm for hunting.   Her indolent habits were no more : she
would rise at daybreak.   The king was extremely gracious.
With his accustomed phlegm he would correct her eagerness
to fire.   Yet she was no mean shot, as the Court News could
vouch : "On Thursday last the queen in gentleman's attire
went a-hunting, and killed two stags and a boar, and shot
from horseback at a rabbit running, leaving it stone dead, to
the admiration of the king and bystanders on seeing her
Majesty's extraordinary agility and skill".[2]   Though Elisabeth had won her husband, she treated him as though he
were still to win, which threw the poor king into ecstasies
of delight.   At every moment he would say to Alberoni a
thousand things expressive of his pleasure, concluding always
with the sentence that it was God who had made him the
precious gift of so lovable a queen.   But pleasure should
always prepare for business.   Alberoni hinted that, without
being inquisitive, the queen might tell her husband that, if
he wished to hold the Despacho in her apartment, it was at
his service.   On the following day Orri and his followers
were summoned to the queen's rooms, and observed that,
though she sat at a distance with her crochet, she listened to

[1] *Arch. Nap.*, C. F. 58, Jan. 7, 1715.   [2] *Ibid.*

all that was being said.   After this experience she told
Alberoni that during her drive with the king she had talked
of nothing but Orri's dismissal, and believed that she had
persuaded him.   Alberoni could scarcely believe that she had
not studied politics all her life; he praised her curiosity for
knowledge, her docility in accepting advice, and the courage
with which she formed her resolutions.   If she were granted
life and health the king could soon say that he had in her a
good prime minister.

The Duke of Parma was assured that his daughter was
as well as she was happy; if Mme. des Ursins could see her
she would withdraw her satirical remarks on her angularity
of outline.   She was growing fat; the shifts supplied in her
trousseau were already too narrow.   Her appetite was excellent.   Elisabeth Farnese, indeed, like her distant relation
Catherine di Medici, ate largely, and was not ashamed.   She
was dissatisfied with the royal table and with Spanish fare.
The late queen, she said, was a Piedmontese, and ate nothing;
she herself was Lombard, and her people ate double and
more.   For long she made requisitions on Alberoni's kitchen
for beans *à la Lombarde,* and the post from Parma rarely
failed to bring Italian delicacies.   In the first days of February she confided to Alberoni, much to his confusion, that
she believed herself to be *enceinte.*   The king, enchanted,
ordered him to write the joyful news to the Court of Parma.

But there were shadows to the picture, and Alberoni was
too realistic to omit them.   The first hint of disquietude
appears in a letter of January 14, 1715.   He already perceived that the character of his mistress would depend upon
her company.   " The whole fate of this great soul depends
upon her being in good hands, in her having trust in men of
honour, void of self-love, and devoted only to her interests,
for her noble generosity and good nature cause her to throw
herself into the arms of any one who has the honour to enjoy
her confidence.   Thank God, she has made no false step at
present !"   Three months later he found her good nature and
familiarity out of keeping with royal dignity, and confessed
himself astounded when he reflected that she had been edu-

cated in the Court of Parma. Her invincible indolence and
dislike of business gave the abbé yet more concern. In vain
he appealed to her conscience, telling her that her husband
thought only of her and of his gun, and that if she persisted
in her neglect of business the government would fall into
the hands of ministers and there remain, and that she would
be discredited and despised. Her boasted vivacity required
the spur rather than the rein. It became clear that in
her vigorous resolutions there was a large element of fear,
and Alberoni was reminded of his beloved patron Vendôme,
always indolent until he found himself in grave predicaments
from which he was perforce obliged to find an exit. The
long and earnest discussions on the situation were at an end.
" Our conversations begin to be on indifferent topics and
merely to pass the time, for I recognise to my very great
grief that it begins to bore her to talk of business. I observe
her to be indolent in society, and yet more indolent in solitude." [1] He felt that if any accident should remove him from
her side this aversion to work would become incurable. For
hours the over-worked minister would sit talking twaddle,
and retailing jokes, partly to relieve her fits of melancholy,
partly to throw in a few words on State affairs of import.
He had, he said, to " take her on the wing ". She would act
on no fixed rule or principle, forgetting and neglecting to do
things which would make her popular. She would not talk
seriously for a quarter of an hour together. Advice had to
be given in the smallest doses and in the most digestible
form. Nor was the queen so docile as at first appeared.
Alberoni represented that among the Spaniards she had to
live and die, but after her first reception she for long refused
to bestow upon them any mark of favour. The Duke of
Parma, to whom alone she did not show indifference, pressed
that she should write to Mme. de Maintenon who had
absolute and despotic power over the King of France, for a
reason that was an open secret ; to write need not humiliate
the queen. Yet she told Alberoni that she would kiss the

---

[1] *Arch. Nap.,* C. F. 58, March 4, 1715.

feet of the King of France if her uncle wished, but would not
write to the old woman. Her extravagance, moreover, was
likely to lead to trouble. She spent largely upon herself,
upon jewellery and dress, and still more largely upon others.
She burdened her income with lavish charges in favour of
her ladies-in-waiting, or charitable and religious objects.
But, above all, Alberoni was haunted by the fear of Maggiali.
It was long before the queen lost her *penchant* for the chaplain, though whether it were an incipient passion or merely
a craving for some closer tie with her old home it is hard to
say. She had promised to summon him to Spain. He had
set on foot a correspondence with the queen's first equerry
and sent letters under cover to the queen. Her chief friend
at Parma, the Countess Somaglia, secretly forwarded others.
Some of these Alberoni intercepted and despatched to the
Duke of Parma. They may still be read, little miniature
billets doux, exquisitely written, folded and sealed with lov-
ing care, their purport the constant craving to be called to
Spain. Alberoni repeatedly urged upon the queen and her
uncle that such a call would be to her eternal dishonour.
He spoke to the former of the gratitude and love which she
owed to her husband, whose adoration for her was pure and
holy, and was the sole delight of his melancholy life ; her
character not only ought to be, but must perforce be, without
stain, lest her step-sons might some day seize upon this pretext to attack her, for the nation, dissolute itself, was
prudish in the extreme with regard to its queens ; even the
saintly life of the mother of Charles II. had not saved her from
suspicion. He told her that Mme. des Ursins was on the
alert for the slightest sign of weakness, that she had sent
two young relations of her own to flirt with her and mar her
fair name ; she had publicly stigmatised her as a coquette.
This, he was pleased to see, had a great effect, and the queen
treated these young gentlemen with cold reserve. The abbé
assured the queen that towards ladies of private station he
was no unbending Cato, but that such leniency could not be
applied to one set upon the candlestick of the throne, not one
of whose actions could be hidden. Her best protection was

her growing affection for her husband. Alberoni wrote on April 28 that the queen was now quite in love with her husband and unable to live a minute without him. She told the abbé that previously her friendship was based on esteem and gratitude, but did not proceed from the heart. He could hardly believe that such an unsought confidence was employed to blind him, for her melancholy fits had ceased. She was enchanted with the king's incessant attentions, the effect of which Alberoni increased by telling her that such had never been lavished on her predecessor, adding that such mutual love would delight the Spaniards and the most Christian king, and that her conduct to her husband was the merit of merits before God and before the world. The queen showed Alberoni Maggiali's letter and her reply, in which she explained that it would be difficult to let him come to Spain. "Yet this ought not to lull us to sleep," he continued; "and make us believe that a great flame is extinct, which with the least fresh fuel might kindle a gigantic blaze, all the more that I know her Majesty to be tenacious in her affections and extremely wily and capable of profiting by a good opportunity and gulling her husband, of whom she is absolute mistress, without his entertaining the slightest suspicion."[1] Long after his description of the mutual love of the royal pair his anxieties were still acute. "I am preparing to speak plainly to her and to make her see that to invite Maggiali to Spain would lead to her complete dishonour and ruin inevitable without a hope of ever rising again, whereas, by a miracle of Providence, and with little exertion to herself, she is surrounded by a halo of glory. I assure her that such a visitor would force me to leave Spain."[2] The danger by no means ceased with the first year of Elisabeth's married life, but it is unnecessary to dwell further upon the subject. A page or two may well be spared for the first and last love episode of the heroine of a tale. It proved that the queen was not devoid, as was sometimes thought, of natural affections, and that she was subject to the

---

[1] *Arch. Nap.*, C. F. 58, March 24, 1715.   [2] *Ibid.*, June 23, 1715.

temptations which so readily assail young girls of high rank, married to husbands whose attractions are not equal to their position. Alberoni, moreover, in his horror of fresh arrivals from Parma, has been credited with mere vulgar jealousy. His most confidential letters prove conclusively that he lived in terror lest every fresh arrival should be the emissary of the empty-headed chaplain, "*jam notus in Judæa*," but thanks to Alberoni's precautions never to be known in Spain.

There was yet another visitor from Parma whose advent caused Alberoni much anxiety, and who ultimately contributed largely to his fall. The Duke of Parma had consented to send Elisabeth's nurse to superintend the coming confinement. The queen was in ecstasies of delight; she urged that she must come at once, that she need not wait for an outfit, but should only bring her linen. The duchess, wrote Alberoni, need not send any dogs and birds for the queen no longer cared for the like beasts; she had two puppies in the palace, but never took the trouble to see them. " She expects this woman," he concluded, " as though she were the Messiah."[1] Alberoni hoped on the one hand that this new favourite might divert her mind from Maggiali, on the other hand she might prove a go-between. There was danger too lest her arrival should check the queen's increasing industry. The queen assured him that she would speak plainly to her, and that he must give her a good lesson. She would tell her to behave herself well, and to act entirely under his guidance. But Alberoni, knowing the queen's character, suspected that if she were a woman capable of abusing her good nature, she could do so with security. Laura Pescatori arrived in September. At first sight she seemed to Alberoni, as to others, a good-natured, jovial woman, who only enjoyed the queen's confidence in menial matters. He soon discovered that pecuniary interest was her sole motive. Alberoni had undertaken the management of the queen's privy purse. He had to provide for the nurse much fine linen and magnificent furniture, silver candlesticks and boxes of cypress wood.

[1] *Arch. Nap.*, C. F. 58, Sept. 2, 1715.

She was accompanied by a young person who gave herself
the airs of a lady and considered herself the mistress of the
palace.   She could not tolerate that the gates should be
shut, and wanted to promenade the town.   The queen promised to send her away, but with her usual good nature continually put it off.[1]

Before long Alberoni's worst fears were realised ; Laura
became the medium of communication with the Countess
Somaglia and Maggiali, and the queen no longer showed him
the chaplain's letters.   The nurse became the centre of a
cabal to keep the queen idle, and, as a means to this, to get
rid of Alberoni.   Money had actually been given for her
return to Italy, but the queen with an excessive innocent
good nature allowed her to see that she was necessary.
" The rascally woman abuses the queen's good temper, and
treats her with such superiority and contempt that it kills
me. . . . I find myself in a palace that has become a Babylon.
I swear to your Highness that she gives me more trouble and
more work than all the interests of the Crown, for I see that
she is labouring to totally undo the reputation which the
queen has acquired, and to which I have so carefully and
jealously contributed."[2]   Nobody more sturdily resisted
Alberoni's economies than this greedy peasant woman.   Her
evil influence upon Elisabeth must not be underrated, yet it
is difficult not to smile at the picture of Laura sitting weeping in the ante-chamber, showing her feet to all the passers-
by, and declaring that she was left in beggary, without so
much as a pair of slippers.   " And yet," concluded Alberoni,
" besides all her food she has 450 lire a-month in cash."[3]

Meanwhile Alberoni's representations were not altogether
without effect.   From pure indolence the queen had long
delayed to appoint an ambassador for France.   At last she
told him, laughing, that he need not scold her any more, for
that the mission was intended for the Prince of Cellamare.

---

[1] This objectionable young person proved to be Laura's daughter, and became a great lady by marriage, if not by manners.

[2] *Arch. Nap.*, C. F. 58, June 25, 1716.   [3] *Ibid.*, March 10, 1716.

She was also persuaded to forward by the prince a letter to Mme. de Maintenon. In June Alberoni wrote: "I am succeeding better every day in accustoming her Majesty to harness and to hard work at State affairs. I try to bring them in the form of mince meat in order to spare her all possible fatigue. . . . Yesterday I told her that up to now I had played the charlatan, letting the world in general and my friends in particular understand that she was most devoted to business and incessantly occupied therein, whereas I really observed a total want of application, not to say aversion. Her Majesty began to laugh, and condescended to tell me that knowing the zeal and affection with which I served her, with so much advantage to her fame, it was her duty to help me also on her side." [1] The queen was at this time reading all urgent despatches and receiving reports from the departmental secretaries, and no important measure was taken without her knowledge. To the great satisfaction of Alberoni and the nation she was at last persuaded to give two high appointments to Spaniards, both of them men who had refused to give the title of Highness to Mme. des Ursins. Notwithstanding her indolence, she was greedy of glory and applause, treating any one who contributed to this end with delicate attention and confidential docility. On this key Alberoni unremittingly struck. "I try to give her greed of glory." "Her love of glory," wrote her step-father, "will be the best bait with which to tempt her." [2]

The queen's character never had a more candid or capable critic than Alberoni, and therefore stress has been laid upon his impressions in these early days. He had opportunities of observation never accorded to others than the king. Day after day he spent hours of *tête-à-tête* in his attempt to educate her to her position. To the Duke of Parma it was his interest to tell the truth after the first burst of unrelieved eulogy. The result is the picture of a rather commonplace Italian girl, a character of not unusual contrasts. She was indolent, but yet ambitious, resolute at

---

[1] *Arch. Nap.*, C. F. 58, June 23, 1715.   [2] *Ibid.*, May 24, 1715.

a crisis, negligent in everyday life. She loved popularity, yet would take no trouble to acquire it. Her pride, as her familiarity, was the result of a somewhat vulgar nature. In one who was fated to be the despot of her husband and the ruler of the nation it was a dangerous feature to be the sport of the first comer. Much would depend on the definite direction which might be given to her ambition, and to the growth of a knowledge of character. All queens of Spain had the same great difficulty to face. To become Spaniards they must sink their individuality and nationality, they must surrender all hope of elevating Spain to the European level, and yet unless they could become Spaniards they could exercise no influence upon the nation. In this there could be no half measures. The barbarous but attractive people either absorbed its visitors or else repelled them.

Alberoni has left a sketch of the queen's daily life, which anticipates the more celebrated description of S. Simon. The queen and her husband at this time retired to rest at half-past ten. At eight in the morning they took light refreshment in their bed. Philip then rose, and the queen remained in bed for two hours and a half, saying her prayers, reading despatches and French books. After Mass and dinner the royal pair would spend an hour together. The king then went a-hunting; and if the queen did not accompany him, Alberoni would entertain her. On Philip's return they took a slight repast and talked or despatched business until supper at eight. Both king and queen took an early dislike to Madrid. They preferred the Pardo or Aranjuez, where the sport was at their doors. Aranjuez was notoriously unhealthy, and Alberoni warned the queen that if any mishap should befall her step-sons the world would say that the spot had been selected for the purpose.

It is time, however, to turn from domestic details to wider Spanish and European interests, which were so largely affected by the queen's marriage and ambitions. When Elisabeth Farnese pushed Mme. des Ursins from her door she gave to Spanish history an impetus which was not quite exhausted throughout the century. Spain was started on an independent course; she was no longer towed in the wake of France. Mme. des Ursins, it is true, was by no means always at accord with the French Court. 'She is charged by S. Simon with being an enemy both to France and to Spain, as leading Spain away from French alliance. Her jealousy had more than once made the position of the French ambassador impossible. She was regarded as the patroness of all the foreign adventurers or exiles who swarmed round the carcass of the Spanish monarchy—Flemings, Irish, and Italians. She was, after all, Italian by marriage, and had spent much of her life in Italy, whither she retired to die. Nevertheless, her influence and her methods of government were French. French modes of thought dominated the Court, and extended as far as Court influence could reach. The history of her supremacy had proved that she could not break away from France, and that the French Court could not permanently discard her. Had not Louis died shortly after her disgrace he might yet have been forced to replace her. Her long and private interviews with the old king and Mme. de Maintenon caused the liveliest alarm at Parma and Madrid, and were the subject of diplomatic representations. In vain Louis XIV. implored Philip to accord a pension to one who had served him so disinterestedly, and to whom he would once have accorded all that she might have asked. The Savoyard ambassador at Paris had predicted that she would spread fine stories in France, and obtain a hearing.[1] Not only was she charged with tempting and defaming the young queen's virtue, but she professed anxiety for the safety of her step-sons, an imputation which for long found echo in the party which gathered round the Prince of Asturias. That her fall was followed by the French king's death was a fact of consummate importance. A new series of ideas had been introduced, and the opportunity was thus given of carrying them into execution.

---

[1] Perrone to King of Sicily, Jan. 28, 1715.

A modern Italian writer[1] justly claims that the resurrection of Spain owed its origin to an Italian princess and an Italian cardinal, who both, for good and evil, left a wide track upon the annals of the nation. Elisabeth Farnese was a thorough Italian. Not merely had she Italian modes of thought and loved to be surrounded by servants and ministers of her own race, but she had definite Italian ambitions and respectable Italian claims. She intended from the first that her issue should continue and increase the power of the Farnesi in Italy. To the Duke of Parma the Spanish marriage was the lever which was to lift Austrian oppression from Italy. Long before Elisabeth reached Spain the Parmesan agent was instructed to spread wide his net for assistance from the Spanish Court. The marriage itself increased the necessity for such aid. The Court of Vienna regarded it as a threat to the neutrality of Italy, and the imperial representative in the Consistory had opposed the concession of Papal consent. Antonio, Elisabeth's uncle, was pressed to marry; and the Austrians threatened both the Courts of Tuscany and Parma. Philip wrote to his grandfather that the honour of both Crowns was concerned in the defence of the Duke of Parma; but Alberoni doubted whether his lively representations would have any effect upon a king whose only thought was now to prolong his life, while, since the death of the Queen of England, the slightest pressure from Germans or from English made his courtiers think that a formidable host was at the gates of Paris. If Spain were in good hands he might hope at once to see her make a show in Europe; but her position was pitiable, without government or ministry, living from hand to mouth, without thought for the present or the future. His master must place no reliance upon either France or England, but temporise and arm himself with patience, and avoid the blows which threatened him as best he could. Orri had even said that the emperor was within his rights, and that France could not by the terms of the Treaty of Baden interfere.

[1] Carutti.

Yet it was essential to cultivate friendly relations with France, and the fall of the princess produced no breach. The queen wrote a dignified apology to Louis XIV. She was resolved, she said, to maintain harmony between the two Crowns, and to protect the French who faithfully served the king. But the sublime merits of the French nation did not extend to all its members; some had abused their usurped authority to overthrow the laws, the customs, and all that the Spaniards held most sacred; those who thus behaved no more merited the protection of the King of France than they should receive that of the Queen of Spain; there were still in Spain persons of little merit, who, not content with the *rôle* of mere administrators, played the despot with an intolerable audacity which made their yoke detested.

Orri, not without reason, trembled in the queen's presence. Her step-father urged the eradication of the evil weeds, and the intendant general's fall was followed by that of Macanaz and the king's confessor, Robinet. Yet, Alberoni suggested the recall of the Cardinal del Giudice, who was high in favour with the French Court, and Louis XIV. gave his sanction. He resumed his office of inquisitor-general, and was entrusted with the governorship of the Infants, a post on which Alberoni believed the peace of the queen greatly depended; for past examples proved that the relation to the Infants was the rock on which almost all queens had suffered shipwreck, even when not step-mothers as was Elisabeth. The education of the Prince of Asturias had been shamefully neglected; his sole companions were the two boys of the late queen's tailoress; Mme. des Ursins' surgeon taught him to read, and a woman superintended his writing and heard his catechism. It would have been desirable to appoint a Spaniard, but no one of high rank could be found who was even moderately capable. Giudice was, moreover, intended to act practically as first minister, to take off the queen's shoulders the unpopularity which a change of system necessarily involves. He had a character for activity and ambition, but was wanting in frankness and good faith. Partners in power were intolerable to him, and he was incapable of moderation if invested with too much authority. No resolution, no enterprise was too bold for him. He was wont to say that a cardinal with a revenue of sixty thousand crowns could make himself respected by small and great, a sentiment which Alberoni doubtless bore in mind. Daubenton, the king's confessor, was French, but in sympathy more Spanish than the Spaniards. He had the reputation of being frank, upright, and well-intentioned, but disposed to interfere in matters very far removed from his calling. Asked to dine with Alberoni he ate well and drank better, and his jovial conversation showed him to be a man of the world. He professed to idolise the queen, and promised to keep Alberoni fully informed ; he already knew the story of Maggiali. It was thought of extreme importance to place the queen and the king's confessor on good terms. Friendship with him would render her perfectly secure, for she had to deal with a husband under the mastery of scruple. Everything proposed to Philip under the cloak of conscience or religion sufficed to throw him into a state of utter indecision and melancholy. This, apart from the confessor's aid, the queen would scarcely overcome without doing violence to her husband's feelings.

An old favourite of the king, the Secretary Grimaldo, upon Orri's fall, showed a disposition to take his place. Alberoni convinced him, as he did Giudice, that the queen intended to be the mistress. Owing, however, to her lamentable indolence he was less successful with the French ambassador. The Duke of S. Aignan, with the audacity of conceited incompetence, deliberately thrust aside the queen and her Italian adviser. He complained at not having been consulted in the dismissal of the late ministers, he urged that they should be replaced by Frenchmen. He discussed with the king the reform of the army, and filled the Board of Marine with his nominees. Sartine, the intendant, was an adventurer who, on Alberoni's authority, had been bankrupt once in Cadiz and twice in Lyons, and had cost the king eight thousand horses. His companions, the Dukes of

Veraguas and Tinachero, were men of bad character, whose appointment scandalised all honest men, and roused at length the indignation of the queen. A letter was shown to her and to the king, which made them believe that France did not wish Spain to be strong at sea, and was not sorry to see the admiralty in the hands of a Frenchman and a scoundrel.

The ambassador proposed to put himself at the head of a Spanish faction, in opposition to the overbearing Italian influence which was represented as becoming so disliked as to make the French regretted. He became a centre for the malcontents who, to make the queen unpopular, complained, as in the days of Vendôme, of the Italian knave who was always at her side. Alberoni, however, did not believe that his influence was objectionable to the Spaniards at large, who knew that he loved their nation and that this was made a ground of complaint in France. The Duke of Parma urged him to give the lie to the rumour that the government was in Italian hands by appointing Spaniards. This he did whenever it was possible. He was, indeed, by no means in complete harmony with the Italian faction, whose influence had in some measure preceded his own. " Some few Italians here," he wrote, " give me more trouble than all the Spaniards put together." [1]

The French Government was more prudent than its ambassador. It was realised from the first that the queen would dominate the king. This was sarcastically implied in the reply of Louis XIV. to her first letter. He regretted that her satisfaction should have been disturbed by the princess's misfortune in displeasing her; his grandson, however, seemed very far from being likely to protect those who might not be agreeable to herself. Torcy was informed that whatever might be the queen's faults the only policy was to win her favour. The important question was whether she in turn would let herself be governed, and if so, by whom ? Before Elisabeth had been at Madrid a week Orri wrote that

Alberoni was master, and that France must act accordingly. Torcy failing to bully the favourite attempted to bribe him with a pension. Alberoni would accept no new gift, no pledge for future service. The pension which had been granted in consideration of his services to Vendôme had been discontinued; its payment might fairly be renewed. This delicacy reserved his freedom of action and secured six years' arrears. He was informed by friends in Paris that Torcy wished to cultivate his friendship in order to open a secret correspondence with the queen. The Duke of Grammont advised Alberoni to win the favour of the old king, who was the honestest man in the country. The Duke of Parma urged the cultivation of the Duke of Orleans. The latter had common ground with the queen in his detestation of Mme. des Ursins. Philip, on the other hand, regarded him with horror. He believed that he had intrigued with the Spaniards of the rebellious provinces to deprive him of his Crown, his life, and his wife. Two servants of the duke, Flotte and Regnault, had long languished in the prisons of Segovia, on vague suspicions of a plot against the king. Alberoni assured Philip that the duke's sole fault consisted in the talk of these two men, who, when it was thought that Philip would leave Spain, hinted that their master would undertake the Spanish cause. The reconciliation with Orleans and with Rome he regarded as his two most essential tasks, and it was probably at his prompting that Torcy, on May 18, wrote a formal despatch to the Duke of S. Aignan on the subject. The prisoners were released. The king and queen interchanged letters with the duke, the latter expressing his pleasure at the change of government, which was a deliverance for Spain, and which had put an end to the unhappy relations between the king and himself. Madame, his mother, expressed her gratitude to the good queen, and the Duke of Parma congratulated Alberoni on his *coup de maître*. The correspondence which Alberoni conducted with the duke was perhaps the origin of the belief, which was later current, that his policy was prompted and paid for by the regent as the only means of reducing the growing power of Spain.

The maintenance of the friendly relations between Spain and France was due partly to the hopes of the Italian party that the French Government might protect its interests in Italy. But a stronger motive was furnished by the imminence of the question of the regency in France, and the probability of that of the succession. The inheritance of the French Crown appeared to be equivalent to sentence of death. Within a few months had died the dauphin, his eldest son, and his eldest grandson. A sickly child, whose rearing appeared to be impossible, stood alone between Philip and the Crown.

Yet Philip's exclusion and that of his heirs had been made an absolute condition of the European peace. He had, after a little struggle, yielded to his grandfather's pressure, and the French succession was settled on the younger lines of Berri and Orleans. During a mission of Giudice to France, the Duke of Berri suddenly met the fate of the preceding heirs. The cardinal forthwith reopened the whole question. Philip had regarded his renunciation as invalid, as extorted by force, as contrary to the fundamental laws of the kingdom. He could not, at all events, prejudice the rights of his children. He had no intention of reigning on both thrones at once—the son should sit on one and the father on the other. The cardinal was instructed to press the claims of the King of Spain to the regency and the guardianship of the young king in the event of the death of Louis XIV. The old king, however, was still under the mastery of the horror of war, which was rendered more probable by the death of Anne and the accession of the militant Whigs. He advised his grandson to recall the cardinal, and to deal tenderly with the prejudices of the English Government. Philip was forced to yield ; but his opinion never changed, and Giudice, who had even outrun his master in his zeal, was now in the position of first minister in Spain. Alberoni also placed before the queen the hopes which she might cherish for the future. The conversation of S. Aignan and the course which Torcy secretly pursued seemed to prove to him that the French themselves regarded the king's speedy

accession as not improbable. In February the Prince of
Cellamare, nephew of Giudice and intimate friend of Alberoni, was destined for an embassy to France. In May he
received his secret instructions to discover the provisions of
the king's will, and to form a party in Philip's favour. The
princes, the marshals, the ministers, the Jesuits were the
objects of his intrigues. The king's death was to be the
signal for a manifesto claiming the regency and the guardianship for Philip to the exclusion of the Duke of Orleans. The
Spanish Court had reasonable grounds for hope. The exclusion of the Spanish line had been purely due to the necessity
of peace with England, the continuance of which appeared
to be impossible. The Duke of Parma, in announcing the
approaching arrival of the English ambassador Methuen,
besought Alberoni to pay him all possible attention, for the
friendship of England would be of incalculable advantage to
the interests of the Farnesi.[1] Alberoni replied that he would
do his best to serve him, but found the English demands for
a revision of the commercial treaty most irregular.[2]

Methuen met with a cold reception : the Court, he perceived, was guided in everything by France ; a few ministers
who had always opposed Giudice had lost their places, but
the system was unchanged. No redress could be obtained
for British grievances, and business was at a standstill.
The ministers had no other aim but to follow the dictates of
the King of France, and to secure their king's going safely
to France when his grandfather died. The eyes of the
whole Court were straining towards France.[3] He rightly
saw French encouragement in the reduction of Majorca
whilst negotiations for its submission were still pending, for
the King of France had written that if measures were to be
taken it must be at once before England had time to interfere.[4]

The fidelity of the French king to his engagements was
shaken. He no longer instructed his grandson to cultivate

---

[1] *Arch. Nap.*, C. F. 58, March 12, 1715.   [2] *Ibid.*, April 15, 1715.
[3] Methuen to Stanhope, July 15, 1715. *R. O. S.*, 155.
[4] The reduction of Majorca was the first exploit of the queen's reign, for
Barcelona had fallen a few days before her marriage.

the Hanoverian *régime.* In August he asked for Spanish money to assist the Pretender's expedition to Scotland. Torcy arranged that 100,000 ducats should be sent to France for this purpose, of which sum half was actually despatched. He wrote to Alberoni that war with England could no longer be avoided, for the Whigs could neither prevail nor indeed exist on a peace footing.[1] The envoy of the States-General told the same tale, and added that his republic was determined to be neutral. It was of no slight importance that the queen's step-father expressed his delight at the intention of France and Spain to help the holy cause. Alberoni informed him that the French Court persisted at all costs in landing the Pretender in one of the three kingdoms; England, if he mistook not, had grave reasons for reflection, for he could not conceive how in its distracted condition it could carry its arms abroad. A landing was, indeed, fixed for September 15. Louis XIV. in one of his last letters urged Philip to recognise the Pretender, and Berwick and Torcy wrote in the same strain.

Yet another moment and Alberoni was in deep dejection. The French projects on England, he wrote, would end in smoke; Spain attacked by England and unassisted by France would fare badly; she was crushed or drooping, she had neither men nor money; all that had been done had but served his principal object of securing the foothold of the queen. In the government there was neither shape nor system; four secretaries ran their own course with the reins on their necks and none to drive them; the sole remedy was to induce Elisabeth to work upon the king, but in this he found greater difficulties than ever, for as far as he could see her character could never adapt itself to business.[2]

But Alberoni's hopes and fears of immediate war were groundless, for as he penned this letter the Grand Monarque was dead.

---

[1] *Arch. Nap.,* C. F. 58, Aug. 26, 1715.   [2] *Ibid.,* Sept. 2, 1715.

CHAPTER IV.

1715-16.

PHILIP AND THE FRENCH REGENCY — RISING POWER OF
ALBERONI — INFLUENCE OF THE DUKE OF PARMA —
ELISABETH'S ITALIAN AMBITIONS—CONDITION OF ITALY
—HOSTILITY OF SPAIN TO THE EMPEROR—PROSPECTS OF
SPANISH INTERVENTION IN ITALY—A SPANISH SQUADRON
AT CORFU—LOUVILLE'S MISSION TO MADRID—COMMER-
CIAL TREATY WITH ENGLAND—TREATY OF WESTMINSTER
—RECONCILIATION OF SPAIN AND THE PAPACY.

HITHERTO the queen, however great her personal influence,
had rather followed than guided the general lines of her
husband's policy. French agents had somewhat ante-dated
her complete ascendency. Philip's eyes were fixed upon the
throne of France; even before his second marriage he had
determined to annul his renunciation. In the part which he
was playing he needed no prompting from his wife. She no
doubt was willing enough to accept the blue ribbon of royalty.
She already had hopes for the future, and probably shared
the opinion of the old Duchess of Orleans that her offspring
would be numerous, that Philip, in Alberoni's phrase, was
destined to people the world with princes. The coming son
might well live to be King of France, while the Prince of
Asturias was left to vegetate in Spain. The latter was,
moreover, delicate, as were his younger brothers, the elder
of whom shortly died.

On the news of the old king's illness the Spanish Court
eagerly expected its summons to France. On September 6
Bubb, who had succeeded Methuen, informed his Government that he felt pretty sure that the Court was preparing to

(58)

proceed to Paris. The crisis was soon decided. On the 9th arrived the tidings of the king's death, and this was immediately followed by intelligence that the Duke of Orleans had been declared regent by virtue of hereditary right, which was practically an official recognition of Philip's renunciation. Cellamare had not even ventured to enter the protest which had been prepared. Prudence is not always policy, even in a diplomat. S. Simon believed that, had Cellamare proclaimed Philip regent, he would have found universal acceptance.

This disappointment led to a marked change in the policy of the Spanish Court. The ideas of Philip gave place to those of Elisabeth, and the execution was transferred from Giudice to Alberoni. The son of the jobbing gardener, born in a two-roomed cottage at Piacenza, was now to become a personage. Hitherto he had no recognised position in Spanish service—he was merely the agent of a petty Italian Court. But among the diplomatic small fry he had long attracted notice. His ability had diminished the friction between his patron, Vendôme, and Mme. des Ursins. He had remained in favour with the princess after his master's death. Yet, but for the matchless skill with which he had steered the Duke of Parma's daughter to the throne, it is hardly probable that he would have taken a front rank in history.

Alberoni had from the first regarded the ministry of Giudice as but a temporary expedient for clearing away the *débris* of the old system and preparing the house for its new inhabitants. Neither Giudice nor Alberoni could bear a partner, and it became evident that one must fall. Giudice delayed the liberation of the servants of the Duke of Orleans that he, in place of Alberoni, might take the credit. So, too, when entrusted with the proposals for the reconciliation with Rome, he delayed conclusion, that it might pass through no other hands. In his diplomatic career he had won a reputation for ability; but the country needed not a clever diplomatist, but an industrious and disinterested administrator.

The fact that the cardinal devoted himself to the prince was sufficient to attach the queen to Alberoni. The real work of the State gradually fell to the latter ; and after the work, the honour. He was entrusted with the reorganisation of the government of Catalonia and Majorca. He never rested until he had ousted from the Department of Marine the satellites of the old French *régime*. Night and day he laboured at schemes for naval reform. By the end of 1715 authority was conceded to him independent of the departmental secretaries. His apartment in the palace adjoined the queen's, and hither the secretaries brought their reports for discussion. The queen added her weight to his policy by personally attending the Despacho. Giudice's long-expected report on the Papal difficulties resulted merely in invective against Macanaz and Orri ; he had no practical proposals to offer. From henceforth Alberoni and Daubenton undertook the matter until it was carried to a successful issue. The friendship of England and Holland was becoming more important than that of France, and it was to Alberoni, and not Giudice, that their envoys, Stanhope and Ripperdá, turned for aid. The king had never approved of Giudice's recall. Within the year both king and queen would have dismissed him, had not Alberoni prayed them to wait for an opportunity. To the last Alberoni appears to have dissuaded his disgrace. Disliked as he was, it was feared that his fall would elevate him in the eyes of the superstitious Spaniards to the rank of a S. Peter Martyr or a S. Thomas of Canterbury. In May, 1716, however, he was relieved of the governorship of the Infants, and in August he was discharged from all his employment. Yet Alberoni did not publicly succeed to his functions, nor had he any official status. There was no formal Minister of State. Grimaldo was but a secretary, and Alberoni still but envoy of the Duke of Parma. This fact was of capital importance, because it compelled the abbé within certain limits to act in the interests and on the suggestion of his master. The queen was naturally subject to the same influences, with the result that the policy of Spain was in great measure directed from the Court of Parma. Spain once more turned its face towards Italy. The queen and her step-father showed the national jealousy of the lesser Italian princes for the power that was *de facto* dominant. This power now possessed also the alleged *de jure* claims of the empire. The empire, it is true, had lost its sentimental significance, and its lien upon its Italian fiefs might safely be neglected when stated only by the Chancery of Vienna. It was different when such claims were urged from the barracks of Milan and Naples.

The young queen, still solely under the influence of her Italian education, naturally wished to utilise her new position to make Spain the nucleus round which Italian discontent should gather. Nor were her motives of a purely political character. Brides, and especially the brides of dull men, have a pardonable craving towards their old homes. If Elisabeth Farnese had indeed been shut up in an attic of the palace of Parma she forgot it in the sombre State apartments of the Buen Retiro. She remembered only the bright Italian life. The Italian of this, as of all ages, was at once material and gay. The Spaniard cared little for the creature comforts, and his gaiety was confined to his domestic circle. The situation of a widowed queen in Spain was so painful, the confinement so close, the allowance so scanty, that from the moment of becoming a wife she was haunted by the fear of widowhood. This may account for the singular attachment of Spanish queens to husbands who, on general grounds, would hardly be regarded as attractive. Elisabeth, in her fortnight's visit to her aunt, had gained some insight into the situation of a dowager. She was resolved from the first not to be subjected to the common fate. Within two years of her marriage, when Philip's health caused anxiety, she discussed, with tears in her eyes, her future fortunes with Alberoni ; her father's agent she regarded as her only stay. Her aim, therefore, was to secure for herself a dignified retreat in her beloved Italy. Even during her journey to Spain the Irish adventurer Burke had realised this, and had pointed out to Torcy that France might gain influence by suggesting and supporting such a course.

There was much in the situation to favour the success of
the queen's policy. It did not require his bride's caresses to
stimulate Philip's indignation against the emperor. He was
wounded in points of sentiment, which most readily affect a
nature at once proud and reserved. The emperor retained
the title of King of Spain ; he formed a so-called Council for
Spain and a Council of the Inquisition. The most virulent
Spanish refugees were among the most favoured admirers
and pensioners of his Court. The Catalonian, Rialp, stood
perhaps above all others in imperial favour. Imperial Italy
was as completely in the hands of refugee Spaniards as was
Spain in those of refugee Italians. Thoughtful Spaniards
recognised that, by the loss of the Netherlands and Italy,
Spain had been relieved of an incubus which had wasted her
strength, and turned her attention from the wealthy West
to the unprofitable East. But the upper classes regretted
the lucrative employment which the governments of Milan
and Naples had provided.

Within Italy there was a reasonable probability of support. The temporal interests of the Pope were still large,
and to a temporally-minded Pope there were many possibilities of friction with a power which ruled at once Lombardy
and Naples, which faced his frontiers both at Bologna and
Benevento. To such possibilities the substitution of the
emperor for the Spanish king had infinitely added. There
might be bickerings between the Papacy and its feudatories
of Parma, but in sight of the common danger they leaned
upon each other. Hence the great importance ascribed by
Alberoni to reconciliation between the Papacy and Spain.

More delicate were the relations of Elisabeth to the
Grand Duke of Tuscany. Siena, a part of his dominions,
was still regarded as a fief of the Spanish Crown, but the
Sienese coast towns, the so-called State of the Presidi, had
passed from Spain to the emperor, and Tuscan access to
the sea was practically confined to the ports of Leghorn
and Porto Ferraio. The claim of the empire to Tuscany
was founded merely on the grant of titles, on the creation
of the dominions actually possessed by the Medici, first into

a Duchy of Florence, and then into a Grand Duchy of Tuscany. In default of heirs male, Elisabeth regarded herself as heiress. The grand duke, however, desired that the succession should pass to his daughter, the wife of the elector palatine. The emperor professed to be offended with this disposition of his estates without imperial sanction, and made consent conditional on the admittance of palatinate garrisons. The situation was complicated by a revival of republican feeling. The people, it was urged, had granted hereditary lordship to the Medici; if the grant lapsed by extinction of the race, to the people it reverted.

The time was passed when Venice could defy Vienna. Yet a friendly neutrality might be expected: Alberoni knew the Venetian maxim that there were two Turks to fear, and that he of Vienna was to be feared the most. More active help might be expected from the inhabitants of the imperial possessions, who realised that they had not changed masters for the better. Spanish oppression of the age of Charles V. was now an old wives' tale. Its rule had become perhaps too incompetent to be unpopular. There had been little interference from the central government, and the administration from very indolence had fallen in with Italian needs and habits, and become almost national. The rising of Masaniello at Naples and the revolt of Messina were but sporadic cases of disorder; their suppression proved that there was no *nidus* for revolutionary germs. No dynasty had existed so long with so little vocal discontent. The Spanish officers at Naples, and doubtless, also, at Milan, abandoned their frugal Spanish customs and spent their money freely. The Germans lived meanly and spent stingily; they saved their pay to send to their wives at home.

The action of Spain in Italy has usually been considered as unwarrantably offensive, as sacrificing the peace of both countries to the dynastic ambitions of Elisabeth Farnese. But Alberoni and the Duke of Parma honestly believed themselves to be stemming the tide of barbarian encroachment. Their belief was well grounded, for the emperor had addressed proposals alternately to France and England for the annexation of Sicily, and the succession to Tuscany, Parma and Piacenza, and Mantua. The Neapolitan viceroy was already taking measures for a move on Sicily. It is unquestionable that the realisation of all bygone imperial claims on Italy was the darling project of the emperor. He believed himself to be the successor of Barbarossa and of Henry of Luxemburg. This being the case, it is not wonderful that on the other side, also, we hear the echoes of the past, the murmurs of the Angevin Robert of Naples on behalf of his adopted country: " The Kings of the Romans have been wont to be chosen from the German people, which cleaveth rather to the savagery of barbarians than to the faith of Christ; . . . since then they have nought in common with the Italians, we must needs watch that German savagery do not turn the sweetness of Italy into bitterness ".[1]

The marriage of Elisabeth had from the first given hopes of future deliverance, but it was fraught with immediate peril. The Duke of Parma was directly threatened, and was instant in his demands for help, which Alberoni deliberately resolved to give upon the earliest opportunity. Towards the close of the reign of Louis XIV., when war with England was regarded as certain, he told the queen that she should keep fifteen or sixteen ships in readiness, and he informed the duke that in a fortnight or a little more Spain could make an attack upon Naples or Sardinia.[2] Immediately on the French king's death the Duke of Parma urged the necessity of alliance with France and Savoy for the defence of Italy. The possessions of the Duke of Savoy (now King of Sicily) were the emperor's chief aim; some cession of long-coveted territory would always win him. The Savoyard ambassador at Madrid courted Alberoni's confidence after a long period of coolness, but the latter would not trust his brother-envoy, and to his wish for a good intelligence between the two Courts replied coldly that it was already perfect.[3]

[1] Bonaini, *Acta Henrici VII.*, i. 237.
[2] *Arch. Nap.*, C. F. 58, Aug. 26, 1715.
[3] *Ibid.*, Feb. 17, 1716.

From France there was little hope. Alberoni had early notice that the regent intended to preserve harmonious relations with Spain; but, to maintain peace and reform finance, he was timidly avoiding every pretext for rupture with the emperor. It was suspected, not without reason, that he had gone further than mere neutrality. The regent, fully aware of the hostility of the Spanish Court to his own claims on the succession, had turned to the emperor for assistance before having recourse to the Court of S. James. He had proposed that the emperor should exclude Philip from the throne of France, and guarantee the Orleanist succession. In return, the regent was prepared to resist the return of the Spaniards to Italy, and to guarantee to the emperor the reversion of Tuscany and Parma. Negotiations had, however, temporarily broken down on the emperor's demand for the restoration of Alsace and Strasburg. It was clear that France would not give active help to Spanish enterprise. Spain, therefore, must stand well with France, avoid rupture with England, cultivate the friendship of Portugal, and prepare for defence against the emperor. Such preparations were going rapidly forward, and Spain was again mistress of a fleet. This fleet, wrote the Duke of Parma,[1] would be not only useful for the Indies, but for an attack upon the emperor in Italy in the ensuing year. Alberoni, in reply, hoped to give the emperor food for reflection within two or three years.[2] It was believed that England and the States-General would offer no resistance. The question of the barrier to the Netherlands caused irritation between the emperor and the latter power, while the English Government had intercepted a letter from the emperor to the Pretender.[3] By both the imperial menaces to Tuscany were regarded with extreme jealousy.

Meanwhile Austrian oppression was increasing. The Genoese police had arrested a Catalan officer in imperial service for wearing his sword in the streets. The

---

[1] *Arch. Nap.*, C. F. 58, Nov. 29, 1715.   [2] *Ibid.*, Dec. 9, 1715.

[3] *Ibid.*, Jan. 11, 1716.

Imperialists thereupon occupied Novi, levied contributions, and imposed upon the Genoese Government a humiliating surrender. With regard to Genoa, the old water-gate of Spain, the Spanish Government was peculiarly sensitive. If no means were taken to check the emperor's aggression, the queen's expectations would be worthless.

Salvation for the oppressed, as often before, came from the Turks. Their progress in the latter half of 1715 threatened to keep the emperor at home, if not to drive him from it. At the beginning of November Cardinal Paulucci inquired whether, in the event of a Turkish war, the King of Spain would respect the neutrality of Italy. The Spanish Government, in the interests of the Pope and of Christianity, signified consent, provided that the emperor was guilty of no fresh encroachments.

This, said Alberoni,[1] left a door open for action in Italy, because the emperor was certain to encroach. The Duke of Parma proposed that a further step should be taken, and that a force should be offered to the Pope, nominally for the protection of his States against the Turk, but really for the defence of Italy against the Austrian, for if Spanish help did not come quickly, Italy was lost.[2] Alberoni's reply proves that from the first the emperor, and not the Sultan, was the objective of the squadron which he was arming. After mature reflection, he believed that it would not be serviceable to the king and queen to send help to the Pope unless it were considerable; the emperor might probably not allow the Pope to accept it, for his aim was believed to be that Italy should be invaded by the Turk, that he might come and rescue it, subjecting it to a yoke more barbarous than the Turk's. A squadron of six ships, four galleys, and ten thousand men was being fitted out, under the Genoese Mari, who, though a novice, appeared to be their ablest officer, industrious and determined to get on. Meantime, he said that his design was "to tickle" the princes of Italy, to make them realise that the Emperor of the West

---

[1] *Arch. Nap.*, C. F. 58, Nov. 4, 1715.   [2] *Ibid.*, Jan. 17, 1716.

was more formidable than the Emperor of the East. The present opportunity was too good to be lost, but without this the Duke of Parma would see that he could not honestly persuade the king to send ships or troops to Italy, for a large force could not be sent, and that which was being despatched was not sufficient to make headway unless it found aid in Italy. If once it got a footing, he did not despair of being able to increase it.[1] If the Pope were forced to refuse this aid, it could be offered to the Venetians. Meanwhile the Duke of Parma was entreated to be cautious : " Let your Highness, for God's sake, take all possible care not to give the Germans cause for picking a quarrel. All my schemes are at present undigested. But I will not be caught napping, and shall try to profit by the friendly relations which I have established with the maritime powers."[2] The duke could only reply by imploring Spain to act at once ; the Grand Duke of Tuscany would gladly receive the squadron, the maritime powers could be moved by commercial bribes and threats of the danger to Leghorn ; the liberty of Italy was in its death agony.[3]

Alberoni was fully aware of the danger of Italy, and believed that if the emperor were wise he would take advantage of the situation ; it needed not an astrologer or philosopher to see that he was waiting for the pretext of a Turkish invasion of Italy. Action could not long be deferred, but it was impossible to send troops to Italy, unless it were certain that the Italian princes were resolved to stem imperial encroachment ; the theatre could not be opened unless the King of Sicily was prepared to make his *début ;* Scotti had been sent to Turin to sound the Savoyard Government ; if a force were lent to the Venetians it should not cross the Adriatic.[4]

The minister began to realise with grief that he must give up all distant views, and in return for such a sacrifice bind the other powers by the closest ties to uphold the

[1] *Arch. Nap.,* C. F. 58, Feb. 17, 1716.   [2] *Ibid.,* March 8, 1716.

[3] *Ibid.,* April 5, 1716.   [4] *Ibid.,* April 20, 1716.

liberties of Italy. The danger was pressing, for the Turks were beaten at Peterwardein. "The German victory makes me fear that those brutes of Turks will make a peace which will be war for Italy."[1] To the reverses of the Turks Alberoni was, much against his will, forced to contribute. Intelligence had arrived from Turin that the King of Sicily would not move, and that it would be perilous to trust him with troops. The Duke of Parma still besought that the Spanish squadron should not sail for the Levant, but should cruise off Genoa, Leghorn, and Civita Vecchia. In spite of Alberoni's promise the little fleet sailed eastwards to seek another Lepanto. It was the appearance of the Spanish sail that in great measure determined "those brutes of Turks" to retire in confusion from the siege of Corfu.

The distant views from which Alberoni sorrowfully turned his eyes were the revival of Spanish commerce in the Indies and possibly the chances of the Crown of France. With regard to the regency he had no regrets ; Spain would have the more friends in France for not having a share in her domestic troubles. The regent would support Philip in Spain to keep him out of France. But Alberoni was not yet master, and the regent, perhaps with reason, did not feel secure on the side of Spain. The leaders of the anti-Orleanist party paid studious attention to Alberoni, who, however, informed his master that their cultivation was a card to be played with extreme caution.[2] Though every care was taken to avoid a rupture, French interference was no longer tolerated. French resident merchants were taxed and in case of resistance were threatened with force in spite of S. Aignan's threats of his withdrawal. The French Government, jealous of the growth of Spanish commerce and manufacture, tried to tempt away by higher wages the skilled artisans whom Alberoni had introduced. With still greater dislike was regarded his activity in the Department of Marine. "They do me much honour," he wrote to the Duke of Parma, "by attributing these and many other ideas to my initiative,

---

[1] *Arch. Nap.*, C. F. 58, Aug. 31, 1716.   [2] *Ibid.*, Oct. 24, 1715.

assuming that I alone, assisted by the active support of the queen, can bring them to a successful issue, with so much advantage to Spain. For this reason they would like to see me removed from the ministry."[1] It was known that the divergence of Spain from the old course was due to the queen and Alberoni, and personal feeling against the abbé was already strong in the regent's government. The French ambassador was ordered to complain that he did not contribute to the harmony so necessary between the two Crowns. An attempt was, however, made to restore French influence at Madrid as a remedy for the dangerous isolation in which France was placed by the Anglo-imperial alliance.

The Marquis de Louville, whom Alberoni describes as a scoundrel of the first class,[2] who had once enjoyed complete ascendency over the king, was despatched to Madrid on a mysterious mission. The object of his secret instructions was to arrive at a settlement of the succession question, and to replace the Italian Government by a national administration which was expected to fall easily under French control. The means to the end was to stimulate jealousy between Giudice, Alberoni, and Daubenton. Giudice had just fallen ; but it is possible that from his visit dates the ill-feeling which grew up between the confessor and the minister. Louville was, however, not allowed to see the king, and was ordered to leave Madrid at once; a command with which he refused to comply until he received instructions from the regent. Louville himself believed that Alberoni was the sole author of so drastic a rebuff. A letter was conveyed to the king, through the medium of his confessor, complaining that Louville's dismissal was due to Alberoni. The king replied in his most dignified manner that the refusal to admit Louville to his presence was due to his express orders, and that any letters addressed to him might, for the future, be entrusted to his ambassador at Paris. Alberoni's letter on this subject illustrates his own hostile feelings towards the French Government. "They tried at

---

[1] *Arch. Nap.*, C. F. 58, Sept. 28, 1716.   [2] *Ibid.*, July 27, 1716.

first to frighten me, but without success. They then thought to bribe me by proposing that I should demand my pension with the certainty of its payment, and though I have never been willing to ask for it, they have meanly tried to throw it at my ribs, by paying the arrears as well. Believing that I had been bribed, they sent Louville with a letter to me, ordering that he should take no steps except under my guidance. However, the real end of this mission was to place at the king's side an insolent fellow who should recover the ascendency which he had of old exercised over the king's mind, and gradually reduce the king to a condition of distrust. . . . But they have seen that we can cut short and sharp, and are in a devil of a taking, knowing well that we do not choose to be any longer under tutelage, and that every man likes to be master in his own house." [1]

Friendship indeed between the two Crowns was impossible, while the king and regent had their eyes fixed on the succession to the French throne. The queen's thoughts were now bent upon such advancement, notwithstanding the disapproval of her step-father, who believed that, in trying to better her condition, she would spoil it.[2] Alberoni spoke with no certain sound. He had himself encouraged her hopes. He had foreseen that she might some day find herself in a position to play a great part in the world and make her name immortal.[3] But now he hesitated; the Spanish Court must act, he wrote, with dissimulation and reserve; it might be that the queen would be exchanging the certain for the uncertain. The Spaniards had willingly undergone much misery in Philip's cause; he had for fifteen years placed Spain and the Indies at the discretion of the French; what would they say, what would they do or think if he now left them to receive a new king at the hands of England and the States-General, with whom the decision would really rest? For this reason the regent was using every endeavour to win the maritime powers; if the prosperity of Spain could be restored, the exchange of thrones would be a matter

---

[1] *Arch. Nap.*, C. F. 58, Oct. 12, 1716.   [2] *Ibid.*, Oct. 30, 1716.
[3] *Ibid.*, March 2, 1716.

for much reflection, for the king could now rule Spain absolutely even while he slept, whereas the French were by nature disorderly, unreliable, and enterprising. A host of peers of the blood would, if the ministry lasted, become a herd of wild horses, speedily capable of giving trouble to the government; the parliament had made itself at once the corrective of royalty and its scourge.[1]

Notwithstanding these considerations it was felt to be intolerable that the regent should rob Philip of his birthright, and that this was his aim could not be doubted. His every action was directed by his hopes of the succession. To win this he would ally himself with the Turk; no reliance could be placed upon him. There was reason to fear an alliance between France and England if Spain continued to support the Pretender's cause. He had treacherously informed George I. that such support had been already given. The king and queen should treat him as though he might some day become an avowed enemy.[2]

The growing hostility of Spain to France implied a reconciliation with England. The alliance of the Hanoverian and Orleanist Governments was known or suspected, but was unpopular in both countries, and seemed unlikely to be durable. At all events the support of one or the other was essential to success in Italy, and England, in Alberoni's opinion, was the only power that need be feared. The attempts to secure the friendship of England was entirely due to the queen and Alberoni; the progress of the negotiations coincided with the decline of Giudice influence, and his fall was decided by the representations of the British minister. Previous to the death of Louis XIV. the latter had been unable to obtain any redress, or even any reply. The commercial clauses of the Treaty of Utrecht had been carelessly drafted, and the explanatory articles issued by the Spanish Government had deprived English commerce of most of the privileges which it had been intended to secure.

[1] *Arch. Nap.*, C. F. 58. Oct. 5, 1716.

[2] *Ibid.*, Nov. 28, 1715; Jan. 20, 1716; Aug. 30, 1716.

The grievances were manifold.   British ships had been
embargoed for the siege of Barcelona.   Others were boarded
and plundered not only in American waters but in the
Mediterranean.   The jurisdiction of the courts established
for the protection of foreign commerce was set at nought,
and the confirmation of the consuls' patents was refused.
The Donativo, a benevolence extracted from municipalities,
was imposed upon British merchants under pretence that
they were Irish Catholics and nationalised subjects.   Arbitrary duties were levied by the intendants at the ports.
The Spanish townspeople themselves realised that they
would lose their best market for fruit and wine, and two
aldermen of Malaga were banished for resisting a new duty
of 4 per cent.   The merchants were thought to be foolish
in continuing to ship, but the duties were generally increased
just as the merchandise was ready.   It was calculated that
the dues on British goods were double those of the reign of
Charles II.   This was aggravated by the fact that the
French, excluded by treaty from direct trade, were flooding
Spanish America with their wares, so that French goods
were as cheap in America as at Cadiz.   Their manufacturers
were beginning to undersell the English in the finer cloths,
because wool exported and woollens imported by land paid
lower duties than when shipped by sea.   Moreover, the
Spanish Government had not only negotiated with Legitimist malcontents in France, but had given encouragement to the Legitimist exiles from England.   Every ridiculous report spread abroad by Irish adventurers in Spain
found ready credence.   England could not be forgiven for
retaining Port Mahon, "the bridle of the Mediterranean,"
and Gibraltar, "the mistress of the Strait".   Methuen believed that Giudice was bent on a rupture with England,
basing his hopes on a rising in favour of the Pretender.
"Our ministers," wrote Alberoni, "have treated Methuen
as if they wished a breach ; their manners might have been
more suave and courteous even if they thought it for the
king's service not to come to an adjustment."[1]   Bubb was

[1] Sept. 30, 1715.

aware that Louis XIV. had established a correspondence between the Pretender and the Court of Spain. But within a fortnight of the old king's death he informed Lord Stanhope that the Queen of Spain was thinking of entering into relations with himself and with the Dutch minister. A few days afterwards the queen instructed Alberoni to negotiate with the British envoy. The medium was the Dutch envoy, who was no less than Ripperdá, as yet unknown to fame, and regarded by Methuen as "a very honest gentleman, heartily zealous for the service of his country".[1] Ripperdá persuaded Alberoni that it was essential to terminate the quarrels with England in order to reorganise the American trade, on which the revival of Spanish power depended. There was, he said, a perfect understanding between France and England to the Pretender's prejudice; the regent had engaged not to assist, directly or indirectly.[2] On October 19 Bubb wrote that he had discovered the man who had complete control over the queen, that he only cared for money, and that he had proposed to arrange a commercial treaty for a consideration of 14,000 pistoles (£12,600), of which 4000 were to be paid on the signature, and the balance on the ratification of the treaty. Lord Stanhope, out of regard for the person mentioned, for whom he had a singular esteem, consented to a payment of 10,000 pistoles, and in a postscript advised the minister, rather than miscarry, to pay 4000 more. On December 9 Bubb drew 4000 pistoles, and on December 15 he wrote for the balance of 10,000. He parted with it, he wrote, with more regret than if it were his own. Such is the celebrated bribe for which Alberoni has been accused by Spanish historians of selling the interests of his adopted country. Naturally enough, there is no reference to it in his own despatches. It is doubtful, however, if he ever demanded or received the money. He afterwards wished Lord Stanhope to contradict the report, which had given him much pain.

---

[1] Methuen to Stanhope, July 22, 1715. *R. O. S.*, 155.

[2] Alberoni, Sept. 30 and Oct. 7, 1715. *Arch. Nap.*, C. F. 58.

Stanhope replied that the money had certainly been paid. Alberoni assured him that in that case it had stuck to the fingers of Ripperdá and Bubb, and Lord Stanhope, who was far from credulous, believed that Bubb had been duped by Ripperdá.[1]

There was, in point of fact, little need for corruption. Alberoni would, indeed, have preferred to rely on the friendship of the States-General. Ripperdá had suggested that his government would provide ships with which the Spaniards might drive both French and English from the Indies ; Holland wished for no exclusive privileges for herself; payment for the ships sold was left to Alberoni's discretion. The Pensionary Heinsius was represented as being extremely jealous of the English monopoly of commerce, and no friend of the Hanoverian dynasty. Though not believing in the Pretender's success, he instructed his ambassador to act according to circumstances, and confessed to Alberoni that it might some day be necessary to restore the Stuarts. But Alberoni early realised that the friendship of either England or France was indispensable, and that of France was for the moment the less valuable and the less obtainable. It was equally important for England to arrive at an adjustment. Spain now and hereafter held a great advantage. She could tempt England by the bribe of commercial privilege, or terrorise her by threats of the Pretender. Thus, while Alberoni was expressing confidence in a favourable conclusion to his negotiations, support was still given to the Jacobites. As late as December money was sent to Cellamare for their cause, and Alberoni expressed regret that he could not send a few ships and troops.[2] The Duke of Parma was delighted at the help accorded; it would please God, and also get rid of a German devoted to the emperor's party. He urged Alberoni to use all endeavour to secure the return of the Tories to power.[3]

---

[1] Lord Stanhope to Craggs, Aug. 15, 1716. *R. O. S.*, 162.

[2] Alberoni, Dec. 2, 1715. *Arch. Nap.*, C. F. 58.

[3] Dec. 20, 1715. *Ibid.*

But the English Treaty was signed before the close of the year, though only after a thousand wranglings. Whatever was settled with the king in the morning Giudice and his party undid at night. The English minister ascribed the merit to Ripperdá and Alberoni, and advised Lord Stanhope that any message from the king or from himself to the latter would be well taken, and might be of service.[1] His own proposals had been accepted, and were put into Latin—" the worst piece of Latin that ever appeared since the monks' time ". The terms were better than the scholarship. The explanatory articles, by which Philip had sworn to his late wife to abide, were virtually withdrawn. Duties were reduced to the rate payable in the time of Charles II., and the privileges then enjoyed were restored. Exports and imports were subjected to the same scale of payment by sea and by land. English ships were allowed to obtain salt from the Tortugas. Bubb's most sanguine hopes were realised, and Lord Stanhope was anxious to make yet another treaty for the South Sea Company by the same expeditious method. The English Government was informed that Spain was prepared to drive the French from the Indies,[2] and that the king had now no dependence upon a change of dynasty in England, and that he gave ear to a minister who would lead him in the right way.[3] He had already shown such marked displeasure with the French that S. Aignan was pressing for his recall. Alberoni found little difficulty in persuading the British envoy that the unbridled ambition of the emperor for the absolute dominion of Italy would be prejudicial to England, and the German princes. By acting in favour of Spain England could permanently divide the Bourbon Crowns, and highly oblige the queen, who was absolute. If George I. would go a step farther and guarantee the reversion of Tuscany to the queen and her heirs, the Spanish Court would grant the most favourable conditions for English

---

[1] Bubb to Stanhope, Dec. 9, 1715. *R. O. S.*, 155.

[2] Bubb to Stanhope, Dec. 23, 1715. *Ibid.*

[3] Holzendorff to Stanhope, Dec. 30, 1715. *Ibid.*

commerce, and security for the Hanoverian succession ; the
Court was disposed to treat the French as the King of England might wish. England, wrote Bubb, could not make
Alberoni too great, for his greatness would imply wider influence in Spain than England had ever yet possessed. He
suggested that England should sell ships to the Spanish
Government through the medium of the South Sea Company. Nor was the queen forgotten. Alberoni mentioned
that she had talked much about English horses, for the
Spanish mounts were too fiery for a lady, and she had lately
been in danger of being thrown. A present of two or three,
wrote Bubb, would be taken as a compliment, and would
certainly keep her a friend more than was to be imagined
from such a trifle. Seven English horses were accordingly
sent to Madrid with English grooms. Two of these were
rendered unfit by sea sickness for a royal present. The
others were trotted out beneath the palace windows by Bubb
and Alberoni, the queen being prevented by her confinement
from at once trying their paces. " Without the queen,"
wrote the envoy, " we should never have done anything
here, and when she desists from supporting our interests we
may take our leave of Spain. I am fully persuaded that she
is hearty for them now, and a sworn enemy to France, and
I believe his Majesty may keep her so as long as he pleases." [1]
Support was no longer accorded to the Pretender. Alberoni
believed that notwithstanding his landing in Scotland he
would have to retire unless assisted by some foreign power,
or backed by a general rising ; if well advised he would not
play a desperate game, for he might be sure that if he did
not succeed to-day he might win to-morrow, for there could
not fail ultimately to be some power who would find it its
own interest to strike such a blow at England ; meanwhile
Spain must take no false step and close her ears to the
Stuart queen's request for arms and for the Irish troops in
Spanish service.[2] In March the Pretender was refused per-

---

[1] Bubb to Stanhope, June 3, 1716. *R. O. S.*, 156.
[2] Alberoni, Feb. 3, 1716. *Arch. Nap.*, C. F. 58.

mission to visit Spain, and no aid was given to his beggared
followers.

Yet it was not found easy to arrive at a final adjustment.
Partly this was due to Spanish methods of business. "There
is no making them do business," Bubb complained, " unless
one is perpetually dunning them."[1] Both parties, the French
and the Spanish, proved an obstacle to British interests. The
Spaniards opposed everything because it was not proposed
by themselves. The grandees were disposed to treat Philip
as a cypher, but this the queen would by no means permit,
however willing the king might be. The French party was
more active, and Giudice was its leader. He still controlled
the Committee for Foreign Affairs, and when British interests had been favourably dealt with in other councils they
were thwarted here. He had now little active power, but
his negative influence was considerable, and the English
minister therefore pressed Alberoni to publicly undertake the
administration. It was expected that Giudice's fall would be
followed by a defensive alliance between Spain and England, and this impression gained ground when Louville was
dismissed without a hearing. Alberoni, however, expected a
quid pro quo. He had protested that the delay was due to
the fact that he was not yet entirely master, and that neither
he nor the queen had a single person on whom they could
rely ; the queen was forced to take her measures and go on
little by little. He added, truly enough, that he could not
always get her to apply herself so much as he could wish,
and that it was difficult to engage a lady to think of matters
of trade.[2] But to the Duke of Parma he confessed that he
had delayed the conclusion of the Assiento Treaty in order to
see whether it would facilitate other matters ; if he could
succeed in making a stroke in the Indies, without which
Spain could never make anything of the wealth of that great
world, he would give King George matter for reflection.
Meanwhile the scarecrow that lived at Avignon might

---

[1] March 30, 1716. *Arch. Nap.*, C. F. 58.

[2] Bubb to Stanhope, May 24, 1716. *R. O. S.*, 156.

frighten him.[1] Nevertheless, in August the treaty was signed, and it only remained to draw up a code of rules for the decision of grievances, a vast sea, which Alberoni confessed to be above his knowledge, and which he would gladly have avoided. He recommended that a commission of merchants from both nations should consult with the English minister.[2]

This early sunshine of Spanish and English friendship was soon clouded. As early as April Ripperdá confided to Bubb that the reason of all difficulties was the information received by the Spanish Court of an offensive alliance between the emperor, England and the States-General. The king had reproached Alberoni with the concessions which he had made ; he had never been known before to be so angry. Bubb assured Alberoni that this information was incredible, and that it was a machination of Monteleone to bring the English into disfavour.[3] He pressed for Monteleone's recall from London ; he was in the interests of France and of the Pretender ; it was not wise that the ambassador of Spain should receive his instructions from Paris ; he was, moreover, no friend of Alberoni, with whom the French were likewise discontented. Alberoni, however, believed that the Whig government would find difficulty in breaking with the emperor ; his hope was that the nation might be won by commercial concessions. " I have always thought," he wrote, "that the union of interests between the emperor and the King of England would keep them at accord, but in the above-named adjustment, and in the Assiento which will follow, my aim has been to gain the nation and consequently the parliament, as one does not know what may happen."

Alberoni believed, not unnaturally, that the English people were Jacobite at heart, and that the national interests were

---

[1] April 20, 1716. *Arch. Nap.,* C. F. 58.   [2] Aug. 3, 1716. *Ibid.*

[3] Yet in March the arrangements were complete. English action was prompted by the desire to retain Bremen and Verden and by the danger in Mecklenburg, where the Russians, called in by the duke against his estates, were in occupation of the duchy.

concerned in commercial friendship with Spain. He therefore suggested a defensive treaty with England and the States-General. It was understood that the two latter powers would prefer a treaty both offensive and defensive, but such would be virtually aimed against France, and the suggestion could not be entertained. Lord Stanhope, however, admitted the necessity of checking the advance of the emperor in Italy by a fresh guarantee of its neutrality. He confessed that the English nation would do more but for the German ministers of George I., who urged the king not to lose the opportunity of profiting by the spoils of the luckless King of Sweden. The emperor's friendship was necessary for the retention of Bremen and Verden by the Electorate of Hanover.[1]

If some chance did not arise to bind England closer to Spain it was becoming clear that Hanoverian influence would predominate. At the end of April, Lord Stanhope confessed that England and the States-General were negotiating a treaty with the emperor, though Ripperdá swore solemnly that he knew nothing of it. To propitiate the Queen of Spain both England and France offered to ratify afresh the Treaty of Utrecht. It was believed, however, that the regent was prompted only by his desire for a guarantee of his claims to the succession, while a renewal of the provisions relating to the neutrality of Italy was thought to be rather prejudicial than advantageous to Spain. The emperor had committed breaches of his engagements which would enable Spain to profit by the first opportunity, which was impossible if these were condoned by a fresh treaty. The maritime powers could under no circumstances allow the emperor to touch Tuscany, and it might therefore be advantageous to Spain if he were given rope. In June Alberoni was able to send to Parma a copy of the terms arranged between England and the emperor, which were embodied in the treaty of June 5, and of a proposed treaty with France and the States-General. Yet it was after this that the Assiento was conceded, and Alberoni expressed

---

[1] Alberoni, April 6, 1716. *Arch. Nap.*, C. F. 58.

neither surprise nor indignation. He would give, he said, fine words to Stanhope, whom, of course, he could not trust, but his intimacy was useful, and if he offered an alliance it should be accepted if only to cause jealousy to the emperor. He admitted that it was with reason that the English complained of commercial grievances which the Spanish ministers would not regulate, and feared that he should have difficulty in satisfying the English nation, with which it was not to the interest of Spain to quarrel. These grievances meanwhile were causing increasing anxiety to the British minister at Madrid. Spanish irritation was on the rise, and British merchants were harshly treated. Alberoni told Bubb that he could do no more, and that the queen had made him promise not to lay further complaints before the king. In this there was probably exaggeration, for Alberoni, at the close of the year, wrote to the Duke of Parma that the king and queen regarded the leagues which were being formed with the greatest calmness ; the Catholic king was courted like a beautiful woman, and so far kept giving fair words to suitors, but was coy in bestowing further favours ; all wished to be his friends, and reserve was the best method of preserving their friendship ; both England and the States-General would fain make a league with Spain, but wished to be pulled by the ears in order to obtain better terms ; meanwhile their Majesties were engaged in reorganising the Departments of Finance and Marine, and consequently the trade of the Indies on which all depended.[1]

The repulse of Louville at Madrid had been followed by the gradual *rapprochement* of France to England. The French proposals, coolly received at first, had been made palatable by the ability of Dubois. The result was the treaty of November 28, 1716, which the accession of the States-General converted into the Triple Alliance of January 14, 1717. By the two systems of alliance Spain appeared completely isolated. Nevertheless, the early months of 1717 were singularly calm. England was offering her mediation

[1] Dec. 14, 1746. *Arch. Nap.*, C. F. 58.

between the emperor and Spain ; but Spain, thought Alberoni, could never make a treaty with the emperor without security as to Tuscany, and this could not long exist while the emperor was in Italy, and especially at Mantua.

This calm was probably in great measure due to the desire to propitiate the Papacy. Alberoni had, in concert with Daubenton, taken up the negotiations which, under the auspices of Louis XIV., had been begun at Paris. Giudice had been forced from the field. Macanaz, who, while still in exile, boldly protested in favour of an extreme view of royal prerogative, was silenced by the threats of the Inquisition, and Alberoni found no difficulty in arranging terms with the Papal envoy, Aldrovandi. The latter was despatched to Rome to bring the question to a conclusion. The Pope, however, raised unexpected difficulties; he modified Aldrovandi's draft, and above all hesitated to confer the cardinalate on Alberoni. The latter was naturally indignant. He had risked the odium of an arrangement which the Spaniards thought prejudicial to the monarchy. He had alone resisted the wish of the Councils of Castile and of State to refer the matter to a council. The terms which he had offered were better than those which the Spanish monarchy had ever deigned to accept. The Pope had failed to answer a letter written by the queen's hand, in which she had urged this favour for her faithful servant in terms so strong that they could be no stronger were she praying for Paradise. The Pope, however, was under the emperor's control ; he was mocking Spain, and taking every measure to frustrate Alberoni's intentions. The latter felt sure that unless Aldrovandi brought with him from Rome the cardinal's hat he would not be permitted by the queen to enter Spain, and it was this that at last brought the Pope to reason. Aldrovandi was stopped upon the frontier, and the negotiations began afresh. Alberoni was careful to suggest that the hat should be given for services rendered against the Turk and not for an adjustment which might bring unpopularity upon the queen. In a Consistory, held June 17, the cardinalate was conferred upon Alberoni ; and on June

26 the Spanish Government declared its dispute with the Papacy to be at an end.

The original demands of the Spanish Government were by no means satisfied. It had required that the right of subjecting the clergy to the Millones, a tax upon the chief articles of consumption, which was renewed by the Papacy every five years, should be granted in perpetuity, that the clergy should be subject to the tax on sales and purchases termed Alcabala, and to an annual charge on its estates in compensation for the loss of revenue on lands held in Mortmain. So also lands and revenues made over to ecclesiastical members of a family were required to contribute to taxation. The imperial sympathies of the Papal government or the pressure exercised upon it by imperial armies had been a cause of annoyance and danger. Bulls had been refused to the bishops appointed by the king, and the Pope had nominated to the sees in his gift persons absolutely disloyal to the reigning dynasty. It was demanded that the Pope should make his nomination from a list presented by the king, and that the king's nominees should enjoy their temporalties from the moment of nomination, and not from that of the receipt of the bulls. The Papacy was required to withdraw its right of imposing charges upon benefices, though a fixed sum levied equally on all benefices was suggested by way of compensation. Finally, the abuse of the episcopal courts caused a demand that a judge should be deputed by the Pope to try ecclesiastical delinquents, and that great restrictions should be placed on the rights of sanctuary. It is clear that some of these articles went beyond any concessions hitherto accorded to Catholic monarchs, and that they could have given almost complete independence to the Spanish Church. If reconciliation with Spain were desirable to the Papacy with a view to a counterpoise to the growth of imperial power, the favour of the Pope was even more essential to the success of Elisabeth Farnese and Alberoni. The terms, therefore, ultimately arranged receded considerably from the high-water mark of the original demands. The Pope agreed to despatch, as usual, the briefs for the Cruzada,[1] and the Millones and other taxes; to grant a tenth on ecclesiastical revenues in Spain and the Indies. The tribunals of the Dataria and the Nunciatura were reopened, and relations between the two courts resumed. The Papacy had refused to abandon any principle, though it made pecuniary concessions which it could withdraw. Ecclesiastical independence was sacrificed to the needs of temporal alliance in Italy. Spaniards were naturally indignant at the Italian queen and her ministers, who had surrendered to ultramontanism for their personal ends.[2] This surrender and the commercial concessions made to England are the chief charges laid against Alberoni by Spanish writers.

[1] The Bull of the Cruzada granted plenary indulgence to those who served personally against the infidels or paid an annual composition of about one shilling. The proceeds of this composition were granted to the Crown, nominally for the defence of Ceuta. It amounted to a general tax, for all persons were obliged to buy the indulgence before confessing or communicating.

[2] Belando, *Hist. Civil*, p. iv. c. 15, speaks of this arrangement as the sacrifice of the rights and the regalian profits of the monarchy.

CHAPTER V

ARREST OF MOLINES—CONQUEST OF SARDINIA—ITS VALUE
TO SPAIN—POLICY OF LORD STANHOPE—THE TRIPLE
ALLIANCE—ATTEMPTS AT MEDIATION—POLICY OF THE
REGENT AND OF THE KING OF SICILY—ALBERONI'S
REFORMS—HIS RELATIONS WITH RUSSIA, SWEDEN, AND
TURKEY—THE KING'S ILLNESS.

IT was from a sky comparatively clear that issued the thunder-
clap which ushered in a new cycle of storms for Europe. At
midnight on June 7 despatches arrived from the Duke of
Parma and the Marquis S. Felipe communicating the outrage committed by the Imperialists upon Molines, the newly-
appointed inquisitor-general, who was on his way back to
Spain. The circumstances were peculiarly aggravating. At
the Pope's instance he had been furnished with some sort of
safe conduct from the imperial minister at Rome. In spite
of this, he was arrested by the governor of Milan, and lodged
in the castle under the charge of the Spanish refugee Colmero. Here he shortly afterwards died.

Seldom has a series of wars found its occasion in so feeble
an old gentleman. Molines was appointed on Giudice's disgrace. A curious letter exists in which Aldrovandi begs that
his nomination may be withdrawn. He could not walk, and
had to be lifted into his litter. He could hardly write, had
almost lost the use of his voice, and had a delicate chest.
He could not perform his duties at Rome, much less could

he act as an efficient inquisitor-general. The Spanish Court, however, insisted, to its cost. It was not easy to find a Spaniard fit for the post. Molines had shown courage in the long campaign which he had conducted at Rome against the Papacy. In Spain he was held in high esteem, which Alberoni, however, did not share. The minister's letter, written immediately after receiving the startling news, indicates extreme irritation : "It is a barbarous outrage ; but it was madness on the part of that wretched Molines to cross the State of Milan. He is one of those people who has passed with this nation for an oracle, while it seems to me that throughout his embassy he has shown nothing but eccentricity and irregularity."[1]

The opportunity for action in Italy had indeed come a little too early, and for this very reason the rupture had perhaps been provoked by the imperial government. No more effectual measure could have been taken to provoke the queen, anxious for an opportunity of interference in Italy, and desirous, also, of completing the reactionary religious policy in Spain. The king was peculiarly sensitive to such an outrage on his dignity. But the reconciliation with Rome was not yet complete, and therefore, though the Spanish squadron was ready for sea, no immediate action was taken. The Duke of Parma, in the letter which conveyed the news of the arrest of Molines, suggested prompt measures : "You will be able to consider whether this might not be a favourable opportunity for changing the course of your squadron to these waters, and for replying to the outrage by some demonstration of resentment. However, such a matter requires much reflection, and we rely entirely on your prudence."[2] Alberoni, in reply, besought his master, for heaven's sake, to be prudent, and not to give the emperor the slightest ground for picking a quarrel, which was what he sought. Spanish money was sent to Italy to prepare against emergencies, but the duke was told that it would be highly imprudent to levy soldiers. The duke returned to the charge. It could

[1] June 8, 1717. *Arch. Nap.*, C. F. 59.   [2] May 27, 1717. *Ibid.*

not be right, he urged, to abandon Italy; its possession by the emperor would enable him to destroy the peace of the Spanish monarchy, which would be never secure if it neglected to apply in good time the strongest remedies; a tardy repentance would avail nothing; stringent orders had come from Vienna with regard to the succession of Tuscany, and it was believed that the Pope's family could be bribed by the promise of a Tuscan principality.[1]

This letter was followed by a long memorial,[2] under the assumed name of a Neapolitan nobleman, urging the conquest of Naples, and proving that that kingdom was ripe for revolt. When the latter letter arrived the Spanish fleet had already sailed. The slip of paper which announced the opening of the coming wars may still be read. "The squadron you wot of will leave the port of Barcelona on the 17th instant, and will proceed to the conquest of Sardinia, as being the easiest to preserve, this being the sole motive which has dissuaded that of Naples. The latter would perhaps force the emperor to make peace with the Turk, and descend into Italy with all his forces. Secrecy is recommended."[3] The secrecy which had been observed was indeed commendable to the Spanish Government. Yet the general intention of the armament, and even its immediate destination, were not unsuspected. Eighteen months before, Bubb had informed his government that the force given to the Pope against the Turk was intended to act against the emperor.[4] It was, in fact, the result of the imperial occupation of Novi. The idea of the conquest of Sardinia was even earlier than this. On August 26, 1715, the Duke of Parma stated his supposition that the dismissal of the French troops implied that the conquest of Majorca would not be followed by that of Sardinia. In his despatches of June 5 and 19 Bubb warned his government that the Spanish armament was intended for Sardinia, and

---

[1] June 2, 1717.   *Arch. Nap.*, C. F. 59.
[2] July 25, 1717.   *Ibid.*
[3] Alberoni, no date.   *Ibid.*
[4] Bubb to Stanhope, Feb. 19, 1716.   *R. O. S.*, 156.

then for Naples, or else for Sicily. He added that when, in 1716, the fleet sailed for the Levant the Council of State suggested that it should test the affections of the Sicilians, and that the infraction of treaties by the King of Sicily justified such a measure. The king had replied that such a step was not convenient yet.

More powers than one were in alarm, and since the great Armada, no fleet was probably watched with more anxiety. The fishermen of the Provencal coast were equally alert with the "gallant merchantman," who "came full sail to Plymouth Bay". The Savoyard ambassador at Madrid warned Vittorio Amedeo as to Sicily, adding, however, that the fleet was unequal to its conquest, and that it was unfit to stand a battle. The king wrote to Maffei, his Sicilian viceroy, that the armament was intended for Sardinia, Sicily, Naples, or Tuscany, and a week later that Sardinia was its probable destination. In the last week of July it was rumoured at Paris that the Spaniards had actually surprised Sardinia. The Austrian diplomatist, Königsegg, who was at Paris, believed that the armament was directed against Languedoc, or was to be employed in the Pretender's service. He could not think that the Spaniards would dare attack Naples or the Milanese. Bubb had long warned the governor of Port Mahon, who was to experience many such alarms, until the cry of wolf had lost its terrors. Yet greater was the alarm of Genoa. Its position was indeed critical. Technically independent since Andrea Doria's adhesion to Charles V., it had been in effect a satellite of Spain. When the Spanish monarchy was dismembered, it was to be expected that Genoa would follow the fortunes of its Italian provinces. This view had been, as has been seen, rudely adopted by the Court of Vienna. On the other hand, it seemed certain that in any Spanish aggression on Italy, Genoa would be one of the objective points. It might easily give to a Spanish invasion the *pied à terre* which Barcelona had offered to the Austrian invaders of Spain.

The fleet did not actually leave Barcelona until the last days of July. It consisted of twelve men-of-war and one hundred transports, collected in great measure by embargo upon neutral merchantmen. It took on board 8000 infantry and 600 horse, commanded by the Marquis of Lede. The two squadrons of which the fleet was composed took a different course, and the delay which occurred before they effected a junction at the mouth of the S. Andrés gave time to the viceroy, Rubi, to send for reinforcements. Little opposition was, however, offered. The inhabitants, Spanish in traditions and customs, welcomed the invader, while the Marquis S. Felipe, recently envoy at Genoa, himself a Sardinian, secured the adhesion of the upper classes. Cagliari was unable to stand a blockade, and by the end of November the island was reduced. It has been believed that, but for the delay in landing, the Spanish forces would have proceeded to attack the State of the Presidi or the Kingdom of Naples; but this supposition has been negatived by Alberoni's despatches, and, moreover, the fleet had only shipped stores for three months.

The intrinsic worth of the island of Sardinia was little, but at this conjuncture it had what may be termed a considerable occupation value to the Spanish Government. By the Treaty of Utrecht parts of the island of Elba had been left to Spain. The possession of Sardinia enabled the Spaniards at very short notice to reinforce the garrison of Porto Longone, and thus to threaten the coast line of Tuscany. But this was not the sole nor the chief motive for its acquisition. The Spanish Government was aware that the emperor intended to add Sicily to his dominions. As long as the maritime powers were opposed to such a project there was little or no danger, but the Treaty of Westminster between the emperor and the King of England guaranteed not only the actual possessions of the contracting powers, but those which they might acquire by mutual consent. By this clause a defensive was virtually converted into an offensive alliance, and it was known that the acquisition of Sicily was in view. The king had expressed himself as not unwilling for its surrender in November,

1716, and in this suggestion, as Dr. Weber well remarks, lay the germ of the Quadruple Alliance. The project took more definite shape in the negotiations for the Triple Alliance. It was intended by France and England that the Duke of Savoy should receive compensation for Sicily, while the Queen of Spain should be propitiated by the reversion of Parma and Tuscany. With this view Bubb had communicated proposals for a mediation between the emperor and Spain, and had sounded Alberoni on the terms. The latter said that the Spanish Court would like to owe such accommodation to England, but that he did not regard Tuscany and Parma as of sufficient importance to establish a balance, for the emperor was so strong in Italy that he could keep his word or not at pleasure ; Spain would deprive herself for ever of a chance of regaining her Italian possession, and this for a reversion which might never fall in, there being three lives in one family and two in the other between the queen and possession ; a verbal promise on the part of the mediatory powers was of no value, though immediate permission to send Spanish garrisons might make some difference.[1]

Spain, by the occupation of Sardinia, had deprived the emperor of the equivalent which might be offered to the King of Sicily. The only alternative was a portion of the Duchy of Milan, the loss of which would materially weaken the emperor's position. Sicily and not Sardinia was the real subject of dispute, and though the tactics of Spain were offensive, she was, in fact, acting on the defensive. She had ample reason for dissatisfaction. When Sicily had been assigned to the Duke of Savoy, the King of Spain had claimed that it should be held as a fief of the Spanish Crown. This had been categorically refused, and the claim was withdrawn. The French Government then supported Spain in the demand that its possession by the house of Savoy should be inalienable. Bolingbroke persuaded Maffei that this was not a matter of capital importance, because the

---

[1] Bubb to Stanhope, April 12, 1717. *R. O. S.*, 159.

only reasonable equivalent was the Duchy of Milan, to the west of the Adda, which the emperor would never cede. In the final draft the inalienability of the island was included, and this, too, mainly in the interests of England. France and Spain, indeed, believed that the possession of Sicily by an Italian power would secure to them the *entrée* to Italy in the event of imperial encroachment. The Venetians alone wished that Sicily should be ceded to the emperor on condition of his evacuating Mantua in favour of some less dangerous power. Bolingbroke replied that nobody would neglect the alliance of the Duke of Savoy for the sake of a republic that was no longer good for anything.[1] It was deliberately intended that the kingdom of Naples should be weak and isolated. The interests of England were more closely involved. She hoped to monopolise the carrying trade of Sicily if occupied by a non-maritime power. The house of Savoy would be dependent for its defence upon the English fleet. To Alberoni it seemed inconceivable that the Whig government, resting in great measure upon the commercial classes, should deliberately resign this invaluable hold upon Mediterranean commerce, and that for the costly friendship of the emperor it should sacrifice that of Spain, which gave England half its livelihood.

But with the Whig government dynastic interests predominated over commercial. The protection and extension of the electorate, and the boycotting of the Pretender by the chief European powers, were the two planks in the platform of George's ministry. The first had been made secure by the Treaty of Westminster, the second, as far as France was concerned, by the Triple Alliance. The opportunity had then offered itself of welding the two alliances into one. In September, 1716, hints had been thrown out by the imperial government that Charles VI. was prepared to surrender his claim to the Spanish throne in consideration for territorial advantages in Italy, and that he would secure the co-operation of France by acknowledging the Orleanist right

[1] Carutti, iii. 453.

of succession. The advantage to the regent seemed clear, for it was unreasonable to expect that Philip would resign his claim to the French throne, as long as that of Spain was rendered insecure by the emperor's pretensions. Lord Stanhope at once became the pivot of the negotiations ; he and his clever agents, S. Saphorin and Schaub, laboured unceasingly to reconcile the ambitions of the various powers. The Quadruple Alliance was the work on which the Stanhopes' reputation must mainly depend. Seldom has so much labour and so much ability been expended on the elaboration of a peace which implied the certainty of war.

The views of the allies were by no means hostile to Spain. The regent long refused to enter the alliance unless conjointly with the sister Bourbon State. Stanhope was honestly anxious to reconcile the emperor to the Kings of Spain and Sicily, to make peace in Southern Europe that his government might turn its whole attention to the North. Yet both France and England miscalculated the forces that were at work in Spain. With Philip the claim to the succession of the French throne was a matter of conscience, which the emperor's renunciation of his Spanish titles could in no way affect. With the queen, on the other hand, Italian liberation from the Germans had become a passion. The emperor's aggrandisement in Italy was the keynote of the Quadruple Alliance ; Elisabeth could not chime in unless the retrenchment of his power were substituted.

The emperor's original demands were indeed none too modest. The King of Sicily was required not only to surrender Sicily, but either Monferrat or the acquisitions of 1703. Tuscany, and Parma and Piacenza were to be recognised as imperial fiefs. Stanhope had demurred to mulcting the Sicilian king of his Northern possessions, and had put in a plea for the ultimate cession of Parma and Piacenza to Elisabeth's son. He did not inform the imperial government that his agents had already proposed to the queen the future investiture of Tuscany. In this condition negotiations lay when Alberoni struck his first blow at the emperor.

Lord Stanhope had acted with a sincere desire for peace, yet it is impossible to acquit the Whig government of the responsibility for the disastrous results of its short-sighted policy. In its reckless disregard for the Treaty of Utrecht, and in its prostration before the continental interests of the house of Hanover, it surrendered not so much the interests of Spain, but those of the house of Savoy, and therefore of Italy, without any possible equivalent. Not only was the carrying trade of Sicily sacrificed, but the trade of Spanish America, while the possession of Gibraltar and Port Mahon were gravely jeopardised. No more disastrous concession was ever made to the house of Hapsburg, and on no occasion might the familiar phrase, "Hands off Austria," have been so appropriately applied. The policy of the English Government was as fatuous as it was unfaithful. No so fair an opportunity of opening to England on honourable terms the riches of South and Central America has ever before or since presented itself. It is hardly romancing to suggest that but for the annexation of Bremen and Verden to the Electorate of Hanover and for the Russian scare, the Family Compact might never have been drafted, the United States might still form part of the United Kingdom, and Spain and the Indies might have developed a common civilisation impervious to pronunciamento, revolution, or presidential speculators.

Had the house of Savoy been loyally supported in the rights accorded to it by recent treaties, the Italianisation of Sicily might have been anticipated by a century and a half. The natural dislike of Sicilian to Savoyard might have been overcome to at least the extent to which it has been overcome at present.

It must be remembered, moreover, that by the Treaty of Utrecht the reversion to Sicily was secured to the Spanish Crown, in the event of the failure of the line of Savoy. This was no impossible contingency. These were the days of free living, copious bleeding, and of sanitation neither natural nor scientific. A drain, a doctor, or a drinking bout might make havoc of the most prolific dynasty. The French

Bourbons were a startling example. The Spanish Crown had fondly regarded the cession of Sicily as a temporary expedient. For its reversion no compensation was offered. A possession of a Spanish house, far older than Granada, far older than the union of Castile and Aragon, passed to a rival power. In the hands of the distant house of Savoy, which possessed no navy, it was, at least, not a source of danger. Now, with its magnificent ports, it was assigned to' the power which would thus hold two of the great harbours of the quadrilateral of the Western Mediterranean, Naples and Palermo, while it controlled the third in Genoa, and had until late in the century all the devotion of Barcelona.

The surprise of Sardinia was the signal for angry remonstrances from the great powers, and for a circular letter from the hands of the Secretary Grimaldo, in which the enormities of the emperor were cleverly set forth. The emperor threatened the Duke of Parma as being prime mover of his daughter's policy, and the Pope as being his accomplice. The Pope threatened to withdraw his nuncio from Madrid, whereon the Spanish minister replied that in that case no nuncio would ever return to Spain. An apologetic brief was addressed to the emperor, an expostulatory brief to the King of Spain, which the king returned unread. The English Government sent Colonel Stanhope to Madrid, and put pressure on the other members of the Triple Alliance to take concerted action. Bubb informed his government that it was owing to his representations that Spanish conquest had stopped short at Sardinia.[1] The loss of Sardinia had made the emperor more disposed to moderate his pretensions, and, on the other hand, Prince Eugene's rescue of the imperial troops by his brilliant victory at Belgrad rendered France and England less desirous to make the emperor supreme in Italy. It was proposed that a Spanish plenipotentiary should be sent to London to negotiate a treaty, by virtue of which Tuscany and Parma should be secured to the queen or her son as fiefs of the empire, under the guarantee of the Triple

[1] Bubb to Addison, Sept. 13, 1717. *R. O. S.*, 160.

Alliance; it was even suggested that Spanish garrisons might be admitted, except into Pisa and Leghorn.[1] Alberoni protested that the queen would never rob her step-father of his independence, and he persuaded the Duke of Parma to protest both against the Spanish garrisons and the imperial suzerainty. Tuscany and Parma, he said, were but *bicoques.* The offensive league which was offered in the event of imperial encroachment he regarded as useless while the emperor remained in Italy, to which Stanhope replied that the powers, in the face of recent treaties, could not be expected to turn him out. The queen and her minister were, in fact, from the first bent upon war. "The resolution of which you know," wrote Alberoni on August 6, " and others which we are going to adopt will serve to shake people out of their indolence, and to show the king who is Jew and who Samaritan. I am sure that the measures which I am taking for the coming spring will give some work this winter to the cabinets of the powers of Europe."[2] In January and February Alberoni's letters to Cellamare at Paris are full of fight. There would be no peace, he wrote, for Italy, and no balance of power for Europe, as long as a single German remained in Italy. The resolution was taken to die fighting, sword in hand. There were reasons to believe that Spain would not stand alone. The later combination of Spain, France, and Savoy was already foreshadowed. It had been regarded as certain in France that in the attack upon Sardinia Spain was acting in concert with Savoy. It was too fine a project, said the regent, to have been hatched at Madrid. Even before the expedition sailed it was reported that it was destined for Naples, and that the King of Sicily would provide the arms and artillery. The King of Sicily was, in fact, innocent, but he realised the full importance of the situation. He instructed his ambassador to take every means to discover whether the attack on Sardinia was made

---

[1] This was with reference to a proposal much affected by the English Government that Pisa and Leghorn should be severed from Tuscany and erected into a free State.

[2] *Arch. Nap.,* C. F. 59.

with the connivance of France. Donaudi replied that the
state of French finance prevented action, but that several
French ministers had told him that this was the best opportunity that the Italians had ever had of freeing themselves
of their fetters by an alliance with Spain for the expulsion of
the Germans.[1] An extraordinary envoy was sent to Paris by
the King of Sicily to press the regent to be loyal to his interests. Three points were urged as equally essential : the
retention of Sicily, the retention of the reversion to the
Crown of Spain, and the cession of Milanese territory
arranged in 1703.

The regent had many grounds for not wishing to be
forced into war against Spain, which would shatter his
finances and threaten his succession. Philip had declared
that he would fight to the last extremity, and if turned out of
Spain he would retire to France where his position as first
prince of the blood would give him consideration. When
Lord Stanhope urged the regent to send a squadron to join
the English fleet he refused on the ground that no breach of
the neutrality of Italy had been committed. But he went
farther than this. The Spaniards had scarcely been a month
in Sardinia when the Duke of Parma received a confidential
communication which was to be transmitted to the Court of
Spain. The regent was prepared to assist in the recovery
of the Spanish possessions in Italy on condition that the
succession of his house to the throne of France should be
guaranteed afresh. The duke strongly urged the acceptance
of these proposals on Alberoni. The guarantee required had
already been solemnly given ; its renewal could do no more,
and it could always be again withdrawn if Philip had sufficient force to back his claims ; the regent would be compelled
to execute his promises at once, the king would make engagements but for a distant contingency. Alberoni eagerly
welcomed the proposal, which, however, he regarded as
shameful as it was unexpected. He urged the duke to assure
the regent that he would act as his advocate and procurator.

---

[1] Aug. 23, 1717. *Rel. Dip. Sav.*

He hoped to complete the negotiation by the means of the Marquis Monti, who was expected at Madrid ; Italy once secured for Spain, an indissoluble union of interests between France and Spain would be assured, and the King of Spain would be in a position to give the Germans much to think about ; the accession of France was all the more important as it would entail the adhesion of Savoy to an anti-imperial alliance.[1]

Disappointment, however, was to follow. The dangerous state of Philip's health caused the regent to reflect that he was offering Italy to Spain without any equivalent that might not otherwise be gained. Alberoni's first despatches of 1718 are of much importance as foreshadowing the hopes and fears of the next two eventful years. . On January 3 he wrote : " It is absolutely impossible to place any reliance on the duke-regent, and consequently on the Duke of Savoy, the principle of the latter being to take no steps unless France engages herself. I, however, stand fast and fixed in my determination to execute our project, hoping in God, who will cause such contingencies to arise as will oblige others to concur in defending the public cause. I have observed that in the trade of war the daring generally succeed and that something must be left to chance."[2] During this month Philip's health improved, and on the 24th Alberoni wrote that the regent was showing a disposition to do all that was desired, that pressure was being exercised on his weak side, and that if France declared herself Savoy was also won. Meanwhile the writer was working without stint or stay to send the fleet to sea early in the year. In March the illusion as to French assistance was. at an end. The English Government had thrown all its weight upon the regent : he had once for all to choose between the Hanoverian and the Bourbon. The terms were now drafted which with slight modifications were ultimately embodied in the articles of the Quadruple Alliance. The Marquis de Nancré was despatched to Madrid with orders to support Colonel Stanhope

[1] Sept. 22, 1717.   *Arch. Nap.*, C. F. 59.
[2] *Ibid.*

in his proposals of mediation and in his threats of armed intervention. This produced temporary discouragement. Immediately after the ambassador's arrival Alberoni wrote that although the wiles of the Germans were known to himself every other power shut its eyes to them. Spain would be left alone, nay, more, the English would support the emperor with a Mediterranean squadron. It seemed to the main promoter of the war that his project must be for the time abandoned, but the interests of Elisabeth Farnese were now thoroughly involved, and the combination of ignorance and resolution by which she was characterised was at this crisis of great importance. Upon the following letter alone is it possible to base the theory which Alberoni elaborated in his own defence, and which has of late been usually accepted by historians, that he was not responsible for the war and that he did all in his power to prevent it. " I have already told your Highness that France will not join the dance and therefore it seems to me a difficult matter for Spain to open the ball alone, because even if she succeeded in conquering Naples it would be in my opinion impossible to retain it. Hence the best policy to adopt at present would be to yield to necessity and either lean towards any adjustment that may be proposed by the mediating powers, or else leave the whole in suspense and gain time by putting off the conclusion of the treaty. The king and queen, however, drawn on by our vast preparations and by the favourable disposition of the people of which we receive news from every side, think that it would be an act of cowardice and vacillation to withdraw from a project so generally known, so that up till now they have not given the least approval to my representations. . . . France is at present wallowing in vice and indolence, the regent dare not detach himself from King George, and the latter has his own private interests which keep him tied to the emperor." [1] The secret articles offered by Nancré were sufficient to tempt both king and queen and minister. They comprised the cession of Gibral-

[1] April 5, 1718. *Arch. Nap.*, C. F. 59.

tar, and the regent's guarantee of the Spanish regency for the queen in the event of Philip's death.

At this moment, however, important negotiations were opened with Savoy. The Duke of Parma had in February suggested that the King of Sicily might be caught by the bait which was known to be the only one at which he would bite and which he was never known to refuse.[1] The future of Italy would clearly in great measure depend upon the relations of Spain and Savoy. They had many interests in common, and also not a little cause for jealousy. Savoy protected herself against the encroachments of the imperial government by threatening the return of the Spaniard. The King of Sicily had insisted that the Spaniards should retain their foothold at Porto Longone until the territory ceded to him by treaty was actually in hand. But Savoy already deliberately had in view the absorption of Italy ; the well-worn metaphor that she would swallow it like an artichoke, leaf by leaf, was familiar to the other Italian princes and to Spain. When it had been proposed that the duke should exchange Piedmont for the far wealthier kingdom of Naples, Melarede had shown that Piedmont would ultimately carry with it Lombardy, Naples and Sicily. But the pressure put upon the King of Sicily to exchange his kingdom for Sardinia brought the two aggrieved powers into negotiations to which indeed there had been a previous inclination. Vittorio Amedeo had believed that the emperor's preparations for the Turkish war were probably but a pretext for an attack on Sicily, and the emperor had on his side feared that while engaged against the Turk he would be exposed to an attack by the combined forces of France, Spain, and Savoy. There was so much of reality in this idea that the Duke of Ossuna confided to Donaudi, the Savoyard secretary of legation at Paris, that he intended to stay in France throughout the winter of 1715-16, nominally to enjoy himself, but really to form an offensive alliance with France ; if, as was expected, the regent refused, Philip

---

[1] Feb. 25, 1718. *Arch. Nap.*, C. F. 59.

would return to France and assume the regency rather than expose his throne to an Austrian attack.[1] How far the Spanish government was implicated in such proposals is uncertain, their execution was delayed by the Duke of Ossuna's sudden death. At first sight the formation of the Triple Alliance seemed likely to counterbalance the danger arising from the Treaty of Westminster, but the action of England served only to increase the suspicion of the Spanish and Savoyard governments. Vittorio Amedeo offered his adhesion provided that the Treaty of Baden instead of that of Utrecht were made the basis, his reason being that in the latter no provision was made for the neutrality of Italy. He instructed his legation that, under pretext of assuring Sardinia to the emperor, for "Italy" should be substituted "Italy and the adjacent islands".[2] He feared that some quibble might arise as to the inclusion of Sicily in the guarantee, a point which was hereafter of some importance. The regent replied that he found neither of these proposals to be practicable. The English government refused point blank to enter into any engagements as to Italy, and insistance would have delayed the signature of the Triple Alliance.[3] On the capture of Belgrad by Prince Eugene the King of Sicily was told that the emperor could throw 16,000 men into Italy, and the promises made by France were insufficient to protect him. He was advised to satisfy the emperor by the cession of Sicily, receiving compensation in the Milanese with the title of king.[4] Such proposals constituted a serious danger for Spain, and it became necessary, at all events, to delay their acceptance by more tempting offers. Alberoni was unwilling to confide his views to the Savoyard minister, Del Maro, with whom he was always on bad terms, but early in 1718 he proposed to Cordero, the secretary of legation, that Spain and Savoy should combine to liberate Italy from the Germans. Lascaris was in April sent to

---

[1] Donaudi, Dec. 15, 1715. *Rel. Dip. Sav.*
[2] King of Sicily to D'Entremont, Nov. 14, 1716. *Ibid.*
[3] D'Entremont to King of Sicily, Nov. 27, 1716. *Ibid.*
[4] Donaudi to Lanfranchi, Feb. 1, 1717. *Ibid.*

Madrid to negotiate the terms of such an alliance. He expressed willingness that Sicily should be added to Spain, on condition that a Bourbon prince should be established in Italy, and that communication should be opened between the Spanish and Savoyard territories. It was taken for granted that Savoy should annex the Milanese, and that the Germans should be expelled. Alberoni proposed that the two Crowns should conquer the Milanese, which should fall to Savoy, but that Sicily should be at once ceded as a sacred deposit. The Savoyard complained that these proposals did not meet his two conditions, and protested against the sailing orders given to the Spanish fleet on the preceding night (May 21, 1718). Vittorio Amedeo's answer, however, did not arrive until June 30. He required large subsidies and a force of 10,000 men to be immediately despatched to Piedmont ; he refused the cession of Sicily on deposit as a thing unheard of. Alberoni retorted that the subsidy was excessive, that the king's answer had come too late, and that Spain had made her dispositions, and, indeed, on July 5 Palermo was in the hands of the Spaniards.

It was impossible that Vittorio Amedeo and Alberoni should trust each other. The latter did not conceal from the Savoyard ambassador that he knew of his master's negotiations with the emperor. And yet the King of Sicily was possibly in earnest, for he withdrew troops from Sicily and massed them on the Milanese frontier. Alberoni had told Cordero that Philip would go all lengths to restore Italy to her original liberty and peace under the gentle sway of Spain, but such was not the ideal of the house of Savoy. Spain after all opened the ball alone, and Sicily was to be the ballroom. Here it was possible to inflict a blow upon the emperor without danger of a counterstroke. Without securing Sicily it was impossible to conquer Naples, but its acquisition would stimulate the disaffection which was being fostered by emissaries and by fly leaves in the emperor's South Italian possessions. Moreover, it could be urged that Sicily was not included in the guarantee accorded to the neutrality of Italy. Spain was, as the event proved, fully a match for the unassisted forces of the emperor and Vittorio Amedeo. For this Elisabeth Farnese can claim some little credit. She had loyally supported Alberoni against French intrigue, against the discontent, at times amounting to mutiny, of the victims of his reforms, against even the cabals of the palace, headed by her prime favourite Laura Pescatori. The results of his administration were regarded by friend and foe as marvellous. He had the merit of believing in the innate vitality of Spain. Before the marriage of the queen he had privately expressed his conviction that in the present condition of Europe the King of Spain might play a great part in Europe, and that in more ways than one. At the close of 1715 he wrote : " I become more and more sure that it only depends upon the king to make a figure in the world, and I can tell your Highness that materials are not lacking ".[1] He began to hope that the affairs of Spain would prosper, more perhaps than those of any other potentate, for the King of Spain alone could call himself free from debt ; his want of credit had proved the salvation of his monarchy. Yet Alberoni would at times despair. Notwithstanding the king's discernment, to which the minister did full justice, he lacked courage and resolution. He was incurably indolent, and yet jealous of his authority, though his secretaries made what use of it they pleased. These secretaries hindered rather than helped. This he experienced during the preparations for the expedition destined for the Levant. " On my return I found that not the least thought had been given for the despatch of the six ships and four galleys. It is death to have to deal with these ministers, who, some from malice, some from ignorance, and others from laziness, will not work   Believe me that the secretariate at Parma does more in a day than these four do in a week, and each one is composed of nine members, and this is no exaggeration." [2]   All the schemes projected for the glorious revival of the monarchy were suspended for want

---

[1] Nov. 25, 1715. *Arch. Nap.*, C. F. 58.
[2] April 6, 1716. *Ibid.*

of a single person to give thought to them. War had ceased, and yet taxation was not reduced; for the king there was neither love nor respect, and all the world was disgusted; it seemed impossible that the country should ever rise—it would soon be without troops, without ships, without credit or commerce, the people beggared by taxation, the nobility lost to all honour and reduced to despair. "To stay these fatal misfortunes I have neither heart nor spirit, unless I am given strength and powerfully assisted, in which case I can without vanity assure your Highness that to all these imminent disasters the remedy could be applied." [1] Heaven helps those who help themselves. Alberoni's depression did not cause any relaxation in his efforts. Night after night he forced the king and queen to consider his reforms. He convinced them that Spain should be a naval and not a military power. She could never engage in a continental war without the aid of France, and a force of 50,000 men would suffice to hold Catalonia down. The expensive Walloon, Italian, and Irish guards should be replaced with the Swiss, which the Crown of France was now disbanding. He wished to tempt the native Spaniards back to agriculture, the neglect of which had been the ruin of the country. The Prince of Havrech, chief of the Flemish party, and one of the most influential noblemen at Court, resisted Alberoni, and, at the Duke of Parma's suggestion, was sent into honourable exile. Extraordinary activity was imparted to the arsenals and shipbuilding yards, and, pending the construction of a national fleet, Alberoni projected the purchase of ships from Holland, Hamburg, Genoa, Russia, and the South Sea Company. Everything depended on the trade with the Indies. If this were reorganised the king would not have to beg a pittance from the Pope. But for the intervention of the Italian question, an early attack would have been made on the English and French contraband trade in the Indies. The disaffected provinces of Catalonia and Valencia

---

[1] July 6, 1716. *Arch. Nap.*, C. F. 58.

were not only fortified from an attack from within or without, but their administration was remodelled and simplified, and they began to contribute to the royal revenues. The department of finance was rigorously overhauled. Official pluralities were abolished, and a large reduction was made in the overgrown staff of the Judicature and Civil Service. The prosperity of the country began to revive. Native manufactures were encouraged and stimulated by the im-portation of foreign instructors. Moreover, such talent as existed in the country was seeking its level. It is true that this was mostly of foreign origin. The best soldier, the Mar-quis of Lede, was a Fleming; the best sailor, the Marquis Mari, a Genoese. The negotiations or conspiracies at the French Court were conducted, as was believed, with consummate skill by the Neapolitan, Cellamare. Of more real ability was Alberoni's countryman, Beretti Landi, who for long frus-trated the endeavours of the allies to make the States-Gene-ral declare against the King of Spain. But it was certainly not Alberoni's wish to exclude native talent from the royal service, and Spain could claim some credit for the two ablest officials whom the great crisis brought to the front. The brothers Patiño were of Spanish origin, but their family had for long been settled at Milan.[1] They had had no small share in determining the disgrace of Giudice, and their talents were fully recognised by Alberoni. The elder of the two, the Marquis Castelar, devoted his energies to the department of war. He was self-indulgent and indolent, but he boasted, not without some justification, that when he worked he could do in one hour what others did in eight. But Alberoni's right-hand was Don José Patiño, intendant of marine. He is heard of now at Cadiz, now at Barcelona — wherever, in fact, there was work to be done. During the siege of Barcelona he was seen in the August sun working on the shore from morning to night, eating on the spot a mouthful of ham, that there might be no delay. And now,

---

[1] Bragadin calls Castelar a Milanese, adding that his ability or penetra-tion would have caused his rapid promotion if not retarded by the dislike of Grimaldo and the fact of his being a foreigner.

again, he was on the mole night and day superintending the embarkation of troops and stores, dealing at once with fifty persons in different departments, never confused by the multiplicity of business, sifting it as it came to hand, and distributing it among his subalterns, who in turn rendered their reports.   To him, perhaps, as much as to Alberoni, Spain owed her magnificent armament, finer, as S. Felipe believed, than any of those which had sailed from Spain in the glorious reigns of Charles V. and Philip II.   Alberoni had just cause for boasting. He could treat with disdain the calumnies industriously spread abroad by the Court of Vienna for the purpose of making him unpopular in Spain. The favour of his mistress was still unshaken. He could hear Spaniards say aloud that through his means they saw a navy such as Spain had not seen for two centuries.   Three hundred sail were on the Mediterranean alone, with 33,000 troops on board, of whom 6000 were cavalry ; 100 pieces of siege artillery, besides a field-train, 20,000 quintals of powder, 100,000 balls, 66,000 trenching tools, bombs, grenades— everything, in fact, that so large a force had need to carry. He was absolutely master of the troops, because he alone had punctually paid them, and the best officers owed him their promotion.   Notwithstanding his protests to Colonel Stan- hope, he was in no mood for peace.   Five days after the sail- ing of the fleet he wrote to Parma that no guarantee should be accepted but the total expulsion of the Germans ; without this Italy could never enjoy peace nor safety.

Yet Alberoni cherished no illusions.   He was fully aware that Spain could not fight the united powers of Europe, when even the Grand Monarque had failed.   He believed that the sole aims of George I. and the regent were to keep king and to become king, and that for this they needed the friendship of the emperor and were prepared to betray to him all the strongholds of Italy.   What else could account for the sacrifice of Sicily, the only means of making the emperor a naval power?   But the regent, he believed, would hesitate to declare against Spain.   His own ambassador, Nancré, had condemned his conduct, and

regarded him as abandoned by God, and brutified by
vice, faithless to his engagements, without hope of being led
back into the right path.[1] Cellamare at Paris pulled the
wires of a conspiracy which might at any moment overthrow
the regent. Notwithstanding Prince Eugene's victory at
Belgrad, it was still hoped that the Turks would keep the
Imperial troops employed upon the Hungarian frontier. It
was as yet uncertain how the negotiations opened at Passarowitz would result, and it was this in great measure that
prevented the regent from taking active measures. No
such formidable charge was ever made against Alberoni as
that he was in alliance with the enemies of the faith. This
in every Apologia he stoutly denied, and indeed his denial
was accepted by the Papacy. Yet his own words prove
that the accusation was not far removed from truth. In his
despatches he confesses his intimacy with Ragotski, Prince
of Transylvania, the emperor's rival and the Turks' ally.
" Ragotski," he wrote on November 29, 1717, " makes me
hope that the Turk will not make peace, if one were willing
to take certain measures, for which purpose I have despatched a person with the character of envoy, and with
full instructions which the prince will be able to utilise with
whomever he may think it necessary." The Duke of Parma
replied that it would be very helpful if the emperor could be
prevented from shaking himself free from the Turkish War.[2]

---

[1] May 16, 1718. C. F. 59.

[2] Alberoni, in a pathetic letter to the Duke of Parma after his disgrace,
thus deals with this question: " As for the Turk, your Highness knows that
there has never been the slightest intercourse. With regard to Ragotski, he
wrote two letters, one to the king and another to me, in which he asked for
some assistance, which was absolutely refused. He begged that his Majesty
would send an officer to reside with him in the character of envoy, saying
that such a mark of distinction would gain him credit with those barbarians.
His Majesty sent a commissioner in order to have a spy at Constantinople to
supply good information about that Court. As soon as he arrived he wrote
that it was inclined towards peace, and that it would certainly bring it about.
His Majesty, therefore, ordered his officer to return, much to Ragotski's disgust, who inveighed against me because I had not written to him. The king,
on despatching his officer, wrote a courteous reply to Ragotski, saying that
in the coming campaign he would make vigorous war upon the emperor, and

But the power chiefly to be feared was England, and for her Alberoni hoped that he could find full employment. He knew of the hostility of the Czar and the King of Sweden to the Hanoverian dynasty. The former had been thwarted in his attempt to extend his power in the Baltic; he was alarmed at the threatened conversion of Hanover into a maritime State by the aid of English resources. He had attempted to draw the regent away from the English alliance. The King of Sweden was naturally unable to forgive the share which the Hanoverian had taken in dividing the spoils during his enforced exile. He was yet more irritated by the somewhat ridiculous collapse of the conspiracy which his agents, Goertz and Gyllenborg, had conducted in the pretender's favour. Yet England seemed secure, for the one power counteracted the other. To reconcile Peter the Great and Charles of Sweden might well have seemed impossible. Yet this it was that Alberoni effected.

It is not clear how far he was implicated in the earlier plots, but his despatches show that from the end of 1717 he was busily engaged in the attempt to form a northern league against England and the emperor. If the northern barbarians could but once be reconciled, Sicily could be conquered within the year, and an attack made upon Italy in the coming spring.[1] "Success," he wrote, "depends upon the northern league, for the consolidation of which I have worked more than eight months, moving heaven and earth; but I have to deal with people born in a cold and changeable climate."[2] Upon this league he believed all hopes of success to depend. "If the Czar, Sweden, and Prussia do not make a

that if he had sufficient power he might perhaps hope to conquer his territories. I wrote another to the same effect, and enclosed that of his Majesty. All this he did with the approval of the theologians, who said that in the case of Ragotski, a Catholic prince, he might have full intercourse with him; there—that is all my intelligence with the Turk." Feb. 29, 1720. C. F. 64.

[1] Aug. 29, 1718. C. F. 59.

[2] Sept. 5, 1718. *Ibid.*

league, we shall be forced to accept the infamous proposal." [1]

It was intended that the Czar, supported by Prussia, should attack the emperor from the north, while the King of Sweden should effect a landing in England, and proclaim the pretender, who was to be conveyed thither by a Spanish fleet. Little doubt was entertained that there would be a general rising against the Hanoverian Government. But for the conclusion of this league it was impossible to wait.

During the Sardinian expedition and the preparations for the Sicilian campaign the King and Queen of Spain almost vanish from sight. Elisabeth was living in an unwholesome atmosphere of palace intrigue. Money had been given to Laura Pescatori for her return to Italy, but the queen's good-nature had at the last moment prevented her departure. She gave Alberoni more trouble than all the interests of the State. She stimulated every intrigue that was formed against him in the Babel of tongues and nations which the palace had become. It seemed inevitable that Maggiali would be invited to Spain, and that the Duke of Parma would lack courage to refuse permission. Philip's health was becoming a source of constant anxiety. He believed himself to be suffering from an internal fire, which the doctors declared to be a pure delusion. By the autumn of 1717 the malady had developed alarming energy. " For the last eight months," wrote Alberoni, " this poor gentleman has been showing symptoms of insanity, his imagination inducing him to believe that he is destined to die immediately, fancying himself attacked by all sorts of diseases in turn." He fancied that the sun had struck his shoulder and penetrated into his weaker organs. To all the arguments that were adduced against the possibility of such a malady he would reply that he had the misfortune not to be believed, and that death alone would justify his statement. Alberoni thought that he might become totally insane, and the doctors feared for his life. He could not

[1] Oct. 10, 1718. C. F. 59.

sleep, and became thinner day by day. Alberoni was advised to lose no time in making preparations for the future, and the king himself pressed him to draw up his will securing the regency for the queen, a subject which led to much anxious correspondence between the cardinal and the Duke of Parma, the former thinking it doubtful whether the stepmother of the Prince of Asturias could constitutionally be appointed regent, even by virtue of the king's will. The situation was rendered the more anxious by the fact that the Regent Orleans was intriguing to overthrow, by force if necessary, the intended regency, and to substitute a Council of Regency, consisting of his own creatures among the Spanish grandees. At the close of the year Philip's bodily health improved, though his mind still halted. He fancied himself to be dying from moment to moment, and would often call the confessor at between two and three o'clock at night. The Duke of Parma sent his own doctor, Cervi, who was destined to become a personage at the Spanish Court, after overcoming the preliminary difficulties of professional and national jealousy. "If Doctor Cervi," wrote Alberoni, "has courage, phlegm, and patience, he may possibly gain the confidence of the king and queen, enjoyed at present exclusively by three men—the doctor, the surgeon, and the chemist—who never stir from the king's room. These are three sly and artful Frenchmen, and I fear that they may turn the Italian doctor to ridicule, just as happened to the poor Sardinian doctor who was reduced to play a pitiable part in the palace, and I fear that poor Cervi may be disgusted at once and make up his mind to leave, but if he will trust to me I will try and illuminate him as to the line he will have to take." [1] The king's health was naturally the all-absorbing subject of interest for the queen. There is little doubt that she was now sincerely attached to him. Alberoni described their touching tenderness for each other. They always hunted together, and their sport took the form of wholesale slaughter—six stags falling in two hours. The

---

[1] Dec. 17, 1717. C. F. 58.

king and queen would eagerly and pleasantly dispute their claim to each head of game.[1] He regarded, however, the queen's indulgence for the king's fancies as most prejudicial to his health, and spoke plainly and earnestly both to herself and her stepfather, but with little permanent result. " Her indulgence," he concluded, "is a subject for pity, because she loves him tenderly, and suffers with a courage that the greatest martyr has never shown." [2] The king's health was indeed the chief cause for anxiety during the early stages of the Sicilian campaign. It was believed that his life could not be long. He could retain nothing that he ate, and yet he was always eating. His legs were swollen, and he was unable to stand upright. His scruples of conscience were increasing, and the worst of all was that there was no hope that he would allow himself to be cured.[3] Other ambassadors regarded the queen as being the absolute mistress of the king. Alberoni describes her as his perfect slave. She would ask no favour for herself or her friends. She was literally unable to be alone for a single moment in the day. The king followed her wherever she might go. " She has so vehement a passion for him that it has reduced her to a blind subjection and to complete loss of will. . . . Would to God that the queen would have had the strength to do that which I have for two years been suggesting, with tears in my eyes, and perhaps we should not now be in the condition in which we are. The king requires governing as he was governed by the late queen." [4]

[1] May 11, 1717. C. F. 58.
[2] Jan. 8, 1718. C. F. 59.
[3] Nov. 22, 1718. *Ibid.*
[4] Nov. 28, 1718. *Ibid.*

CHAPTER VI

INVASION OF SICILY—BATTLE OF CAPE PASSARO—RUPTURE
WITH ENGLAND, FRANCE AND THE PAPACY—FRENCH
INVASION OF SPAIN.

THE Spanish fleet set sail from Barcelona on June 17. As
in the recent Garibaldian invasion Palermo was the objective, and as Garibaldi landed at Marsala, so the Spaniards
had intended to make the neighbouring port of Trapani. It
is from the land side that it is most difficult to defend
Palermo. A storm, however, drove the Spaniards from the
west coast, and the landing was effected some twelve miles
east of Palermo in the little bay which lies beneath the ruins
of the old Roman town of Salunto. An easy march across
the base of the promontory brought the Spaniards to Palermo.
The viceroy Maffei evacuated the town, and the citadel made
only a nominal resistance. A large ship was taken in the
bay. The Spanish Government had protested its intention
to hold the island in deposit for the King of Sicily until the
danger of its transference to the emperor had passed away,
but as soon as Palermo was secured no secret was made of
the real object of the invasion. The Spanish commanders
issued a proclamation that they had come to liberate the
island from the tyranny of the Savoyard. This was no mere
form of speech. The whole country rose for Spain, and it is
this national enthusiasm which gives the Sicilian expedition
its peculiar interest as compared with the other wars of the
reign of Elisabeth Farnese.

To the present day the traveller in Sicily feels the island
to be in character rather an annex of the Iberian than of the

Italian peninsula. A common substratum of Moorish blood may partly account for this, but apart from this it is the natural result of four and a-half centuries of Spanish rule, voluntarily accepted. The island from its architecture to its donkeys bears the mark of Spain. The recent Neapolitan, the present Italian government appear to the natives as a foreign domination, much more so the Savoyard government which had existed but some three years. The Savoyard had indeed been welcomed as an alternative for the German. Vittorio Amedeo had visited the island and been well received. He was generally supported in the quarrel with the Papacy with regard to the legatine authority of the king, which he had inherited from the Spanish government. Pope and king had come to an open breach. Recalcitrant clergy were expelled the island and landed on the coasts of Italy. Sicilians vied with Savoyards in enforcing the royal edicts. But all had changed with the king's withdrawal. Palermo was not after all to be the seat of a monarchy. The supreme council for Sicily was established at Turin. The island was again to become a province, and that not of a boundless empire which stretched from world to world but of a poor and paltry principality on the Alpine slopes. Spain though dismembered could still offer valuable employ, Savoy regarded Sicily as a preserve for the benefit of its needy officials. The Savoyard economy was regarded as parsimony, no credit was given for the order introduced into the finances. There are countries where the possession of a balance is regarded as a grave indictment against the government. The character of the Savoyard then as now was incompatible with the Sicilian temperament. He was a foreigner far more than was the Spaniard. The nobles believed their privileges betrayed by the introduction of modern methods of monarchical government, there was a reaction even in favour of the persecuted clergy.

None but Savoyards followed Maffei out of Palermo. All the large towns, and even the little hill villages, shut their gates against the viceroy. He could get neither bread nor water, he represented the natives as being far more formidable than the Spaniards. The Sicilian squadron at Malta mutinied, and the seamen went off to Palermo. In the south the scenes of the Sicilian vespers were re-enacted against the isolated Savoyard detachments. At Girgenti there was desperate fighting. Throughout the campaign the aid of the natives was of incalculable advantage to Spain. The nobility enthusiastically raised levies among their retainers, nor was there any symptom of change until the situation had become desperate. While the viceroy was wearily forcing his way across the mountainous heart of the island, the Spanish cavalry followed the coast-road and the infantry was conveyed by sea to effect the conquest of the eastern section.

At this moment the English fleet made its appearance in Sicilian waters. No sooner had the capture of Palermo become generally known than Admiral Byng informed the Spanish government that he was empowered to offer English mediation, and that he was ordered to resist any attack upon the emperor's dominions. Alberoni returned his letter with a marginal note : " His Catholic Majesty commands me to inform you that the Chevalier Byng may execute the orders which he has received from the king, his master. Escurial, July 15." The Spanish Court had no fear that it would be interrupted in its Sicilian operations, and when it was ready to attack upon the Imperial territories the English squadron would doubtless be otherwise employed. But the Spanish and English fleets found themselves at too close quarters in the Straits of Messina to part without fighting. It has always remained uncertain which squadron fired the first shot. But the action of the English admiral was undoubtedly offensive. He had "shadowed" the Spanish fleet down the Straits, and had prevented its divisions from effecting a junction. The Spaniards were unprepared for fighting ; they had troops and stores on board, they lost the wind, and were in dangerous proximity to the shore. Ships are more easily manufactured than sailors. The Spanish admiral, Gastañeta, had no experience in manœuvring a fleet, he was not at complete accord with his more able subordinate Mari, and was perplexed by the orders of Patiño. A squadron under Guevara had been foolishly despatched to Malta, and only returned when the action was practically decided.

The battle off Cape Passaro does not rank among the great achievements of the English navy. It may be classed with Navarino and the bombardment of Alexandria as one of its untoward incidents. Cordial alliance with the Bourbon dynasty of Spain was perhaps impossible, but this action, fought in a cause which was not that of England, alienated the Spanish people always well disposed towards English friendship. The queen whose favour had been regarded as indispensable to British commerce never forgave the total destruction of her great minister's work. On the arrival of the news of the disaster an embargo was laid upon English ships and English merchants were imprisoned. Alberoni indeed assured Lord Stanhope who was now in Madrid that this was against his orders, and would not allow him to go to the Escurial for fear he should be insulted. He told Nancré that he should like to hear that the Spaniards had lost 10,000 men; this alone would bring the king to think of peace.[1] He as well as Daubenton protested to Nancré that they were anxious for an accommodation, but that the king and queen were inflexible. Even before the action Alberoni had told Lord Stanhope that he was not the author of the war and that if he were master it should cease; Spain would be more powerful by confining itself to the peninsula and the Indies and ruling them well; he himself would prefer Oran to Italy; peace and the friendship of neighbouring powers would suit his private interests, and place him in a condition to sustain the form of government which he had established and which would not last three days after his fall. Lord Stanhope believed that Alberoni was not quite straightforward, but also not quite master.

The attack on Sicily had precipitated the conclusion of the Quadruple Alliance. Early in July a convention was signed

[1] Stanhope, Oct. 31, 1718. *R. O. S.*, 162.

I

by Lord Stair and Dubois, and was subsequently approved by the French council. On August 2 the Imperial minister in London had affixed his signature. Beretti Landi still dissuaded the States-General from taking any decisive step, but Vittorio Amedeo made over his remaining fortresses to the Imperial government, and Austrian troops were conveyed to Sicily by English ships. The king received in exchange the title of King of Sardinia and the reversion to the crown of Spain. The secret articles of the treaty provided for concerted action against the King of Spain if within three months he declined to accept the terms of the allies. In addition to the acknowledgment of the queen's claims to the Italian duchies Lord Stanhope held out the cession of Gibraltar as a further bait. But the Spanish Court was hoping that the northern powers would declare themselves, and neither Lord Stanhope nor Nancré could obtain any satisfactory reply. In October letters of reprisal were issued to Spanish privateers. Nancré left Madrid early in November and the English minister shortly followed.

The year closed disastrously for Spain. The agreement between Russia and Sweden had at length been concluded. Charles opened the campaign for the conquest of Norway and the recovery of Bremen and Verden which was to be the prelude for the invasion of England. But on December 11, he was shot at Frederickshall. The confederacy upon which alone the Spanish government placed reliance crumbled to pieces, and Goertz, the Alberoni of the north, met his death upon the scaffold. The inaction of the Czar and the conclusion of the peace of Passarowitz enabled the emperor to pour troops into Italy. Naples was now safe and the Spaniards were in danger of being besieged in Sicily. The action off Cape Passaro had not prevented the capture of the citadel of Messina. Trapani, and Syracuse, the sole fortresses left to the Germans were blockaded by the Spanish cavalry, but the bulk of their forces were concentrated before the entrenched camp of Melazzo. Daun the Viceroy of Naples had landed a large force in their rear and they were forced in turn to entrench themselves, with scarcely a hope of receiving renforcements.

Meanwhile, in Spain, discontent already manifested itself. The depreciation of the coinage produced dissatisfaction. In Guipuscoa and Biscay there was a rising in consequence of Alberoni's fiscal measures. He had abolished internal impediments to traffic, but had established a common system of customs upon the frontiers. The trade of the northern provinces was with France rather than with Spain, and they had hitherto been free upon that side. The royal judges were unable to enter Biscay, and it became necessary to send troops to reestablish order. The Duke of S. Aignan had long tampered with the fidelity of the grandees hostile to the queen and Alberoni, and spread rumours abroad with regard to the undue influence exercised upon the king in the matter of the regency. Alberoni's old enemy, Veraguas, was arrested, and S. Aignan was sent under guard to Alcalá, whence he thought it prudent to escape in disguise to France. This rendered certain the expulsion of Cellamare. He was ordered to hold on until the last moment, and then to publish his protests and fire his mines. These mines comprised the seizure of the regent, for which purpose a band of salt smugglers was collected in the neighbourhood of Paris, a rising in Brittany, which was suffering from fiscal oppression, and the convocation of the Estates-General, which were intended to proclaim Philip V. as regent. Measures were taken to form the *cadres* of a military force by securing the services of unemployed officers. Proclamations were in print addressed to the Estates-General and the Parliament, as were also the replies which it was intended that they should present. Discontent and distress were so universal in France, that this conspiracy was perhaps not so chimerical as it may appear. Some of the princes of the blood were deeply implicated; the marshals regarded Philip's claims with favour, and the acceptance of the Quadruple Alliance had pleased no one but Dubois. But Cellamare's mines fired themselves prematurely, and at the expense of those who had laid them. He took the oppor-

tunity of the departure of the young Abbé Porto-Carrero and
the son of Monteleone, Spanish ambassador in England, to
convey to Alberoni copies of the various proclamations, and
a list of the conspirators. The French Government was
already on the track of the conspiracy, and it now had the
opportunity of striking. The *dénouement* was due either to
information given by one of Dubois' numerous acquaintances
among the *demi-monde* or to the imprudent anxiety of Porto-
Carrero for his portmanteau. The two young men were over-
taken at Poitiers, and relieved of their papers. Cellamare's
house was searched, and full information fell into the regent's
hands. The Duke and Duchess of Maine, the Cardinal
Polignac, the Marquis of Pompadour, the Duke of Richelieu,
and many others were arrested. Marshal Villars narrowly
escaped. Cellamare was conducted to the frontier, and
France declared war on January 9, 1719, twelve days after
its declaration by England.

It had become a matter of general belief that Alberoni
was the author of the war, or at least that Spain could not
continue the war after his fall. The allies therefore directed
their efforts to his overthrow. This had been the object of
the accusation brought against him of alliance with the
Porte, and of the Court intrigues fomented by the French
ambassador. Alberoni was early aware of this aim. "It is
obvious," he wrote on October, 1718, " that my presence in
this Court is displeasing to the regent, but he will be
deceived if he thinks that I shall leave it unless I choose to
leave it."[1] The main attack was, however, directed through
the Pope. The Imperial government affected to believe
that the Pope had acted in concert with Spain. It demanded therefore that the Papacy should abandon its claim
to the investiture of the two Sicilies, and surrender the
Duchy of Benevento. The emperor, as King of Naples, demanded the right of nomination to the bishoprics of the
kingdom, while the nomination to the lesser benefices
should rest with the bishops; charges or benefices and

[1] Oct. 27, 1718. *Arch. Nap.*, C. F. 59.

annates should be abolished, and the Tribunal of the Nunciatura closed. It was intended by these unexampled demands to force the Pope to deprive Alberoni of his Cardinalate, or at least to refuse the Bull for the Archbishopric of Seville to which he had been nominated by the king. The Pope did in effect delay the transmission of the Bull, and by these means provoked a rupture with Spain. In June, 1718, Aldrovandi was ordered to close the Nunciatura and to retire from Spain. Spanish subjects were instructed to leave Rome. Edicts forbidding any kind of communication with Rome were posted at the street corners, a measure which occasioned much comment, as on previous occasions such decrees had been privately addressed to the tribunals. The Pope was urged to take further action, but Alberoni thought that this would turn to his own advantage. His letter of October 27 gives a curious insight into his ecclesiastical position. " If the Pope persists in his unmannerly behaviour he will find himself more befooled than he expects, for this rupture will in the long run be just the thing to open the eyes of Spain and make her abandon the stupid and blind superstition from which above all things the Court of Rome derives so much advantage.[1] The queen speaks as furiously and passionately as a Megæra against Rome, and I have only to show indifference to see some fine fun." Clement XI. Alberoni regarded with scathing contempt. " In accordance with his weak and miserable character he shifts with the shifting of every breeze."[2] Alberoni enjoyed the fruits of his archbishopric independently of Bulls ; yet the time was to come when he would feel how heavy was the displeasure of the feeblest of Popes : " Ah me, unhappy ! for I have lost the favour of the king, and won the enmity of the Pope ".

The allies were unaware that with the disasters of the winter the war had passed out of the minister's control. It was due to the Duke of Parma's pressure that it had been prematurely opened. Now, under his assumed name, he

---

[1] Oct. 27, 1718. *Arch. Nap.*, C. F. 59. [2] *Ibid.*

urged Alberoni to alarm England with privateers, to mollify
the regent, to complete the conquest of Sicily, and while
making war to negotiate for peace through the mediation of
the States-General. Alberoni's reply proves how fully he
realised the situation : " The reasoning of your highness as
to the duke regent could not be more sound nor sensible ; it
has always been my own view, but the king and queen will
not persuade themselves of this. They believe that when
they are in presence of the French army the whole of it will
pass over to their service. I, however, who know the temper
of the nation, think differently. After the disclosure in
France, by means of such black treachery, after the death of
the King of Sweden, who was to cross to Scotland while we
simultaneously landed in England, after the seizure by
Holland of the arms and munitions purchased there by us,
after their accession to the league, and finally after seeing
that Portugal will undoubtedly join it also, it seems to me
that the king must yield to necessity after having given so
many proofs of his courage and his power. And yet, so far,
I have laboured in vain to persuade him of this truth." [1]

    Henceforth, Alberoni could at most modify, he could not
direct. Philip shook off his languor and depression, and
with his queen prepared for war. The French forces crossed
he frontier in March and burnt the ships and stores at
Pasajes, under the advice of Colonel Stanhope, who accompanied the expedition. The siege of Fuenterrabia was then
opened. Philip and Elisabeth left Madrid on April 26 for
Pamplona. Here they found themselves at the head of an
organised force, though greatly inferior to the French. The
queen showed great activity in this her first and last campaign. She was continually on horseback, reviewing and
encouraging her troops. Her shapely figure was set off by a
habit of pale blue and silver. The *modistes* of Madrid failed
to satisfy her taste, and her dresses made at Paris were
courteously delivered to the Spanish outposts. Philip's
main confidence lay in the defection of the French army.

For this there was some little ground. The southern provinces and their garrisons had long been disaffected to the
regent, he had been obliged to change the commanders of
the latter. It had been feared that the Sardinian expedition
was intended for Languedoc. Some difficulty had been experienced in finding a general. Marshal Hasfeld had shown
his golden fleece and asked to be excused. Marshal Villars
could not be trusted. The Minister of War, Marshal
d'Huxelles, had refused to sign the Convention for the
Quadruple Alliance, until threatened with dismissal. The
command had finally been entrusted to the Duke of Berwick,
whose acceptance, however, was the subject of much
criticism. He owed his reputation to his campaigns in
Philip's cause ; he wore the golden fleece ; his son, the Duke
of Liria, was a grandee of Spain, and served against him in
the Spanish army. But the duke was no politician, his sole
interest lay in soldiering, he cared little for whom or against
whom he might be told to fight, he had few of the prejudices
of the legitimate Stuarts. Some little disaffection seems
actually to have occurred. It was thought prudent to
relieve the Prince of Conti of his command of the cavalry
at Fuenterrabia, while Stanhope wrote that the French lost
some 2000 men by desertion, and that most stringent
measures were taken to prevent it.[1] Yet Alberoni was probably well advised in preventing the king from a personal
appeal to the French army. It is said that he sent orders
to the governor of Fuenterrabia to surrender before the
king's arrival, and Villars states that he[2] instructed the commander of the king's escort to lose his way.

Alberoni's short letters from the front give a lively
picture of the general demoralisation and want of plan.
Defection on the Spanish side was more serious, if Belando
is true in asserting that the province of Guipuscoa offered
allegiance to the Crown of France. It has been seen that
its material interests wedded it to France, and that its fiscal

---

[1] Stanhope to Craggs. June 27, 1719, *R. O. S.*, 165.
[2] Villars, iii. 37.

union with Castile had excited a rising. Berwick was doubtless prudent in declining the offer, if ever made, and indeed Colonel Stanhope saw little inclination among the inhabitants to join the French, though it was expected that the Catalans would do so.   With the capture of Fuenterrabia and S. Sebastian Berwick's campaign in the North West was practically closed.   He did not dare attack Pamplona, and the king and queen retired to Madrid, the king sulkily indignant at the loss of his military reputation which he ascribed to Alberoni.   The Prince Pio was sent to command the Spanish forces in Catalonia, where the French undertook the siege of Urgel.

Meanwhile, the expedition directed against England ended in complete failure.   The Pretender had travelled in disguise to Nettuno, and thence sailed to Sardinia and to Spain.   He was lodged in royal state at the Buen Retiro. The Duke of Ormond was placed in command of a considerable fleet with 5000 men, and arms for 30,000 Highlanders.[1] But his transports were dispersed off Finisterre by heavy weather, and only two frigates succeeded in making Kintail with 300 Spanish troops and the Lords Marischal, Seaforth, and Tullibardine.   They were joined by some 1700 Highlanders, but the whole force was easily broken up by General Wightman.   The storm off Finisterre was perhaps an advantage to the Spanish Government and to Ormond, on whose head a reward of £10,000 was placed.   He had represented to Alberoni that success depended solely on surprise, and the English Government was fully informed of the details of the expedition by Dubois, and probably also by the Pretender's confidential agent, the Baron Waleff.[2]   The relics of the scattered armament were intended to give support to a rising in Brittany, but this was crushed before

---

[1] The preparations for this expedition are described in the Duke of Ormond's letter book, recently acquired by the British Museum, MSS. 33, 950. The letters extend from Nov. 4, 1716 to Sept. 27, 1719. The main invasion was intended for England, while a subsidiary force should supply arms to the Highlanders.

[2] Belando, iv. 34.

the Spaniards could appear. On the other hand, an English squadron conveyed French troops to Santoña, and burnt the arsenal; and a more powerful force, under Lord Cobham, took Vigo in October, sacked the neighbouring towns, and destroyed the remains of Ormond's expedition. It was feared that the English troops would march upon Madrid, but for this the land forces were insufficient, though little organised resistance was possible. In Sicily Merci arrived to reinforce the Imperialists, under Zuminghen, and Lede was forced to retire from Melazzo. He won during his retreat a brilliant victory, on June 27, at Franca Villa, but he was too weak or too cautious to follow up his success, and Alberoni believed that the possession of an intact army would be of more service to negotiations than the chance of a victory. Montemar, who advocated a more dashing strategy, was recalled. Messina fell, and by the end of the autumn the Spaniards held little more than Palermo and Castel Vetrano. The inhabitants were forced to recognise the Austrian dominion, which was all the harder as being exercised by Spanish refugees. " Why," they complained, " should the emperor take so much trouble to expel the Spaniards, merely to replace them by others ? "

Alberoni had taken advantage of the victory of Franca Villa to propose terms of peace. It was suggested that Sicily and Sardinia should be ceded in return for the French conquests, and Gibraltar and Port Mahon. The Parmesan minister, Scotti, was despatched to the Hague with these proposals, but the French Government refused him passports until it had communicated with Lord Stanhope. The latter made the dismissal of Alberoni a preliminary to all negotiations. He represented in his celebrated letter to Dubois that no peace could be secure while Alberoni was still minister. To this conclusion everything was now tending. The king actively disliked him. Daubenton had from his friend become his enemy. Laura Pescatori had ceaselessly intrigued against him. The grandees hated the minister who had curtailed their pensions and despised their counsels. Their exclusion during the king's illness was greatly resented.

The Duke of Escalona had insisted on admittance in his official quality. Alberoni, after vainly requesting him to withdraw, took him by the arm. The duke fell into a chair, and, exasperated by his fall, belaboured Alberoni with his cane, calling him a despicable thief. The queen had watched the scene in silence from the king's bedside. The French suite of Philip was in constant communication with the regent. Daubenton was won by the promise of the regent to remove Fleury and to give the young king a Jesuit confessor. When Elisabeth gave birth to her daughter he complimented her on the appearance of a future queen of France, the rainbow of peace between the two nations. From Giudice came to the king the letter in which Alberoni had engaged to frame the concordat in accordance with the Pope's desires in return for the cardinal's hat. But it was still thought impossible to win the queen without the intervention of the Duke of Parma. This was secured by Lord Peterborough, who was sent by the regent to promise the succession of the Italian duchess to the queen's son, Don Carlos, to whom should be given in marriage the regent's daughter. The Marquis Scotti was instructed to visit Paris, and thence to proceed to Madrid to strike the final blow. This intrigue was by no means entirely concealed from Alberoni, either by the Duke of Parma or by Scotti. On November 13 he wrote to the duke, that but for a principle of honour and gratitude it would not require the instance of the regent to make him lay aside a yoke which he could no longer bear. On the 29th, he assured him that all the offers suggested by the duke had been made to the regent and rejected with scorn ; the Englishman who had visited the duke with such proposals was regarded in Spain as a most pretentious fool and consummate blackguard, and his very name was sufficient to make his terms disliked. "As for myself I have no reason for disquietude, for, if I were obliged to leave Spain in the manner thought of, it would be an exit only too glorious, and, if I had any vanity, my self-satisfaction would be complete. This is what the queen means to express in the letter which you will receive

from me."[1]   In the ensuing fortnight, however, Scotti appears
to have betrayed his fellow-countryman, and a discreditable
backstairs' intrigue, in which perhaps the Duke of Parma
played the shabbiest part, led to Alberoni's fall.[2]   On
December 14 Alberoni attended the Despacho and had a long
interview with Scotti.   On the following morning the king
and queen when leaving for the Pardo handed to Duran,
Secretary of State, a decree commanding Alberoni to leave
Madrid in eight days and Spain within three weeks, to take
no further part in government, and not to appear in Court
or anywhere where the king and queen might chance to be.
Alberoni vainly begged for a last interview.   No notice was
taken of the letter which he was permitted to address to the
king and queen.   He left Madrid for Barcelona, but was
stopped at Lerida and his papers taken from him, among
which was the king's will appointing the queen as regent.
Near Gerona his escort was attacked by Miquelets, and he
escaped in disguise and on foot with great difficulty.   He
was escorted through Southern France and took refuge at
Sestri Levante, the port from which his mistress, who owed
so much to him, had set sail for Spain.   The King of Spain,
the Duke of Parma, and the Pope used all their endeavours
to induce the Genoese Government to surrender the fallen
minister, but in vain.   Alberoni, to relieve his hosts of his
dangerous presence, fled to Switzerland, where he lay *perdu*
until the death of Clement XI. in 1721, when he returned in
disguise to take part in the election of his successor.

For six months abuse of Alberoni was the surest passport to favour at the Court of Madrid.   His crimes were of
the most heterogeneous character.   He had at once deceived
and misrepresented the king and queen, ascribing to them
sentiments of which they were incapable.   Men were in his
pay who copied all hands, and produced forged letters to
procure the removal of the objects of his suspicion, who

---

[1] *Arch. Nap.,* C. F. 64.

[2] A voluminous correspondence on this subject, with the names thinly
disguised, may be read in the Farnese Archives at Naples.

were always the most honourable persons. His malversation was universal. During the king's illness he had made
improper use of the royal seal. He was capable of any crime
down to assassination and poisoning. The king and queen
professed gratitude to the allies for opening their eyes to so
pernicious a minister, they urged the Pope to deprive him of
his purple and secure his person. His sins of omission as an
ecclesiastic were only equalled by his sins of commission in
the field of morals. For six years he had never said mass
nor communicated, nor attended a sermon, nor worn long
robes. His conversation was as blasphemous as it was improper. In his terrible accesses of passion he spared neither
ecclesiastical dignity, prince, nor lord. His relations to the
other sex ill became an ecclesiastic, even " the old and stolid
Camilla " was believed to be his mistress.

The queen set the example in this abuse, and the courtiers
only too willingly re-echoed it. Alberoni had spared neither
courtiers nor malcontent grandees, and no foreign minister
could be popular in Spain. Yet, it seems possible that this
abuse was only superficial, and his real services were soon
recognised. His personal enemy, Macanaz, and his political
opponent, S. Felipe, both render homage to the energy displayed in the revival of Spain. It may or may not be true
that on his fall the grandees called in crowds to show their
chivalrous condolence, it is certain that in later years the
Spanish soldiers quartered at Piacenza showed him every
honour.

The influence of Alberoni upon Elizabeth Farnese can
hardly be overrated. Without him she would doubtless
have cherished Italian ambitions, but would have lacked the
energy to give them reality. He guided her over the dangerous portion of her journey and set her feet upon the high
road, from which she could hardly stray. It is true that
these Italian ambitions caused his own ruin, they were in
great measure forced upon him by his connection with the
Court of Parma, and were not the objects which interested
him most. How far as a foreigner he could have succeeded
in reviving Spain and her colonies it is impossible to decide,

but almost all the beneficial projects of the century may be traced back to him. His natural bent, like that of the younger Pitt, was rather towards administration and reform than to the guidance of a gigantic war. His diplomacy was over fanciful, but luck turned against him to an unforeseen extent. The seizure of Cellamare's papers, the death of Charles of Sweden, even the battle of Cape Passaro were adverse accidents, for which fortune gave no compensation. His surest title to distinction is perhaps the fear which he inspired. He might well boast in the words of Bragadin, that the greatest powers of Europe were more fearful of his counsels and his impetuous resolutions than of the material force of Spain. The English Whigs recognised that the old campaign against the Bourbons must be fought out anew, that their capital had been transferred from Paris to Madrid, and that their diplomatic armoury had been taken with them. The Spanish, as the French, Bourbons under Alberoni's auspices, endeavoured to gain a hold in Italy whereby to strike the Hapsburgs, their good wishes if not their active help were given to the Turk, they renewed the old connection of their race with Sweden, while the more powerful Russia replaced the decadent Poland in their system of alliance. They strove to cut the States-General adrift from England, and while preparing to rival and to ruin English commerce, determined in Bourbon and in Catholic interests to restore the exiled Stuarts. Philip V. was indeed an unworthy successor to the Grand Monarque, but Alberoni trod not unsteadily in the footsteps of Colbert and of Torcy. With such a master and with fellow-scholars inspired by him it would be strange indeed if Elisabeth Farnese left Europe to slumber at its ease.

CHAPTER VII.

1720-3.

DIFFICUTIES OF PEACE—PROPOSED CESSION OF GIBRALTAR—
TREATISES WITH ENGLAND AND FRANCE—THE FRENCH
MARRIAGES—FRENCH INFLUENCE AT MADRID—PHILIP'S
ABDICATION.

THE fall of Alberoni was by no means followed by the
immediate conclusion of peace. The continuance of the
war had been due rather to the obstinacy of the king and
queen than to the deliberate judgment of the minister.
Spanish prospects had to some slight extent improved.
Their privateers cruised off the entrance of the Channel, and
caused considerable losses to English trade. The French
army had failed to take Urgel ; it had been surprised by an
early winter, and retired in complete demoralisation across
the frontier. Six regiments of Spanish cavalry wintered in
Cerdagne, where they were not ill received by a population
essentially Spanish. The spirit of the Sicilian army was still
unbroken. For several months a collision with the Imperial
troops was thought imminent, and there were those who
believed that the latter would come off second best.

Strange rumours were afloat. The Portuguese Ambassador heard from Magni, a recent refugee from France, that
he had persuaded the king to make peace in order to recall
his army from Sicily and march it into France, where nineteen out of every twenty Frenchmen would join him.[1] A
separate treaty with the emperor seemed not impossible.
This extreme measure had been recommended by Alberoni

---

[1] Schaub to Lord Stanhope. March 13, 1720. *R. O. S.*, 165.

shortly before his disgrace, and he had suggested that it should be cemented by intermarriage. The rumour that he was concealed on imperial territory gave some uneasiness to the allies. The queen already regretted that she had dismissed him without a further bargain. From the diplomatic jealousy between England and France the Spanish Court partly regained the position which it had lost from their joint military action. Sir Luke Schaub was sent to represent English interests at Madrid, and his despatches are of much interest, as being an epitome of the see-saw between English and French influence, which was to characterise Spanish history for the next half century. The Duke of Parma had no intention of losing his hold upon his stepdaughter. He might well believe that he pulled the wires by which Spain moved. The war and the peace had been alike his handiwork. Beretti Landi had been intended to replace Alberoni, but his services were required for the coming Congress. The Marquis Scotti, therefore, attempted to fill the void. The queen appreciated his abilities at their worth, and was the first to laugh at him. Yet her constant attachment to him, and the honours and wealth which were subsequently lavished upon him, were probably the result of her craving in these early years for some connecting link with her old home. He was, says S. Simon, a large, fat, heavy man, whose thickness appeared in everything he said or did. Schaub's more detailed description is equally uncomplimentary.

"Scotti has all the appearance of an honest man, or rather of a good fellow. His intellect is marvellously encumbered and confused. He is full of subtle speculations, which he has great difficulty in disentangling. He is jealous, and suspicious while not wishing to appear so. He would like to dissimulate, but does not know how. He has little knowledge and much presumption. He makes a show of great unselfishness, and yet he allows us to see glimpses of an inclination for honourable profits. His ideas have little fixity, and I am much deceived if he has so far formed any policy. At all events, he changes his plans from day to day.

Ordinarily, he is taken up with France, and I see that it is chiefly because he expects from France the deliverance of the Italians, who groan beneath the emperor's yoke. He is afraid of the emperor by nature, and we must help him to be afraid of France."[1]

This was the task set to Schaub, to persuade the king and queen that the emperor was not dangerous, and to inspire them with the fear of France. The latter was the easier, for the king hated the regent, but the ambassador feared that France could lead Spain into any enterprise she pleased as long as the Italian queen had power. The Court of Vienna seemed incapable of propitiating her; it treated the Duke of Parma more harshly than any other Italian prince. It was necessary, therefore, to bring the emperor to reason, and offer to Spain as a nation and to Scotti as a man higher terms than the regent could concede.

The immediate object of the Spanish Government was to obtain the restitution of Gibraltar and Port Mahon from England and that of Pensacola from France. The regent pressed the former even more eagerly than did the King of Spain. Indeed Scotti, representing the queen, hinted that these demands were urged merely to prevent the Spaniards from saying that a peace, which they regarded as disgraceful, was made solely for her Italian interests.[2] The regent, however, felt that to the surrender of Gibraltar his word was pledged. He had but recently promised its restoration, while the English offer was regarded as annulled by the outbreak of war.[3] On the other hand, the queen did not doubt that England was interested in the restitution of Pensacola.

" I should not hesitate," she said, "to lose the succession of Parma and Tuscany for my son, rather than Pensacola for my husband. And the King of Great Britain is no less interested than ourselves in getting this place restored to us."[4] Schaub found it impossible to persuade the king

---

[1] Schaub to Lord Stanhope. Feb. 17, 1720. R. O. S., 165.
[2] Ibid.
[3] Schaub to Lord Stanhope. Feb. 12. Ibid.
[4] Schaub to Lord Stanhope. Feb. 17. Ibid.

and queen that Gibraltar could not be ceded without the consent of Parliament. Yet he earnestly urged such cession ; the king was bent on having the fortress, and would never oblige England until he had it ; his conscience was as much concerned as his punctilio ; his mind would never be easy as long as there was a Protestant garrison on the continent of Spain ; it was less important to England to keep so use-less a place than to take away from France so dangerous an advantage, for the king would look to its restoration by the help of France. The licence for the South Sea Company's ship was refused, and the king and queen assured Schaub that it would never be granted until Gibraltar was sur-rendered. English affairs were, in fact, not prospering, and Schaub doubted whether to attribute it to the king's passionate though weak character, to a cabal against Scotti, to Spanish slowness, to Italian *ruse*, or to French perfidy. Probably, he added, it was due to a little of all.[1]

No pains were spared by both parties to secure Scotti's favour ; while from France he received a portrait of the king, by George I. he was honoured with a service of plate. He complained of the regent's parsimony during his dangerous intrigue against Alberoni, and spoke pathetically of his large family.[2] " I should be badly off here if Scotti were well off," wrote Schaub ; " but, luckily, he is quite as greedy for money as I for letters, and his needs supply mine a little. Do not be surprised, he has a large family and is in debt." [3] Scotti had not the power nor the opportunities of Alberoni. He could only dispose of places and pensions through the ordinary channels. He was afraid to take money for fear the Spaniards should tell the king, and if the latter sur-passed himself in liberality it would not come to much, for he was said to be as stingy as he was devout.[4] But the English drafts which followed the plate were somewhat

---

[1] Schaub to Lord Stanhope. March 13, 1720. *R. O. S.*, 165.
[2] Schaub to Lord Stanhope. Feb. 17, 1720. *Ibid.*
[3] Schaub to Lord Stanhope. March 7, 1720. *Ibid.*
[4] *Ibid.*

K

wasted, for Scotti's influence began to decline before that of Grimaldo, and in fits of depression he would declare that he had no more power than his own footman. It was thought that Scotti might be supplanted by Daubenton, who would be promoted to the cardinalate, and become first minister. This would have been not unfavourable to England, for it was becoming known that from his pen, and not from that of Alberoni, had proceeded the scathing manifestoes which the regent could not forgive. It was now also clear that the designs on the regency and on the Crown proceeded not "from the brain of Alberoni, but from the hearts of the king and queen".[1] Schaub informed his Government that the queen held even more to France than to Italy, and would become Imperialist at once if England would but declare against the regent; it was not without reason that the regent was arming, for he was a greater danger in peace than in war.

Meanwhile negotiations proceeded slowly. Schaub roundly taxed Scotti with accepting the terms of the Quadruple Alliance merely to prevent the evacuation of Sicily and Sardinia; he had removed from Spain the person of the cardinal and not his principles. The lack of a responsible minister made Alberoni regretted, for the foreign ambassadors had known to whom to apply, and the cardinal had spoken clearly. In June the convention for the evacuation of Sicily was completed, but this served only to increase the irritation of the king and queen, who professed that it was without their orders. The slightest movement of troops in Spain caused excitement and alarm. Preparations were made for an expedition to Barbary, but it was observed that Ormond was constantly with the ministers, and that the Lord Marischal and other supporters of the Pretender had left for the ports of Biscay. On the other hand, it was rumoured that the Spanish force at Cadiz was intended to drive the French from the Indies.[2] The Spanish people were indeed more jealous

[1] Schaub to Lord Stanhope. Mar. 27, 1720. *R. O. S.*, 165.
[2] Col. Stanhope to Craggs. Aug. 5, 1720. *Ibid.*, 166.

of French expansion in the Indies than their sovereigns were
of imperial encroachment in Italy. It was believed that
France intended to ruin the English and Dutch trade and
monopolise that of Spain. A French ship had been sent
with orders to the colonists to extend their settlements
towards the Spanish silver mines, where they would be supported by a squadron of ten sail and by troops.[1] The
Indians were to be incited to rise against the English. Consul Walker reported that the Spanish troops had been really
intended for Barbary, but had been detained owing to
rumours of a revolution in France.

Spanish confidence was reviving, and it was believed at
Court that, owing to the circumstances of her neighbours,
Spain had never been so powerful. France, disabled by the
plague and by the collapse of Law's financial projects, was
incapable of taking the offensive, or even of defending herself if attacked. The disorders in England put her in at
least as bad a condition, and the Dutch would shortly be in
no better a state. Spain was courted on every side. It is
quite possible that Scotti was correct in his confidences to
Colonel Stanhope, who had replaced Schaub, that the
emperor was trying by all imaginable means to make a
separate alliance with Spain for the ruin both of France and
England. The advantages offered were such that only the
piety of the king could resist. Among other proposals, a
double marriage was suggested between the emperor's
daughters and two of the Spanish princes.[2] These rumours
reached not only the English but the French Government,
and were for long a source of disquietude.[3]

At length in June, 1721, the defensive alliance between
Spain, England, and France was concluded. It contained
guarantees for the maintenance of the Treaties of Utrecht,

---

[1] Col. Stanhope to Craggs. Oct. 28, 1720. *R. O. S.*, 166.

[2] Col. Stanhope to Craggs. Nov. 18, 1720. *Ibid.*

[3] Il'y a quelque temps que nous étions dans une inquietude assez vive sur
les traités et les alliances que l'on prétendist, non sans fondement, se former
entre le Roi d'Espagne et l'Empereur, et sur le marriage du prince des
Asturias avec l'Archiduchesse. Sept. 14, 1721. *Villars* iii. 100.

Baden, and London, and determined the contingents to be provided by the contracting powers in the event of an attack. The queen's influence was evident in the protection accorded to the Duke of Parma, for whom the English Government engaged to obtain the coveted districts of Castro and Ronciglione. It also promised the duke to oppose the introduction of Spanish garrisons into Tuscany and Parma. The points under dispute with the emperor were reserved for the Congress of Cambray. These comprised the questions of investiture of the Italian duchies and the composition of their garrisons, the disputed title to the Crown of Spain, and the right to confer the Golden Fleece. A separate treaty between Spain and England confirmed the commercial clauses of the Treaty of Utrecht as modified by the agreements of December 14, 1715, and May 26, 1716. To Spain was conceded the free exercise of the Catholic religion in Minorca, a matter in which English officers appear to have behaved with some brutality, and the privileges hitherto enjoyed in the Newfoundland cod fisheries. Both nations agreed to restore their prizes, among which were included the ships taken in the action off Cape Passaro. The queen condescended to write in person to George I. to congratulate him on the *accouchement* of the Princess of Wales.[1] Dubois had, in fact, feared the possibility of a triple alliance between the emperor, Spain, and England. In March, 1721, news arrived from Bruninx, the ambassador of the States-General at Vienna, that the King of Spain had proposed the marriage of his heir with the second daughter of the Emperor Joseph, and of Ferdinand and Carlos with the present emperor's two younger daughters. In these schemes there were several variations, but Dubois informed

---

[1] A Madrid le 16ᵉ Juin, 1721.

Monsieur Mon Frère.   Comme je m'interesse particulièrement à tout ce qui regarde la prosperité de votre maison vous vous persuaderez facilement le plaisir que j'ai eu en recevant la nouvelle que vous me donnez de l'heureux accouchement de la Princesse de Galles, et de l'augmentation de votre famille Royale, dont je suis d'autant plus aise que vous me donnez occasion de vous témoigner l'estime particulière que j'ay pour vous.

Monsieur Mon Frère.   Votre bonne Sœur, Elisabeth S.   *E. O. S.*, 167.

the French ambassador at Madrid that the king had shown the greatest eagerness to arrange the conditions of a union which would serve to re-establish all the power which Charles V. had combined upon his head and in his] house. Whatever such projects were, it is certain that they were due rather to the queen than to the king.

English satisfaction was marred by the growing intelligence between Spain and France. The separate articles between the two powers were conceived in the spirit of the more celebrated family compacts. Their union was described as eternal and indissoluble. It was not long before the treaty was followed by tangible results. The wild projects for the marriage of the Spanish princes with the archduchesses, or even with the Princess Anne of England, were dropped in favour of a general system of intermarriage with the regent's family. This had been long in the air. It was believed to have been rejected by the King of Spain in the spring of 1720, when a marriage between the Prince of Asturias and the regent's daughter was suggested. The regent might well believe that he would find security in such a marriage, for the prince and his father, said Schaub, were as like as two drops of water, both in body and mind, so that the prince as his father would probably let himself be governed by his wife. The regent might be sure that his daughter, who to all appearance would be pretty and *spirituelle*, would be able to prevent the prince from disputing the title of the regent or his family to the Crown of France, or from aiding his younger brothers to do so.[1] On the other hand, it was pointed out that the king's aversion to the regent would make him unwilling to accept such a proposal, while the queen, who could not count upon her husband's life, would be naturally jealous of a French princess. Whatever difficulties there were had now been smoothed away. In July Daubenton informed the French ambassador that since the end of March the negotiations with the emperor had entirely ceased. "I know," he added, "another thing which would still further console you, but I cannot speak. I will tell you,

---

[1] Schaub to Lord Stanhope. April 20, 1720. *R. O. S.*, 165.

however, that your suspicions have so little real foundation
that since the period mentioned his majesty is resolved to
live more and more on friendly terms with his royal highness, and so fixed and serious is this idea becoming that he
will some day be surprised." This intelligence was confirmed by the king himself, and Grimaldo, who had been prepared by the present of a ring, was then approached. The
French ambassador was informed by the minister that the
king asked for Mademoiselle de Montpensier for the Prince
of Asturias, and proposed the marriage of his own daughter
with Louis XV. This, he added, was no new idea of the
king, who eagerly desired to bind closer the ties which united
the House of Bourbon, and believed nothing more advantageous to both families than such marriages. On August 4
the regent wrote to express his delight at the project of the
double marriage. It is probable that in order not to exas-
perate the regent's enemies, Dubois insisted that the marriage
of the Prince of Asturias should not be published until after
the announcement of that between Louis XV. and the Infanta.[1]

On September 14, 1721, the regent announced that the
King of Spain had offered the Infanta to the King of France,
and on September 30 he told Villars that he requested his
own daughter's hand for his eldest son. The Infanta was in
the winter despatched to France, and on January 20, 1722,
Mademoiselle de Montpensier was married to Don Luis.

The effect of this new departure was at once apparent.
Shortly before the marriage Stanhope wrote that the French
influence was not only strong enough to demolish the Congress, but to bring about whatever else they should have a
mind to. Madrid was flooded with French envoys, who had
their different provinces assigned to them. The regent had
playfully warned S. Simon that he must conceal his Jan-
senism if he wished to return whole from Spain. The hint
was taken, for he was described by Stanhope as winning

---

[1] This is, perhaps, the explanation of S. Simon's inaccurate statement
that Philip had been delighted that Louis XV. asked for his daughter's hand,
and that the regent had made the marriage of his own daughter with the heir
of Spain an absolute condition of the Infanta's marriage.

Philip's favour by his bigotry. Maulevrier, the object of S. Simon's ill-natured rivalry, had won the queen's heart by his powers of match-making. La Fare was attached to the prince and princess, while Robin was the man of business for Grimaldo.[1] Couriers passed daily between Paris and Madrid. Elisabeth looked no longer to her stepfather, whose favour England had secured. He had forwarded the project of an imperial marriage, and was kept in complete ignorance of the negotiation with France. The result, wrote S. Simon, fell upon him like a bomb and threw him into despair.[2] Scotti was nearly sent back to Italy. He was at swords and daggers drawn with Laura Pescatori ; they skirmished in the queen's presence, and he was always beaten. Twice he was reduced to tears. Laura, jealous of the Italians, was well disposed to France. S. Simon even condescended to ask her son-in-law to dinner, and plied him with eulogies on her good intentions and her merits. French influence was farther increased by the engagement of Don Carlos to the regent's younger daughter, Mademoiselle de Beaujolais. The regent could hardly hope for a grander marriage, and he secured a double hold on Spain. The queen directly interested him in her Italian ambitions ; Don Carlos would be protected from the jealousy felt by the emperor and by the King of Sardinia when he found himself shut in by Bourbon States. " I must be carried away," wrote Stanhope, " by that torrent of French power and favour which increases every day, and particularly since this last marriage, upon which the queen shows a joy inexpressible and even greater than upon the first." [3]

French influence, however, extended no further at present than the king and queen and the Foreign Office. No commercial privileges could be secured for France, and the minister for the Indies, De Pez, an implacable enemy of the

[1] Stanhope to Carteret. Aug. 6, 1722. *R. O. S.*, 169.

S. Simon, however, wrote that the king and queen, Daubenton, and the secretaries did not conceal their disgust at the number of these emissaries ; they knew not which to trust. S. Simon to Belle Isle. Feb. 20, 1722.

[2] S. Simon to Belle Isle. Feb. 20, 1722.

[3] Stanhope to Carteret. Aug. 29, 1722. *Ibid.*, 169.

French, sturdily resisted their attempts to remove him. Daubenton, whose ill-feeling for Grimaldo was scarcely veiled, was in close correspondence with the Italian party. Yet this revival of the union between France and Spain was sufficient to cause alarm. It was thought that Spain was only waiting for the failure of the Congress for a combined attack upon Italy. A fleet was in readiness, which was supposed to be intended for Don Carlos. Elisabeth earnestly urged that he should be sent to Italy in the character of heir to his future dominions. In this she was supported by her stepfather. A force of 6000 men, of which he would be the real commander, would give him weight in Italy, and would cool the rising Republican enthusiasm at Florence. The Pretender's adherents were active and hopeful, and were in high favour with Patiño, Minister of Marine. The movements of Ormond and Lord Marischal were anxiously watched by Colonel Stanhope. He had secured as a spy one Cammock, an officer of high repute in the Spanish navy, who was intended for a command in the Pretender's service, and who had been informed by Patiño that his services would shortly be required.[1] Orders were sent to the admiral at Gibraltar to seize a ship named the "Resolution,"[2] which was intended to convey the Pretender to Ireland and Scotland, and the vessel was in effect boarded in the port of Genoa. Danger from Spain was again complicated by danger from the North. Cammock was told by the Russian minister that his master was resolved to aid the Pretender.[3]

Death and disease were, however, powerful allies to the one nation whose policy did not depend upon an individual's health or life. In August, 1723, died Dubois. On November 1, 1723, died the Grand Duke of Tuscany, and this event, while it rendered more imminent a rupture with the emperor, gave a greater value to the friendship or neutrality of England. Far more important was the circumstance

---

[1] Col. Stanhope to Carteret. Aug. 6, 1722. *R. O. S.*, 169.
[2] Col. Stanhope to Carteret. Sept. 15, 1723. *Ibid.*, 170.
[3] Col. Stanhope to Carteret. Feb. 15, 1723. *Ibid.*

that the Duke of Orleans, once too often dined too well. He had retired after dinner to the apartments of his mistress, Madame de Falari, and was preparing to transact business with his ministers when he was stricken by apoplexy, and never spoke again. He was still in the prime of life; he had apparently weathered the storm which shook the unsubstantial fabric of his regency. He could stand now without the aid of Hanoverian support. He had every hope of ruling Spain through his daughter and her husband. An Orleanist family compact might even have forestalled that of the later Bourbons.

Philip, also, was desperately ill. If he did not drink too deeply, he habitually ate too much. In the summer of 1723 he again fell into deep depression. He was ordered horse exercise, but fits of giddiness obliged him to discontinue it. Religious scruples obtained an overwhelming mastery over his mind. His old friend and confessor, Daubenton, was no longer by his side to combat them,[1] for he had died in August in his eighty-third year. In January, 1724, within a few weeks of the regent's death, Europe was electrified by another royal sensation. The King of Spain had resigned his throne.[2]

[1] Bragadin, 1725. But the Venetian ambassador also mentions the belief that Daubenton's correspondence with the regent was with a view to Philip's abdication that the Princess of Asturias might ascend the throne.

[2] Belando asserts that Daubenton confided to the regent the secret of Philip's scruples, and that the regent, in the hope of dissuading him from abdication, forwarded Daubenton's letter, which contained also reasons against this step. The result was unexpected. Philip upbraided the confessor with his betrayal, and told him that, having sold the country to the regent, he had now sold his master and his God. Daubenton was dismissed, and his disgrace was followed by a paralytic stroke which caused his death, while the *contretemps* threw the regent into a deep depression which contributed to his end. The Jesuits have always denied Daubenton's betrayal of the secrets of the confessional, asserting that his resignation was due to old age and infirmity, and that he was buried with honour. Belando, a warm adherent of Macanaz, was an enemy of the Jesuits in general and of Daubenton in particular, and the balance of evidence is against his statement. His book before publication was read and approved by Philip, and it has been thought strange that he should have overlooked this important passage in his own life or given it his sanction if false. Yet it is not clear that Philip read the third volume in which this passage occurs.

CHAPTER VIII.

1720-3.

INCREASED INFLUENCE OF ELISABETH—S. SIMON'S MISSION
TO SPAIN—HIS DESCRIPTION OF THE COURT—DAILY
LIFE OF THE KING AND QUEEN—ELISABETH'S CHA-
RACTER—HER UNPOPULARITY—THE ITALIAN PARTY AT
MADRID—THE SPANISH ADHERENTS OF THE QUEEN.

IT was to the action of Elisabeth Farnese that the disgrace of Alberoni had been finally due. Yet she alone had
reason to regret the fallen minister. Her isolation was now
complete. Her stepfather's agent, Scotti, was quite incapable of filling the void. To Alberoni's position as chief
minister and royal confidant Grimaldo gradually succeeded.
On his assistance the queen could place no reliance. While
professing descent from the noble Genoese house of Grimaldi,
he was, in fact, a plodding Biscayan *roturier*. His heart
was with Spain and the Spaniards. He detested the Italian
party at Madrid. He had neither genius nor inclination for
a forward European policy. Spain, he thought, should lean
upon France and England, and avoid Italian complications.
Apart from a total divergence in policy, the queen was averse
to Grimaldo on personal grounds. She had been prejudiced
against him by Alberoni, who had secured his removal from
office. He was, moreover, likely to be her chief rival for the
monopoly of her husband's affections. The king had refused
to acquiesce in his removal from Spain or from Madrid. He
had instinctively realised that he was an honest and trust-
worthy servant, had even from time to time procured his
secret admission to the palace during the late *régime*.

It appeared extremely doubtful whether Elisabeth would

be able to retain the control over her husband which she had exercised in conjunction with Alberoni, and which her predecessor had enjoyed with the aid of Madame des Ursins. For this reason, the few years that elapsed between the ministries of Alberoni and Ripperdá are of high importance in this biography. It was in this short period that Elisabeth consolidated her influence over Philip, and learnt to play upon his mind as upon an instrument. She began to take an independent view of European politics and to realise their possibilities. She taught herself to compensate for her want of education and complete ignorance of the world by her natural powers of attraction, and by unwearied observation and study of character. These few years are also of supreme interest to the biographer from the accident that within them falls the embassy of S. Simon to the Court of Madrid. The punctilious French nobleman was promoted to great honour; his Spanish visit was an episode on which he loved to dwell, and it is perhaps the most complete and studied portion of his memoirs. To this posterity owes a detailed description of social life and political parties at Madrid; a perfect portrait gallery of all important, and many unimportant, personages in the country, and an unrivalled picture of the daily life of the royal household.

S. Simon was fortunate in the period at which he saw Elisabeth. She had all the self-confidence of recent emancipation from control, and still possessed the fresh charm of youth. The French noble knew that she was no friend to France, and accordingly had no predisposition to draw a flattering portrait. His description may be taken therefore as approximately just. "The Queen of Spain has such grace in her figure, in everything that she does and says, in the play of her wit and in her manners, she is so natural, moreover, and so evidently at her ease, that in a few minutes the injuries wrought by the smallpox are forgotten; her charm and the impression of her intelligence are only increased. The latter, however, would have a better and a wider range, but for the total absence of all culture and

education.　　Her familiarity, great as it is, never detracts
from her dignity, and only serves to make her lovable."[1]　Such
was the external impression which an impartial stranger
might receive of Elisabeth Farnese.　In the Court of Spain
religion was an important factor.　The queen carefully
observed the practices of her own, and of her adopted
country, but she had none of the scruples of the king, and he
never could inspire her with his liking for the Jesuits, nor
would she confide to her confessor other secrets than her
sins.　She was proud, and passionate to violence, even with
the king.　This was due partly to natural temper, partly to
design, in which, however, her success was chequered.　Her
ignorance, owing to the exigencies of her daily life, was incurable.　She could neither be taught nor educate herself.
For this reason and from natural disposition she was not
a good woman of business, and was confused by details.
Nevertheless, she liked power, she wished to know everything and to have share in it, though appearing not to do
so.　Italy and all Italians were dear to the queen, though
her love for her parents was, S. Simon believed, more
the result of good breeding and family pride than of affection.　She was no longer subservient to the views of the
Court of Parma, and it was improbable that she would be
controlled by its minister.　Passionately fond of her
children from affection and policy, it was already clear
that she would lend herself to any measures which would
further their advancement.　Her apparent attachment to
her husband was such that she seemed to forget herself.
Her actions, her conversation, her broad, unceasing flattery,
were all directed to give him pleasure.　In meeting his
every wish, she was so easy and so natural, that she
deceived spectators into thinking that she really liked the
task, ceaseless, dangerous, and tiresome as it was.　For
Philip's pleasure she had to devote herself day after day to
hunting, whether she was well or ill, whether her confine-

---

[1] This and the other descriptions contained in this chapter are derived
from *Mémoires du Duc de S. Simon*, Vol. xviii., Chéruel et Regnier, 1875,
and from *Papiers inedits du Duc de S. Simon*, E. Drumont, 1880.

ments were approaching or scarcely over. The stranger would imagine that she had a genuine dislike for all that she loved best; for cards and music, in which she was extremely skilful, for fêtes, and all the amusements of a Court, in which she was by nature adapted to shine, for conversation, to which she could contribute most agreeably, and with much versatility. Naturally gay, good tempered, and sympathetic, she was given to badinage, and had a keen sense of the ridiculous, and could mimic to perfection. Yet her fun was almost always kindly. Her manners were unequal and sometimes rough. This arose from her keen sensibility, for she felt offence acutely, though she never lost her head. Any kind of affectation was Elisabeth's abhorrence, and dissimulation she practised as little as possible. Nor did she like the artificial additions to her toilet which etiquette and the king's taste compelled her to adopt. She felt and gave expression to the difference between her present and her former fortunes, she spoke openly of her defects of appearance and character, and had none of the ordinary reticence of ladies in such matters. Alberoni had described the palace as a Babel of petty intrigue. Yet this was not to the taste of the queen, who severely criticised this tendency of her sex, and made no concealment of her preference for men's society. It may be concluded that her character, like that of her great English namesake, was somewhat masculine.[1] Her most feminine characteristic, says S. Simon, was her love of amusing herself with all kinds of birds and beasts, which, he adds, were not perhaps without value to her in the extreme retirement in which she lived. It is pleasant to think that the puppies of whom Alberoni pathetically wrote were no longer subject to their mistress' neglect.

Alberoni's despatches will have made it clear that Elisabeth was singularly open to the influence of those who were

---

[1] Belando, in his dedication, pays a somewhat doubtful compliment to the masculine character of his mistress. "It must be added that in your Majesty nothing that is feminine is to be found; on the contrary, your Majesty is in all things of masculine strength."

brought into close contact with her. Much depended upon the character of her ministers, and not less upon that of her personal surroundings. There was no Court life in the ordinary sense, but a few officials of the household were brought into daily relations with the queen, and these were not without influence upon her life. Among these, the most important at this point were the Duke of Arco, the grand equerry, and the Marquis of Santa Cruz, the queen's major domo. To the former Philip was devotedly attached. He combined the pride and dignity of a Spanish noble with the polish and modern graces of a Frenchman, for which, even in Paris, he would have passed. He was one of the few Spaniards who could give an eatable dinner, and his company was, therefore, appreciated by French ministers and residents. In all martial and athletic exercises he was supremely skilful. He had saved the king's life from a boar. His physical and courtly address had been displayed in an accident which had happened to the queen of Charles II. She had fallen from her horse, and was dragged with her foot in the stirrup. The duke sprang to the ground, reached the runaway, and freed the queen's foot. He then rode without drawing rein to sanctuary, for to touch the foot of a Queen of Spain was treason. To Alberoni he had never bowed the knee, and the new queen realised that she must admit him to her friendship.

The Marquis of Santa Cruz was a favourite both with Philip and the queen, notwithstanding his expressed aversion for Frenchmen and Italians. Up till the War of Succession he had lived in obscurity on his estate in La Mancha. He had been unfortunate in his relations to women. His wife had obtained a divorce on the ground of impotence. A successful affiliation action had been brought against him by a *bourgeoise*. With his peasants he had bravely defended an important pass in La Mancha, and the Duke of Berwick insisted on bringing him to Court. Rough and wild at first, he had been gradually tamed. He was tall and strongly built, with a ruddy, brown complexion, large, black eyebrows, and a sidelong glance. His knowledge was respectable, his mind subtle and acute. He talked little, but was fond of gossip, and his expressive, sardonic laugh was often heard. People feared his silence, his sarcasms, his speaking eyes, and his sullen indifference. Yet he was assiduous in his duties, unostentatiously polite, respected by all, and beloved by his friends.

These two nobles were in constant attendance on the king throughout the year, they dressed and undressed him, accompanied him in his walks and drives, lighted him from his carriage to his room. They were devoted friends, and with their inseparable companion, the Duke of Liria, formed a trio which enlivened the monotony of the Court. The chief lady-in-waiting, the Countess of Altamira, also stood high in the queen's esteem. She was small and ugly, and at sixty might be taken for seventy-five. Yet, notwithstanding her bad figure, she had a dignified and imposing presence. She ruled the ladies of the household with a courteous absolutism, which none ever dared to question. S. Simon found her always sitting on a square of carpet at the end of her apartment, and he was accorded an arm-chair in front of her. Upon one occasion she was alone. S. Simon knew not a word of Spanish, nor she of French. The conversation was carried on by signs, with an occasional interchange of smiles. " This visit," he writes, " I cut extremely short."

Another highly respected member of the interior circle was Don Gaspard Giron, the senior of the major domos for the week. He was the living picture of Don Quixote, tall, dark, and dried up. The typical gravity of his nature and his rank was tempered by his gaiety and politeness, by the unpretentious ease of his manners. His importance was due to his unequalled knowledge of the laws of etiquette new or old, of gradations of rank, of ceremonies and customs. He had outlived many ministries ; he knew the secret springs of the rise and fall of Court influence. To him the king, the ministers, the foreign ambassadors constantly referred as to a living Court almanac. He was the chosen cicerone of all foreign magnates who visited the Court. Though poor, he was greedy neither of promotion nor of gain ; he was the

soul of honour and of disinterested loyalty.   S. Simon mar-
velled to see him stranded in the very mid-channel of all
fortune. This was due, he believed, to the fact that he was so
indispensable that he could not be promoted. His want of
distinction was compensated by the intimate friendship of
the king and queen, who were glad at times to talk to him in
private, and to whom he would freely speak his mind.

Such was the interior circle in which Philip and his
queen passed such part of their daily life as was not exclusively devoted to each other's company.   Its character
redounds to their credit. The high standard of honour, of
dignity, and moral respectability compares favourably with
the venality of Vienna, the vulgarity of the Georgian, and
the profligacy of the Orleanist Courts. No member, however,
of this circle possessed any direct political influence. All
authority and all State business centred in the king.   To
manage the king was to govern Spain ; and it was to this
task that the queen addressed herself with untiring patience.
The seclusion, the unvarying regularity of life to which
Philip had become habituated under the *régime* of Madame
des Ursins doubtless contributed to Elisabeth's success,
though it added infinitely to her labour. S. Simon is probably right in regarding the petty details of this monotonous
daily life as giving the key of the political situation. To the
biographer, at all events, they are essential. Without a
knowledge of them it is impossible to understand the character and influence of the queen, or to realise the tragedy
underlying an outwardly prosaic existence.

If Elisabeth would govern Spain, the nuptial couch must
be the seat of government. To this Philip was unswervingly
faithful. The king and queen never occupied a separate bed-
chamber nor a separate bed. The latter was scarcely four
feet wide, was a four-poster, and, according to Spanish
fashion, very low. No night was ever spent apart. Towards 9 A.M. the curtains of the bed were drawn by the azafata. Behind her appeared a valet bearing a basin of gruel
composed of broth, wine, milk, and yolk of egg, sweetened
with sugar, and flavoured with cinnamon and clove. It was

white, greasy, and very hot.[1]   While the king drank this the
azafata brought to the queen her tapestry, enveloped the
royal persons in their dressing-jackets, and placed upon the
bed the papers lying on the chairs.   The king and queen
then said their prayers and read books of devotion; for
secular works had been discarded, and no more is heard of
French romances.   Grimaldo, at a stated hour, appeared at
the door; but sometimes the king would beckon to him to
wait until the prayers were finished.   The minister spread
out his papers on the bed, drew his writing case from his
pocket, and discussed public business; for the queen's work
did not disable her from giving an opinion.   The valet, on
seeing Grimaldo retire, gave notice to the azafata, on which
she brought to the king his slippers and dressing-gown.
Retiring to his dressing-room, he was attended by the Duke
of Arco, the Marquis of Santa Cruz, and three French valets.
The toilet completed, the confessor was summoned, and
with him the king conversed in the window, while the two
lords waited by the door.

Meantime the azafata had given a dressing-gown to the
queen and put on her shoes and stockings.   This was sometimes the only moment when the queen could speak to her
old servant alone, and this was a quarter of an hour at most;
for if it were longer the king inquired the cause of the delay.
The queen's toilet was one of the most sociable hours of the
day.   It was attended by the king and his two lords, the
infants and their governors, some of the principal ladies of
the household, and the Cardinal Borgia.   Conversation
turned on the royal journeys, or sport, or on the fine clothes
of the king and the infants.   Occasionally there was a little
word of advice or reprimand from the queen to her attendants as to their assiduity, their friendships, or the regularity of their devotions.   In these matters Elisabeth was
somewhat of a martinet.   To be on good terms with her it
was essential to be seldom ill, but frequently confined, to

[1] The Irish court physician, Higgins, once brewed a dose of this mixture
for S. Simon, who found it not disagreeable, but would prefer not to make it
his meal.

avoid the fashionable world, and, above all, to go to church
once a week.　The butt of the party was the Cardinal Borgia,
and many were the jokes made at his expense.　He was a
good natured person, utterly unsuited to his exalted ecclesiastical position.　His blundering celebration of the Prince
of Asturias' wedding was a standing joke.　The royal party
was kept waiting while he was carefully coached by his two
almoners, for he could hardly read.　Notwithstanding the
rehearsal, he was far from word perfect ; for during the ceremony he knew not where he was nor what he was doing, his
face was as red as his cap, and the whole Court was in con-
vulsions.

After the queen's toilet the king gave private audiences to
ambassadors and others, at which the queen was always present.　Every Monday a public audience was granted to all
whose names were entered on the official list.　They entered
one by one, and said whatever they liked, but the interviews
took but little time, for the Spaniards, unlike the French,
were measured, respectful, and short.　The Council of Castile also presented its weekly report, and this and the business which followed might occupy an hour and a-half.　This
was the only time which the queen had to herself, with the
exception of the daily quarter of an hour, and these audiences
only took place when the Court was at Madrid.　In these
short and precious moments the queen could, in fear and
trembling, give a private interview, or receive and write a
letter, but the greatest care was requisite to destroy all
papers, and to conceal the presence of the visitor.　It must
not be supposed that these stolen moments had any sentimental bearing ; they were utilised chiefly for political
intercourse with the outside world.　Hence arose the
remarkable influence of the azafata.　She alone could introduce visitors or pass on the secret correspondence.　Laura
Pescatori had been promoted to this post, and had become
an important factor in the queen's life and in the foreign
policy and domestic government of Spain.　Ambassadors
found to their convenience that she was open to bribes.
Cucurani, one of the most ambitious *intrigants* in Spain,

thought it worth while to marry her daughter. Even the king treated her well, and courtiers put up with her bad temper, for the queen said that they might well endure it as she had much to bear from it herself.

After audience the king and queen amused themselves together or went to mass. Dinner was served in the queen's apartments. Philip and Elisabeth differed only in their dishes. Both had large appetites, but while the queen liked variety, the monotony of the king's daily life extended to his fare. It consisted of soup, poultry, and an invariable loin of veal, no fruit, nor salad, nor cheese, rarely pastry or fish. The *menu* was occasionally varied by eggs or caviare.

The king drank old Burgundy; the queen preferred champagne, now much in fashion at the regent's Court. Elisabeth was much addicted to snuff, in which she was a connoisseur. The king never quite got over his aversion at this habit of his wife, who would deplore that she had never succeeded in sacrificing this taste to her husband's wish. Dinner was a pleasant meal, the conversation continual and varied, the queen always gay and agreeable.

Shooting was the one real pleasure of the king, and shooting was, therefore, perforce the queen's amusement. But even this excitement was dulled by Philip's growing bulk and indolence. He had ceased to ride and to shoot from the saddle. Sport had degenerated to the battue. Big game was not to be found within easy distance of Madrid. In the country toward the mountains the ground was so hard and rough and scored with crevices that hunting was dangerous for dogs and horses, and the coarse, strong scrub was an obstacle to scent. The royal carriages were driven at full speed to the place selected by the Duke of Arco. Here were erected two bowers with a common partition wall. They were completely closed but for their wide windows, the sills of which formed a rest. In the one were stationed the king, the queen, the captains of the guards, the equerry, and four loaders with twenty guns. One lady attended the queen, but she was left in her carriage with her work or a book, for nobody came near her. In the second bower was the Prince of Asturias with a large suite. The carriages and horses with the lady-in-waiting were then dismissed to a distance for fear of disturbing the game. For the next hour and a-half not a word was spoken, no movement was permitted. The king and queen sat on straw-bottomed chairs, their suite upon their cloaks. "This part of the entertainment," says S. Simon, "did not appear to me to be very amusing." At last distant halloo-ings were heard from the lungs of some three hundred peasants, who had since night been beating and driving the game. Silence was, if possible, redoubled, a cough would then be completely out of place. Then all of a sudden herds of animals, deer, wolves, foxes, badgers, martins rushed past the sportsmen within easy range. The king and the queen fired first, and no one from the prince's bower might shoot until the royal pair had ceased firing, consequently there was often little for the prince to shoot and nothing for his suite.[1] "This amusement or butchery," adds S. Simon, "lasted half-an-hour." The game was then collected for the king's inspection and packed behind the carriages. The bag on the occasion of S. Simon's visit consisted of a dozen or more of deer and some hares, foxes, and martins. Occasionally pigeons were shot from horseback, and the queen could kill the strongest flyers on the wing. Such was the amusement of their Catholic majesties every working day.

From February till April a close time was given to the game, and then the royal exercise consisted in a walk in the Park of Buen Retiro, and a visit to the Mall. Philip played three full rounds with his officers, the queen accompanying him, and changing her place so as to be always on his left. The king played well but unevenly, and his pleasure obviously depended on his strokes, which

---

[1] The king, at the queen's request, sent a gun to S. Simon, who, though he had not shot for a year, killed a fox, a miracle for which, he wrote, he had to come to Spain. He paid dearly for his triumph, for on the next occasion, with true French impatience, he fired before the king. Long afterwards he recognised his error, and excuses proved the subject for much talk and pleasantry.

the queen applauded if they were good, and found excuses for when bad. The first equerry played very badly, and she gracefully condoled with him as if she were really sorry, though she could not help being delighted. She always had some badinage with the grand equerry, whose game was correct and elegant, but wanting in dash; when the queen joked him about his age it was a pleasure to watch the skirmish, for he was capital at repartee. The principal courtiers joined in, but all this with grave familiarity and majesty on the one side, and perfect respect upon the other. The queen's freedom and gaiety were delightful, and attracted the Court to the Mall. Elisabeth tried hard to make her husband talk; she drew him on with an unequalled charm, and sometimes joked him, though with an air of respect. Occasionally she succeeded in making him say a word or two to the company. To the rest she talked of anything and everything, telling amusing stories, or inquiring after their families. She found means to entertain every one, and without chattering managed that conversation should never flag. The time at the Mall always seemed too short.

When the hours of exercise were over, the king ate a piece of bread or a biscuit, and drank some wine and water; the queen preferred fruit, pastry, and sometimes cheese. Thus fortified they entertained the infants for a few minutes, and then Grimaldo entered, and work began. When the queen confessed it was at this hour, and she had no other time to speak to her spiritual director. The confession was necessarily short, for, if longer than usual, the king would open the door and call her. On Grimaldo's departure husband and wife said prayers together, or read a religious book, until supper. After this *tête à tête* conversation or prayer carried them to bedtime. The ceremony of undressing the queen resembled the morning toilet, except that the infants and the Cardinal Borgia were not admitted.

This daily routine was rarely broken. Long journeys were seldom undertaken, and the stages were so short that the time usually appropriated to shooting sufficed for travel.

The shorter and more constant trips to Aranjuez, the Escurial, or Balsain, merely entailed a somewhat earlier drive than usual. The very rough accommodation at Balsain may indeed have afforded a little variety. But the journey was invariably the same, the eternal *tête à tête* in the queen's big carriage with its seven windows. The identical arrangement of the furniture at the various palaces was suggestive of marital unity. It is no small matter that a married couple should occupy in peace a common wardrobe, but other domestic details which S. Simon gives are even more expressive and extraordinary. Of the customary gaiety and splendour of Court life there was next to none. State balls and theatrical entertainments were rarely given, but both king and queen were fond of dancing, and the informal dances given in the palace were perhaps the most cheerful moments of the queen's life. Philip, when dancing, lost his awkwardness of gait and figure, and the queen danced with a grace which S. Simon had never seen surpassed, and rarely equalled. Yet even here her choice of partners was not extensive, it was limited to the king and the infants.

To any ordinary woman the tragic monotony of this daily life must have been destructive to either morality or reason. Since the departure of Maggiali no breath of scandal ever clouded the mirror of Elisabeth's conjugal fame, her reason and her wit she carried with her to her grave. She was saved no doubt by her natural high spirits, by the entire absence of morbid self-consciousness, and by the growing activity of her intellect. She was never without opinions, without wishes, without interests. Her opinions were so decided, her wishes so vehement, so consistent, and her interests so dear, and so apparently great, that no price was too high if only she could attain her end. On this end, worthy and unworthy, she meditated day and night. Thus she was never dull. Notwithstanding the outward constraint of her life, it was really one of unceasing agitation. She never had a doubt that the game was worth the candle. But others thought the cost too high. " Great as was her power," writes S. Simon, "she owed it to so much skill, flexibility, management and patience, that it is not too much to say that she paid too dearly for it." Part of the price was unquestionably paid by the temper. Her acquiescence in *ennui* was not the unconsidered and virtueless acquiescence of the stupidly good-tempered wife. Her childhood had taught her self-restraint, but the fiery temper which she had doubtless inherited from her mother was but banked up. As far as can be judged the outbreaks were sharp and short. Her sense of humour was so keen that a witty answer would turn away wrath. Moreover, if the fussiness of Philip were provocative of irritation, his gentleness was the antidote to anger. Husband and wife may safely lose temper if the loss be not simultaneous. Apart from this, if any suffered from the queen's temper it was not the king. For him she was all sweetness and patience. Her attentions and her flattery were incessant. It pleased him to have his beauty praised in the presence of courtiers or foreign ministers. Everything that the king did or said, if the queen's own projects were not affected, was right. His wishes were constantly anticipated by her thoughtfulness. The weariness, the weight of the daily burden, never let itself be seen.

This unbroken *tête à tête* had given the queen the opportunity of learning her husband's mind by heart. She had learnt her lesson beyond the possibility of mistake. The king's manner, his answers, the condition of his temper, were the compass by which she steered. She would throw out insinuations and suggestions to prepare her way. The king was gradually induced to assimilate her likes and dislikes. If there was resistance, she knew its cause and the means of overcoming it ; she realised that there were moments to yield in order to return to the charge again, moments to hold firm in order to carry the position by storm. There is reason to fear that the king's sensuous and uxorious temperament was the strongest piece on her board, and she occasionally pushed her advantage to extreme lengths. The coarse-grained azafata was not always reticent

on the subject of the king's cries and threats, and the
queen's tears, and the gossiping Irishman, Burke, who
hung about the back-stairs of royalty, would retail the
unsavoury stories.   Such tiffs as these were so many
ultimate triumphs for the queen.   The strain of such a life
was terrible.   Many a clever woman has ruled her husband
by making him believe himself the ruler, by crediting
him with the origination of her own suggestions.   But the
influence of the king in Spain was so all important that in
this task, sufficiently easy in private life, the wife had many
rivals.   Continual watchfulness was needed.   If for a moment she lost touch of the king's mind, the game might well
be lost.[1]   The difficulty was increased by the complexity of
Philip's character.   His weakness of purpose was combined
with strong prejudices, which rose at times to chivalrous
attachments.   His indolent self-effacement was counteracted by a conceited sense of self-importance.   The queen
felt that no reliance could be placed upon her husband's
actions.   Thus, in the pursuit of her political ambitions, she,
the wife of the most immaculate of husbands, suffered from
all the pangs of jealousy.   She must be always by his side.
She assisted in his interviews with the Secretaries of State.
Every judicious courtier, every well-informed ambassador
knew that it was useless to request a private audience without her presence.   She questioned the king as to everything
he said or did or read.   His engagements, indeed, came to
little ; for his desire to gain time to consult the queen had
made him a master of indefinite reply.   Of such scenes S.
Simon gives a picture, of which there must have been many
a *replica*.   He had been granted a private audience with the
king.   As he approached their majesties, the queen came
towards him, and said in an easy and natural manner : " Now

---

[1] The Savoyard ambassador, Del Maro, attributed the queen's conduct to
Alberoni. The first lesson instilled into the queen by Alberoni, and which
since served as the fundamental basis of her conduct, was to manifest such
a tender attachment for the king's person as not to be able to be separated
from him even for the shortest time without suffering from faintness. —*Me
morie della R. Accad. delle Scienze di Torino, Serie II. vol. ix.*

then, sir, no ceremony. You have something that you wish to say to the king in private; I shall go to the window and let you talk." S. Simon protested that he had nothing to say in private, that, in fact, if he had had the disappointment of not seeing her, he should have been obliged to ask for a separate audience to thank her for the brilliant reception of the previous evening. "No, no," she replied, with much liveliness, "I leave you with the king, and shall rejoin you when you have finished." So saying, the queen took two skips to the window, which was a long way off, closely followed by the ambassador, who protested that he would not open his mouth till she returned. At last she allowed herself to be persuaded, and returned to the side of the king, who had stood still and silent throughout this interview. "She would have known just as well from the king," concludes S. Simon, "anything that I might have said without her, and would never have pardoned me." It was, doubtless, to these private audiences that the queen owed her growing experience in men and measures. Her presence, by degrees, became absolutely necessary for their conduct. Questions, answers, and discussion rested entirely with her. She possessed, to a marvellous degree, the art of leading while pretending to follow the conversation, of effacing herself before the king while relieving him of the burden of the audience, and of placing the person to whom it was granted completely at his ease by importing an element of cheerfulness, even into the most serious subjects. The king, meanwhile, shifted from foot to foot, then stood on his two heels, he half coughed without occasion, kept turning his head towards the queen, and when he wished the ambassador to retire these movements became more frequent and he finally pulled the queen's gown, upon which she gracefully dismissed the visitor.

It is not surprising that, to a slave of habit as was Philip, his wife's constant presence became a necessity of life. His jealousy at her short absences was carried to such a pitch that if, during a walk on the Mall, she dropped a few paces behind while talking or listening to an anecdote, he would anxiously look round, and she had hurriedly to regain his side. After Alberoni's departure the queen indeed attempted to enlarge the prison house and to relax the chains; but great as was her influence she could not master Philip's habits, which had become a second nature. To the conduct of State affairs the constant presence of the queen was not altogether advantageous. If, indeed, she had had no interests apart from those of the Spanish Crown, her natural good sense and quickness of vision would have been of service. She would have drawn full advantage from her wit, her charm of manner, and her blameless character. But her inordinate mania for the establishment of her children distorted her vision. She had not sufficient knowledge nor experience to realise at once how far a given proposal would bring her nearer to or farther from her goal. Her suspicions extended themselves to subjects which were entirely foreign and indifferent to her aims. If ministers and ambassadors could have conversed with the queen alone, she had ample intelligence to understand their proposals and judgment to discuss them. But such discussion was impossible in the king's presence, because she feared that the king might take impressions which might conceivably be unfavourable to her aims. She, therefore, gave no room for explanation, and barred suggestions which might have facilitated her projects; because she did not grasp their consequences. To induce her to return to proposals previously made required such delicate manipulation and such round-about methods that the opportunity for action was often lost. Thus her dominating influence was frequently the despair both of ministers and diplomats. Nothing could be done without her; and yet ambassadors could make no progress, and chafed at the humiliating futility of their position; while Spanish ministers were constantly checked by the fear of losing office. The queen had, in fact, that peculiar quality of mind at once suspicious and acute which bars the way to honourable and reasonable advice and throws it open to the subtle approaches of the charlatan.

It would have been well for the Spanish monarchy had

the queen been impartial or had she been popular. Her partiality and her unpopularity were indeed closely connected. It was the latter which threw her into the unfortunate position of a faction leader. The Spaniards had disliked the marriage as being derogatory to the dignity of their Crown, and above all, as being the work of Madame des Ursins. The queen's hard treatment of the princess did not cause the Spaniards to forgive the marriage, the sins of the tyrant still rested on the new comer's head. The Spaniards seemed irreconcilable. Frenchmen would have bent before the girlish gaiety and natural charm of the young Italian. Under Alberoni's iron rule the tongues of the Spaniards had been tied. His disgrace gave full vent to their pent-up feelings, and they were so outspoken in their dislike that the queen disdained to try to win them. "The extent of this mutual aversion," writes S. Simon, "seems incredible. Whenever the queen drove out with the king the people kept crying incessantly, the bourgeois in their shops and all : 'Long live the king and the Savoyard—and the Savoyard,' and they kept on repeating, 'The Savoyard' at the top of their voices, so that there should be no chance of a mistake. Never a voice shouted : 'Long live the queen'. The queen pretended to despise all this, but it could be seen that she was inwardly furious, and she could never get used to it. She used to speak her mind on the subject freely, and has more than once said to me with a piqued and angry expression : 'The Spaniards do not like me, but I hate them too'." [1] For the French followers of the king and for the small party which gathered round the French ambassador the queen had little natural liking, but she concealed her feelings from respect to her husband. For the same reason she was at this time studiously kind to her predecessor's children. This was probably no mere affectation. It was her nature to be

---

[1] Her want of care in concealing her bitterness and her satirical remarks at the expense of Spanish ladies completed the alienation. One source of the unpopularity of Philip and Elisabeth was their continual absence from Madrid, where they only resided from December to March. The rest of the year was spent between the Escurial and Balsain, the Pardo and Aranjuez.

kind, until her temper was soured by evident want of appreciation.

It was natural that in her state of isolation Elisabeth
should draw nearer to the Italian clique. It has been seen
that this had existed before her marriage.[1] The ill-success
of the late war could probably have disorganised this party,
but for the queen's accession to its ranks. This conjunction
was inevitable. The Italians could alone appreciate the
queen's ambitions; they alone could understand her modes
of life and thought; they in common with her felt con-
strained by the social *ennui* and the intellectual depression
of Spain. Yet too much stress must not be laid upon this
natural sympathy. A native of Parma would have little in
common with a Neapolitan noble, and many of the leading
members of the Italian party were of Neapolitan extraction.
Peculiarly distasteful to Elisabeth was the leader of the
party, the Duke of Popoli, a Neapolitan noble, whose splendid appearance and polished manners could not be improved
upon. But his fine intelligence degenerated into intrigue,
and his eloquence into a mastery of the art of lying.
Haughty by nature, he would cringe if it suited his needs.
He would sacrifice all for advancement or for money. One
of such sacrifices was pretty certainly his wife. The queen,
whose friend she was, openly reproached him with her
murder. Yet he had obtained the important post of governor to the prince. The same suspicion rested upon the
governor of one of the younger infants, Salazar, which gave
occasion to the *mot* that wife murder was a necessary quali-
fication for the post. The appointments held by these
Italians was regarded as a scandal, for two men less capable
of giving a wholesome education to the princes could hardly
have been found. Such criticisms, indeed, would not apply
to all the Italian party. The Duke of Mirandola, Elisabeth's
former suitor, was honourable, pious, and universally beloved. His wife, the queen's great friend, was equally re-

---

[1] Alberoni had discouraged it, but the outbreak of the war in Sicily had
given it fresh influence.

spected.[1]   The Duke of Solferino, a Gonzaga, had improved both in character and appearance with the certainty of his daily bread.   The little, dark, thick-set man with hair unbrushed, at whom the Parisians had laughed as at a poor college exhibitioner, had been married by the wealthy and widowed Duchess of Alva, had on her death turned Capuchin, and confined himself to rush-bottomed chairs for grief, and had then married the only pretty woman in Madrid.   No wonder that he was highly esteemed and well received, and regarded as a leader of fashion.   The Prince of Santo Buono had as governor of Peru discovered a specific for gout, but, having omitted to bring it home, was allowed a stool when waiting for the king, and a sedan chair, though not a councillor. The Prince of Cellamare, notwithstanding the failure of his plot and the fall of his friend Alberoni, retained his credit till his death, and the Duke of S. Pierre, a Spinola from Genoa, had finally done credit to the educational efforts of his wife, a sister of Torcy, and for long the queen's intimate friend. On her husband's death in 1727 her mode of consolation became a scandal, and she retired for a time to Paris, whence she wrote amusing letters to the queen, with whose replies she entertained the Cardinal Fleury.   Would that these could be discovered!

To the Italians were still attached the Flemings, and to some extent the Irish.   They all had this in common that they possessed not an acre of land in Spain, they had no vested interest in the country.   Dispossessed princes or *parvenu* adventurers, they were all forced to seek their fortunes by Court favour, to jostle for place and pension. The heads of the Flemish and Irish parties, the Marquis of Lede and the Duke of Ormond, stood indeed aloof from faction, and were on good terms with all parties.   The former attended to his military duties, while the fact that the latter sacrificed high promotion to his fidelity to Anglicanism, proved that he was no dangerous rival in a Court.

If the queen suffered, or even pressed the promotion of

[1] She was drowned in her oratory in the celebrated flood of 1723. See *Murray's Magazine*, Sept., 1890.

disreputable men, personally repulsive to herself, it must be remembered to what an extent her hands were tied. Owing to her secluded life she could not always be well informed. The members of such councils as were left, and the lower departmental officials, were almost exclusively Spaniards. The great lords opposed to the Italian faction still had some access to the king notwithstanding his seclusion. The queen therefore resolved to follow the lead of Madame des Ursins, to push the promotion of members of her own party, to bind them to her interests by their own. This was not always easy. She could indeed compass the exclusion of a distasteful candidate, but was not invariably able to secure a friend's appointment. Yet by raising objections to every other, she would sometimes gain a post for one whom Philip had rejected. It was seen that her favour was the surest path to honour, and consequently a few Spaniards began to be drawn within her radius, or, for other reasons, attached themselves to the Italian party. It is noticeable that some of these were suspected of Austrian sympathies. Such was the Count of Montijo, who became grand equerry and major-domo, major of the queen, and filled successively the English and Imperial embassies. He had shown courage in the war of succession which crippled his finances, and his complete retirement with his young wife until his affairs were readjusted had done him credit. His reappearance on the occasion of the prince's marriage was universally welcomed. The presence of such men in the queen's party, and her liking or respect for some of the highest of the Spanish nobility, such as the Duke of Arco, and the Marquis of Santa Cruz, served to relieve the tension, and to create some neutral ground between the two extreme wings of either party. Yet to the end of her life Elisabeth was an alien in her adopted country.

CHAPTER IX

REASONS OF PHILIP'S ABDICATION—THE ROYAL RETREAT AT
  S. ILDEFONSO—GOVERNMENT OF KING LUIS—CHARAC-
  TER OF THE YOUNG KING AND QUEEN—DEATH OF LUIS—
  PHILIP AND ELISABETH RESUME THE GOVERNMENT.

PHILIP's abdication, though it took Europe by surprise, was
not the result of a sudden freak. The queen told Scotti
that it had been in his mind for four years, and much the
same estimate was formed by the king's Irish adherent,
Cammock, who had reliable information on the subject.
The disgrace and disappointment of the Sicilian war had
doubtless largely contributed to Philip's resolution. Grimaldo had been in the secret for a year, and both the king's
confessor and the queen's had vainly used their influence
to prevent it. The French Government had some idea of
the king's intention. Scotti and others believed it to have
been fostered by the regent, in the hope that by his
daughter's aid he would, from the hour of Philip's abdication, control Spanish policy. This, however, is hardly
consistent with subsequent events. At the end of 1723, it
was known at Paris that Philip was suffering from religious
mania, and intended to resign the throne, and the Marshal
de Tessé was sent to watch the situation, and to counteract
the tendencies of the Spanish ministers who were believed
to be influenced or corrupted by the English Government.
Before his departure the resignation had already taken
place.

It is tolerably certain that Philip's abdication was due
exclusively to religious scruples ; he was constantly subject

to agonies of fear that he had offended his Maker, and he craved for the time and solitude necessary to reconciliation. He felt that he was totally unequal to the duties of sovereignty, and this indeed was no hallucination. When the final farewell to his children and his ministers was over, he cried: "Thank God I am no longer a king, and that the remainder of my days I shall apply myself to the service of God and to solitude".[1] Most persons, however, who were in their sound senses, and especially the foreign ministers, were unable to believe in so simple an explanation for so extraordinary a step. They were at a loss to account for the queen's assent. "No one can understand," wrote Scotti, "how the queen, with her high spirit and intelligence, could have concurred in so extravagant a proceeding, of which every one disapproves, unless it is due to some great intrigue, or to some great deception under the shape of advantage."[2] To account for this, it was generally believed that Philip was actuated by an *arrière pensée* of facilitating his accession to the throne of France in the event of the death of Louis XV. If he were no longer King of Spain, the renunciation of the Crown of France no longer bound him. He would leave his dynasty firmly established in Spain, while the queen, if left a widow, would not be subject to the humiliating position of a dowager of Spain. In this view there was probably so much truth that Philip's acceptance of the Crown of Spain, and his renunciation of that of France, formed no unimportant element in the religious mania by which he was tortured. It is possible that had Louis XV. died the king would have immediately exchanged reconciliation with Heaven for return to France. The queen eagerly desired translation to the French throne, but it may be safely asserted that she assented to abdication because she could not prevent it; her absolutism was not unfrequently tempered by abject servitude. There was gossip indeed about a projected visit

---

[1] Cammock to Burchell, Jan. 17, 1724, *R. O. S.*, 173.
[2] January 24, 1724, Arch. Nap., C.F 63.

to France to form the acquaintance of the young king; but such visitors would have been far from welcome, and Philip and Elisabeth retired to the gorgeous solitude of S. Ildefonso.

This new palace had been for some years past the royal plaything. The forest of Segovia was the king's favourite hunting ground, as it had been that of Philip II., but the accommodation at the royal lodge at Balsain was quite inadequate, and the ministers and ambassadors were forced to reside at Segovia, a most inconvenient distance. In one of his hunting expeditions, Philip had fixed upon a new site, and the name of S. Ildefonso was given to it from the patron saint of the neighbouring church. Enormous sums were spent upon the building, and especially upon the gardens, which were artificially created in the midst of the most unpromising surroundings. Alberoni had been irritated beyond endurance at the constant drain on the revenues in the midst of his schemes for the revival of the Spanish monarchy. He had told his mistress that all she wished was to be Countess of S. Ildefonso. Yet architects, sculptors and workmen were most irregularly paid, and at times the queen was subject to the visits of her duns. The palace and gardens were one of the shows of Europe in the last century, but the climate was detestable, and Colonel Stanhope's Protestant secretary, Holzendorf, found difficulty in appreciating devotion under such inclement conditions. "The good King Philip goes on with his earnest devotions at S. Ildefonso, notwithstanding he lives in a very cold climate and country which in this season is surrounded with mountains of snow of a very hideous aspect, and is reckoned the coldest country in Spain. That prince has hitherto manifested nothing but what may confirm your opinion of his being in true earnest, and perhaps would he give stronger proofs of his sincerity, by retiring into a Carthusian convent, which is about a league from S. Ildefonso, if it was not for bands of matrimony which he cannot so easily dissolve, and which he seems as yet to have no aversion to. As for you, sir, I hope you are

M

in a good English country house and garden, with a chapel
to attend your devotions. I shall be very happy to have
the honour to pay you my respects there, being persuaded
that I have done sufficient penance by having lived nine
long years in Spain." [1]

Nothing could have been more formal than Philip's renunciation of power. He had bound himself never to
resume it ; he had even donned the little habit of S.
Francis. The suite that followed the king was very
moderate ; he intended to abandon hunting and the other
pleasures of the world, and the stables were reduced to the
modest proportions of a private establishment. Yet from
the first Spain was ruled, not from Madrid, but from S.
Ildefonso. This was perhaps partly due to the persuasions
of the Marshal de Tessé, who visited the king before proceeding to the Court. He begged Philip to retain control
over his son, and in this he was warmly supported by the
queen and by Grimaldo. " King Philip is not dead," said
the minister, " no more are we." Steps, however, had
already been taken to secure the subordination of the young
king. The Italian party had feared the complete loss of their
influence on the queen's retirement, while the Spaniards
were equally delighted. S. Simon had noticed that Luis
was the dominating passion of the Spaniards. They were
never tired of following in crowds and cheering him. He
returned their affection, and detested his Italian governor
and the memory of Alberoni. Spaniards pardoned his total
lack of education, and his surprising rudeness to ladies.
He shot well, was skilful at all games, and danced divinely.
" If he and Elisabeth," wrote S. Simon, " had to dance
for their livelihood the price of stalls would rise on the
nights of their appearance." In person he was " made for a
picture," tall, thin, and slight, with an ugly face, but a fair
complexion, and beautiful hair.

Very popular was the formation of a Cabinet Council, to
which Philip would previously never consent. But this

---

[1] Holzendorf to Temple Stanyer, March 20, 1724. *R. O. S.*, 173.

council was composed either of nonentities or of adherents of Grimaldo, who was at this time regarded as the depositary of the queen's views, and, moreover, all the public offices were full of his creatures. The President of Castile was known as a bad ambassador, and as a good-natured sociable member of society. The Archbishop of Toledo was the son of a blacksmith, at Gibraltar, and of as mean parts as extraction. His devotion to Philip, as a country *curé*, in Catalonia, had raised him to the episcopate, and the Jesuits had promoted him to the primacy as being incapable of doing injury to their order. De Guerra was too old, the Inquisitor-General too exclusively a courtier, to be active statesmen. The President of the Indies was rich, covetous, and entirely governed by Grimaldo. The one member of ability was Castelar, whose character did not command respect, and his interest was slight. The king at first attended council regularly, but soon showed as little inclination for business as his father. At the instigation of the ladies-in-waiting he made lavish grants of pensions and places, to the disgust of Castelar and Lede, and was forced to cancel them by Philip's representations. The substance of power lay with Grimaldo, who had three secretaries working with him at S. Ildefonso, and the packets daily brought to Madrid were fully as large as before the renunciation. The secretary, Orendayn, had been Grimaldo's page and then his head clerk. This station he really still occupied, though under a higher title. De Guerra confessed that the cabinet was really a cypher, and desired that it should be no secret, for it was better the world should know they had no authority, than imagine they were neglectful of their duty.[1] Keene's description of the two Courts is entirely confirmed by Scotti. "The Court of S. Ildefonso continues to have a hand in all important matters, many of which are not communicated to the cabinet.[2] . . . Affairs of State are only communicated to the

---

[1] Keene to Walpole, Feb. 24, 1725. *R. O. S.*, 173.

[2] Feb. 26, 1724. *Arch. Nap.*, C.F. 63.

cabinet in general terms, the majority of decisions are taken
without consulting it, extraordinary delay is caused by
waiting for the views of the Court of S. Ildefonso, and
yet there they deny any meddling." [1] The conduct of Luis
was partly the cause, and partly the result of his subordination.   He was in character a mere child.   He had been
strictly brought up, and he enjoyed his liberty in childish
fashion.   He would prowl the streets at night, and rob his
own gardens, for the fun of watching the gardener's vexa-
tion.   More objectionable was his habit of bursting open
the bedroom doors of the ladies-in-waiting in company with
servants of low rank.   Yet greater anxiety was caused by
the conduct of his queen.   She had always despised her
husband, and disliked his step-mother.   This dislike she
now openly avowed.   The blame is not to be attributed to
Elisabeth.   She had affectionately welcomed the young
bride, had nursed her through an attack of erysipelas, had
given her gruel with her own hands, and arranged her bed.
These attentions had from the first met with unmannerly
return.   The girl refused to attend the State ball given in
her honour; she hated dancing, for she danced incredibly
badly, and it kept her up; whereas, unlike the queen, her
maxim was early to bed and early to rise.   She did not
care for plays, and refused to hunt, for she detested
shooting.   Her only amusement consisted in childish jokes
which she practised at table and upon the queen.   S.
Simon was the witness and the victim of the incredible
vulgarity of her manners.   Since her marriage she had
sulked; she now gave the rein to her naturally high spirits.
But at Madrid the possibilities of amusement were few, and
the queen's tastes were not refined.   Tired of rambling
through the palace, she would take walks in the rain with
her petticoats up to her knees, and not return till night-
fall.   Philip himself was horrified to see her running round
the gardens at S. Ildefonso with no clothing but a dressing-

---

[1] N.D., C.F. 63   *Cf.* Bragadin, 1725: "In every petty matter the
oracle was consulted at S. Ildefonso, so that it might be said that the royal
title was at Madrid, its essence at Ildefonso".

gown with which the curious wind took liberties. She ate enormously, and at all hours, and would force her ladies to do likewise, waiting upon them herself, and slapping them if they refused to eat. To her husband she would never speak, and it was believed that she had always refused to consummate the marriage. She publicly insulted the Court of S. Ildefonso by refusing to allow Elisabeth's friend, the Duchess of S. Pierre, to kiss her hand. The young king at length inflicted a summary chastisement. Her coach was stopped on its return from one of her wild excursions, she was not allowed to return to the palace, and was placed in confinement. No attention was paid to her paroxysms of passion and shame. The old Marshal de Tessé took the opportunity to lecture her on her behaviour, and to prescribe a reconciliation. Her husband met her on her release, kissed her affectionately, and took her into his own carriage.[1]

The incident had produced a revulsion in her favour; the Spaniards thought the punishment too severe and too public for her offence, and attributed it to the vindictive nature of Elisabeth Farnese. Philip, whose scruples had forced him to abandon his crown, was now tormented by the thought that he was the cause of all disorders. Early in the spring there were those who believed that he

---

[1] The letter of Elisabeth to her step-son on his trouble has a genuine ring of sympathy and affection. " The letter of your Majesty, my very dear son, has pierced my heart, as I very well understand the grief in which you must be, and I am more sorry for you than I can possibly express. If I could comfort or console you in any way, there is nothing which I would not do ; but I am good for nothing, and, such as I am, I commend you to God, that it may please Him to apply a remedy. If after all this she continues in the same course, it is enough to make one lose one's senses. In God's name try and get as much distraction as you can, and take care of your health, which is so dear to us that if you fell ill we should be in despair."—July, 3, 1724. Alcalá, 2489.

Luis took his step-mother's advice, and distracted his mind with sport. She writes on July 23: " I am very angry with that rascally woman who drove your stags away yesterday, but there is nothing which women do not spoil. We must hope that she will not always be there, and that you will have the pleasure of seeing and killing them."—*Ibid.*

would reassume the crown. Tessé was likely to forward
such a scheme, for the council was beginning to feel its
way towards independence, and Frenchmen were gradually being replaced by Spaniards.[1] Rumours came from
Paris that it was intended to send the infanta back to
Spain; and at Madrid there was talk of annulling
the marriage of the king, and the engagement of
Don Carlos, and of substituting Bourbon princesses for
the daughters of the late regent who had now lost their
value.

The young king's death came almost as a relief. He was
ill but a week. His malady was attributed to tennis immediately after dinner in excessive heat, and to an immoderate
appetite for fruit and iced wine. Children are warned that
if they swallow cherry stones they may die of scarlet fever,
and it was on the same principles perhaps that Luis' small-
pox was ascribed to his own defects. His wife, prompted
by her confessor, bravely moved to his apartments, and
nursed him till his death, whereas his father and step-mother
would not go near him. His death took place on the last
day of August. For Spaniards, wrote Bragadin, it might
well be called a fatal loss. On September 2 the Council of
Castile, filled with Elisabeth's partisans, met at her desire
and petitioned the old king to resume the throne, but it is
interesting to find that it was debated whether conditions
should be imposed upon his absolutism. Among the Spaniards who had already begun to worship Ferdinand, Philip's
return was regarded with great disfavour. Scotti believed that
but for Ferdinand's absence at S. Ildefonso he would have
been proclaimed by acclamation.[2] Philip was as usual in

---

[1] Tessé himself was out of favour. The President of Castile, to whom
the French department of Foreign Affairs was assigned, disliked the nation.
Tessé, under pretence of gout, stayed at home, where it was contrary to
etiquette for the president to visit him.—Bragadin, 1725.

[2] "The number of those who would much have preferred the continuance
of Philip's retirement was not small; yet, though many even of the distinguished personages in their hearts desired the Council of Regency, in
order that power might return to the grandees, who are at present held down

agonies of doubt. His confessor, Bermudez, entreated him to abide by his oath of renunciation. A meeting of theologians was divided, some thinking that Philip would only hold the regency until Ferdinand should be of age. Elisabeth summoned another which was unanimously in favour of resumption, and the Nuncio Aldobrandini was so skilful that he succeeded in calming the king's scruples. Before he left the palace, Philip came out into the antechamber and announced his resolution. The queen's influence was probably decisive. She told her husband that to please him she was prepared to sacrifice her life and her blood, but not her honour and the interests of her children. Her entreaties were accompanied with floods of tears, which she always had readily at command. Her confessor urged her to persist and not lose courage. She doubled the guards, and ordered Bournonville to allow no one to approach Prince Ferdinand that could put independent ideas into his head. The king was at length persuaded, and left for Madrid to receive again the oath of allegiance from his subjects, but much discontent was caused by his rapid return to S. Ildefonso. Care was taken that Ferdinand should accompany the Court and great uneasiness was manifested at the chance of a revolution. It is indeed highly probable that, but for the armed force at the disposal of the Court, the smothered discontent of the Spaniards might have for once found utterance.[1] The young dowager, the crisis over, continued her irregularities, and made small case of her husband's death. Her presence in Spain caused such scandal that,

---

and kept aloof from the slightest share in government, yet every one concealed his private feelings, striving to rival each other in appearing to be amongst the most constant and most genuine in their acclamations and benedictions upon the king's decision."—Bragadin.

[1] "The fact that the infant happened to be at S. Ildefonso when his brother was seized with smallpox contributed greatly to the disappearance of any ideas which some malcontents may have conceived; besides which the two battalions of infantry and the three companies of horse guards always act as a powerful check on any who might cherish thoughts of revolution."—Bragadin, 1725.

contrary to the invariable practice, it was determined to send her back to France.[1]

[1] Scotti, Sept. 7, 1724. C. F. 63.

After her return, the disreputability of the young dowager's life became a public scandal, and she was finally deprived of her Spanish pension. Lord Percival's description of her at dinner at Vincennes fully bears out the criticisms of S. Simon and others on her manners. "She was fat, not seventeen, gluttonous, ate with both hands ; the two men attendants carried her off swinging in their arms, like a fat spirit in Henry VIII.; her feet did not touch the ground till she landed in the third room, and then she fell a-boxing them ; she never reads or works, seldom plays cards, and cuts her hair like an English schoolboy."—Paris, April 2, 1726. *Hist. MSS. Commission,* vol. vi. Report 7. App. 248c.

Madame, her grandmother, thus describes the princess in a letter of December 6, 1721 : " One cannot say that she is ugly ; she has pretty eyes, a smooth, white skin, a well-shaped nose, though rather small, and a very tiny mouth. With all this she is the most disagreeable person that I have ever seen. In all her manners, whether she be talking, or eating, or drinking, she annoys one. So I did not shed any tears when we said good-bye, no more did she."

CHAPTER X.

1724-6.

RUMOURS OF ALBERONI'S RECALL—ELISABETH LEANS TO-
WARDS AN IMPERIAL ALLIANCE—RISE OF RIPPERDÁ—HIS
MISSION TO VIENNA—THE INFANTA'S BETROTHAL AN-
NULLED—BREACH WITH FRANCE—TREATY OF VIENNA—
HOSTILITY TO FRANCE AND ENGLAND—ALLIANCE OF
HANOVER—THE SECRET ARTICLES OF VIENNA—RETURN
OF RIPPERDÁ—INTRIGUES WITH THE PRETENDER—
ALLIANCE WITH RUSSIA—ADMINISTRATION OF RIPPERDÁ
—HIS DISGRACE.

SPAIN was a country of surprises. Europe had scarce recovered from the sensations of Philip's abdication and
restoration when it was startled by the news of a Spanish
imperial alliance. To those who were not behind the
scenes this seemed a monstrous combination. Yet indica-
tions of such a possibility had not been infrequent. Alberoni
had suggested it before his fall, and the French Government
had, until the treaty of 1721, been seriously alarmed at the
prospect. During the reign of Luis, Ripperdá, who had
risen in Court favour, informed Scotti of a scheme for marrying Ferdinand to a daughter of the emperor, adding that he
felt confident of success. Scotti replied in general terms,
but assured his master that since Daubenton's death there
could be no insuperable obstacle.

After the restoration, however, Scotti believed that
Elisabeth inclined towards a Russian marriage, for the Czar
would be more willing to grant his daughter, now that Ferdinand was heir, and such an alliance would imply the

liberation of Italy from the barbarians.[1]   He spoke to the
queen of the rumour of an imperial marriage. She replied
that it would be well if the emperor would grant good terms,
but that at present it was not to be thought of or hoped for.[2]
Four months later she assured him that the reports were
merely gossip, and that such a marriage would be dangerous,
for the lords, still imbued with Austrian sympathies, might
instil into the mind of the prince sentiments adverse to his
father.[3] Shortly afterwards it was reported that the emperor,
relying on a secret treaty with Spain, was demanding places
in Alsace from France. Yet another month and Scotti taxed
the king and queen with Ripperdá's mission.[4] The king
only smiled, while the queen reddened a little, and replied
that she knew that the baron had gone to Holland, and if
he had gone to Vienna also she could not help it.   The
Parmesan minister understood that she was unwilling either
to deny or admit, but felt sure that Ripperdá's commission
had a royal source.[5]

Rumours were simultaneously afloat that Alberoni was
expected to return, and that a rich bishopric was awaiting
him.   The Duke of Parma, reconciled to him since he had
become a *persona grata* at the Papal Court, had for some
time pleaded for the forgiveness of the king and queen.
Scotti mentions a rumour of his recall immediately after the
restoration, but believed it to be impossible owing to the
king's dislike to the idea of a first minister.[6] To Alberoni
was ascribed the attempt to conclude a fresh reconciliation
with Rome, and the scheme for intermarriage with the imperial family.[7] Early in the year the king's health became
so bad that it seemed certain that he must either resign
afresh or allow some minister to relieve him of the weight of
government.   Both the Pope and the Pretender were believed to be urging Alberoni's recall. Men began to speak
well of the cardinal, and to think that his financial ability

---

[1] Sept. 23, 1724. C. F. 63.   [2] Oct. 6, 1724. *Ibid.*
[3] Feb. 17, 1725. C. F. 65.   [4] Feb. 24, 1725. *Ibid.*
[5] March 24, 1725. *Ibid.*   [6] Aug. 13. Sept. 23, 1725. *Ibid.*
[7] Jan. 15, 1725. *Ibid.*

might again restore Spain to power. The queen's confessor said that apart from the violence of his character Alberoni was a useful servant to the queen and the nation, and that past misfortunes might induce him to reform customs which were not becoming.[1]

The queen had probably long forgiven him; in the ensuing year he is found engaged in friendly correspondence with herself and Philip.[2] Yet even without Alberoni's prompting it was not strange that Elisabeth should at length turn towards Vienna. Before her marriage she had been Austrian at heart, as was natural in a descendant of Charles V. Her mother was a German and connected with the imperial family. Her earliest reminiscences were associated with the fears of Bourbon domination in Italy. The heat of the great conflict was over before she reached Spain, and she did not therefore cherish her husband's personal hatred for Charles VI. In Spain she had attached herself to the Italian Flemish party and had favoured Spaniards suspected of Austrian sympathies. The French alliance had brought nothing but disappointment. The regent had deceived her as to the restoration of Gibraltar, and he had supported England in opposing her favourite scheme that Don Carlos should pass into Italy as heir presumptive to his ·future States. The reconciliation with the House of Orleans had never been sincere, but it was hoped that Don Carlos, married to the regent's daughter, would be backed by the power of France. This hope had vanished with the regent's death. Don Carlos, whose prospects depended on a brilliant marriage, was tied to a lady who was now of little more than private rank, who would rather injure than advance him in the favour of the French Court. His establishment in Italy now rested solely upon Austrian goodwill. The

---

[1] Feb. 17, 1725. C. F. 65.

[2] Alberoni wrote from Rome on Sept. 6, and Dec. 8, 1725. The king replied on Feb. 15, 1726: "I assure you that I shall always value your memory and pray for your prosperity from the esteem which I have for your person". The queen replied in an equally friendly strain.—Alcalá. 4823, 2460.

king's physical and mental condition was such that delay
was dangerous and time of supreme importance. Yet the
congress had drifted into a round of dinner-parties to which
there was no natural conclusion. The queen's influence
over Philip had been strengthened by the solitude of S. Ildefonso. His return to the throne was in the main her work,
she was now to complete her triumph by converting him to
the imperial alliance. Accidental circumstances favoured
her schemes. Bermudez, the king's confessor, was not a
politician, but he had Austrian sympathies, and hated all
that was French. He was hand-in-glove with the Italian-
Flemish party, and this was eager for the imperial alliance,
partly out of spite to French and Spaniards, partly in the
hope of reinstatement or pecuniary compensation. Grimaldo
could not now safely thwart the queen, for his opposition to
King Luis' ministers and his harshness to his adherents
upon his death, had alienated the Spaniards upon whom he
usually relied. To the king, in his remorse for his son's unhappy marriage, the connection with the House of Orleans
now seemed a deadly sin. England was in little less disfavour. Her fleet had wrecked the queen's hopes when near
fulfilment. Her king had stultified the Spanish Government by his fallacious engagement to restore Gibraltar.
Her competition and her contraband were crushing the
commercial classes.

The emperor on his side had strong incentives to reconciliation. The Ostend Company was his peculiar plaything.
He believed that the natural lines of commerce could be
diverted at will, and that his new foundations at Ostend and
Trieste would revive the traffic of Germany from sea to sea,
reopen old trade routes long grass-grown, restore old towns
long crumbled. Ostend alone could pay for the keep of the
Austrian white elephant—the Netherlands. Monopoly was
then the infallible creed of all intelligence, the postulate of
civilised commerce. The suppression of the Ostend Company and the stifling of Austrian and German trade has been
regarded as one of the proudest feats of the Maritime
Powers. Yet the emperor naturally resented their inter-

ference, and hoped to gain by an exclusive treaty with Spain the advantages which England was deriving from legitimate commerce and illicit contraband.

A yet stronger motive for reconciliation with Spain was the security which it offered for the imperial schemes in Italy. Not content with the territories added to his hereditary possessions, the emperor definitely intended to reassert the old imperial claims, to make Italy again a province of the empire, and with her resources to consolidate his power in Germany. Measures were taken to create a Chancery for Italy, which would imply its formal inclusion in the empire. The Elector of Cologne would cease to be a merely titular official. Recent events had shown how dangerous the arms and intrigues of Spain could be to such a scheme. She was the natural refuge for affrighted or disaffected Italian princes. Bragadin informed the Venetian Government that the recovery of Italy was not only a desire of the king, but the prayer of the whole Spanish nation; and that the ministry, using less violent measures than Alberoni, was winning the favour of the Italian princes in order to secure a foothold. He added that, considering these views, it would be to the Senate's interest to cultivate the friendship of the queen. If, however, Spain recognised the imperial overlordship of provinces to which the imperial title was of the weakest, the backbone was taken from the opposition. Moreover, the hostility of Spain made the emperor disagreeably dependent upon England, for the English fleet could alone secure his hold on Italy against the Spaniard. The unfriendly action of England with reference to the Ostend Company and the Barrier, and the intermittent jealousy between the Elector of Hanover and the emperor, made it desirable that this humiliating dependence should cease.

Some weight may be attached to another consideration. Until recently, commerce, the balance of power, and religion had been the three ingredients of which, in varying proportions, European politics had been composed. The latter element had become at times a *quantité négligeable*, but it was always liable to reappear. A religious revival had been experienced under Mme. de Maintenon, and the flame just extinguished in the West of Europe seemed not unlikely to burst out in the East. Events in Saxony and Poland contributed to this possibility. A revival of Catholicism might be a valuable instrument in the emperor's hands for the fulfilment of designs in the East of Europe, while it might bribe the Pope to acquiescence in his Italian policy. For this purpose no reliance could be placed on France, notwithstanding the regent's death. France was undergoing a reaction from the religious strain of the latter years of Louis XIV.; she had made her last attempt to be religious, and had obviously failed. But in Spain king and queen and people were genuinely Catholic. Gentle as was the present Grand Inquisitor, the office was still alive and active. Its exclusion from Gibraltar and Minorca was felt to be a national disgrace. In commercial disputes with England its action frequently occupied a prominent place. Complaints against the Inquisition formed the English answer to Spanish remonstrances on smuggling. Spain, therefore, and the emperor might well find common ground in religious revival, and the special form which this might take was the restoration of the Catholic dynasty of Stuart.

The first overtures came apparently from Vienna through the medium of the Pope. But the way had been prepared by the queen's growing confidence in Ripperdá. His association with her and its sudden and violent cessation forms one of the most striking episodes of her life. His personality undoubtedly for a time exercised a strong influence on her imagination. His character has usually been drawn from sources avowedly hostile. He was not a mere adventurer nor completely a charlatan. He possessed powers of invention and organisation. His imagination was rapid, and his criticism acute, qualities well adapted to attract the queen. His knowledge of commerce and manufacture Alberoni had recognised by employing him in commercial negotiations for which he himself had not sufficient experience. Like Patiño, Ripperdá was of Spanish origin but of

alien birth.   His family had long been settled in Groningen ;
he had served with the Dutch forces in the War of Succession and had been sent to Spain to conclude the commercial
arrangements made with the States-General under the terms
of the peace.   Seeing a brilliant career before him in
Spanish service, he divulged to the king his unalterable intention of embracing Catholicism for the salvation of his
soul and as a passport to the service of so great and good a
monarch.   His reward was the superintendence of the cloth
factory of Guadalajara.   No subordinate office could have
been more skilfully chosen to bring him into contact with
the king and queen.   Guadalajara was the scene of their first
meeting, and their sentimental associations took the practical
form of the establishment of a cloth working industry, as
part of a general scheme for the revival of woollen manufacture.   Ousted for a time by Alberoni, he had intrigued with
Daubenton and Grimaldo for his fall, and was afterwards
established at Segovia as inspector-general of national
manufactures.   He was now on intimate terms with the
queen and began to unfold schemes of a more directly political character.   He lived extravagantly, was always in need
of money, and not scrupulous in his means of getting it.
Both the English and Imperial Governments had simultaneously employed him as paid agent.   Prince Eugene had
a high opinion of his abilities and attached him to imperial
interests.   It is an illustration of his foresight that he procured his introduction to the queen through the emperor at
whose request the Court of Parma gave him letters of introduction.   Than this there could be no surer passport to
success.

In one of his confidential but contradictory conversations
with Stanhope, Ripperdá asserted that his master-passion
was hatred for France.   This was possibly true, but it was
long before circumstances were favourable to the avowal of
his animus.   He had largely contributed to the English
Commercial Treaty, but he then occupied no official position
in Spain, and his handsome reward he might regard as a
professional fee due to an impartial specialist.   Opposition to

England was now a necessary result of his position, and hence his far-reaching schemes for crippling the commercial supremacy of England and stifling the prosperity of her colonies.

Ripperdá's influence with the queen had become so great that but for Philip's abdication he might possibly have replaced Grimaldo. If not the author of the proposals for an Imperial Alliance, he was the natural agent to employ when overtures reached the queen's ears in the autumn of 1724. In great secrecy he was despatched to Vienna, it being given out that he was on his way to Holland to engage skilled artisans, or that he was sent on a commercial mission to Russia. He received apparently formal instructions to remove the difficulties which prevented a permanent peace, to arrange a marriage between the Prince of Asturias and an archduchess, who should bring the Low Countries as her dower, and to secure the reversion of Tuscany and Parma for Don Carlos. The queen, however, seems to have given him private instructions to obtain the hand of Maria Theresa for Don Carlos. If this negotiation succeeded she reached the summit of her ambitions. While her daughter sat upon the throne of France her son could wield the forces of the empire. Two bad lives alone stood between Don Carlos and the throne of Spain, and possibly not more than two barred his accession to the crown of France. It is not surprising that Elisabeth's imagination was intoxicated by such a prospect.

Ripperdá reached Vienna in November, 1714. Von Arneth denies the usual statement that he passed under an assumed name,[1] and indeed his want of precaution caused some anxiety. The Spanish agent's task was not easy.

[1] *Prinz Eugen*, iii. 171.

S. Saphorin's statements as to Ripperdá's disguise are very circumstantial. On February 18, 1725, he wrote that a Dutchman going by the name of Phastenberg had been in close conference with Sinzendorff for five days past, going generally in the evening. Finding himself narrowly watched, he afterwards held his conferences with Buol. March 10: Sinzendorff, finding the intrigue discovered, brought the matter into conference. April 25: Ripperdá was no longer *incognito.*—*R. O. S.*, 176.

Prince Eugene and Staremberg were opposed to a Spanish alliance. Perlas and Sinzendorff and the emperor himself were favourable. Over and over again negotiations would have broken down but for the emperor's desire to float the Ostend Company and to separate the two lines of Bourbon, whilst Elisabeth's passion for her son's advancement prevented Ripperdá's retirement.

The conclusion was perhaps hastened by the breach with France on the subject of the infanta's marriage. There was a close connection between the two sets of events, and it is difficult to distinguish between cause and effect. Early in 1725 the French Government received warning of Ripperdá's negotiations at Vienna, and, on the other hand, it seems certain that the Court of Spain had intimations of the intention to annul the young king's marriage. The Duke of Bourbon had no desire to break with Spain, but the situation was too difficult for his feeble nerves. If Louis died the succession seemed an open question between the Spanish and the Orleanist lines. The latter was irreconcilable with the Duke of Bourbon, and hence Tessé, a veteran adherent of Legitimist succession, had been sent to propitiate the Court of Spain, and to offer or request support. But it was becoming clear that Philip's chances in France were on the decline, that he was the subject of some ridicule even among Legitimists, and that, in the event of a vacancy, the succession of the Duke of Orleans would be unquestioned. The alarming illness of Louis XV. made such a contingency entirely probable. The Council determined to return the infanta to her parents, and for this purpose the Abbé Livry was summoned from Portugal to replace Tessé. On March 8 Livry received orders to announce the resolution of the Council, and to deliver a memorial containing the reasons for this step, and letters from Louis XV. and the Duke of Bourbon to the king. The abbé read the first, but Philip declined to receive the other documents.[1] The matter was

---

[1] Richelieu relates that Livry, on being presented, burst into tears. Philip fumbled for a pair of scissors to cut the tape of the letters, but Elisabeth, guessing their contents, passionately prevented him.—II. 215.

kept as secret as the agitation of the king and queen and Livry would allow; but on the 18th a courier arrived from Lawless, stating that the resolution had been officially communicated to him by the Court of France.

The Court of Madrid showed all the indignation of genuine surprise. Mlle. de Beaujolais was ordered to join her sister, who was already on her homeward journey. Surely, as S. Simon said, these marriages had not been made in heaven.[1] French consuls were expelled, and French subjects ordered to naturalise or leave Spain. This inconsiderate order extracted from Philip one of the few jokes with which he has been credited. The queen found his boxes and portmanteaus open and his wardrobes emptied. She asked in astonishment the cause of these unexpected preparations. " Why ! " replied the king, " have not all Frenchmen been ordered to leave Spain ? Well, then, I am French, and so I am getting ready to be off." Elisabeth might lose her temper, but not her sense of humour. She broke into a merry laugh, and the order was recalled. Philip's own indignation was very real ; he declared that his subjects would shed their last drop of blood to avenge the insult ; that he would never forgive France until the duke asked for pardon on his knees. He assured Stanhope that he would never be reconciled to France, and that his plenipotentiaries at Cambrai should decline her mediation, his differences with the emperor should be submitted to the King of England. Now, if ever, the queen deserved the

---

[1] Mlle. de Beaujolais was well liked by Elisabeth and the Spaniards, and was the only one of the regent's daughters whose death was regretted by the French. She was pretty, sweet-tempered, and *spirituelle*, romantic, and, as her father said, babyish. It was said that she was passionately devoted to Don Carlos until her death. It is true that her head was turned by the Duke of Richelieu, to whom she wrote in terms so warm that they " burnt the paper ". But the life of no lady of quality was complete without a passion for this lady-killing duke.—See Mme. de Tessé, i. 314.

The Duke of Richelieu draws a picture of the meeting of the three disgraced ladies. The infanta, unconscious of her wrongs, was playing with her toys. Mlle. de Beaujolais was weeping for her lost lover, while the widowed queen could not conceal her joy at escaping from Spain on any terms.

soubriquet of termagant. "The Bourbons," she cried to Philip, as she trampled upon the portrait of the King of France, "are a race of devils!" And then, recollecting herself, she added : "Always excepting your Majesty". To Stanhope her expressions were yet broader. "The rascal, this malformation, has given my daughter her *congé*, because the king would not make his concubine's husband a grandee of Spain!"

Yet for the furtherance of her present designs no event could have been more opportune. The infanta had left home too young to be subject to her mother's influence ; there was no certainty that, as Queen of France, she would have furthered her mother's projects. The queen had laughingly confessed this to S. Simon. They found the child learning French, and the king said that she would soon forget Spain. "Oh!" said the queen, "not only Spain, but the king and me, to devote herself to nobody but her husband."[1] It had already been decided to annul the betrothal of Don Carlos, and the dismissal of the infanta provided a plausible pretext for the breach of faith. Thus it must be confessed that the indignant reprisals of the Court of Spain contained an element of art. Above all the prospect of an immediate rupture convinced Philip of the necessity of alliance with the House of Hapsburg. French and Spanish troops were on the march to the common frontier, and the Spaniards at all events were prepared to fight ; Spanish pride was deeply wounded, the French king's effigy was dragged in the mud, and the mountaineers harried the French border and hamstrung the cattle. Santa Cruz, who was sent to conduct the infanta, entered S. Jean de Pied de Port as if he were heading a storming party, and brought back pieces of black bread on which he said the infanta had been fed in France. Ripperdá was instructed to give way on the disputed points, and he arrived at an agreement with Sinzendorff. Yet the opposition was still vehement at Vienna. The empress and the archduchess herself refused

[1] S. Simon to Louis XV. Nov. 24, 1721.

to abandon the Prince of Lorraine. Ministers of German blood felt that fresh power would be thrown into the hands of Spaniards and Italians, already too high in the emperor's favour. Staremberg reproached Sinzendorff with wishing to make Austria a Spanish province. But Ripperdá promised boundless subsidies, and the emperor convinced Windischgratz of the value of these for reducing the German States to dependence on Vienna. The aid of Spain was promised for the recovery of Strasburg and Alsace, and the Three Bishoprics. The big Prussian grenadier, urged Ripperdá, was too fond of his toy soldiers to let them fight, but if he did he should be turned out of Prussia, and the Elector of Hanover out of both his German and his English possessions.

The Spanish price was, however, again rising. A condition was made that all three archduchesses must marry all three infants ; a clean sweep must be made of the imperial matrimonial board. Sinzendorff protested that such a proposal would alarm all Europe ; it would be well to wait for quieter times. Ripperdá rejoined that the queen's heart was chiefly set on the marriage of Don Carlos, but he assented to the omission of the proposal from the treaties. Of these there were three. The first, signed on April 30, took for its basis the Treaties of Utrecht, Baden, and London. The emperor and king agreed to bear during life the titles which they claimed, while renouncing each other's dominions. The reversion to the Italian duchies was ceded to Don Carlos, but the Spanish Crown was excluded from sovereignty or guardianship over any States in Italy. The dispossessed partisans of either claimant were reinstated, and the debts of the Imperialist Government in Catalonia and those of Spain in Sicily were recognised. The second and third treaties were signed on the following day. The former provided for an offensive and defensive alliance, and the emperor pledged his friendly offices for the recovery of Gibraltar. The latter placed the emperor's subjects and the Hanse Towns on the footing of the most favoured nation, and gave express recognition to the Ostend Company. It is clear that so far the

emperor was the gainer. But it was unlikely that the Queen
of Spain should abandon her ambitions even under pressure
of the breach with France. At this time the project of Don
Ferdinand's marriage seems to have dropped. There were
obvious difficulties in its way. It was not expedient that
the elder infant should marry the younger archduchess, and
if he married the elder the direct prospect of the union of the
dominions of Spain and Austria would provoke all Europe.
It is doubtful if the proposal had ever been seriously made,
for negotiations for the hand of the Princess of Portugal had
been opened the very week after King Luis's death. The
name of Don Philip now became more prominent; the interests of the offspring of Philip's first marriage were subordinated to those of the second family. How far the emperor
at this time entered into any definite engagements is uncertain. Belando, whose book received the king's approval,
asserts that the emperor and empress wrote a letter to the
king and queen containing a promise of Maria Theresa's
hand for Don Carlos, and that this letter was the consideration for the formal treaties.

The European powers were perhaps more surprised at
the manner than at the matter of the Treaties of Vienna.
Colonel Stanhope expressed his astonishment that a man
of Ripperdá's infamous character should in so short a time
have produced between two such inveterate enemies an accommodation which had for five years resisted the mediation
of the two greatest powers of Europe, whose guarantee was
thought by Spain an insufficient security. The ambassador
was assured by Grimaldo that the treaty was in no sense
prejudicial to England, and it was thought that it was due
merely to the desire of the emperor to increase his influence
by being appointed mediator in the disputes between England and Spain. Such mediation was indeed offered, but
Lord Townshend replied that there was absolutely no
dispute, that his Government did not need, and would not
admit of mediation. The chief dangers of a rupture lay in
Ripperdá's intemperate talk. His main failing as a diplomat
was his incapacity to hold his tongue. He declared that

England and France had purposely delayed peace between the emperor and Spain to enjoy their contraband trade, but that they should now be confined to the indirect trade through Cadiz, while Spain and the emperor shared the profits of the Indies. He boasted of the enormous subsidies to be placed at the emperor's disposal for war against the Protestants. He told the envoy of Parma that he would offer to England the alternative between Gibraltar and the American trade; for the King of England and his treaties he cared nothing, but this matter would be brought before Parliament, which would not sacrifice the nation's commerce. S. Saphorin, English minister at Vienna, heard that the emperor intended to offer to the English king, or rather his Parliament, to exclude the French from Spain and the Indies if England would cede Gibraltar and join the allies against France. Alberoni was the subject of Ripperdá's patronising remarks; he was not, he said, wanting in talent, but had made capital mistakes; he should have attacked Naples instead of stopping at Sicily; and, above all, should have invaded England and dethroned the king; failure was impossible, and all else would have followed. The Danish ambassador disconcerted him by asking if the English fleet which had destroyed the Spanish ships off Sicily would not have done so off Gravesend. Sinzendorff, with an air of embarrassment and mortification, confessed that Ripperdá might cause more disturbance with his tongue than he had given pleasure by his promises. Stanhope was instructed to ruin Ripperdá, at Madrid, if his talk were the result of his own madness, but if it expressed the sense of his Government, to speak plain and threaten a rupture. From Stanhope's despatches such a rupture seemed only too imminent. "As to Ripperdá's disposition towards his Majesty, nothing could be worse, he having long been a zealous Jacobite, and hath nothing nearer to his heart than the ruin of our country, except that of his own, to which he is still a more implacable enemy."[1] Under pretence of

---

[1] Col. Stanhope to Newcastle, June 22, 1725. *R. O. S.*, 176.

changing the African garrisons, he had projected the surprise of Jamaica. The Jesuits were busy collecting money for the Pretender's service. The Pope and Alberoni were eager to convert the coming war into a crusade. The Courts of Vienna and Madrid were equally governed by "the same wild, turbulent and wicked spirit of that infamous incendiary Ripperdá".[1] The Court of Madrid was so elated as to seem drunk with joy; the heads of the king and queen were filled with such wild presumptuous notions that they regarded themselves as the arbiters of all Europe.

Yet the boasted treaty was represented by Stanhope as being generally disapproved and ridiculed.[2] Grimaldo was opposed to its anti-English spirit, but he had lost all credit and was kept in ignorance. The queen would gladly have dismissed him, but the king retained some remains of kindness for him, and he hoped by patience and submission to weather the present storm, as he formerly had others. Monteleone, who had belonged to the queen's party, lost favour by his defence of the Duke of Bourbon and his opposition to the treaty. He now supplied all the information in his power to England. The queen, he said, was absolute, and Orendayn and Ripperdá alone were entrusted with her secrets; the king had no wish to break with England, but the queen, knowing what store he placed upon Gibraltar, pressed its acquisition to reconcile him to the treaty, which she regarded as her own work.

In July a peremptory demand was made for the immediate cession of Gibraltar. Stanhope complained to the king in person of the precipitate character of this ultimatum, pointing out that the consent of Parliament was essential and that the writs could not be issued owing to the king's absence in Hanover. "Then make the king," replied Elisabeth, "return immediately and summon his Parliament. . . . I am convinced that in the two Houses there will not be a

---

[1] Col. Stanhope to Newcastle, June 22, 1725. *R. O. S.*, 176.

[2] The Venetian envoy Bragadin is at variance with Stanhope on this point.

single vote against the restitution of Gibraltar. To make the proposal more urgent offer this alternative : Choose between the loss of Gibraltar and that of your trade with the Indies. The question will not admit of a moment's doubt nor suffer the slightest delay." [1]

The feeling of the Court was yet stronger against France. It was suggested that a marshal or duke or peer should be sent to offer an apology, but Philip replied two or three times : "That is not enough ". As the Duke of Bourbon had been the author of the affront, from him alone satisfaction was expected. The duke, however, professed to be unable to leave the young king for a single day. He was not courageous, and had no mind to expose himself to the now notorious temper of the queen. When the famine in France was discussed at the royal table, the king showed tenderness, and said : " We must not let the people die of hunger"; upon which the queen exclaimed : " Yes, let them all die," and Philip let the conversation drop. Grimaldo told Stanhope that they were persuaded that the Court of France had neither courage nor means for war, and Stanhope believed that its abject conduct encouraged the haughtiness of Spain. At Madrid all was done to stimulate warlike enthusiasm. The king and queen, as other imported sovereigns, had discouraged bull fights, but they now attended one on the Plaza Mayor, where sixty bulls were killed.[2] Philip was roused from his lethargy, and allowed himself to be washed and shaved. The white cockades which the troops had worn since Philip's accession were pulled from their ribbons. In the fireworks the device of the spread eagle replaced the *fleur de lys.* Yet the popular joy abated on hearing the conditions of the treaty, and it was not dared to publish the commercial articles. Warlike preparations were actively carried forward. " Yet no prince," wrote Stanhope, " ever entered a war with less visible means, there

---

[1] Col. Stanhope to Townshend, Aug. 6, 1725. *R. O. S.*, 176.

[2] Their humanity, however, was not blunted. On a later occasion when an accident occurred they stopped the sport, until it was ascertained that no human bones were broken.

being no money in the treasury, and no means of finding subsistence for the troops." The army in Catalonia was daily reinforced, but difficulties of commissariat and desertion of French and Irish soldiers seemed likely to bring the Court to reason.

The Court, however, was becoming more and more Germanised. Keene described the queen as constantly fed with hopes from Vienna, and as ready to take the wildest resolutions ; she was encouraged by her confessor, who was but a weak man, but could repeat his lesson with an air of integrity which never failed to leave an impression. " I need not tell your lordship," he concludes, " why I do not mention the king." Stanhope, in August, informed Lord Townshend that a rupture could only be avoided by a breach with France or by the cession of Gibraltar, and that the effect of the latter would not be permanent, while the former was what the emperor desired.

It was full time that the threatened powers should take defensive measures. Gibraltar and Port Mahon had already been put in a condition of defence. " God be thanked," wrote Townshend to Stanhope on September 26, " we signed on the 3rd of this month N.S. a defensive alliance with France and Prussia." The ambassador was instructed to say nothing further as to a possible equivalent for Gibraltar. " I must tell your excellency in confidence that the offers my Lord Stanhope made in relation to Gibraltar were done absolutely without the king's order. It cannot be alienated without consent of Parliament, and the behaviour of the Spanish Court since they entered into measures with that of Vienna has been such that it is impossible they themselves can think his Majesty any longer under the least obligation even of laying their demand before the Parliament."[1]

---

[1] *R. O. S.*, 176. The curious parallel between the cases of Gibraltar and Heligoland will doubtless be noticed. Both were regarded as accidental acquisitions and expensive possessions, until capitalised for purposes of Parliamentary opposition. For both the equivalent was offered in the shape of commercial or territorial advantages in the current El Dorado. In both cases

The Treaty of Hanover was strictly defensive. It contained guarantees for the integrity of the territory of the contracting powers, with special relation to Gibraltar and Minorca, and was expressly directed against the existence of the Ostend Company. The King of Prussia was induced, after great hesitation, to accede by the recognition of his claims on Juliers, and the alliance was ultimately joined by Sweden, Denmark, and the States-General.

The attitude of the allies drew the emperor and Spain more closely together. The former, quite unprepared for war, implored Ripperdá for immediate subsidies. He was promised all that he asked, and more, if only he would formally concede the Queen of Spain's demands. Ripperdá had already prepared the way. " I only know," wrote Scotti in June, " that Ripperdá has powers to spend all the money he pleases to win the ministers at Vienna to gain advantages for the infants, and this he will not have neglected, for everybody knows that at Vienna anything can be done for money." [1]

Whatever the means the result was a most secret and sensational treaty, signed on November 5 by Prince Eugene, Staremberg, Sinzendorff, and Ripperdá, and ratified on January 26, 1726. The emperor agreed to give two of the three archduchesses then living to Don Carlos and Don Philip, as soon as the girls should be of marriageable age (Article 2). He promised that Maria Theresa, his eldest daughter, should be married to Don Carlos, if before such a period he himself should die (Art. 3). The Crown of Spain was declared untenable with that of France, and the possessions of the Hapsburgs with the Crown of France or Spain (Art. 5). The King of Spain guaranteed the Pragmatic Sanction (Art. 5). Emperor and king agreed not to give their daughters to the King of France or to princes of the French royal house (Art. 6). Both powers promised mutual assist-

there was the same doubt as to the respective powers of executive and legislature. The authority of Philip and his termagant queen is in favour of Mr. Gladstone and Sir W. Harcourt.

[1] *Arch. Nap.*, C. F. 65.

ance in all cases that might arise (Art. 7). These included the retention of the empire in the House of Hapsburg, the candidature for the throne of Poland, for which the King of Spain would give 500,000 florins or more to purchase the election of the Austrian nominee, the support of the rights of the Palatine of Sulzbach and the imperial family in the succession to Juliers and Berg (Art. 8). In the event of a successful war with France the king engaged to assist the emperor in the recovery of the Belgic provinces. Burgundy was to pass to the infant or, were he otherwise provided, to the emperor. Alsace, saving the rights of the German princes, should be restored to the emperor, Roussillon Cerdagne and Lower Navarre be ceded to Spain (Art. 10). Should emperor or king be involved in war with England in consequence of the previous treaty, the emperor engaged to assist in the forcible recovery of Gibraltar and Port Mahon, and meanwhile to continue his offices for their cession (Art. 11). The commercial clauses of the former treaty were recapitulated (Art. 12).[1]

It is not surprising that both Courts were elated by the anticipation of such a rearrangement of the map of Europe.

---

[1] Alcalá, 3369.

The terms of this treaty were a profound secret. Patiño more than once said that neither he nor any other minister had seen it, and that the king kept it under lock and key (Keene, Jan. 9, 1730). Von Arneth (*Prinz Eugen*, iii. 547) states that he had never found it, which would seem to prove that the imperial copy has ceased to exist. He believes, however, that he was aware of its contents from the MSS. of Bartenstein and from Prince Eugene's letters. Nevertheless his dates are incorrect, and he apparently has no knowledge of Article 3 relating to the marriage of Don Carlos and Maria Theresa, in which lies the whole gist of the dispute. An examination of the precise terms of the treaty throws an entirely new light upon the conduct of Elisabeth Farnese and of the emperor, which is much in favour of the former. It is perhaps strange that the artifice underlying the separation of Articles 2 and 3 was not seen through by the Spanish minister, but Orendayn was both stupid and ingenious. On the other hand, the document proves that the English Government was misinformed as to an article respecting the Pretender, and that Count Palm was justified in his flat denial. Most curious of all perhaps was the provision for the dismemberment of France. Rumours had indeed got abroad, but it was not suspected that such a scheme was embodied in a formal treaty.

Elisabeth was previously sullen and depressed, not speaking a word, which for her was most unusual. Grimaldo told Stanhope that this was due to the news of the Treaty of Hanover, and the encouragement given to the desires of the Florentines for a republic by the French and English ministers. Even Orendayn was saying that no stress was to be laid on what Ripperdá wrote, and that there was no comprehending what he did. Stanhope prophesied that the queen, losing heart, would break out and be more inveterate against the emperor than against England. He intended to let her first fury vent itself before making his advances. But the situation was changed by the news of the secret treaty and by Ripperdá's return on December 11, 1725. To give *éclat* to his arrival, he appeared before the king and queen in travelling dress. Honours were showered upon the brilliant diplomat; he received the title of duke and grandee, and the Order of the Golden Fleece. Philip would never suffer the nominal existence of a prime minister, he professed to be his own, but Ripperdá now occupied a position fully equal to that of Alberoni. The king and queen expressed themselves with infinitely greater rage against England and France than ever, and Stanhope assured Lord Townshend that he had absolute proofs of their intention to begin the war in the spring. The queen, in an access of religious fervour, pressed for a crusade which should exterminate Protestantism. In this she found support in Philip's piety. He was prepared, it was afterwards said by Ripperdá, in this cause to put up grandeeships and appointments in the Indies, and the Crown domains to auction; he would sell the very shirt from off his back. The Pretender's restoration became a prominent feature of the programme. The imperial ministers always strenuously denied that there was any agreement on this subject. It was not included in the secret treaty, and they were probably substantially accurate in stating that they should only utilise the Pretender in the event of war. Ripperdá assured Stanhope that there was no concert between the two Courts in this matter, and that his talk had proceeded from his opinion of making his court to their Catholic Majesties but more especially to appear zealous in his religion, which was much suspected, and to avoid passing for a heretic, and falling into the hands of the Inquisition, who were very watchful over him, and as they looked upon him as a *Christiano nuevo* would lay hold of any pretext for falling upon him. The queen, however, was unquestionably in earnest. The Pretender had always possessed her warm sympathy. The Duke of Ormond stood high in Court favour. S. Simon during his embassy was instructed not to associate with him publicly, but found that he was a member of the interior circle and could scarcely be avoided. The duke was now in constant communication with king and queen; the Pretender's disagreement with his wife seemed an inadequate reason for interviews so frequent. Stanhope's purse and the home-sickness of some of the Pretender's adherents gave the ambassador a great advantage. Admiral Cammock constantly supplied him with information.[1] He was now suddenly arrested; his Irish friends had lodged information with the Inquisition that he had a wife at Madrid and another at Dublin, but his correspondence with Stanhope was the real cause, and it was intended to keep him out of the way in case of operations. Stanhope was endeavouring to replace him by Captain Morgan who was much in Ormond's confidence, and by the duke's favourite valet who carried his letters to the post.

At this juncture the Duke of Wharton arrived from Vienna. He was invited to S. Ildefonso, but his personal peculiarities were not such as to make him appreciated by so severe a Court. He was described by Holzendorf as a formidable hero over his bottle. He was always drunk, wrote Keene, and never had a pipe out of his mouth. This enterprising English agent made good use of Wharton's babbling and bibulous propensities. " Upon the whole

---

[1] Cammock was equally open to bribing or being bribed. In 1718 he had attempted to seduce Byng and the English fleet from their allegiance. He offered £10,000 to any captain who would bring his ship over to the Pretender. —*English Hist. Rev. Oct.*, 1886.

behaviour of this gentleman," he continues, "it is easy to observe that some project in their (the Stuarts') favour was certainly laid at Vienna, but Ripperdá must have found himself not able to sustain it, since he was better informed of the true state of Spain. . . . Wharton, Liria, and the young Jacks are yet fond of it, and if it depends on them would now put it in execution. But the graver sort of them are not so confident, nor so much on their mettle. Wharton was telling the Duke of Ormond that his master did not love fox-hunting, but that he promised to go to Newmarket, to which he answered he saw no great probability of it on a sudden but wished the Pretender might take such care of his affairs that he might be able to keep his word."

The mention of the Duke of Liria is significant. He was a member of the trio with whom the Court was in daily contact. As son of the Duke of Berwick, he was the natural head of any movement in Spain in favour of the Stuarts. Married to a Spanish wife, and possessing large estates in Spain, he was perhaps the solitary foreigner who met with real acceptance. As a man of fashion and of pleasure, and as possessing the French gift of social initiative which the Spaniards lacked, he was eminently a person of light and leading among "the young Jacks," and this might readily be turned to political account. Stanhope obtained through the agency of the Bavarian minister a detailed project of Ripperdá and Liria, for an invasion in the Pretender's interest. It was for this purpose, and not from fear of an English disembarkment, that troops were massed in the north-western provinces. The plan comprised the landing of six thousand men from Ostend, and the destruction of Chatham, while a Russian expeditionary force would convey the Pretender from the Baltic. Anxiety was felt with regard to three Russian ships which were suspected of having landed arms at Lewis. They had then sailed for Cadiz and back to Santander, and information was received that they would next be found upon the Irish coast. Lord Townshend wrote that two more Russian ships had sailed to join them, and that a squadron was being collected for an invasion of England in the spring. In reply to diplomatic representations, Orendayn wrote that the Muscovite merchantmen had been admitted to Spanish ports in accordance with the liberty vouchsafed to other friendly nations. " Your Government," he concluded, " must be extremely timid and suspicious."

The English Government had reason to be nervous. Ripperdá had been empowered in July, 1725, to effect an offensive and defensive alliance with the Czarina. She was mainly prompted by the hope of recovering Schleswig from Denmark for her son-in-law, the Duke of Holstein, and her desire was stimulated by Spanish subsidies. A well-known Jacobite was expected to be sent as minister from Spain, and Ormond was constantly conferring with the Russian envoy. Stanhope was busily engaged in unravelling the intrigue. " I bribed his (the envoy's) secretary, a poor Frenchman, with a wife and six children, who only makes three shillings a day. I gave him fifty pistoles, which saved his wife's life he said, and he brings me copies of all letters his master receives, but it has not as yet answered my expectations. The minister evidently knows nothing as yet of any concert between his Court and Spain for the Pretender."[1]

The Czarina had a strong party in Sweden and in Denmark. The allies of Hanover had to buy the Swedish Government by sums which Walpole, an expert in such matters, regarded as extravagant. In Germany, the adhesion of the Spiritual Electors, and of Bavaria and the Palatinate to the emperor, outweighed the accession of Hesse Cassel to the Alliance of Hanover. The belief that the King of Prussia would not fight was justified by his rapid withdrawal from this alliance.[2] Nor could absolute reliance be placed upon the States-General. Vandermeer,

---

[1] Col. Stanhope to Townshend, Dec. 5, 1725. *R. O. S.*, 179.

[2] The emperor and King of Prussia concluded the Treaty of Wusterhausen, October 12, 1726. The emperor engaged to secure for the king the succession to Berg and Ravenstein.

their minister at Madrid, was loyal to the English alliance,
but Orendayn made this fidelity a charge against him in his
despatches to the Pensionary. The Spanish Government
recognised that in Holland *la haute politique* depended on
differential duties on cloves and nutmeg; it proposed to
admit Dutch spices on advantageous terms. It held out a
prospect of the assiento and licence for an annual American
ship, with the privilege of entering the Spanish ports in the
East Indies and abatement of duties in Spain. There was
always a strong Spanish party in Holland. If the Dutch
acceded to the Treaty of Hanover, exclaimed Ripperdá, it
would only be due to the bribe of £50,000 given by Townshend to De Buys. Much depended upon the loyalty of
France to her allies. Ripperdá assured Stanhope that he
was, and ever would be, a mortal enemy to the French; he
wished God Almighty might never have mercy upon him if
ever he neglected any opportunity of confounding that nation,
or if ever he suffered a reconciliation with the Spanish Court.
The king and queen, he added, were of the same mind, even
though Bourbon should consent to apologise in person, which
he was vile enough to do. Yet the Spanish Government
was trying to detach France from the English alliance and
to induce her to take part in a religious war in Germany.
Holzendorf wrote in January that it was reported that reconciliation with France would soon be concluded. Ripperdá boasted that he could bring it about in half-an-hour if
he pleased, and that his doing so would depend on the
behaviour of England and Holland. Stanhope discovered
that some of the most considerable people in France were
negotiating for Bourbon's overthrow, the abandonment of
the Alliance of Hanover, and the Pretender's restoration.
Ripperdá, perhaps, truly represented that the chief obstacle
was Philip's fear lest the Duke of Orleans should replace
Bourbon, whilst Ripperdá's own fall would follow the revival
of French influence in Madrid. Yet Stanhope read a letter
from Stalpart, an agent of Ripperdá's, to Morville, suggesting that France should enter the Alliance of Vienna, that
the emperor should guarantee Philip's renunciation of the

French crown, that the House of Hapsburg should be excluded from that of Spain, and that the two lines of Bourbon should form an eternal alliance for the general re-establishment of the Catholic religion. Even Fleury was asserted by Ripperdá to be concerned in the intrigue ; and of this Stanhope believed he had certain proofs, though he was afterwards persuaded that Fleury's agents had exceeded their instructions.

In April the queen's confessor was heard to exclaim in a passion that Fleury had turned his coat. The duke's Government was unstable and incompetent ; he might at any moment be sent into the wilderness as the scapegoat for the sins of the French Bourbons towards the Spanish line. Bourbon was credited with none of the virtues, and debited with all the vices, of the late regent. The one had been governed by Dubois, the other was tied to the apron string of Madame de Prie. Superior to the cardinal in personal charms, and equal to him in the disreputability of her life, she was in political capacity infinitely his inferior. The aerial grace of her figure, the delicate and sympathetic beauty of her face, might well have charmed a less susceptible prince than Bourbon. Yet the Duke of Orleans, who was a connoisseur, had passed her by as lacking wits.

In the face of the weak and divided condition of France, the combination which the queen had, by Ripperdá's agency, effected was far more powerful than that which, under Alberoni, had been the bugbear of Europe. Spain had then fought Austria with one hand tied. Now both were free : one could strike for Gibraltar, the other at the commerce and colonies of England, or it might be held out to Jacobite friends in Scotland and Ireland. It was the turn of England to be one-handed, for the king's possessions in Hanover needed protection from an imperial invasion.

Yet the return of Ripperdá was but the beginning of disillusion. Spain was behind the world, and was always failing to overtake it. The indispensable requisite was time. Alberoni had begged the queen for time. Ripperdá, outpacing his mistress in rapidity of thought, had seized time by

the forelock. Yet time remained behind, and the captor
hurried on with but its wig. Ripperdá's designs were admirable. Many of them were carried into execution by the
plodding Spanish administrators of the future, by Patiño,
Ensenada, and Florida Blanca. It was to their realisation
in great measure that Spain owed the revival of her prosperity., The stagnation of Spanish manufacture under
French and English competition was unnatural. Spanish
wool was unrivalled. Ripperdá would utilise this superiority
in native looms. Skilled labour, tempted from abroad, might
revive decaying knowledge in the long-established manufac-
tories of Spain. Competition would be reduced by prohibi-
tive duties, the Spanish Court should set the example of
wearing only Spanish homespun. That Spain could produce
the finest cloths was proved by the fact that fastidious
Italian prelates were content with nothing but the soft black
fabric of Segovia. Those who wished to set up the manufacture of lace thread, fine paper, and other articles not made
in Spain, were directed to apply to Ripperdá. He designed
Ferrol not only for an arsenal and naval station of the first
class, but as a centre for a fishing industry which should wrest
from England the enormous profits annually drawn for the
supply of salt fish. A Bank of Madrid was projected, based
on the uninvested capital belonging to ecclesiastical corporations, and the accumulations of the Charitable Treasure of S.
Just. The prosperity of Spain depended, however, mainly
upon the development of her colonial trade. Ripperdá urged
the formation of light squadrons and flying detachments to
sweep the English smugglers from sea and shore; a tax of
six per cent. on colonial appointments, and the profits of
vacant benefices, would meet the. expenses. English commerce without being prohibited could be rendered valueless
by vexatious regulations. Safe conducts should only be
granted after the Spanish merchant fleet had placed its cargoes, and when the great annual fairs were over. Colonial
governors should allow no foreign fabrics, and especial
prohibitions should be placed on those of English make.
Were the colonial trade carried on in royal vessels, they

could at once be converted into a naval force, and their expenses would be defrayed by their freights. Attention was directed to the neglected Philippines, for Ripperdá was struck by the importance which the Dutch attributed to trade with these islands. A project was formed for regular communication between Cadiz, Chili, the Philippines, China and Siam, a scheme which was afterwards partially executed.

Such reforms would have needed a quarter of a century of profound peace. The Duke of Richelieu was indeed a witness hostile to Ripperdá, whose rival he had been at Vienna. Not content with the well-designed accident which sent the Dutchman spinning down the dusty stairs, he has visited him with ridicule sometimes undeserved. Yet there is truth in his criticism that Ripperdá's predictions were but brag, his projects dreams, and his system hallucination. In one respect Ripperdá realised the value of time. Time meant money. If he could hold out till the summer, the arrival of the treasure fleet would enable him to meet his obligations to the emperor. This was probably the secret of his confidences to Stanhope, of his assurance that the king would never fight for Gibraltar, and that no peculiar privileges had been conferred on the Ostend Company. But the English Government was too anxious to be thus amused. The North of Spain was carefully watched. A consul was established at S. Sebastian, whom however the authorities promptly removed, and " in order," as Belando writes, " that he might see more of the interior he was conducted to that emporium of letters, the city of Salamanca ". The same course could not be pursued towards the squadron which hovered off the northern ports, and might easily repeat the devastation of the previous year. The Spanish fleet had not recovered the destruction of her dockyards, and the real object of the suspected Russian ships was probably the supply of naval stores. But the chief obstacle to Ripperdá's success was Admiral Hosier's squadron, which blockaded the treasure fleet at Porto Bello. The administration was reduced to living from hand to mouth. The departmental staffs were cut down to such an extent that the minister was overworked, and his nervous system shaken. The dismissed officials served to swell the ranks of the opposition. All payments from the treasury were suspended, to the despair of the merchants to whom large sums were due. Ripperdá would say that he had six friends : God, the Virgin, the emperor and empress, and the king and queen. He was nearer the truth when he told Stanhope that he had not a single friend in Spain except the queen. Philip had never really liked him ; creature of habit as he was, he missed the familiar presence of Grimaldo. The ostentatious vulgarity of Ripperdá, the *soupçon* of beer and wine and garlic, of which the Duke of Richelieu complained, were distasteful to the reserved and dignified Bourbon. The harmony of the royal circle was interrupted. There were days when the king would scold the queen, and she would weep from morning to night. Philip already repented of his breach with France, and would gladly have extricated himself from his engagements to the emperor. " Yet," wrote Stanhope, " the queen's absolute ascendant over him, and more particularly now that she is with child, leaves but little room to hope for his coming to any resolution contrary to her inclinations." Ripperdá's future now depended solely on the continuance of the queen's support, and the opposition was attempting to gain her ear. He had endeavoured to get rid of his most dangerous enemies, Patiño and Castelar, by sending them as exiles to Brussels and Venice. They now worked upon the queen's mind through the medium of her confessor, the Bishop of Amida. Patiño made a special study of him. This amiable but timid bishop *in partibus* lived in agonies of wonder as to the queen's real sentiments, which he would not dare to traverse, but which she did not always divulge. Recently he had said that Spain had at last found the minister of whom she had so long been in need. But now Ripperdá, the bishop assured his visitors, was quite an ordinary man. The confessor was, says Montgon, the barometer of Court favour, which announced fair or foul weather. His apartment was an observatory, and his legs, which he shuffled when agitated, were delicate instruments which marked the shifting of the wind. The least coolness in the queen's voice, the slightest alteration of her face, was enough to give the bishop a fit.

The minister's fate was decided by the arrival of Marshal Königsegg, the imperial ambassador. The queen discovered that many of the alleged engagements of the emperor were the fabrications of Ripperdá's brain. The Court of Vienna had been made to believe that the King of Spain had more ready money than all the Courts of Europe together, whereas Königsegg found him more distressed than the emperor himself. Ripperdá complained that the Imperial Government was insatiable, and would strip Spain to the last pistole. The emperor expressed indignation at Ripperdá's indiscreet confidences to the English ambassador. The queen, flattered by proofs of imperial favour, fell under Königsegg's influence, and determined on her minister's fall. The first hint of disfavour was shown in an interview in which he explained to Königsegg the impossibility of meeting the stipulated subsidies. The queen interrupted him with a frown, and said : " What is that to you ? " On the pretext of overwork, he was relieved of the ministry of finance on May 14. After a long interview between the king and queen and Königsegg, he was informed by Orendayn that he was discharged from the royal service on a pension. On the morrow he left the palace, but fearing violence from the populace, escaped in Vandermeer's coach to the English embassy ; and here he was found by Stanhope on his return to Madrid, much to the ambassador's embarrassment. Königsegg, in alarm for the results to which further confidences might lead, urged his forcible removal. This was done, but not before Stanhope had read some valuable papers and taken down some incoherent utterances. It is still difficult to determine what weight, if any, may be attributed to Ripperdá's confessions before and after his disgrace. He was an excitable person, whose lies were not always conscious. But contradictory statements were not unnatural. Since his return to Spain his sole efforts were directed to maintaining himself in power. His revelations were . intended partly to frighten the English Government into the cession of Gibraltar, or to delay its action, partly perhaps to purchase a retreat. On the other hand, he was at times forced by the growing confusion into wild schemes of immediate war, in which something might have turned out to his advantage.

Prince Eugene, while congratulating Königsegg on Ripperdá's fall, alone, perhaps, did justice to his talents.

" Yet one must also confess that Ripperdá possessed very good qualities which, in a certain position, might have won him fame and distinction. I believe that, violent and desperate as he was, he might have been able to do the king services which were not to be expected of any one else, certainly not of any born Spaniard. For the Spaniard will never venture to lay his hand on certain malpractices which have so long taken deep root, and are extremely injurious to the king's interests. On these subjects, at all events, Ripperdá has imparted ideas to me, which, if carried into execution, might have been of great value to the king's finances and the revival of trade. For their development, however, a man was needed who would not mind bringing upon himself general dislike, who possessed sufficient resolution to follow out his plans, and who would have spared no one in order to reach his ends." [1]

---

[1] Von Arneth, *Prinz Eugen*, iii. 190.

Ripperdá's career was adventurous to the end. He was taken from the British embassy to the Castle of Segovia, leaving, as the story went at Paris, his papers behind, but taking a bottle in each hand. He was liberally treated, the charge of treason was not pressed, and a part of his pension was granted to him. As the Duke of Richelieu said, even " le crapaud trouve sa crapaude," and Ripperdá won the affection or sympathy of the governor's servant-maid, who, in conjunction with his valet and a corporal, contrived his escape. Both the governor and the English Government were suspected of complicity not without some reason. Stanhope, on September 18, 1726, promised that he would omit nothing for facilitating his escape, though it was difficult from his perpetually being laid up with gout—an indirect confirmation perhaps of the tale of the two bottles. On October 30 Stanhope wrote: " All my endeavours have proved ineffectual, though I have omitted nothing. I have even met in private and in disguise with the governor of the castle, with whom I always used to lodge, and who is my particular friend, but found by him that the thing was impracticable, both from Ripperdá's indisposition, and from the governor's being watched by the Alcalde, who carried him from my house." From Segovia, Ripperdá repaired to Soho Square, where he led a merry if not reputable life. Then he paid a visit to Holland, but not finding scope for his diplomatic abilities in Europe, he took service in Morocco. "The incredible news I sent you about Ripperdá is confirmed," wrote Keene, on July 4, 1732. "He is actually at Tetuan, and would have been a captain-general could his conscience have allowed him to turn Mussulman; but as yet they have only taken his presents, and as the country is cheap, they have granted him leave to spend the surplus of his income in the service of Muley Abdelah." His religious scruples are generally supposed to have been overcome, and he is said to have shown conduct and courage in the war against Spain, and to have won the heart of the mother of his sovereign. He took part in the dynastic disturbance in Morocco, and was suspected of having a hand in the romantic enterprise of King Theodore of Corsica. To the end he seems to have retained his fancy for startling combinations, for he was stated to be elaborating a scheme for the union of Catholicism, Islamism, and Protestantism. Having gone the religious round, he is reported on his deathbed to have re-entered the bosom of the Catholic Church in which he was reared, a thing which he would certainly have done, sarcastically wrote Keene, if he thought it conducive to his present interests.

CHAPTER XI.

1726-8.

ELISABETH AND HER MINISTERS—ASCENDANCY OF KÖNIGSEGG
—THE KING'S CONFESSORS—RUPTURE WITH ENGLAND—
BLOCKADE OF PORTO BELLO AND SIEGE OF GIBRALTAR—
THE SPANISH PARTY IN FRANCE—MISSION OF MONTGON
TO PARIS—THE PRELIMINARIES OF VIENNA—ELISABETH'S
HOSTILITY TO ENGLAND—CONVENTION OF THE PARDO.

FEW sovereigns have in the space of ten years been responsible for ministers so adventurous as Alberoni, so reckless as
Ripperdá. Yet, granted Elisabeth's character and her
ambitions, they were a necessary condition of her rule.
They, like herself, were devoid of national prejudices, regardless possibly of national interests. To her nothing was
impossible that was desired; in their vocabulary also impossibility found no place, their position depended on finding
nothing impossible which the queen willed. Neither
minister had struck root in Spain, and their detachment
made them the more serviceable to their alien mistress.
The laborious indolence, the methodical and cautious procrastination, which characterised the best Spanish administrators, were intolerable to her impatient temper. The
health of the king contributed to this. Elisabeth could not
afford to wait, and yet when she cried "to-day" the Spaniard,
with a shrug, replied "to-morrow". Had she been more able
or more artful, had she been born and bred in a wider diplomatic atmosphere, she might have governed and negotiated
for herself. But though for thirty years she was the pivot on
which the diplomacy of Europe turned, she never possessed
the talent, nor acquired the experience of a *diplomate*.

(200)

Disliked by Spaniards, devoted to her children's interests, absorbed by one dominant idea, she abandoned herself to those who alone seemed capable of appreciating her views and executing her projects. Professional assistance was indispensable.

Alberoni was a *diplomate* by nature, Ripperdá by opportunity and self-assertion. Yet the ascendancy of each was not so much that of personality as of circumstance. The ministers who seemed to be the architects were but the tools. As soon as the edge of her tools was blunted, as soon as the material proved too stubborn, as soon as she found others ready to her hand, Elisabeth dropped them without difficulty, and apparently without regret. She possessed the permanent strength of vehement and consistent desires. She might change her methods and her ministers, but never her ends.[1] Alberoni was abandoned because reconciliation with the regent seemed necessary to the attainment of their ends; Ripperdá was sacrificed to the continuance of the Imperial Alliance. Yet the queen was not self-sufficing; an adviser, a factotum, was still required, and the post was once more occupied by a foreigner. Marshal Königsegg, an ally's ambassador in name, became in fact first minister of Spain. His influence with Elisabeth was fully as complete as that of her two former ministers. She had reason to be dazzled by his qualities. Never yet had she been brought in contact with a personality so imposing, with a man of equal position, ability, and character. Chafing at the monotonous stupidity of her husband and her Court, she had not unnaturally mistaken audacity for talent and vulgarity for *esprit*. Short as was the imperial ambassador's influence, it was perhaps of no small weight in the formation of her future estimate of men. Her imagination was struck by

---

[1] "The aggrandisement of her children is the sole law and the sole secret of her policy. This is the solitary motive in the choice and change of ministers. Persons are not wanted who are likely to raise a shade of opposition. Alliances are sought when they promise well, abandoned when they do not answer expectation. The interests of Spain serve merely as a cover for the real object of her wars."—P. A. Capello. Relazione, 1738.

the contemptuous aristocratic ease with which he brushed
Ripperdá aside. The presumption which offended Spaniards
not impossibly engaged the Italian's fancy. The escutcheon
above his door proclaimed his master's title to the crown of
Spain. He usurped the royal privilege of driving six mules.[1]
He was one of the tallest and handsomest men in Germany.
Prince Eugene had found the marshal not only a most
capable general, but an invaluable negotiator; he combined
to perfection the military and the diplomatic bearing. The
Imperial Government appreciated his gift of making contradictory engagements, and of taking the consequent blame
upon himself. Elisabeth as a woman was attracted by
Königsegg, and as a mother she looked to him alone for the
fulfilment of her maternal ambitions. Prince Eugene had instructed him at all hazards to preserve the alliance with Spain,
and for this purpose he must gain complete influence over the
king, and more especially over the queen. He was warned
of the danger that Elisabeth in pursuit of her Italian aims
might suddenly veer round towards France or England, in
which case the imperial provinces would be exposed to risk.
Yet he was recommended to be modest in his display of
royal favour, for it was advisable to conciliate the Spanish
magnates. This was recognised as difficult, for they were
strenuously opposed to the Austrian Alliance. They had
never forgiven the loss of their employments in Italy and the
Netherlands; the infants' establishment was of no service to
Spain or to themselves, it would be the recognition by Spain
of the robbery of her possessions. Prince Eugene believed
that no Spanish minister could be trusted except Orendayn,
now Marquis de la Paz, who was dependent on the queen,
and therefore at present devoted to the Imperial Alliance.

The circumstances of Ripperdá's disgrace made Königsegg's task the easier. Stanhope indignantly demanded reparation for the violation of his embassy. A rupture with England
seemed inevitable, and thus apart from the queen's desires it

---

[1] Other ambassadors felt compelled to do likewise until the diplomatic
block in the public highway forced the municipal authorities to interfere.

became necessary that Spain should cling to the Imperial Alliance. Königsegg was master of the situation. He had been instructed indeed not to interfere with internal politics, but the line between home and foreign affairs was hard to draw. Stanhope described him as not only first minister but regent, as the idol or rather the governor of their Catholic Majesties. The other ministers were but cyphers, reduced to mechanical employment. Contrary to custom he was lodged in a royal residence at Balsain, and the Dutch envoy on protesting was told by the king that he was master in his own house. He walked alone with the king and queen in their gardens, and the ministers brought their portfolios to his apartments when required. He was the fount of honour ; Orendayn told Monteleone that the only means to obtain a diplomatic post was to interest the marshal in his favour. Spaniards said that no imperial ambassador in the days of the Austrian kings had possessèd such power.

Grimaldo was regarded as sold to England, and was discharged from the Viennese Department of Foreign Affairs. All who were suspected of English and French predilections shared his fate. Among these was Bermudez, the king's confessor. The queen had long tried in vain to procure his dismissal. She charged him with forming seditious cabals, and fomenting and spreading scurrilous aspersions on herself. He was engaged in a secret correspondence with Fleury, and during the king's confession handed to him a letter from the cardinal, and another from the King of France. At that unlucky moment the queen entered, but pretended to withdraw. "You can come in," said the king ; "we are not busy. Father Bermudez was only telling me about his letter from Cardinal Fleury, and he has given me another for myself." The queen took the letters, and before the sun was down the confessor was sent back pensionless to his college. He was replaced by a Jesuit, Father Clarke, who had been Königsegg's confessor. He was, according to Stanhope, the most violent Jacobite on earth, and, as Rector of the Scotch College, had useful means of information with regard to the Pretender's cause. He spoke French badly, and was therefore not peculiarly suitable for his present post. Arriaza, Secretary of Finance, was dismissed because he objected to the Austrian subsidies. Castelar and Patiño, who had been instrumental in Ripperdá's fall, were rewarded by the Departments of War and Marine. Stanhope was in dire disgrace. Prince Ferdinand had expressed discontent at the present policy, as being destructive of his own interests and those of the monarchy, and as carried on by the queen purely for the aggrandisement of her children. He refused to tell who prompted him, showing only an anonymous letter. Ferdinand was believed to be of a haughty, unquiet spirit, and as he would shortly be of age it was feared that he might intend assuming the government by virtue of his father's renunciation. The queen's confessor alleged that Stanhope had dropped the letter into the prince's pocket, and told the queen that he was more dangerous than the devil himself. Since Ripperdá's disgrace, nobody dared come near the ambassador; he was, he said, as solitary as if he were in the deserts of Arabia. On a visit to Aranjuez, the queen would not deign to notice him, and every one dropped off as if he had the plague. It was believed that Ripperdá's escape to the embassy had been concerted with the ambassador, and he daily expected his dismissal. The insolence of the Jacobites, who swarmed at S. Ildefonso, increased. The Duke of Liria said publicly that in a month it would be a crime to mention King George as King of England. They played the tune of "The king shall have his own again" before the Court, and explained the meaning to the queen, who exclaimed aloud: "I wish Stanhope would come hither that we might welcome him with this tune".[1]

Stanhope saw no hope for the king's being brought to a juster way of thinking or acting, considering the queen's violent temper, her present views, and her absolute ascendancy. Of the latter, the dismissal of Grimaldo and

[1] Stanhope to Newcastle, Oct. 4, 1726. *R. O. S.*, 179.

Bermudez, the only persons for whom he had a genuine affection, was regarded as a signal proof. The foreign character of the queen's government was perhaps never so apparent. "All approaches to the king must now be made either through herself, Count Königsegg, First Minister, a Scotch Jacobite confessor, or an Irish physician of the same inveterate principles. I mention the last from the great attention which his Catholic Majesty's extreme timidity and carefulness for the health of his body always make him show to those who have been in that employment, as the like concern for that of his soul led him· to do to his confessor. Consequently, no one seems to expect anything from this Court that is not directly opposed to his Majesty's interests and destructive to his government."[1]

The queen was full of confidence. Forgetting that the Bourbons were a race of devils, she now repeatedly boasted that they should sit on the throne of the Hapsburgs. In September she heard that Russia had definitely acceded to the Treaty of Vienna. The Court was in ecstasies of joy. It was taken for granted that the Russian fleet had broken the blockade and destroyed the English squadron, and that the King of Prussia, if he would not desert his allies, would be driven from his dominions. In the winter war seemed inevitable. Patiño was building ships in Catalonia, Andalusia, and Biscay, and was buying at Venice, Genoa, and S. Malo. He promised to have twenty ships at Cadiz ready for any enterprise in February. All the seafaring population of Spain was enrolled, as was the custom in France.

The King of England's speech to Parliament in January, 1727, referred in no measured terms to the alleged secret articles of the Treaty of Vienna.[2] Count Palm, the im-

---

[1] Stanhope to Newcastle, Oct. 4, 1726. *R. O. S.*, 179.

[2] The terms of the Secret Treaty prove that the English Government was wrong in its belief that it contained an article for the Pretender's restoration. Yet it asserted that it had positive evidence. This evidence consisted in an imaginary draft of the treaty given to Walpole at Paris by the Sicilian abbots, and accepted as unimpeachable by that minister and by the Duke of New-

perial minister in London, angrily refuted the statements, and was dismissed, while S. Saphorin received his *congé* from Vienna. The negotiations with Russia became a reality. The Duke of Liria was despatched, as the first Spanish ambassador to the Muscovite Court, with instructions to form an alliance between the Czar and the Catholic king, and to arrange a Russian attack upon the English coast.[1] In February the Spaniards opened the siege of Gibraltar, and on March 11 Stanhope left Madrid. War became more possible to Spain, because the treasure fleet from Porto Bello arrived in safety. Admiral Hozier had been unable to maintain the blockade with his rotting ships and fever-stricken crews. The treasure ships slipped by Sir Charles Wager in " thick, blowing weather," and arrived in detail at different Spanish ports. Prince Eugene, who

---

castle. It contains much that was curiously right and much that was curiously wrong, and was probably founded on wild conversation in the palace. If good offices failed, Gibraltar was to·be recovered by an attack upon Hanover. In the event of the death of Louis XV., the emperor engaged to establish the Spanish line on the French throne. If success were not complete, the French low countries, Franche-Comté, Burgundy, and Alsace, should be detached to form a State for Don Carlos; while Roussillon and Cerdagne, Lower Navarre, and such other conquests as might be made, were added to Spain. The same partition was to take effect if war broke out with France in consequence of the treaty. The emperor agreed that Don Carlos should marry his eldest daughter, and succeed him, the King of Spain supplying the *fumée* necessary to induce the electors to elect him as King of the Romans. The final article was the re-establishment of the Pretender. To obtain a pretext, it was arranged that the Catholic king should demand the restoration of Gibraltar immediately after the publication of the Treaty of Vienna.

This fictitious treaty, and the correspondence relating to it, may be read in Brit. Mus. MSS., 32752, 32772. It is strange that so able a diplomatist as Walpole should have swallowed such a farrago. The English Government subsequently attributed too much weight to the information supplied by these ecclesiastical refugees, and in this it has been followed by Coxe. Montgon, who knew them, rejected the advances which they made to him; and Keene wrote contemptuously on their views of Spanish politics. These, which are contained in the Walpole papers, have been so largely quoted that it is necessary to give a note of warning.

[1] Liria's interesting diary of this memoir is printed in *Documentos ineditos para la historia de España*, vol. xciii., 1889. See *Quarterly Review*, Jan., 1892.

knew more about soldiering than seafaring, was sarcastically exultant. The English admiral wrote : " I believe I had better have been at Parson's Green looking after my garden, for I know that people generally suppose that it is as easy to intercept ships at sea as to stop a coach at the end of a street ". He asked for reinforcements, for though the Spaniards were generally slow in their movements, they were working very hard at Cadiz to fit out a squadron to drive him off the coast. Yet war was not declared, and such fighting as there was confined itself to the futile siege of Gibraltar. It was feared that this would force France to give active aid to England ; and it was, therefore, pretended that it was a reprisal for the blockade of the Spanish galleons and not a *casus fœderis* for France. The same pretence was made for the seizure of the South Sea ship the " Prince Frederick," which became the subject of a voluminous correspondence.

The Duke of Richelieu was probably correct in saying that the queen was the only person in Spain who wished for war. Even the king was believed to desire reconciliation with the maritime powers. It was feared that a French invasion would be followed by revolt, for not only Catalonia but all the provinces of the Crown of Aragon were profoundly disaffected. Even Orendayn was scandalised at the subsidies sent to Vienna, and there was a general outcry against the queen for selling and sacrificing the monarchy to the emperor. Spaniards were astounded at the subsidies paid to German princes while Spain was more visibly in want of money than any nation in Europe. National feeling was outraged by Clarke's appointment as confessor. Allowance was made for the king's affection for his countrymen, " but this pitching upon a Scotchman, and one scarce ever heard of amongst them, they say must have proceeded from the queen's hatred or contempt of the Spanish nation, or from the consciousness of the designs she is carrying on being too destructive to that nation for her to find a Spaniard capable of not dissuading the king from suffering her to put them in execution." [1]   Disaffection existed in the highest quarters. Stanhope was told by one of his informants that Patiño and Castelar suggested a surprise of Leghorn by French troops in English ships as a means of detaching Spain from the emperor. [2] The ambassador carried on a secret correspondence with Patiño too risky to be confided to the post. [3] The Council of Castile ventured to protest against the prohibition to wear silks or woollens of foreign manufacture. Even the siege of Gibraltar was not popular. Ormond was believed to be its chief promoter, relying on supposed intelligence in the town. [4]

The Count de las Torres owed his command to brag. He engaged to finish off Gibraltar in a few days, which would give his troops time to meet the French upon the northern frontier. But the other Spanish generals and engineers protested that success was hopeless while the sea was open. Supplies were constantly being thrown in. There was much fire, but little damage to the garrison. The Spanish army began to melt away. Forty or fifty men were killed a day, and the engineers said that this would rise to two or three hundred if the general persisted in pushing his works along the spit. [5] Castelar hinted to the officers that they should

[1] Stanhope to Newcastle, Oct. 4, 1726. *R. O. S.*, 179.

[2] Stanhope to Newcastle, July 22, 1726. *Ibid.*

[3] Stanhope to Newcastle, Oct. 7, 1726. *Ibid.*

" Patiño, with whom I have a very secret intimate correspondence, is most certainly in his heart against a war, and has assured me in the strongest terms of his laying hold of every favourable occasion of dissuading his Catholic Majesty from the measures he is at present pursuing ; though hitherto he has not dared to oppose himself to the queen's sentiments, he assures me the king himself acts against his own judgment, which makes him hope that he will on the first misfortune shake off the absolute ascendance that the queen hath at present over him."—Stanhope to Newcastle, Oct. 30, 1726. *R. O. S.*, 179.

[4] Ormond possibly relied on the devoted attachment of General Sabine, the governor, who had served with him in the wars in Flanders under William III., and had been his fellow-prisoner at Neerwinden.—Montgon, viii. 208.

[5] Among the casualties was the Duke of Wharton, who showed as much courage in the siege as over the bottle. He consoled himself by marrying a young lady with no fortune but her beauty. After vainly repenting of his Jacobitism, he retired to the Monastery of Poblet to repent, with more success it is to be hoped, of his other transgressions.

sign a round robin against this sacrifice of life. Such guns as were not useless were served by infantry, for the gunners had been killed off. The celebrated mine, nicknamed the Cave of Montesinos, made little progress in two months, and if it were fired it would only make the rock more precipitous and defensible than before. The soldiers said that their beards would be grey before the place was taken. The king, wrote Vandermeer, was well aware of the ridiculous character of the project. Marshal Villars admitted that he should be delighted to see the English turned out of Gibraltar, but believed that the siege would drag on, and that it would become impossible to resist Walpole's pressure.

More important was the fact that the Court of Vienna withheld assistance. The emperor and Prince Eugene had strongly opposed the siege. It would absorb the whole army, wrote the former; it would render operations elsewhere impossible; the strength of the country would be sapped. and the end not obtained; it were far better to mass the Spanish forces in Catalonia, and on the first outbreak of war throw them upon France. Prince Eugene severely criticised the incompetency of De las Torres, and the faction and want of discipline in the besieging force. Peace, he added, was necessary to save the honour of the king.

The emperor began to realise that war was impossible. Stanhope had truly prophesied that war could not last six months because the Spanish subsidies would fail. They were now already in arrear, and the emperor became convinced that the Ostend Company would not exist in the teeth of an Anglo-French alliance. The present attitude of France likewise contributed to peace. England could not induce her to fight Spain, nor Spain tempt her to desert England. In the summer the tension between the Courts of Spain and France had been increased by the news of the marriage of Louis XV. with the ex-King of Poland's daughter. "It is impossible for me," wrote Stanhope, "to express the violent things the queen said, not only against the duke, but even against the king himself, and the whole

P

nation."[1] When it was suggested that Bourbon's brother should apologise in his place, she cried: "What! he is a madman—what shall we do with that lunatic here!—no, let him come himself". But Ripperdá's disgrace was closely followed by the dismissal of the Duke of Bourbon, and the Spanish Government was given to understand that this was mainly due to a desire for reconciliation. It was hoped both at Vienna and Madrid that it would be possible to detach France from England. Bourbon's fall was greeted with rejoicings by the Spanish Court. It was believed by the King of Prussia and others that it would be followed by the return of France to the Catholic system. Nothing was talked of at Madrid as more certain than the immediate accession of France to the Treaty of Vienna, the establishment of the Pretender in England, and the destruction of Protestants in general. The King and Queen of Spain were too proud to open direct negotiations, but a brisk correspondence was carried on between the queen's subordinate agents at Paris and Madrid, much of which came into Stanhope's hands. The sense of personal injury was now diminished. The queen had indeed dismissed the king's confessor because he had intrigued with Fleury, but his offence probably consisted less in his French proclivities than in his attempt to treat behind her back. None but a raw ecclesiastic would have ventured this.

The dismissal of the infanta had been far from popular in France. A president of Parliament declared to Bourbon that each of its members would willingly sacrifice sufficient of his remaining years to make her of marriageable age. Many nobles detested, as did Villars, the English alliance and the treaty with Spain. Villars, already a member of the Royal Council, was reinforced by the Legitimists Tallard and D'Uxelles. Fleury was indeed forced by his conviction that France needed a recuperative period, and by mature consideration of the political forces of Europe, into a continuance of the Orleanist alliance with England. But he was also

<hr />

[1] Stanhope to Newcastle, July 19, 1726. *R. O. S*₄ 179.

sincerely desirous of reconciliation with Spain. Alliance
with Spain implied its subordination to France. Its hostility increased its pretensions to pose as the characteristic
Bourbon power, as continuing the traditions and usurping
the influence of the Grand Monarque.

It was with great difficulty that Fleury kept France firm
to the Alliance of Hanover. Villars and other members of
the council boldly criticised his policy. It was indeed extraordinary, said Villars, that the Bourbon King of Spain should
subsidise his Austrian rival for an attack on France, but it
was no less strange that France should have contributed to
expel from Sicily the same monarch that she seated upon the
throne of Spain. It was not Elisabeth alone who said that
Fleury was a coward who cringed to the arch-heretic Walpole. The cardinal's colleagues repeatedly denounced his
Anglomania. England was aiming, they believed, at the
monopoly of the world's commerce; her extravagant
demands were as prejudicial to the trade of France as to
that of Spain.

If, therefore, Fleury desired a better understanding with
the Court of Spain, much more eager were those statesmen
who had remained faithful to the traditions of the late reign.
The French Government recognised that it must take the
Queen of Spain into its confidence in future overtures.
Fresh attempts at conciliation on Fleury's part were met
with reproaches at his having allied his country with the
enemies of God, but Philip and Elisabeth were preparing to
draw nearer to France, if not to Fleury. An immediate
motive for this change was the dangerous illness of Louis
towards the end of 1726. Philip's old ambitions returned
with their original force, and were further fortified by Elisabeth's persuasions. Never had he stated his claims more
strongly than he now did to his confidant, the Abbé Montgon, to whom a secret mission was entrusted. "If it please
God that the king, my nephew, should die without male
heirs, I, the nearest relative, or my descendants, ought to
and will succeed to the crown of my ancestors."

The purport of Montgon's instructions was unmistakable.　He was intended to be in France on the young king's death ; and, meanwhile, to prepare the way for Philip's subsequent accession.　He was ordered to make his way, without appearing to push, into general society, to ascertain the exact position of parties, to tabulate the Legitimist and Orleanist supporters, and the Indifferentist residuum.　Communication with Fleury on the subject was forbidden, for he was Opportunist if not Orleanist.　Morville was dangerous as being Anglophil ; information might, therefore, be extracted but not imparted.　Above all, Montgon was urged to establish friendly relations with the Duke of Bourbon, to assure him that not only full forgiveness for the past but every favour for the future should reward devotion to Philip's cause.　To allay the natural suspicions of the emperor's agents, the envoy was urged to treat them in an easy social spirit, and not allow them to suspect that he had instructions from the king, and to avoid any mention of reconciliation with France.　So confident was Philip of the issue of this mission, that he entrusted to his agent a proclamation of his accession to be submitted to the Parliament of Paris on the moment of the king's death.　This confidence was not entirely without foundation.　The Parliament claimed " to sit upon the lilies ".　It was strongly Legitimist, it had never ceased to oppose the Duke of Orleans, and had witnessed, with deep regret, the infanta's dismissal by the Duke of Bourbon.　It was left to Montgon to decide whether addresses should be forwarded to the various ecclesiastical and secular corporations of the realm, and whether it were desirable to appoint a cabinet or a regent pending the king's arrival.　Should the young queen be left with expectations, it was intended that a competent jury should watch events and superintend results.　For the success of this mission the utmost caution and reticence were necessary, and Montgon was warned by no means to assume the airs or surround himself with the retinue of an ambassador.　He was instructed finally to despatch a courier as soon as the king's illness took a fatal turn, and another on the moment of his death.

Elisabeth was well aware that Montgon's arrival would not escape the notice of Fleury, and that her agent must be prepared with an ostensible reason for his journey. She gave him separate instructions to the effect that Spain was not indisposed to reconciliation, if France would accede to the Treaty of Vienna. She advised him to hint that his visit to Paris was in reality a disgrace inflicted upon him at the instance of Königsegg. Subsequently, a suggestion was made through the medium of the queen's confessor that in the event of the death of Louis XV., the French succession should be settled on her son, while Ferdinand received the heritage of Spain.

Montgon was a vain and vapid, but insinuating ecclesiastical *intrigant* of the second class. He had been a *protégé* of Daubenton and of Bourbon. He believed that for him, as for Alberoni, there was an opening in Spain. He chose, however, piety rather than policy as the basis of his operations. By attaching himself to Philip, not in his royal state, but in his retirement at S. Ildefonso, he could save his soul by striving to imitate the self-renunciation of his master. His hopes for a future life were diminished by Philip's resumption of the throne, but his immediate prospects were improved. The Abbé became one of the tame French poodles of the royal circle. He had many pretty tricks, but he was not quite safe, and his companions partly laughed at him and partly feared him. The success of his present mission required a combination of the highest diplomatic reticence and the most favourable circumstances. Louis XV. proved now, as always, a disappointing invalid, and Montgon was a better talker than a listener. Fleury's artless and ingenuous attitude extracted at the first interview the purport of his mission. He was even induced to unbosom himself to Morville. Valuable information was gained from him as to the *personnel* and views of the opposition, and it is noticeable that it is from this date that Villars complains of Fleury's want of confidence in his colleagues of the council.

Montgon, however, was not without honesty nor talent,

and he acquitted himself not altogether to his master's disadvantage. His very expansiveness was of utility. Relations were re-established with Villars and many others. Legitimist theories became a subject of fashionable conversation, and in France the *salon* melted into the state. Long after Montgon's return, correspondence was maintained with Bourbon and Villars, and doubtless with others.[1] Bourbon professed himself ready to devote himself to Philip's service, and on the death of Louis, to act as his first minister until he should arrive. Yet the luck and the play were on the side of the cardinal, and against the abbé.

This mission had no direct results, and to general European history is of the slightest importance. It was, however, by no means a trivial episode in the lives of Elisabeth and her consort. The will-o'-the-wisp of the French crown frequently flickered before their eyes, tempting them from the more solid ground on which their lot was cast. The intermittent character of its appearance prevented consistency in thought or action. This and the queen's dreams of establishment in Italy were the cause of their lack of popularity in Spain. They could not feel that they were in their permanent home, that they had, in Alberoni's phrase, to live and die among the Spaniards.

The intrigues of Montgon with the opposition convinced Fleury that reconciliation with Spain was essential to the stability of his government. Early in 1727 he is found in active and secret correspondence with the queen. The king had indeed sworn not to reconcile himself with France without the emperor's consent, but she urged that the emperor himself had made overtures to France. She implored Fleury to accept his terms, and, if necessary, to break away from England, which would be forced to drop its ears and beg for peace upon its knees. "I am quite aware," she wrote, "that it is not my business to give advice to so enlightened a person as yourself, but sometimes too some

---

[1] Bourbon's letters at Alcalá fall between June, 1727, and September, 1729.

atom of reason may be found in the least reasonable people. What I say is prompted solely by my wish to see the uncle and nephew reconciled. That done, I most certainly have no further views than the good of the world at large. I am convinced that it is not fear of war that makes you speak as you do, but the welfare of the two crowns. It is just the same on my part, and so we two are playing on the same side. As to fear, we have none, and I have never seen any one have less than the king; he might be called with reason Philip the Fearless." Friendship for France, the queen urged, might induce the king to overlook the offences of England. She bade Fleury remember how Louis XIV. refused to join in a war against his grandson; were he alive that would be his wish in the present conjuncture. The correspondence should be kept secret from English, Dutch, and Imperialists, and he must burn her letter. " Here is a very long letter, and very bad writing, and composition still worse, but I believe that, as my object is the restoration of friendship between two great kings so nearly related, you will be kind enough to forgive me." In conclusion, Fleury was asked to pardon her for showing his letter to the king, for their union was so close that she never concealed a letter from him.[1]

Fleury was not strong enough to give to England the aid which she expected; the opposition was not sufficiently powerful to draw France over to Spain in despite of Fleury. A general peace was, therefore, the natural compromise. For this the Court of Vienna had made advances throughout the spring, and their progress was shown by the marked rudeness with which Elisabeth from time to time treated Königsegg and his wife. She hastily left the card-table when she heard that the latter was approaching, and scarcely any one would accept the marshal's dinner invitations. Patiño kept the purse-strings tight, and the marshal was unable to pay his servants or his debts. Yet his influence was not substan-

---

[1] This letter is undated, but it refers to the siege of Gibraltar as just opening. Baudrillart, *Arch. des Missions Sc. et Pol cxv.* 110.

tially shaken, and it was probably at his instigation that the two Sicilian abbots, Platania and Caraccioli, were arrested and exiled. They were on intimate terms with the king, had been concerned in Ripperdá's fall, and were believed to have French or English inclinations.

The Court of Vienna has been accused of negotiating the peace without the knowledge of its ally. But a letter from Orendayn to Prince Eugene [1] proves that the Spanish Government, however unwillingly, concurred, and this is confirmed by the statements of Villars and Montgon. A conference was held at Vienna between Sinzendorff, Richelieu, the Dutch minister, and the Duke of Bournon- ville. The latter disputed every clause. He ultimately signed, but his court professed to disown his act, though Philip at last acceded. It was agreed that the Ostend Company should be suspended for seven years, the siege of Gibraltar raised, and the " Prince Frederick " restored. The terms of a per- manent peace were left to a congress which was afterwards held at Soissons.

The signature of the Preliminaries of Vienna for some time scarcely altered the situation. The death of George I. inspired Elisabeth with new hopes for the Pretender, which were actively stimulated by Father Clarke, and the siege of Gibraltar was continued. In this unsettled condition, and with a view to obtaining better terms at the congress, it was certain that on either side attempts would be made to break up the solidarity of the opposite alliance; that Spain would make renewed efforts to detach France from England, while England and France attempted to separate the Courts of Madrid and Vienna.

The informal correspondence between Paris and Madrid soon assumed a formal and governmental character. The birth of Don Luis in July, 1727, presented an opening for advances. Louis XV., with his own hand, wrote to con- gratulate the king and queen. Philip, whose feeble will vacillated between ambition and affection, was touched by

[1] Von Arneth, *Prinz Eugen*, iii. 557.

this friendly act of the head of his house. He replied in an equally cordial spirit. The French Court expressed a wish that diplomatic intercourse should be renewed, and sent a list of six ambassadors, from whom Philip was asked to make his choice. The Count of Rothembourg, an old supporter of the legitimate succession, was selected. His instructions prove how accurately Fleury had gauged the situation. There were some matters which the envoy was advised to confide to the king alone and to his second self. "For these the King of France will be gratified if his Majesty has no other minister but the queen, his consort. This manner of flattering the queen is necessary, because she is not ignorant that her designs have been much suspected. . . . Though the queen has great influence over her husband, yet she is occasionally obliged to yield in things which are repugnant to his sentiments in favour of France. Hence great caution must be employed not to induce her to suspect that endeavours are used to lessen her influence or the confidence which the king reposes in her."

Rothembourg's negotiations were conducted almost entirely with Elisabeth, and she did not make his task the easier, though Duclos' story that he was forced to beg pardon on his knees for the sins of his predecessors lacks confirmation. At his first audience the queen was seated by the king occupied in her needlework, from which she never raised her eyes. She seemed not to notice the ambassador's presence. Philip lifted him and presented him to her, praying her to think only of their nephew, and of the harmony which should exist between them. The queen then became more cordial, but twenty times in the short interview repeated that the French had sold themselves to the English, who lorded it over them like masters. As Rothembourg left he heard sounds of a hot dispute, and the queen cried out in loud and angry tones : "Will your Majesty again trust your family, who have so often deceived you ?"

The presence of a French envoy implied the renewal of diplomatic intercourse with England, and choice fell upon Benjamin Keene, who as agent for the South Sea Company and consul-general had become well acquainted with the procedure and the peculiarities of the Spanish Government. It was long, however, before the queen would admit him to the royal presence, and Rothembourg acted for both nations. [1] The French envoy's despatches are full of lively passages-at-arms with the queen on the subject of the allies' demands. These practically reduced themselves to the withdrawal of the troops from before Gibraltar, the restitution of the South Sea ship, "Prince Frederick," and the distribution of the cargoes of the galleons to the foreign consignees. He was warned by those who had most influence at Court that everything would be done for France and nothing for England. The very name of England was sufficient to cause an outbreak of the queen's temper. Nothing would induce her to allow the execution of the preliminaries. For a moment, at the close of the year, she was pacified by the withdrawal of the English fleet from the Spanish coast. But her obstinacy soon returned. She was not to be tempted by suggestions as to her Italian interests. " I have no other interests," she cried, "than those of my husband," and again when Rothembourg pointed out the imprudence of offending the English, who were joint-guarantors of her succession : " You are come again," she exclaimed,

---

[1] Keene arrived on Sept. 26, but his letter to M. Delafaye of Oct. 6 shows that he might almost as well have been at home. " If it was possible for me to think any place disagreeable where I had the least prospect of doing his Majesty service, certainly I should be of that opinion at present, when both friends and enemies avoid me. The greatest compliment I can pay to the princes is to take no notice of them, and they are sure to return it in the same manner, though I have several hints that they should be glad to see M. Keene if I could contrive to leave the Englishman behind me, and as to the latter, even some of the Jacobites that I have acquaintance with dare not come nigh me for fear of losing their influence at Court. I am lodged in a tent just big enough to hold my bed, but when I go out I have the king's walks and gardens to myself, for no one joins with me. If I could give you an idea of my present situation you would find it so dismal and so ridiculous that you would both pity and laugh at me. . . . You cannot expect much news from me in this condition. All I know is that there was a bull feast in this place on Thursday last, and that the whole family is perfectly in health."—S. Ildefonso.

" to your successions. I voluntarily abandon them if Gibraltar is restored to the king. You see by what I say in his presence that his glory and interests only affect me." If the envoy pressed for the restoration of the " Prince Frederick," Elisabeth declared that if it were his ship the King of France should have it, but the English never, unless they would give Gibraltar for it. She justified its detention on the score of smuggling. When it was urged that there was no proof of this, the king, who rarely spoke, broke in : "There is contraband! There is contraband!" Capital was naturally made of the promise of George I. to restore Gibraltar ; Elisabeth even showed the letter to the French envoy. She asked the king for the key of his casket, and went towards the head of his bed to open it. Meanwhile Rothembourg urged the king, the depositary of all the riches of the world, not to incur the reproach of war for the sake of a single ship. Elisabeth instantly turned and interrupted him : "Is it not just that the English who are so rich should give the king a few millions? . . . True, the riches of the world pass through the king's hands, but the smallest part remains in Spain, and this you would wrest from us to give to your friends the English. . . . You in France are nothing but English. You were not enemies to the emperor till his alliance with my husband. Before, he was your great friend. Do you remember that during the Congress of Cambrai we pressed you to procure satisfaction for Spain from the emperor? Yet you never would. But no sooner had we made peace than you joined against us from caprice, and not knowing why." By this time she found King George's letter. "Perhaps it is forged?" she sarcastically asked as the Frenchman read it. Rothembourg replied that he believed it to be genuine. "I am glad," she answered, laughing, "to furnish you with such an excuse. . . . Let your allies fulfil their part, we will fulfil ours. Let them restore to us what they have. With what right do they come to blockade our ports ?"

French subjects were chiefly interested in the cargoes of the galleons, and Rothembourg pressed for their distribution. " Yes," replied the queen, "when the English have quitted the coasts of Spain and America." In answer to further remonstrances, she imposed a duty of 25 per cent. on this foreign merchandise. French traders were loud in their complaints; they would receive but 12 per cent. upon their capital. The king, urged Elisabeth, was master in his own dominions; he could levy what tax he pleased, foreigners had nothing to do with the fleet; the King of Spain had not interfered in France when the currency had been debased.

Rothembourg possibly regarded the matters of Gibraltar and the " Prince Frederick " among what Villars christened the petty interests of England. He at all events, in despair of a conclusion, signed an article drafted by the Marquis de la Paz, which indeed consented to the restoration of the "Prince Frederick," but stipulated that the congress should decide whether it should not be held as a security for the damages inflicted by the English blockade. Keene was induced to give his unofficial consent. This brought matters to a climax. The English Government insisted that the French king should disown his minister's act, otherwise the Alliance of Hanover must be regarded as dissolved. The condition of the English ministry was critical. The nation clamoured for war; it was less expensive than a state which was neither war nor peace, entailing enormous armaments which rotted away without results. The concert between England and France was far from perfect. Spanish obstinacy was encouraged by letters from France, to the effect that France would forsake England if Spain held firm. Elisabeth had well-nigh succeeded in separating the two powers. Villars represents his party as indignant at the selfish pertinacity of England, as urging that France should express satisfaction with the Spanish offers; those who were not content could only wish to involve Europe in a general war. "We have reduced our demands," said the queen, " more than could possibly be asked. If people are not now content, why—patience!"

Fleury, hesitating for a moment, cast in his lot with the

English ministry. The result amounted to an ultimatum to the Spanish Government. The queen assured Rothembourg that there would be no war. " The allies will never incur such a disproportionate expense, while five or six millions will suffice to defend the Spanish position. If we should lose a few places, they will be restored at the peace, and we have effects enough in our hands to render the allies accountable for them." Patiño was consulted as to whether the country could sustain a war. He sorrowfully admitted that it could not; that the sequestration of the foreign merchandise would only meet the expenses of defensive measures. Both English and French ministries had always believed that the queen's obstinacy was due to Königsegg, though she emphatically denied it, assuming the whole responsibility. Now, at all events, the imperial ambassador threw his weight on the side of peace. Elisabeth frequently lost her temper, but she rarely completely lost her head. She felt that Spain was isolated in Europe, she herself might at any moment be isolated in Spain. The king had been carried to the Pardo desperately ill. Notwithstanding her protestations, her Italian interests carried the day. The Convention of the Pardo, signed in March, 1728, contained the full acceptance of the Preliminaries of Vienna, slightly modified by concessions, from England. The congress could now begin its work.

CONGRESS OF SOISSONS—PROPOSALS FOR CESSION OF GIB-
RALTAR—ELISABETH'S DISAPPOINTMENT WITH REGARD
TO THE IMPERIAL MARRIAGES—HER COOLNESS TOWARDS
THE COURT OF VIENNA—NEGOTIATIONS WITH FRANCE
AND ENGLAND—RISE OF PATIÑO—TREATY OF SEVILLE.

IT is perhaps surprising that the experience of the Congress
of Cambrai had not taught the European powers the futility
of these diplomatic picnics.   They might indeed conceivably
postpone a war, but it was impossible that they should promote a peace.   Each power unearthed old grievances and
developed new desires.   Irritation was as often intensified as
allayed by the dilatory character of the procedure.   Long
before a congress concluded its labours the proposed
European concert was replaced by smaller combinations.
If a general tendency is to be traced, it is that previous allies
were disappointed in each other and previous enemies
agreeably surprised.   But to the superficial observer the
term congress in the diplomatic game corresponded to the
cry of "General Post" at a children's party.   Each power
left its former place, and each was nervous lest it alone
should be excluded from the new settlement.

The Congress of Soissons was no exception to the rule.
It was rendered the less expeditious by the fact that the
plenipotentiaries were rarely in the town.   Fleury could not
remain absent from the capital, and as he was by general
admission the leading member of the congress, other repre-

sentatives were as frequently at Paris as at Soissons. Others again were recalled to their Courts, to report progress, to receive instructions, or merely to delay negotiations. This peculiarity may be illustrated by the case of the Spanish envoys. Macanaz, still prevented by the Inquisition from entering Spain, devoted his talents to the Spanish Government. But he soon left the congress to be within reach of Fleury. Bournonville was recalled to Madrid, nominally to give information, but really, as was supposed, to delay a settlement, and a convenient illness prolonged his absence. Barrenechea and Santa Cruz remained indeed at Soissons, but the caustic temper of the latter and his strong Spanish prejudices were not calculated to promote the harmony of the meetings, which he would abruptly leave if the discussion were distasteful. Barrenechea had been recommended to the English Government as being probably open to pecuniary conviction.

Elisabeth had only consented to the preliminaries under the pressure of imminent danger. The existence of the congress precluded the possibility of immediate war; it gave Patiño time to press on his armaments. The Spanish fleet was assuming formidable proportions both in American and European waters. The negotiations were, as far as Spain was concerned, entirely under the queen's control. It was natural that the old difficulties should reappear. According to the statement of Macanaz, it appears that the points raised by the Spanish plenipotentiaries were as follows: England and France had evaded their engagements for the restoration of Gibraltar. England had therefore forfeited the trade privileges conceded in the Indies. These privileges had been abused, and the conditions transgressed by English traders. The Assiento Treaty was highly injurious to all Europe. The engagements made by sovereigns by letter or even by word of mouth were as binding as those contained in formal treaties.

The Spanish position was strengthened by the belief of the other powers that the concert between the Courts of Vienna and Madrid was intact, and that Elisabeth was still acting under Königsegg's guidance. This belief was confirmed by the fact that Spain was not as yet pressing for the execution of the stipulations of the Quadruple Alliance respecting the Italian Duchies. Fleury knew more than he professed with respect to the changing relations of the Spanish and Imperial Courts, but to his colleagues, since Montgon's revelations as to Philip's intrigues in France, he was singularly uncommunicative. By both emperor and queen the English Government was at first regarded as the prime offender and the most inveterate opponent. Much, therefore, depended upon its readiness to make concessions. With it rested the disentangling of the diplomatic knot. Its position, however, was peculiarly difficult. Fleury had hitherto been loyal. In his most private correspondence with Elisabeth he had tried to induce her to include England in the reconciliation. England, he urged, was not so ill-disposed towards Spain as she thought. But, in the autumn of 1727, Morville had been superseded as keeper of the seals by Chauvelin, who chiefly from dislike of England, was an active partisan of the Spanish Bourbons. Mr. Walpole felt that his own influence with Fleury was on the wane, and was anxious to resign the French embassy. Chauvelin was suspected of being in separate communication with the Queen of Spain, and of preparing to surprise Fleury into acquiescence with demands that England could not accept. Such an attempt was, indeed, actually made shortly before the proposals for the Treaty of Seville were formulated. Mr. Walpole only frustrated it by throwing the whole weight of his long-standing influence upon Fleury, aided by the refusal of his friend, the cardinal's valet, to admit Chauvelin or deliver his message until the interview was ended and Fleury convinced. Thus the English Government was in danger of being exposed on the one side to the hostility of the emperor, supported by Russia, Poland, and Prussia, and on the other to a family alliance of the Bourbons. Hence it was necessary to gratify either the emperor or the Queen of Spain, to make sure at all events of separating the interests of these two powers.

Throughout 1728 there seemed no possibility of accord with Spain except at the price of Gibraltar. "I see no daylight yet in the affairs of the congress," wrote Poyntz, one of the English plenipotentiaries, on June 9, "only this much, that after we carry the point of Gibraltar, the Spaniards will leave no stone unturned to hurt our commerce, in order to distress us into a compliance upon the other point. The Queen of Spain may have other views, but the Catholic king and the true Spaniards are animated against us by this single consideration. . . . This and some advantages for the Queen of Spain's family might perhaps produce a general pacification, and reduce the emperor to reason. Without something of this kind I fear no peace can be of long duration, nor our commerce ever be free from losses and interruption."[1]

The price of Gibraltar Sir R. Walpole and Lord Townshend were prepared to pay, as Lord Stanhope before them, and the elder Pitt hereafter. But on this point of honour the rank and file of England was as punctilious as that of Spain. "What you propose, in relation to Gibraltar," replied Lord Townshend, "is certainly very reasonable ; and is exactly conformable to the opinion which you know I have always entertained concerning that place. But you cannot but be sensible of the violent and almost superstitious zeal which has of late prevailed among all parties in this kingdom against any scheme for the restitution of Gibraltar upon any conditions whatever. And I am afraid that the bare mention of a proposal which carried the most distant appearance of laying England under an obligation of ever parting with that place would be sufficient to put the whole nation in a flame."[2] The suggestion to tempt the queen by proposals for the advancement of her family was more feasible. Such proposals were, indeed, made by Fleury in the name of the allies in October, 1728, and were contemptuously rejected. The reason of this is made clear by the correspondence of Prince Eugene. The proffered assistance of the allies in

[1] Coxe, Sir R. Walpole, p. 628. [2] Coxe, Sir R. Walpole, p. 631.

Q

Italy was of little worth as long as there was still a possibility of Don Carlos' marriage with Maria Theresa. Its
acceptance would only serve to embroil the queen with
the emperor. Throughout the autumn Brancas, who had
succeeded Rothembourg, had represented Elisabeth as
being more devoted to the emperor, and more under
Königsegg's influence than ever.   .

There were, however, already rifts in the Spanish
Imperial Alliance, which were soon to widen. De la Paz,
its main supporter, was being attacked by a formidable
opposition, headed by Castelar and Patiño. Notwithstanding the arrival of the treasure ships, the latter obstinately
refused to forward the overdue subsidies. Prince Eugene
regretted the weakness of De la Paz, who was not the
man to keep the machine going by himself, nor to discover
and baffle the intrigues of the ill-disposed; yet he urged
Königsegg to do all in his power to keep him in his good
intentions, and to bring him nearer and nearer to the queen.
Still more necessary was it to procure the dismissal of
Castelar and Patiño. "As long as the Patiños were in
office," wrote the prince, " they would find means to thwart
the best intentions of the king to give assistance."

The dismissal of the Patiños, however, depended on the
queen ; and it was with her that the Court of Vienna now
had to make a reckoning. It mattered little to her that the
professed objects of the Treaty of Vienna, the Ostend
Company, and the recovery of Gibraltar had proved impracticable. These were mere outworks which did not
affect the security of her main position. This, however,
now appears to have been founded on the shifting sands of
an equivocal article.

It is impossible to exculpate the virtuous emperor and
his advisers from gross deceit. Reading Articles 2 and 3 of
the Secret Treaty together, it seemed pretty clear that
Maria Theresa was destined for Don Carlos, and doubt only
remained as to which archduchess should be granted to Don
Philip. Königsegg throughout had deliberately encouraged
Elisabeth's natural belief. She had, however, in September,

1727, received disquieting information from Fleury that
Charles VI. had with his own hand written to the Elector
of Bavaria denying the matrimonial engagements with Spain,
and that he had also given the most solemn assurance to
the Duke of Lorraine that none should marry the two archduchesses but his two sons. He likewise warned her that
the emperor was busily hunting up documents bearing on
the imperial fiefs, with a view of leaving to Don Carlos, on
his accession to Tuscany, a mere skeleton of a State. The
cardinal told Montgon that the Austrians would amuse
Elisabeth, as long as they could, with the marriage of Don
Carlos, which would certainly never be executed ; why, he
asked, did she fly from the light which was shown to her,
and even shut her eyes not to see it ?[1]

The queen was not at the time disposed to accept suggestions from France, but she doubtless did not forget the hint.
Her position was strengthened by the death of the youngest
of the emperor's daughters. There could now be no am-
biguity ; the remaining two daughters were destined for her
sons. She wrote, therefore, to the empress pressing for
an immediate fulfilment of the contract. The embarrassment of the Imperial Court was extreme. Apart from its
strong attachment for the house of Lorraine, it was resolved
on political grounds not to concede Elisabeth's demand.
Philip's condition was still critical ; if he died the queen's
influence was gone, the grandees would reject the Austrian
Alliance as being her favourite project, and as being on other
grounds avowedly distasteful ; the prince would head the
reaction against his step-mother's system, and cherish no
friendly feelings towards his half-brother to whose interests
his own had been subordinated ; the happiness of Maria
Theresa would be sacrificed, and the heritage of the Hapsburgs
conferred upon a Bourbon cadet, without any equivalent
advantage.

The Spanish Alliance had been a disappointment from
the first. Yet isolation was perilous, and the emperor's

---

[1] Montgon, iv. 187.

Italian possessions would be endangered by the defection of Spain. It was equally difficult to grant and to reject the queen's demands. Her hasty temper was at this time rendered more irritable by anxiety. Any offence might lead to an immediate breach, and Königsegg's influence be superseded by that of Patiño. Charles VI., with a distorted sense of truthfulness not unparalleled by other persons of much general virtue, persuaded himself that circumstances had altered cases, and that by his youngest daughter's death he was liberated from his contract. Yet he dared not say so, and the only possible policy was that of procrastination, which had indeed some justification in the terms of the obnoxious articles.

" The emperor," wrote Prince Eugene to Königsegg, " is anxious to humour the queen, and to avoid anything that might give offence . . . being well aware that in the present state of Spain it is on her support alone that the maintenance of the alliance with this Court depends, and that it would be at an end directly she gives way to the dangerous suggestions of Patiño, to whom she already gives only too much ear, and to the secret intrigues of the allies of Hanover, who spare neither offers nor promises to detach her from the emperor. . . . Her character being such as it is, it is not without good cause that you fear that her vanity might prompt her on the spur of the moment to some decision which would overthrow at one stroke the system of our alliance, and of which she would be perhaps the first to repent. . . . It is, however, easier to foresee the danger than to find the means of preventing it. If the queen only acted on principles of moderation, and if on these principles she took a correct view of the interests of Spain and of her own, there would be no cause to fear such a decision, but it appears that the excitable condition in which she is owing to the king's health, instead of making her more cautious, renders her all the more wayward, and that given up as she is solely to her ambitious views, she only thinks of what can gratify her mania without thinking whether circumstances are such as to admit of such ideas. It is very difficult to have to deal with a character so suspicious and so hard to please as the queen has been for some time past, and it needs no less than your Excellency's ability to be able to keep her in spite of her suspicions within due bounds, and in a condition of good-will towards his Majesty without either increasing or diminishing her hopes on the principal subject."[1]

Königsegg did not dare take upon himself the risk of answering the queen, and even Prince Eugene declined the responsibility. A reply to the formal demand presented by De la Paz was drafted in the imperial council. It was pointed out that the betrothal of Maria Theresa to Don Carlos would alarm all Europe and alienate some of the emperor's most faithful supporters in Germany ; there had been indeed hopes of detaching France from the views held by her allies, but Fleury had decisively declared that he would take no separate action ; the archduchess was as yet too young to marry ; in Germany young ladies were not married so early as in more southern countries ; experience had shown the disastrous results of a departure from the custom ; the archduchess was peculiarly delicate ; a premature marriage would be highly undesirable and hazardous ; before the marriage could take place changes might ensue in the imperial or royal families or in the condition of Europe which might altogether upset any arrangement that might be made ; it would be prudent therefore for the emperor without in any way altering the treaties to keep his hands completely free, as at present, with reference to the marriage of the archduchess, and not to incur the certainty of an European war for the sake of a contingency which might never arise ; such a war would lay upon Spain a far heavier burden than that which so recently she had found herself unable to bear. These remarks led naturally to a hint as to the irregular payment of the Spanish subsidies, and were concluded by the expression of the unalterable attachment of the Imperial Court to the Spanish

[1] November 3, 1728. Von Arneth, *Prinz Eugen*, iii. 561.

Alliance.[1] The empress also wrote to the queen in a similar strain.

Elisabeth in public restrained her temper to a degree which would have been creditable in a less irritable lady. The Marquis de la Paz gave assurance of unshaken fidelity to the Imperial Alliance ; to the outward eye no change was to be observed in the queen's relations towards Königsegg. To have broken with the emperor at this moment would have implied a total surrender to France or England, or a war with these powers for which Spain was not yet ready. The English ministry was urging the French Government to declare war on Spain if she refused to execute the pre-liminaries. It was no doubt due to the imperial letters that, at a moment when it was least expected, the queen showed herself more ready to conciliate the allies of Hanover. She had at length forced the Imperial Government not indeed to declare but to] insinuate its intentions. She realised that upon the marriage of Don Carlos depended the future prospects of her family. If her eldest son married the heiress of the Hapsburgs, the heritage of the Farnesi and the Medici was secure. Otherwise it was certain that the emperor would do his uttermost to prevent the Spanish monarchy from recovering foothold in Italy. Fleury had notified his machinations in Tuscany. In Parma his un-friendly attitude had been yet more obvious. The succession of Don Carlos had been brought one step nearer by the death of Elisabeth's step-father in February, 1727. His suc-cessor, Antonio Farnese, who had long resisted the emperor's persuasions, was induced at length to sacrifice his comfort-able and corpulent celibacy to the charms of Henrietta of Modena. The fortunes of Elisabeth's children and the con-solation of her widowhood were subjected to the chances of the birth of a genuine, or the introduction of a supposititious baby. The queen had experienced that it was impossible to attain her ends in Italy without the help of the Western

---

[1] Prince Eugene to Marquis de la Paz, Dec. 19, 1728. Von Arneth, *Prinz Eugen,* iii. 563.

powers. It was fully time that she should reconsider her relations to France and England. The active resentment against France had died away, the insult to her daughter was forgotten in the injury to her son. She was likely to find no resistance in her husband. With him devotion to France was not only a sentiment, but a habit to which he would only too readily return. It was to Fleury that Elisabeth first privately addressed herself, but more decisive news from Vienna at the end of March led to formal proposals, which were forwarded by Brancas, and laid before the council on April 27. It was demanded as a *sine quâ non* that Spanish garrisons should be introduced into the Italian Duchies, in return for which the Spanish Government was prepared to deliver the cargoes of the galleons subject to a duty of 14 %. The delight of the merchants was unbounded, but the council regarded the admission of Spanish garrisons as impossible, and meanwhile England was clamouring for war. The proposals for peace well-nigh led to immediate rupture. "Passion," wrote Vandermeer, " acts much more than reason on the queen's mind, and a sudden determination for war might easily come about." Elisabeth told Brancas that if they had such cruel relations they could easily find good friends ; that Fleury was utterly given over to the English. Yet not only Fleury but the council at large had regarded the queen's proposals as absurd. " This letter," writes Villars, " containing no explanation of the means of establishing garrisons in imperial territory without any mention of the emperor, nor of the Treaty of Vienna between that monarch and Spain, seemed to us to be mad."[1]

But there was always method in Elisabeth's madness. The Spanish proposals to Fleury had not been at once communicated to England, but as soon as they were understood the English Government realised that the sole arbitress of the destinies of Spain might be won by concessions which would cost it nothing. The conclusion of a despatch from Lord

---

[1] *Mémoires*, iii. 389.

Chesterfield, envoy at the Hague, gives a clear view of the situation in the summer of 1729 : "I think a previous and separate accommodation with Spain is infinitely preferable to a general one with Spain and the emperor together. It has always been a maxim that to treat to advantage with allies one should endeavour to disunite them and treat separately with each, and surely it is a very lucky circumstance if the Queen of Spain, enraged at the disappointment she has met with from the emperor, is willing to throw herself into the arms of the allies. Her private views are very different from the true interests of Spain, and it is very probable that she will make no difficulty of sacrificing the latter to the former, so that we may by gratifying her in that one point obtain conditions from Spain more advantageous than we could at any other time hope for. It is the Austrian pride and power that in my opinion requires humiliation, and which it is likely may be effected by these means. For what can the emperor do when left without an ally in the world, and consequently without a shilling of money? He can no longer rely upon the inaction of France, when Spain, who was the chief cause of that inaction, is become their friend. He will have everything to fear, and nothing to hope for but from his old allies, whose friendship he must then endeavour to regain by a different behaviour from what he has lately had." [1]

The task of the English Government was made easier by the queen's genuine resentment against the emperor and her indignation at Fleury's supposed cowardice and duplicity. Brancas derived no unmixed advantage from his facilities of intercourse with the queen. He bore the brunt of her wrath and satire. The iniquities of the cardinal were her constant theme. He was afraid, she said, of the emperor ; he had contradicted himself at every moment ; she had always suspected him, and now had convincing proof of his double dealing : his tender treatment of the emperor was, she supposed, due to suspicion that she was not really disgusted with Charles VI., and that there was some

---

[1] Coxe, Sir R. Walpole, 649-50.

subterfuge in her advances to the allies; but though Fleury might be false and double, he should not form the same judgment of others: she herself never spoke but what she really thought: the cardinal had always opened his arms to her; had besought her with prayers and supplications to repose herself on France: yet when any action had to be taken against Spain fleets and armies were ready, and all necessary measures were concerted between the allies; but when Spain demanded any favour, the scene was changed: new alliances and preparations then must be made, and the allies were naked and defenceless: they were strong enough to fight emperor and Spain together, but the emperor by himself was too strong for them.

The queen's first aim was to secure Don Carlos in the Italian Duchies, and the second to have her revenge upon the emperor. Both points would be gained by the intro- duction of Spanish garrisons, and to this she believed Fleury to be the chief obstacle. She pointed out that his assistance was not needed for the introduction of neutral garrisons, for that was accorded by the Quadruple Alliance. She told Brancas that the terms now offered were less advantageous than those already granted; whereupon the king, who had been, as usual, silent, broke in: "They have given me nothing at all!"[1] When Brancas pressed for delivery of the cargoes of the galleons in which French merchants were chiefly interested, the queen replied that the king was incapable of injustice, and would not use the property of others, but that he was entitled to reimburse himself for his expenses, and was under no obligation to pay a million and a half out of his own pocket. Business was at a standstill. The flota for Vera Cruz was being laded, but the French merchants held back, and it was believed that few goods would be sent.

Patiño confided to Keene that Fleury was piqued at the direct application which was being made to England, and which he believed was caused by discontent and suspicion

---

[1] Keene to Newcastle, June 16, 1729. *R. O. S.*, 186.

against himself. " In this," says Patiño, "he is in the right, for we shall never have any confidence in France as long as he lives. He has deceived us too often. We are now persuaded that the promises he frequently made to us, and the letters wrote by his Majesty's own hand to the queen, were only to break our alliance with the emperor, and then to leave us in the lurch, or oblige us to submit to such conditions as he might think fit to impose. It is impossible for you to imagine what pains have been taken to bring the king to the temper he is in at present, and now all is likely to be frustrated." He concluded by saying that it would be better for his master to send a *carte blanche*, and give himself absolutely to the power of his Britannic Majesty than to have anything further to do with the cardinal.[1]

The queen's only hope lay, in fact, in England, for she was too indignant with the emperor to revert to his alliance. Her anger affected her outwardly, and Königsegg's melancholy confirmed the impression that it was not assumed. The king's death or abdication might happen at any moment, and the queen felt forced to take measures for her family, and procure for herself an honourable retreat. She had sounded Fleury on the possibility of a substantial establishment, in the event of her widowhood, in France, and had met with no encouragement. Her only resource, therefore, was the settlement of Don Carlos in Italy under the protection of Spanish garrisons. Without these, she urged, his position would always be precarious, for if the emperor and the other contracting powers were backward in their payment of Swiss or other neutral troops, they would soon desert, and the provinces be left defenceless.

For these reasons the queen practically abandoned the demand for Gibraltar, while the English forced the reluctant consent of the French to the introduction of Spanish instead of neutral garrisons. At the end of June, Keene and Brancas gave notice of this concession. The Marquis de la Paz

---

[1] Keene to Newcastle, June 16, 1729. *R. O. S.*, 186.

ministerially concealed his satisfaction and received the agreeable overture with affected *sang-froid*, while the king and queen expressed their pleasure by their looks and their assurances of gratitude. The queen, however, had become suspicious of diplomatists, for she looked at the king and prompted him twice in a low voice to demand in writing what the two ministers had stated by word of mouth. The king's more genuinely suspicious and irresolute nature delayed the immediate execution of the preliminaries. He rallied Brancas on the conditional character of the allies' memorial; there was, he said, one "If" which contained three, and he was so pleased with his joke that he constantly repeated it. Inactive and careless as he was, he was roused by any supposed offence to his dignity, and was then immovably obstinate. The queen's interest to see the matter settled convinced Keene that she was far from raising difficulties, and was applying all her art to remove the king's scruples. These, however, were encouraged by De la Paz, who applauded his master's penetration. The minister was perhaps actuated by imperial sympathies, but he was also like his master haughty and irresolute. He was too timid to advance a step without special orders, and his dry exactness in their execution made it almost impossible to treat with him. To remedy this inconvenience Patiño, who was more communicative and more in his mistress's confidence, was admitted to the conferences.

But for Patiño it is doubtful if negotiations could ever have been carried to a successful issue. Apart from his sterling common-sense and high practical qualities, it was of great advantage that he was heartily averse to the Austrian Alliance and that his fortunes depended upon Königsegg's removal. Since the arrival of the courier from Vienna in the spring had dashed Elisabeth's last hopes Patiño had risen yet higher. Keene describes him as possessing the greatest, indeed the sole, influence over the queen, and as having her confessor at his disposal. Villars speaks of him as first minister without the title. He had regarded the subsidies to Vienna as suicidal to Spanish finance, and though intensely jealous of English encroachment he believed that English friendship was indispensable until a fleet had been recreated and finances reorganised. His diplomatic method was totally opposed to that of De la Paz, who was a Spaniard of the old-fashioned, florid and argumentative school. The divergence was amusingly apparent in the tedious negotiations of the spring of 1729. The marquis " had a great mind to give a loose to his eloquence and ramble away among the antecedents as he calls them ".[1] But Patiño advised that in a crisis like the present it was necessary only to touch upon the essential points and to lop off all that were accessory and superfluous. He told his colleague that provided things went well he should think it of little importance whether a letter of his were said to be writ well or ill ; they were indeed able to prove to the world that France had behaved badly, and to make her ashamed of herself, but the Spanish Government would at the same time expose its own weakness in having been so long led by the nose ; their answer therefore should be clear, precise and free from verbiage ; he could not understand why the marquis required so much time to write four words, but he supposed that he felt his honour to be at stake, and write he must.[2]

De la Paz was painfully conscious of his declining influence. He told Keene, with affected raillery, which was only too serious, that everybody said that the Irish had left him as rats leave a sinking ship. Keene consoled him by replying that he would now believe how little faith could be placed in Irishmen. The king was, as S. Simon said, a kind master, but he sometimes killed his friends with kindness. He insisted that all negotiations should pass through the hands of De la Paz. The orders of the Court were not executed to its satisfaction, and the minister had the mortification of seeing his measures set aside. The queen was less patient. When Brancas reproached her with the divergent replies which he received from the two ministers, she re-

---

[1] Keene to Newcastle, May 26, 1729. *R. O. S.*, 186.
[2] Keene to Newcastle, May 31, 1729. *Ibid.*

plied : " Then you must stand by what Patiño said ; the marquis is not informed of our intentions on that point ".

Philip was now again animated by his old personal hatred for the emperor, and was longing to fight him. He told the French ambassador that he needed no assistance in Italy ; he could cope with the emperor there, as he would have proved to the world, if England had not helped the Austrians in the late war. Königsegg was involved in the disfavour of this Court. The king and queen were ungenerous to their quondam friend. Acting under instructions from Prince Eugene, he assumed indifference on hearing of the allies' concessions. He insisted on an audience late in the evening of June 27. The king and queen had thoughts of refusing, but reflected that such conduct would be too marked. Elisabeth told him the important news. He affected to be pleased, and replied that he had reason to believe that his master would concur. The queen then took her revenge by turning the conversation upon the formidable armaments of the Grand Turk, and the warlike character of the new vizier. In another interview, on August 2, he defended the emperor against the imputations on his good faith. He denied that troops had been marched into Italy ; a few only had been sent to Massa to prevent the prince, an extravagant debauchee, from selling his State to the first bidder. The queen taxed him with intimations sent to the Italian princes to put themselves into a state of defence ; she knew that this had been done in the case of the King of Sardinia, and that the emperor had even suggested to the Pope to send troops to Parma. " Would the emperor by this," she asked, "recede from the right of investiture, granted to him by the Quadruple Alliance, and yield it to the Holy See ? If he is willing, we are so too." Of her intention to send Don Carlos to Italy she spoke with feeling and dignity, if not with a strict regard to truth. " We have too much affection to our son to trust him, unless the grand duke and the Duke of Parma would receive him as we wish. He is but a child of thirteen, but had he strength and maturity to put himself at the head of his troops and demand the gates to be opened, he should then go." [1]

Brancas was assured by Elisabeth that she was well aware of Königsegg's artifices to raise jealousy between herself and the allies by the lateness and length of his audiences. To give them an air of greater importance, he was reduced, she said, to talking of the fine weather and the rain, and tried to turn the most trivial circumstance to his advantage. He had pressed, for instance, upon the king his stud of Neapolitan horses, which had in happier days called forth Philip's admiration. Selfish and ungenerous as Philip often was, he said that Königsegg only offered them because he was too poor to keep them, but he would not refuse the gift, for generals accepted presents from one another, even in open war. [2] There was perhaps some truth in Philip's taunt. The ambassador's ostentatious magnificence, his teams of mules which exceeded the bye-laws of Madrid bumbledom, had doubtless eaten into his resources, even as dinners to Patiño were a heavy charge on Keene's too slender salary. Königsegg was no adventurer like Ripperdá, no carpet-bagger like the French, who in the War of Succession had travelled south to acquire *chateaux d'Espagne*. [3] He had only stayed in Spain at Prince Eugene's express request. His treatment is a slur upon the natural kindliness with which Elisabeth may sometimes be credited, it is another example of her facility in changing tools. The marshal had the humiliation of feeling that he had been out-manœuvred by a woman. He was forced by his Government to remain, but his influence was at an end.

The beginning of the final stage in the negotiations was reached at the end of July. The English Government determined to persuade Stanhope to return to Madrid to give the finishing stroke. "If there be any man living," wrote

---

[1] Keene to Newcastle, Aug. 4, 1729. *R. O. S.*, 186.

[2] *Ibid.*

[3] The Duke of Richelieu attributes the origin of this phrase to the rush for fortunes in Spain during the War of Succession.

Poyntz, "who can bring this about it is Mr. Stanhope. The King of Spain loves him personally, and says he is the only minister who never told him a falsehood. Besides which he has a most universal and deserved credit with the whole Spanish Court and nation."[1] Stanhope arrived in Seville on October 25, and on November 9 the Treaty of Seville was signed by the English and French envoys and by De la Paz and Patiño. The States-General acceded a few days later.

In the late Treaty of Vienna Elisabeth had intended that the profits should be divided between herself and the nation. . To her own family was to fall the heritage of the Hapsburgs, but in the recovery of Gibraltar and in the destruction of the oppressive monopoly of English commerce Spanish interests had been definitely involved. By the Treaty of Seville the queen was the sole gainer. English trade to the Indies and the Assiento were restored to their former footing; the privileges granted to the Ostend Company were withdrawn, and the question of Gibraltar was passed over in silence. But the queen had moved one step further towards the fulfilment of her desires. The presence of Spanish garrisons and the guarantee of the allies of Hanover would make the succession of Don Carlos to the Italian Duchies a certainty. It would no longer depend on the relations of the Courts of Vienna and Madrid, at the moment of the death of either prince.

Yet the King of Sardinia, who was no mean judge of the political situation, expressed admiration for the skill of the allies in inducing an Italian princess to destroy her own handiwork, the Treaty of Vienna, and in contenting her with the Treaty of Seville, which was no better than "humbug".[2] He thought that it would end in smoke, like that of Hanover, and told Blondel, the French envoy, not to believe in war, for England and France would never fight in Italy, and Fleury was waiting for the death of the emperor and Philip.[3]

[1] Coxe, Sir R. Walpole, p. 53.
[2] "Erba trastulla."
[3] Carutti, iv. 579.

CHAPTER XIII.

1729-31.

RECALL OF KÖNIGSEGG—DELAY IN THE EXECUTION OF THE
TREATY OF SEVILLE—DIFFERENCES BETWEEN FRANCE
AND ENGLAND—SPAIN HAMPERS ENGLISH COMMERCE AND
THREATENS GIBRALTAR—DEATH OF THE DUKE OF PARMA
—DON CARLOS' SUCCESSION TO THE ITALIAN DUCHIES—
THE SECOND TREATY OF VIENNA—DON CARLOS SAILS TO
ITALY—ELISABETH'S SUCCESS.

THE prophecy of the King of Sardinia proved in great part
correct. Elisabeth had a weary waiting time before the
provisions of the Treaty of Seville were executed. The air
of imperturbable indifference which Königsegg assumed,
much to her irritation, did not represent the feelings of his
Court. The emperor and Prince Eugene were loudly indignant. They recalled their ambassador from Madrid, and
poured troops into Italy until their forces amounted to
80,000 men. The allies were given to understand that the
secession of Spain could at any moment be bought by the
grant of an archduchess to Don Carlos. Charles VI. was
wounded in his most sensitive point, the imperial suzerainty
over the Italian fiefs. The German nation was roused at the
pretensions of the allies to instal an imperial vassal in his
fief on their own conditions, and without the consent of the
empire. There were threats that Don Carlos should forfeit
the succession, and that the fiefs on the decease of the present possessors should be administered directly for the profit
of the empire. The grand duke was encouraged in his
natural dislike to admitting foreign garrisons, and he was
ordered to repudiate the title of the Spanish crown to the

suzerainty of Siena by receiving investiture from the emperor. Spain threatened him with forfeiture, if he consented, and France declared that such investiture would be regarded as the beginning of hostilities. Over against the allies of Hanover stood a formidable combination of the powers of Eastern Europe, which had for long been preparing with a view to the possibility of Spanish defection.

In all this the Queen of Spain could see no difficulty. The Court would remove to Catalonia and superintend the embarkment of the Spanish troops for Italy; resistance by the Imperial Government would enable her to extend the dominion of Don Carlos to Naples and Sicily. She believed, perhaps not without reason, that the inhabitants would revolt at the first appearance of the Spanish fleet; the allies would invade the Austrian dominions at every point from Palermo to Ostend. To the French and English Governments the situation did not appear so simple. They were not perfectly united within themselves, nor were they entirely at accord one with the other. In England the Treaty of Seville was the pretext for sharp attacks from the opposition, consisting of Tories and discontented Whigs. A minority of twenty-four lords signed a protest against it, as being a flagrant breach of the Quadruple Alliance. On the other hand, Lord Townshend was at variance with his colleagues. He had for some time been urging an immediate attack upon the emperor. He wished at once to enter into engagements with the Rhenish electors to facilitate a combined French and English advance from the westward. Vandermeer, who had acted as the sole representative of the allies of Hanover at Madrid, had also advised the employment of force, even before the Treaty of Seville. The majority of the English ministry was indeed prepared to exercise force, but only after exhausting the resources of mediation. If force were necessary it should be limited to an attack on Sicily, or at all events confined to the emperor's dominions in Italy; an engagement with the Rhenish electors would tie the hands of the Government in the event of the emperor's death, and prevent it from giving

R

support to the Pragmatic Sanction. Above all it concurred with the States-General in the wish to avoid a French attack upon the Austrian Netherlands, on which side the emperor was undoubtedly most vulnerable. It was desirous, in fact, of executing the provisions of the Treaty of Seville with as little injury to the emperor as was consistent with good faith to Spain. There were hopes from the first that the emperor might be induced to admit the Spanish garrisons in return for a guarantee of the Pragmatic Sanction, which would protect his dominions in Italy from future aggression.

In France the old war party was eager to seize the opportunity for further weakening the house of Hapsburg. To the Duke of Orleans, who said that a king's first duty was to spare his people, Villars replied that it was dishonourable to fail Spain, and dangerous from the character of the queen, who was not unlikely to throw herself into the emperor's arms. Townshend, he added, the best political head in England, was disquieted by this danger. Fleury was still averse to a war in Spain's behalf; the enterprises of the Amadis, he said, were less surprising than those expected of France by Philip and his queen. Yet he was opposed to any guarantee of the Pragmatic Sanction. The Austrian dominions would, he believed, if not artificially bolstered up, fall asunder of themselves; forcible disintegration was therefore unnecessary. The Duke of Orleans suggested that war could be averted by the acceptance of the Pragmatic Sanction, for which the emperor would make valuable territorial concessions to France. Fleury replied that three lost battles would not induce him to consent. All parties naturally concurred in resistance to limitations on the objective of an attack. Spain and the maritime powers, it was urged, expected to enjoy the chestnuts which France had the task of drawing from the bars of the imperial fire. Villars broke out upon the subject in the presence of the king. " I have no patience with the injustice of the allies; it seems that they alone have a right to win, while we pay all the costs. I cannot restrain my wrath; I would fain swear, and I believe your Majesty would pardon me." " It is not right to swear before the king," rejoined the cardinal.

The differences of opinion between the allies appeared not only in the interchange of diplomatic notes, but in a Council of War, held in Paris in April, 1730, at which Spinola, who was destined to lead the Spanish expeditionary force, represented his Government. The queen soon perceived that this council only afforded a decent pretext for delay, and this was the case also with a remonstrance, termed an ultimatum, addressed by the allies of Hanover to the emperor. She reproached both England and France with purposely deferring action until the year was too far advanced for a campaign. Patiño had originally incurred only such expenditure as would have been useful in time of peace, but when Fleury in April reproached him with delay he completed the mobilisation. It was keenly felt that this outlay was wasted and could not be repeated for another year. Spinola, who was regarded as having been hoodwinked, was deprived of his command. Castelar was sent on a special embassy to Paris, in the hope that his high position and Patiño's credit would be proof against the temptation which Spinola had been unable to resist. He too, however, was for a time won over and threw the blame of delay upon England. Yet it appears from the Duke of Newcastle's letters that it was on Fleury that the responsibility rested, and that the English Government was prepared to take action in Italy in the spring of 1730. It offered to accept Castelar's own plan for a general war, or any modification which Fleury might propose, provided only that the Netherlands were not attacked. It was even willing to provide troops to assail the emperor in his hereditary dominions.

Whatever may have been Fleury's loyalty to England in the past there is little doubt that he was now striving to detach Spain by intimating that the English would never go to war in her behalf. He flattered the queen by holding out hopes calculated to excite the jealousy of the maritime powers, while he prevented her from swinging back towards the emperor. He wrote to dissuade her from listening to the amusements of the Court of Vienna, while the allies of Hanover had it in their power to make such solid establishments for her children in Italy and Flanders. The queen and Patiño early realised that the cardinal dreaded to see England and Spain united, in which case France, instead of acting as mediator, would be forced into their measures, even against her will. Patiño told Keene that he had convincing proofs that Fleury was surprised into the Treaty of Seville; that he had only wished to separate Spain from the emperor without healing her differences with England; he had now become an advocate of the emperor and the Quadruple Alliance. Brancas met with a cold reception from the king, who complained that he was being cheated and laughed at. The queen desired him not to make her talk, for it would be in too warm a manner; if she did not regard him as a friend rather than as the minister of France she would treat him to some strong language.[1] Philip, always sensitive as to his own importance, fancied that the French ministry despised him. Fleury left unanswered a long letter written in his own hand, and especial offence was caused by the rumours in France that the King of Spain was governed by his queen. This resentment was fanned by Elisabeth, who had heard that either Fleury or Chauvelin had held slighting discourses on her private character. It was feared that the king's punctilio and the queen's petulance would force them to employ the troops which they had mobilised at such expense. Patiño had the greatest difficulty in keeping them from some rash enterprise. The situation was critical, for if any reverse happened to the troops destined for the expedition, which consisted of the *élite* of the army, the rest would scarcely be able to guard the frontier and overawe the Catalans, and it would be years before the Spanish troops could be reorganised on any tolerable footing.

Patiño confessed that he had two extraordinary geniuses to deal with who would not stick to gratify their passions at

[1] "Elle luy chanterait des pouilles." Keene to Newcastle, May 19, 1730. *R. O. S.*, 189.

the expense of a rash action, though he was sure they would repent of it; there were, moreover, those who would not fail to animate their vivacity for their private advantage, and would push them on to the wildest projects in the hope of embarrassing and ruining their favourite minister. Alberoni's fall was ever before Patiño's eyes. There was still danger lest the queen should throw herself into the emperor's arms. It was believed that her refusal to enumerate the instances of his bad faith was due to a wish not to render the breach too wide.

Before the end of the year the congress had practically broken up, and the relations between the French and Spanish Courts were strained to the uttermost. All the diligence of the temporary *chargé d'affaires*, Hulin, failed to change the feelings of the king and queen towards Fleury. They believed that he wished the allies to await the king's death or abdication; that he would do nothing to relieve the present suspense, and everything to keep Spain and England from a perfect understanding.

To such an understanding both crowns had long been tending. In January, 1730, Philip informed Patiño that he was nearly telling Brancas that he should address himself to England and Holland apart from France, and Keene believed that this was purposely repeated to sound the English Government. In June the queen expressed herself willing to accept the English plan, and confine operations to Italy. She repeated several times that from a bad payer one must draw all one can. In July Patiño made definite proposals for separate action. Personal reasons contributed to this policy. The Duke of Bournonville was now in high favour with Patiño. Fleury and Brancas had favoured the duke's recall from France. He was full of resentment, and trying to gain the good graces of England, and this assisted not a little to a better understanding. " His scheme is," wrote Keene, " that there are two interests in Spain, that of the country, the other of the queen, which will always get the better of the former; and that her Catholic Majesty is resolved to try all ways to secure Tuscany for herself and

son ; and if the Turk were to come and offer to introduce
her troops, she would make an alliance with him.   Her
vivacity, he says, is too great to let her principal concern
lie dormant.   It is impossible, without France, to finish it by
force, but he hints it may be done by negotiation ; and that
the first proposals of the emperor will be made by the
means of England, for the Imperial Court knows the
cardinal too well to trust him.   His dark ways would give
to understand that England, Spain, and the emperor are to
enter into an alliance in three months.   It is certain he has
presented a project to her Catholic Majesty ; and she, as he
tells me, is pleased with it, and begins to come back to
his sentiments." [1]   In this proposal of Bournonville is foreshadowed the Second Treaty of Vienna.

Weak as Spain was, she could exercise no inconsiderable
pressure upon the allies of Hanover.   France was intimi-
dated by the prospect of a renewed alliance with the
emperor, and her trade was again affected by the refusal to
distribute the cargoes of the flota.   It was yet easier to
prove the importance of friendship to the English Government.   The commercial engagements of the Treaty of
Seville remained as yet a dead letter.   The English
members of the commission, which was to frame regulations
for the future, and assess compensation for the past, were
already in Spain ; yet it was long before their Spanish
colleagues were appointed.   Meanwhile the old grievances
were unredressed.   The Spanish Government had merely to
hold its hand.   Local authorities and local adventurers
needed no encouragement to harass English trade.   The
governors of Spanish America protected their colonies from
contraband traffic by granting licences to privateers who
acted as *guarda-costas*.   This was a source of no small profit
to the governors and to the speculators in privateering.
There was no fixed line of demarcation to Spanish waters :
it was hard to prove that the Bristol or the Boston sloop
was not deflecting from her course.   The *guarda-costas*

---

[1] Keene to Newcastle, Aug. 20, 1730.   *R. O. S.*, 192.

frequently asserted their right of search wherever a ship might be. They boarded vessels within cannon shot of Jamaica. Sometimes ships were plundered and allowed to go their way, at others the crews were turned adrift in boats or marooned. Frightful tales were told of women tied naked to the rigging and lashed to death. With crews consisting of mulattoes, negroes, Indians, and the offscourings of all nations, such stories are not impossible. The more legitimate course was to carry the suspected ship into the Spanish ports for trial. No redress could be obtained in the local courts ; and, as the ship's papers, her only proof of innocence, were detained, there was little hope of acquittal on appeal. The possession of logwood, cocoa, or pieces of eight was regarded as conclusive of guilt. Yet pieces of eight could be obtained of the South Sea Company, and cocoa and logwood shipped from British settlements. Outward-bound ships which had not broken bulk were convicted on the ground that their cargoes were intended not for British but for Spanish colonies.

It is significant that these outrages became peculiarly frequent at the end of 1730 and in the early months of 1731. It was in the latter year that the "Rebecca" was boarded, and her skipper, Jenkins, lost his ear. More important was the fact that an English man-of-war was forced to fight for four hours to save a convoy of thirty sail, which was ultimately scattered.

To the repeated complaints of the English Government the Spanish ministers replied that the outrages were due, not to *guarda-costas*, but to pirates, who were not necessarily Spaniards. As to the right of search, it was urged that English ships trading to their own colonies had no business in Spanish waters. English men-of-war were charged with protecting or even carrying contraband goods : the licensed South Sea vessels were accompanied by unauthorised tenders : Spanish outrages were matched by those of English or Anglo-American sailors. Nor were these statements altogether unworthy of credit. English memorialists admitted that many of the logwood cutters were converted

privateers or pirates, and relapses were probably not un-
frequent. A Boston captain published accounts of the
Spanish ships which he took and the crews which he
marooned. Admiral Stewart, who commanded the English
squadron, wrote of the brutality of English sailors who
landed in Cuba and murdered harmless inhabitants. Outrage, he urged, could be no more prevented in American
waters than in the streets of London ; the charges of the
English merchants were grossly exaggerated and incapable
of proof. A case in which the Government was anxious to
secure conviction collapsed because the only Spanish sailor
who survived the massacre died of his injuries before he
could make his deposition. There was at all events no
question that a large proportion of the wares introduced into
Spanish America were contraband, and it is more than possible that innocent and inexperienced traders suffered for the
sins of the professional smugglers who evaded the *guarda-
costas* and corrupted the officials. Keene, in his more private letters, concurs with Admiral Stewart in regarding the
English merchants as uncompromising, selfish, and inconsiderate. They could only be matched, he thinks, by the
clergy. "You would never have paired our merchants so
well with any set of mortals as parsons. Thank God that I
have none of the latter upon my back, and I fear that, let me
do my utmost, as I assure you I do, the former would be
sufficient to break it." [1]

English grievances were not confined to America. In
Spain itself much vexatious interference was practised.
Ships were detained under pretence of quarantine, or
searched for heretical books. Government packets were
boarded and overhauled by custom-house officials. The
courts of law interfered with the administration of the
estates of English merchants who died in Spain. English
seamen were pressed, and English ships embargoed for trans-
port service. Merchants had soldiers quartered upon them,
or were forced to purchase exemption. Tobacco, sugar, and

[1] Keene to Delafaye, Aug. 20, 1780. *R. O. S.*, 192.

other products of English colonies were prohibited; new imposts, unknown in the reign of Charles II., were levied. Ships employed in provisioning Gibraltar were stopped and searched, and their Moorish passengers forcibly removed.

Other disputes were of a territorial character. The colony of Georgia had quite recently been founded, and its boundaries were already a matter for angry argument. Of more immediate importance was the question of Campeachy Bay. The logwood cutters having cleared the coasts had advanced into the interior, had built shelter and provision huts, which were converted into permanent settlements. Settlement led to claim of possession, and that to claim of sovereignty. Their rights, they urged, dated from the reign of Charles II.; they had cut and built unhindered; the coasts were unoccupied by Spaniards; Spaniards, in fact, were rarely seen. The Spaniards were now, however, disposed to deny their rights and destroy their settlements, which lay within territory intermittently occupied but invariably claimed by Spain. The recent Anglo-Portuguese dispute in Africa will serve to illustrate the position of the contending parties, if mission stations be substituted for logwood cutters' settlements.

All these grievances were of long standing, but the Spanish Government now adopted a more direct method of forcing England to a determination. Towards the close of 1730 lines were raised opposite Gibraltar. It was at first professed that the operations consisted merely of the repair of huts, but it became clear that the garrison was threatened. General Sabine reported that troops were on the move, that masons and bricklayers were being collected from all parts, and worked so hard that it was difficult to believe that they were Spaniards. Consul Cayley wrote that cannon were being shipped from Cadiz. No redress could be obtained from the Spanish Court. The king insisted on his right to build upon his own territory. The work was probably begun to force the English to execute the Treaty of Seville, and continued to gratify the king's passionate feelings on this subject. In the final and friendly negotiations, Keene was obliged to neglect his instructions, and keep

this matter out of discussion. Patiño told him that its bare
mention would break off all further measures, for, however
fond the queen might be of the Italian succession, the king
would sacrifice a hundred Parmas rather than abandon the
work which kept Gibraltar out of his sight and thoughts;
that were he, Patiño, to be pushed on by drawn bayonets,
he would rather be killed on the spot than open his mouth
to the king on this subject.[1]

The climax was hastened by the death of the Duke of
Parma in January, 1731.   Imperial troops were marched
into the Duchies, though under pretext of securing them for
Don Carlos.   Almost simultaneously with this, Castelar, the
Spanish minister at Paris, made a declaration that his Court
regarded the Treaty of Seville as void.[2]   It is doubtful
whether his Court had authorised or even approved this
declaration, but it was too proud to withdraw it or explain
it away.   It was felt that a rupture might ensue at any
moment.   Robinson was instructed to push on the negotiations into which his Government had entered with the
Court of Vienna.   The Spanish Court expressed disquietude
at the news.   The Duke of Liria had left Russia for Vienna,
and informed his Government that a treaty was being
negotiated which would be highly prejudicial to Spain.
Patiño, however, knew or guessed the truth, and, after re-
proaching Keene with the secret action of his Government,
concluded by saying that he should not be sorry if the report
were true.   The Duke of Liria was instructed to change his
tone, and to communicate with Robinson ; he was, however, wrote Keene, a vain, weak creature, full of projects
and suspicion, and consequently difficult to deal with.[3]   The
French Government, also fearing isolation, instructed Bussy
to treat with Prince Eugene, but, with Fleury's determina-

---

[1] Keene to Newcastle, May, 2, 1731. *R. O. S.*, 196.

[2] Montgon states that Castelar's declaration was concerted with the
maritime powers, and that its object was to relieve Spain from engagements to France. English indignation, he adds, was merely affected to
deceive Fleury.

[3] Keene to Delafaye, April 6, 1731. *R. O. S.*, 196.

tion not to guarantee the Pragmatic Sanction, it was hopeless to expect success.

Rothembourg meanwhile did his utmost to irritate the Court of Spain against the English Government. He laid stress on the fact that it had disbanded troops immediately after the Treaty of Seville, and that the opening of Parliament had been purposely postponed. He had, however, a formidable rival in Patiño, who felt that it was due to the French ambassador that the king and queen had been fed by hopes of conquest; he personally was anxious to escape from the difficulty by neutral troops or any other expedient. He confessed that he regarded Spain as stronger when freed from the incumbrance of any foreign possessions, while the French, and especially Brancas, put other notions into the queen's head. He regarded Spanish or any other garrisons in Tuscany as no security, for even the inhabitants could annihilate them in a night, and he should be sorry to command them. Keene was privately assured that Castelar's declaration need make no substantial difference; Spain was now at liberty to join with any ally who did or would do her most service; if it were England, she would be English—if France, French; or she would assist herself and negotiate without concealment with the emperor; if the King of England could procure the emperor's consent for the immediate admission of Don Carlos into Parma, and reasonable security for the eventual succession of Tuscany, the English should enjoy all the privileges accorded by previous treaties; nay, more, for if it should prove true that the King of England had made a treaty with the emperor which provided for the succession of Don Carlos, and contained nothing prejudicial to Spain, she would immediately accede and enter into a guarantee of the emperor's succession, which was believed to be one of the conditions.

The relations between Spain and England were undoubtedly improving. On January 10 Keene had written to Delafaye that what with the vivacity and inconstancy of the masters of Spain, the cunning and want of sincerity of one minister, and the mysterious buckram of the other, all was incomprehensible, and amongst them there was not a foundation solid enough to bear a probable guess. But on March 2 he was able to report that though he could not be responsible either for the constancy or integrity of the Court, yet he felt obliged to state that he never saw a greater appearance of both than at that moment. The governors of Spanish America were induced to repress outrages on British trade; one *guarda-costa* had been even arrested and condemned.

Yet the difficulties were by no means over. The works over against Gibraltar were continued, and the king was as obstinate as ever. On reading a number of the *Craftsman*, in which it was stated that a certain district before Gibraltar would be demanded as one of the conditions of the treaty, he fell into such a passion that Patiño would not repeat his words.[1] The queen was equally irritable. Every trifling dispute about the Dowager Duchess of Parma, who " proved herself to be the queen's own mother," made Elisabeth ready to fall out with the Court of Vienna. "Who, therefore," wrote Keene, " can reconcile their conduct; they are at variance with all mankind; they say they cannot live long in a state of suspense, though it is their own fault they are in one; they are courted by the principal powers of Europe, and are continually balancing about what they are to do, and for this reason are doing nothing."[2]

This balancing arose in great measure from the different ends of the main personages of Spain. The king was eager for Gibraltar, and therefore hostile to England; he cared little for Italy, much for reunion with France. The queen had been insulted by the emperor, and yet felt that through the emperor alone she could compass her ends in Italy, nor had she entirely abandoned her darling project of an imperial marriage. The English fleet which had destroyed her prospects in Sicily might be instrumental in planting her family in Central Italy. Patiño, jealous of English naval and mercantile superiority, felt that the re-establish-

---

[1] Keene to Newcastle, May 20, 1730. *R. O. S.*, 196.
[2] Keene to Delafaye. May 20, 1731. *Ibid.*

ment of Spanish trade and finance was impossible in the
face of its hostility. Accommodation with the emperor
would be his own ruin, and war with the emperor his
country's. He cared nothing for Italy, and yet his power
depended on the queen, whose only interests were Italian.
Both the queen and Patiño were haunted by the fear of
Philip's death or resignation. Fleury, hating the queen
and fearing her ministers, had won the ear of the prince
or his advisers, and an opposition was forming in the
prince's circle to the influence of the queen.

The alleged pregnancy of the widowed Duchess of Parma
caused another serious hitch in the negotiations. Shortly
before her husband's death she had called for iced chocolate
when heated with dancing, and on the strength of this her
husband had in his will declared her pregnant. The old
duchess had won her confidence, and in July she confessed
that she knew not whether she were with child or no.
Patiño said that she seemed to be but a silly princess, and
the Spanish Court made merry over the story. But to the
emperor and to England it had a more serious aspect. If
the supposition were true there was an end to Elisabeth's
hopes, and, therefore, to an alliance of the two powers with
Spain ; the imperial troops would be obliged to hold for
the new-born babe the territories which they professedly
occupied for Don Carlos. Spain long pressed for professional advice, and this was at length conceded. The duchess
was visited by the Court doctors and a commission of
matrons, who declared her to be pregnant. The Spanish
Government rejected the report, and expressed its intention
of entering a protest against the legitimacy of offspring. It
was believed that there was an intention of foisting upon
European credulity a supposititious child. Suspicion pointed
to the wife of a palace gardener who was likely to become
a mother at a convenient moment.

The French Government naturally did everything in its
power to hinder an accommodation with the emperor.
When it was clear that its overtures at Vienna could
not succeed, it encouraged the Grand Duke of Tuscany

to offer resistance to the proposals made. Rothembourg had orders to state that France would regard what the King of Spain might think fit to do, in consequence of the English treaty with the emperor, with the same indifference that she regarded her other allies, who had by this separated themselves from her. No remark was better calculated to wound the king. He instructed Castelar to reply that as France was so indifferent to Spain, the king would take such measures as he thought proper without deference to France. The next move of the French Government was ingenious. In June the accession of Spain to the new Treaty of Vienna was so far certain that the English squadron was being fitted out which was to convey Don Carlos to Italy. Rothembourg for a moment succeeded in alarming the Spanish Court by representing that it was intended to force Spain to accept the treaty. The Prince of Asturias was made the cat's paw, and he spoke on the subject at the Despacho, though he seldom opened his lips. Rothembourg even offered forty-four French ships to join a Spanish squadron in resisting an English attack. He warned Patiño not to trust Don Carlos to an English fleet, which might sail away with him and keep him as an hostage. The queen's good sense was proof against alarm; and she treated the ambassador with such asperity that he pressed for his recall. She even ventured to say in Philip's presence that it was disgraceful that France should sit idle and let the king and his family lie under such obligation to England. He replied that it was not France, but the present ministry.

The Court of Vienna consented to the peaceable admission of the Spanish garrisons, in return for the guarantee of the Pragmatic Sanction by the maritime powers, subject to the proviso that Maria Theresa should not marry a Bourbon, nor any prince strong enough to endanger the balance of power. The English Government originally proposed to disqualify by name the heir-apparent of Prussia, but the emperor urged that this would needlessly embroil him with the Prussian Court. Negotiations were finally facilitated by the Duke of

Liria. The intimate friend of Philip and Elisabeth, he was also a favourite of Prince Eugene. His lively manners and love for society propitiated the Viennese: he was more at home in Vienna than in Madrid; he had never accustomed himself to Spanish cooking, or to Spanish ladies ; politically a Spaniard, he was socially a Parisian.

The treaty with the emperor was signed on the part of Spain on July 22, 1731. It differed from that between the emperor and the maritime powers in that no direct guarantee of the Pragmatic Sanction was exacted. The Courts of Madrid and Florence then arranged the terms for the succession of Don Carlos to the grand duchy. The grand duke retained his sovereignty during life, and in default of heirs male recognised Don Carlos as his successor. To his sister the electress palatine was granted, on his death, the title of grand duchess. In the absence of Don Carlos the office of regent devolved to the electress. This separate treaty between the two Courts threatened to produce a fresh rupture with the emperor as being a contravention of imperial rights and of the Treaty of Vienna. The dignity of all parties was finally saved by the expedient of calling the Treaty of Florence a mere family arrangement. Don Carlos was as yet a minor, and his parents were precluded by the terms of the Quadruple Alliance from acting as his guardians in the government of Parma. The guardianship was therefore bestowed upon the Grand Duke of Tuscany and the Dowager Duchess Dorothea. Philip wrote to the emperor saying, that in sending his son to Italy he entrusted him to his care, and placed him beneath the defence and wardship of the empire.

The final danger was lest the German Diet should raise objections before Don Carlos was in actual possession. " If this," wrote Keene, " comes upon us when we think that we have the bird in our hands, I foresee the fury the queen will fall into ; . . . she will be calling upon us to avenge the insult done to England and Spain. All the veins of the blood of Bourbon will be set a-trickling to waken the king to resentment. It is for such an incident as this that France is

daily in hopes of." [1]   But matters were hastening towards a
conclusion, if the word haste could be applied to Spain.
Sir Charles Wager had arrived at Cadiz.   The admiral's dry
humour charmed the Spanish nobles.   Patiño was believed
to have never had more pleasure than in seeing the English
fleet and officers, nor more displeasure than in comparing
them with his own. [2]   The hopes of the Duchess of Parma
had vanished.   The Court of Vienna shared in the general
reconciliation, and Liria began to negotiate afresh for an
imperial bride for Don Carlos.   This the queen was prepared to purchase at any price ; there could be no better
security for her son's establishment.   France alone was out of
favour.   Rothembourg made his swollen legs an excuse for
not visiting the palace.   Fleury and Chauvelin applauded
his affectation of indifference.   When at length he made his
congratulations to the queen she thanked him for the compliment and expressed her satisfaction that the success so
hardly won could not have caused the least inconvenience
to the Government of France. [3]   When Castelar informed
Fleury of the conclusion of the treaty he expressed surprise
at the separate action of his allies, but assured him that if
they were satisfied he was content.   But the maritime
powers and the Imperial Government flattered themselves
that the conclusion of the Second Treaty of Vienna without
the co-operation of France was a serious check to the fresh
growth of Bourbonism.

In October, 1731, the Spanish troops sailed from Barcelona, escorted by Wager's fleet.   The imperial garrisons
withdrew, and the Spaniards occupied the towns stipulated
in the treaties.   All Italy was in movement to see the new
Italian prince.   The Tuscans, smarting under the memory
of imperial exactions, eagerly awaited him.   Throughout
Italy the Spaniards were certain to find a welcome and a
desire to forward their aims.   Don Carlos arrived at Leghorn

---

[1] Keene to Delafaye, Oct. 11, 1731.   *R. O. S.*, 197.
[2] Keene to Delafaye, Sept. 30, 1731.   *Ibid.*
[3] Keene to Newcastle, Oct. 17, 1731.   *Ibid.*

on December 27 after a stormy voyage from Antibes, a fitting conclusion to the troubled waters through which the succession question had been steered. He entered the town at night, and through triumphal arches and torchlit streets passed on his way to the cathedral, where the Archbishop of Pisa received him, and a Te Deum was chanted in thankfulness for his safe arrival. In March, 1732, he made his entry into Florence, and was subsequently installed in his capital of Parma. The only discordant note in the harmony of the installation ceremonies was a protest from the Pope, declaring the illegality of these proceedings and the reversion of the fief of Parma to the Holy See.

Elisabeth Farnese had won her first substantial triumph. The obstinacy of motherly ambition had withstood two unsuccessful wars, had worn out three hostile combinations. The untrained *pensionnaire* of a Parmesan convent had outplayed the diplomats of the empire, of France, of England, and of Holland, who had all from time to time resisted her claims, or the means which she demanded for securing them. The son of the victim of the palace attics became the sovereign of her domineering mother. The ultramontane Queen of Spain, the patroness of a revived Inquisition, the persecutor of anti-Papal bureaucracy, had braved the protests of the Pope. A sprig of the Farnesi had denied the claims of the Holy See to the principality which it had conferred upon the house at the expense of Papal reputation.

These, it may be said, were mere personal triumphs or defeats, the passing tittle-tattle of crowned heads. The historian exhumes the dust of decayed institutions, or stands god-father at the genesis of political ideas. The biographer has to estimate in his scales the weight of a strong personality, though it has no comprehensive constitutional conception. The marriages or quarrels of interesting or uninteresting individuals have probably done more to consolidate or divide the nations of Europe than ethnological yearnings, or antipathies grounded on the diversity of institutions. The influence which a comparatively commonplace person can exercise upon the destinies of nations can scarcely be better illustrated than by the results of Elisabeth's first success. The petty Italian princess, in spite of the scars of small-pox, and the sharp edge of her temper, had, with little support but what she had created for herself, once more made Spain a European nation, and given it again a foothold in Italy. She had thrown open to the Bourbons the preserves which all French dynasties had coveted, and some had occupied. She had thrust in between the German possessions in the north and south an Italian principality, with sufficient power to make itself fresh elbow-room. The waste-paper basket was awaiting the Treaty of Utrecht. Everything, writes Galuzzi, presaged an imminent revolution in Italy. The medal that was struck in Don Carlos' honour at Parma was accepted as an omen. Its device was a lady with a lily in her hand, and its motto was *Spes Publica.*

CHAPTER XIV.

1726-31.

ALL is well that ends well, but the years between the fall of
Ripperdá and the Second Treaty of Vienna formed perhaps
one of the least happy periods of Elisabeth's life. The
course of negotiations can hardly be understood without an
appreciation of the interior of Court life during this period.

The excitement of the Austrian Alliance and of the siege
of Gibraltar had soon given place to much personal anxiety,
if not unhappiness. In the spring of 1727 Philip became so
ill that the queen was forced openly to assume the government. She issued all orders, and Königsegg and the
secretaries worked with her alone. In the following January
he seemed near his end. His melancholy was succeeded by
violent fits of passion ; he struck his doctor, and even, it was
said, his confessor. He could not sleep, and was extremely
thin ; he suffered from want of appetite and would only eat
sweetmeats. He was taken to the Pardo in order that he
might be out of sight. In February it was reported that he
could not possibly live ; the Pardo did not suit him, but he
was too ill to be moved. Elisabeth's agitation was extreme,
and was redoubled by her vacillation between a French and
an imperial alliance. She attempted to propitiate her step-
son by associating him with her in the government. In
April, however, Philip recovered his general health, and was
able to receive the French ambassador. He looked well and
fat, and had consented to cut his hair and nails, but there
seemed no doubt that his brain was affected. His melancholy

(259)

fancies soon took a practical turn. In June he contrived, without the queen's knowledge, to write a note to the president of the Council of Castile empowering him to give immediate effect to his previous deed of renunciation, and to proclaim Ferdinand king. Notwithstanding the general desire for Philip's abdication, the council postponed the execution of the order until the following day. After dinner, while hunting, Philip divulged his action to Elisabeth, in the belief that all steps had now been taken. The queen, with wonderful presence of mind, concealed her grief and anger, and insisted only on the return of his note, in order that she might alter the provision made for herself and her children. On its recovery she tore it in pieces, and then passing from gentle and insinuating persuasion to violent reproach, she protested that she would never consent to his abdication, and that his action on his previous resignation proved that without such consent it was not legal. Philip bowed beneath his wife's reproaches, but it was believed that during his life he would nurse this idea of retirement, and it was thought prudent to deprive him of pen and paper. Though he had a Papal brief absolving him from his vow, his conscience could not be calmed; he believed himself to be a usurper keeping the kingdom from its rightful possessor. Religious as he was, when these conscientious scruples overpowered him he would think himself unworthy of the sacraments, and his abstinence shocked the thoroughly Italian formalism of the queen.[1]

Philip, humiliated by his disgrace, took to his bed and refused to stir, though he was in good health and ate well, sometimes too well. It was almost a political event when he consented to rise for half-an-hour in order that his room might be matted and hung afresh. He was roused, however, in October by the news that Louis XV. was attacked by small-pox and in serious danger. Montgon's services were

---

[1] This description of Philip's abdication is taken from the detailed account of N. Erizzo, the Venetian ambassador. According to other statements, the president of the council withheld the king's note until he could communicate with the queen.

again called into requisition. Courier after courier was despatched with letters to the plenipotentiaries, to Fleury and to Bourbon, empowering them to act in Philip's name. Other letters were intended for the Parliament of Paris, and a formal act revoking the renunciation of the French crown was included. Yet Philip was not without his scruples, and there exists a curious letter in which the king's difficulties are laid before the Pope.[1]

Notwithstanding these preparations the news of the French king's recovery was greeted with rejoicings, and Philip was shaved for the first time for eight months, and went to church and to the hunt. In spite of the doubtful relations between the Courts of Madrid and Vienna, Königsegg was still believed to retain much personal influence over the queen. Prince Eugene, feeling that the Spanish Alliance rested entirely upon the continuance of the queen's power, was instant in his entreaties to the marshal to lead her into more prudent courses. The dangers to which she was exposed are clearly reflected in his letters. He was sceptical as to the mutual regard between the queen and her step-son, which recent advices had described as " quite charming " ; he valued at their true worth the demonstrative manifestations of tenderness which she had lately lavished on the prince. Yet nothing, he believed, was so important as to win his affections and to quietly gain the attachment of his favourites, who would probably take the lead on a change of government. The king might die, or he might again resign when the queen least expected it. The prince, it was true, was said to have taken an oath not to accept the crown if his father abdicated, but it might not be in his power to keep his oath. " It is possible that the Cortes might oblige him to accept the crown on the pretext of public welfare, or that, tired of the government and the king's long illness, they would proclaim him regent during his father's life, when they once realise that there is no hope of complete recovery, for the nation naturally dislikes to see itself governed by a

---

[1] *Arch. Miss. Sc. Dip.*, 1880, p. 123 ; also Compte Rendu, *De l'Acad. Sc. Mor. et Pol.*, Dec. 18, 1886, April, 1887.

king admitted to be idiotic, and a queen who has never
shown anything but contempt for the natives, who is not the
mother of the heir-apparent, and who is generally supposed
to sacrifice the interests of the monarchy to those of herself
and her children. The extraordinary gathering of the
grandees on the prince's return, their eagerness to pay court
to him, and the joy which the public has shown at his reappearance, are so many proofs of their desire to see him at
the head of the government, and this will increase as he
approaches his majority, owing to the idea which the
Spaniards have as to his dislike for foreigners, and to their
hopes of having a larger share in the government than they
have at present." [1]   The moral drawn by Prince Eugene was
that the queen should not be lulled to sleep by the king's
oaths, nor by the prince's natural timidity, which might be
overcome by years or by persuasion. It was essential to win
the prince, to manufacture a party among the grandees, to
show more consideration for the nation, and to dismiss the
ministers whom it regarded as the authors of the present
disorder. Friendship once established between the queen
and the prince, there would be more hope of internal peace
and order during Philip's life, the queen need fear no unpleasant reaction on his death, she might even hope to retain
a portion of her authority.

Elisabeth had taken advantage of the king's partial
recovery to resign her functions as regent, but Philip
was perfectly incapable of business, and the uncertainty led
to much disorder, which was increased by the opposition of
Patiño and Castelar to Orendayn. The secretaries of the
departments went each his own way. Königsegg was urged
to press upon the queen some plan for increasing the
efficiency of the government, and for this purpose it was
necessary that she should take a more direct part. Under
the present system, Prince Eugene complained, the king
would always be in debt, even if he had twenty Indies, and
his reputation would fall in foreign as it had already fallen

---

[1] Von Arneth, *Prinz Eugen*, iii. 560.

in home affairs. " The wretched administration of finance, the want of the necessary supplies for the siege of Gibraltar, the irregularity in the payment of the troops, the household and the law officers, the failure of our subsidies, the interest which the queen has to continue these, in order to enable the emperor to advance her children, the hatred of the nation for Patiño . . . all these are so many reasons which may be suggested to his prejudice. . . . The queen could not fail to recognise their importance, and clever as she is, she must also realise that matters cannot continue on their present footing of inactivity, and that one of two alternatives is necessary : either she must induce the king, if his health admits, to give his time to State affairs . . . or she must make him give her wider authority to do the work herself."[1]

It is significant that Prince Eugene's advice remained without effect. The queen neither reassumed the regency, nor did she cultivate the Prince of Asturias and his friends, nor did she dismiss Patiño. Königsegg had failed to serve her ends, and he, too, must be laid aside, as Alberoni and as Ripperdá. Patiño was the new tool ready to her hand. Between the lines of Prince Eugene's diatribe on Spanish finance it could be read that Patiño refused to furnish the imperial subsidies even after the arrival of the galleons. This was no longer a cause for incontinent dismissal. Yet it is fair to Prince Eugene to add that the French ambassador had reported that, under the queen's direct superintendence, more work was done in a month than had been previously done in a year. The scheme of centralisation was to be carried out, though not according to the wishes of the Viennese Government, for the central bureau was to be Patiño's.

At the beginning of 1729 the Court quitted Madrid and its neighbouring palaces, Aranjuez and S. Ildefonso, and did not return until the spring of 1733. This long absence brought additional unpopularity upon Elisabeth. The expenses of the Court were increased, the administration

---

[1] Von Arneth, *Prinz Eugen*, iii. 559.

deranged, and Madrid, which had no means of existence
but the Court, became, according to the Venetian envoy,
"little less than a corpse". But for this, he added, the
queen cared little as long as she could attain her ends.[1] A
motive was attributed to every act of Elisabeth Farnese,
and it was believed that her aim was to make the king's
abdication more difficult by removing him from the neighbourhood of the Council of Castille. It is certain that she
wished to interest and amuse her husband and possibly
herself. The celebrated sights of Spain lay in the south,
and the south was also the centre of the naval activity
which was now exciting much attention. The immediate
object of the journey was, however, the double marriage
between the houses of Spain and Portugal. That of the
infanta had been delayed for a year, and there had been
repeated rumours that she was destined for the young
Czar of Russia. The Court left Madrid on January 7, with
the snow falling heavily, and on the 16th it arrived at
Badajoz. Spain was an uncomfortable country, and Badajoz
not its most comfortable town. No preparations had been
made, and the marriage party shivered over brasiers.
Meanwhile the Portuguese Court arrived at the frontier town
of Elvas.[2] On the bridge over the Caya, which divided the two
kingdoms, a temporary palace was erected, with a spacious
hall and two ante-chambers. In the middle was a long
table, with four chairs on either side reserved for the king,
queen, prince, and princess of their respective nations.
Over one door were the arms of Spain, over the other, those
of Portugal. If the Spanish side of the table were covered
with cloth of silver, trimmed with silver fringe, the Portuguese was adorned with crimson velvet, embroidered with
gold. Spaniards, however, noticed with pride that means
had been taken on their side alone to slip a carpet beneath their monarchs' feet. The kings and queens entered
the hall precisely at the same moment from opposite sides,

[1] N. Erizzo, 1730.

[2] An account of this wedding by an eye-witness may be found in the
Historical Register for 1729.

and advanced to the table step for step. After the deeds were signed, the princesses were interchanged. It was noticed that Ferdinand could not restrain his emotion at the ugliness of his bride. She was in fact, said Noailles in after years, so plain that it was painful to look at her. Fortunately, plain women are occasionally pleasant, and the Portuguese princess soon won all hearts, and made the happiness of her husband's life. Her plainness was redeemed by the beauty of her manners, and the knowledge of six languages. At the final parting both young girls were removed with difficulty, and with many tears from their parents' sides. The marriages were followed by some days of mutual entertainment, varied by fireworks and concerts. The Spanish nobles outshone the Portuguese in the value of their jewels, but their clothes were far inferior, for the king refused to suspend the sumptuary law of his own creation against the wearing of gold and silver lace. The superior smartness of the Spanish troops compensated in some measure for the sombre simplicity of the grandees.

On January 27 the Court left Badajoz for Seville, and this town became their headquarters until their return to Madrid. The king and queen, however, made frequent excursions, dropping down the river to San Lucar, stopping for a day's hunting on the way, and then passing by land to Cadiz. Here they paid their first visit in February; they sailed about the harbour in a magnificent gondola presented by the town, visited the forts and arsenals, and saw the launch of the " Hercules," a seventy-gun ship, the first product of the new arsenal at Puntal. Like the modern tourist they returned to Seville for the pageants of Holy Week and Easter. The pretty and clean little town of S. Maria, opposite Cadiz, was a favourite haunt. Hence the king and queen inspected the equipment of a squadron on the arrival and departure of the American galleons. Patiño, Minister of Marine, was now much in fashion. Keene, on his return to Spain in 1728, had noticed with wonder the progress which had been made in the Spanish fleet. All the money which was not spent on furthering the queen's ambition was spent upon the fleet ; neither the subsidies paid to the emperor, nor the rags and tatters of the Spanish troops, nor the unpaid salaries of the Household and the Law Courts diverted Patiño from his expenditure.   The interest shown by the queen added a fresh impulse to the development of the naval and commercial enterprises of the minister.   Constant movement was necessary to divert the king from his craving to return to the solitude of S. Ildefonso.   Occasionally he was unpleasantly reminded of its existence.   The statuary appeared at Seville and requested to be paid.   Some money was found to satisfy his needs ; but he was ordered to return to his work and never to show his face again.   The king's amusements were simple.   When the Court was stationary he spent the day in fishing, and the evening in drawing with a pencil, for a pen was not allowed for fear he should sign a form of abdication.   So, says Villars, in his Italian campaign he had passed the day in shooting pigeons in the castle of Milan ; he was a man that never changed.   Unusually few persons were at this time admitted to the royal society.   Scotti had recovered favour and was entrusted with the management of the delicate Italian negotiations for which he was thought quite unfitted.   The queen's favourite attendant was a young Flemish lady named La Pellegrina, who was modest, disinterested, and extremely skilful in the dressing of the queen's hair.[1]   Court life in Spain was naturally dull ; there were none of the amusements and daily social interests of other Courts.   Its very respectability became a failing, because its members were from *ennui* forced into politics, or rather intrigue, and the very ladies'-maids and valets were affected by this passion.   Occasionally the flirtations of some Court lady, notably the Duchess of S. Pierre, would give occasion for lighter conversation.

The queen herself was in these days anxious and irritable —fearful with regard to her husband's health, and eagerly awaiting the couriers from Paris or Vienna.   It was dangerous

---

[1] Da Lezze and Montgon.

to contradict her, wrote Brancas; and, indeed, he was so complaisant that she made him grandee of Spain. She knew the weakness of her temper. " Speak to Patiño," she would say, " for I may not be mistress of myself if you talk to me." Occasionally the king would break in and tell the ambassador that if his Court did not keep its word he did not lack of friends; whereupon the queen cried out: " People always make out that it is I who am the scold— now just look at the king ". Relations with the Prince of Asturias were far from pleasant, and there is some probability in the story told in the scurrilous *Life of Isabella Farnesio*, that the prince was followed home by a crowd of the inhabitants of Seville amid rapturous acclamations, and that the queen was so jealous of his popularity that she forbade him to appear again in public. Elisabeth was equally jealous of the princess. The modesty and resignation of the latter, wrote the Venetian envoy Da Lezze, could not be overpraised. She made every effort to win the queen's affection, " but the complimentary remarks commonly heard on the princess were so many mortal wounds to the queen's sensitive heart ; and it is necessary to use the greatest delicacy and reserve in paying court to the princess, in order not to give supreme displeasure to the sovereign, who is in constant fear, though appearances are completely different ". Philip, who had loved Luis, had no affection for Ferdinand, and this it was said was the chief reason against his abdication. The nuncio constantly interviewed the king, and was believed to be endeavouring to satisfy his scruples on keeping the crown from his son. His fits of melancholy were so frequent that it was thought fortunate that the Council of Castile was at a distance, and also that the queen was with child, for his tenderness to her in that condition was extreme. Otherwise it seemed that she would hardly have time as queen to insist upon the introduction of Spanish garrisons in the Italian Duchies. Philip could only be roused by talk of war, and this was one of the reasons for the constant naval and military stir. The ships at Cadiz, wrote Consul Cayley, were only intended to make a show, and to make more of them they were anchored in line : the ships were strong, but clumsy and misshapen : the crews were the worst that were ever put on board. A serious mutiny had lately taken place on board the "Incendio"; the men it is said had forced the officers to pay their prize-money from the treasure which the ship was carrying. Cayley wondered that all crews did not do likewise, for the treatment of officers and men would scarce be believed in any other country.[1]

Early in 1730 a new diversion was found for Philip in a visit to Granada. The journey was interrupted at the petty town of Antiquera by an attack of influenza which confined the king and queen and prince to their quarters for four days.[2] At Granada the royal *cortège* passed through triumphal arches and along the stately avenue to the Moorish palace on the hill. Here the queen was lodged in apartments commanding the lovely view over the expanse of the Vega of Granada. The floor of her room was pierced with holes through which, it was said, in Moorish times perfumes had been injected,[3] and the walls were covered with Arabic inscriptions. Much time also was spent in the cool gardens of the Generalife. A feeble form of Moorish novel became the fashionable literature of the Court. The king and queen, however, soon wearied of the drive down the hill and through the town, and retired to a shooting box in an adjoining wood. The political situation was still exciting, and the road between Granada and Soto de Roma became a diplomatic promenade. Later in the summer the Court removed to Cazalla in the Sierra Morena. From these burn-

---

[1] Cayley was always severe upon Patiño's naval efforts. "Such ships, such seamen, such commanders were never seen upon the waters, unless sent by the same nation."—October 3, 1730. *R. O. S.*, 189.

[2] In the winter this malady had been prevalent throughout Europe, universal around Paris, and in London, killing eight hundred people in a week. In April, 1729, Liria found it raging in Russia, two-thirds of every family being attacked.

[3] This apparently corresponds to the chamber called Tocador de la Reina, but it would be an uncomfortably draughty boudoir to a convalescent from influenza.

ing mountains the king and queen were driven back to Seville, where the sight of the flota would be refreshing at least to Patiño's eyes. Here was received the news of the abdication of the old King of Sardinia, who had almost without warning driven away from the palace into private life with the lady of his heart. This action was represented to Philip as a proof of madness, and much use was made of the *mariage de conscience.* "I perceive," wrote Keene, "they have set it in such a light as will be far from tempting the king to follow his example, and they think they may safely speak against abdication, since he appears to be more fond of governing at present than at any other time, but, were it otherwise, the queen would easily turn this event to her advantage by working upon his pride to prevent him from taking his pattern from any other prince whatsoever." [1] It was believed at first that Vittorio Amedeo intended to retire to France and assume the government. Patiño remarked that he would be a worthy successor to Fleury in the matter of good faith. In the following year the Court was informed of the tragic sequel of the abdication. The old king was arrested by his son on a suspicion of a wish to resume the crown, and died in prison. On hearing this Philip was very silent, and his wife reminded him of her prophecy at the time of abdication. Patiño had to read in the royal presence a letter saying that it was a proper lesson for kings who had an inclination to abdicate, and should, therefore, be sent to Seville.

The constant change had the desired effect upon the king's health, though his habits became peculiar. Keene had never known him so well, and added that his way of life was a proof of the strength of his constitution. He had half killed the greater part of the Court by fatigue, and only the queen could support the hours which he kept. He supped usually at 3 a.m., and went to bed at 5, rising to hear Mass at 3 p.m. Shortly afterwards he would retire at 10 a.m., and rise at 5 p.m. This occasioned a little friction

---

[1] Keene to Newcastle, Sept. 28, 1730. *R. O. S.*, 189.

with the queen, who had scruples as to the hour of Mass, but in married life bad habits are rapidly contagious, and the queen continued these practices for twenty years after her husband's death. Patiño and Keene were, perhaps, the chief sufferers. "Patiño, who is charged with the whole of this unwieldy, ill-regulated monarchy, loses five or six hours every day or night (for we have no distinction) in base attendance on the palace, and I as many in looking after him."[1]

Ordinary business was conducted in the morning, when the Prince of Asturias attended the Despacho. This meeting was, however, a pure form, the secretary read a few reports, and in a few minutes business was concluded. Affairs in which Elisabeth was interested were only produced in the prince's absence, and after midnight, Patiño generally attended, and stayed till supper, at 3 or 4 a.m.[2]

The best proof of the king's health was that he would talk freely of the scruples which led to his abdication, and he resented strongly the current reports in France that he was governed by his queen. Yet this government was a fact that now seemed likely to outlive him. "According to my little lights," wrote Keene, "I can see no reason to doubt, in the common course of things, of the government continuing in the same hands for many years to come, to which I beg leave to add that the queen has the fairest possible prospect of fixing her power here even after the death or abdication of the king, from the delicacy of the prince's constitution, and from the little appearance there is of his ever having issue, of which they that are nighest him are very apprehensive." The childlessness of the sons of Philip's first marriage was a source of genuine grief to all true Spaniards. No wonder that a nervous opposition believed or invented stories of the malpractices of Elisabeth's Italian nurse and doctor.

---

[1] Keene, Nov. 25, 1731. *R. O. S.*, 197. Business in Spain was conducted under difficulties, but Keene never lost his sense of humour. "I have been obliged to keep Bineham (the messenger) until this evening, because Patiño's chief secretary had not finished his siesta. I suppose you know that a siesta is a small nap of about six hours after dinner."—Aug. 5, 1730. *R. O. S.*, 189.

[2] A. da Lezze, 1733.

CHAPTER XV.

1732.

DON CARLOS IN ITALY—THREATENED RUPTURE WITH THE EMPEROR — THE EXPEDITION TO ORAN — DIPLOMATIC STRUGGLE BETWEEN ENGLAND AND FRANCE—PROSPECTS OF ALLIANCE BETWEEN SPAIN AND FRANCE—COMMERCIAL DISPUTES WITH ENGLAND—THE COMMISSION OF CLAIMS —PHILIP'S MALADY.

THE year 1732 opened brightly for the royal household. The queen was happy at her hardly-earned success. The king had never been in better health. Don Carlos, indeed, had been attacked by small-pox shortly after his arrival in Italy; but it was reported to be of the "right sort," and it caused but a slight delay in his progress through his present and future dominions. The very festivities with which he was greeted seemed to improve his prospects. The grand duke, by way of welcome to his heir, "had eat or drunk too much, and it was thought that he would be carried off by an indigestion ".[1]

The English Government was in high favour. Philip addressed stringent orders to the colonial governors to discourage depredations. In France there was no outward manifestation of ill-will. The year promised to be happily uneventful; and this promise was so far fulfilled that the peace of Europe was not actually broken. Yet it was within these twelve months that the plans were maturing which resulted in half-a-century of war, and it was probably but the accident of Philip's health which saved the reputation of the year.

[1] Keene to Newcastle, April 26, 1732. *R. O. S.*, 202.

It was in Italy that sunshine was first clouded. Don Carlos was not prudent, the imperial officials were not conciliatory, and the queen's agent, Monteleone, was not sufficiently stiff-backed. As Don Carlos was already in possession of Parma, Spanish garrisons were no longer necessary as a security for his succession, while the Grand Duke of Tuscany was unwilling that the whole force of 6000 should be quartered on his territories. Monteleone without instructions acceded to a declaration that no troops which were or had been in Spanish service should enter Parma or Piacenza, that the overplus of 6000 men should be dismissed at once, that the said 6000 should be reduced to 3000, and that the King of Spain should formally oppose the pretensions of the Pope. The king and queen disavowed Monteleone's declaration and protested that they would never reduce the garrisons. On the Austrian side Count Stampa's aggressive diplomatic measures were backed by rude threats from Marshal Daun. These menaces struck deep, wrote Keene, and caused more heartburnings than could be well imagined; he tried in vain to mitigate the queen, showing that they were the effect of the marshal's vivacity, and not the consequence of orders from Vienna.

In this state of tension much importance was attached to the powerful armament which was being collected in the eastern ports of Spain. It seemed a menace to the peace of Europe, and Keene warmly commented on so injudicious a measure. He could get no clearer answer from Patiño than that he was minister not master, that several of such enterprises had been begun and laid aside, and this would be another of them. Patiño made light of the whole affair, giving positive assurances that it was not directed against any European power.

The fears which this armament aroused illustrate the critical condition of Europe and the universal nervousness of its powers. Keene believed that its pretext was an attack upon Oran, which would enable Patiño to draw the proceeds of the Cruzada which the inquisitor-general obstinately refused to let him handle. He imagined also that it was immediately due to Daun's threats, and was a bravado to show Europe that Philip could support his garrisons in Tuscany; if terms were not arranged they would be kept under arms until the Grand Duke's death, and then conveyed to Italy; meanwhile an attack on Oran was probable, and its conquest would place Spain in a position to annoy Gibraltar.

The Court of Vienna feared more immediate hostilities. It was reported that six ships being fitted out at Cadiz were intended as a present for Don Carlos. Yet more nervous was the Sardinian envoy, who asked if the fleet was designed against his master's dominions. He was prepared to advise his king to take the offensive and attack Don Carlos in Italy. The resemblance of this mysterious armament to that of Alberoni led, not unnaturally, to the belief that Sardinia might be the first object of attack. The queen, it was believed, was eager to place a royal crown upon her son's head, and that of Sardinia could doubtless be obtained at the lowest cost. The wild ideas which she had already entertained with regard to the crown of Poland give some substance to this idea.

In Spain itself the secret was well kept. Keene's spies confessed that they were in the dark. The secretary's clerks received counter orders to copy with the orders, and they did not know which documents were despatched. The captains of the six suspected ships each received separate instructions to be opened only at a given latitude. Keene thought that the queen and Patiño would be extremely mortified to find themselves engaged farther than they expected, for the queen had much to lose; and her minister would find it hard to provide means for a campaign however short. "But the king," he added, "is of such a martial disposition that he is willing to make war upon his friends or foes." [1]

On June 15 the dreaded armament set sail for Africa. Even at the last moment Philip's proclamation caused fresh

---

[1] Keene to Newcastle, May 14, 1732. *R. O. S.*, 202.

T

consternation. He called for the prayers of the nation to further his endeavour to recover territories now separated from the Catholic Church. The nervous Protestantism of the English Government foresaw from this an attempt upon Gibraltar and Port Mahon ; and, in reply to its remonstrances, it was satirically pointed out that the population of these towns had not withdrawn from the faith. The land forces consisted of 27,000 men, besides numerous volunteers, including many nobles of high rank. They were sufficient, wrote Keene, to take two Orans and twenty Mazalquivirs. After a slight skirmish, Oran was evacuated. The Bey, who had taken it in 1707, and who passed by the formidable name of Don Whiskerando, decamped in the night with 200 camels laden with his wealth. His house was found furnished with carpets and mirrors of the largest size, with gold frames. The seraglio was still scented with the rose water and perfumes of the ladies. The tents were lined with crimson damask—in short, the defenders seemed to be Persians rather than Moors. The fortifications were in such good order that, if it had been known, the Spaniards would probably not have attacked ; but the powder was Dutch, and very bad.

The dean and chapter at Seville had dressed the Giralda tower with fireworks, ready for the match. The king, who was the sole author of the project, was jubilant. "There is scarce a Spaniard," wrote Keene, " who does not think himself half way to his salvation by the merits of this conquest." [1] True Spaniards desired that the success should be followed up by an attack upon Algiers. Keene also pressed this course upon Patiño ; it would be a blessing, he urged, to the whole Mediterranean. Patiño was astute enough to guess his motives, and his bad humour at this time was attributed to the king's martial mania. The Moors of Algiers were of a very different temper to those of Oran. " If they would but attack Algiers, they would lose so many of their men that they would be cooled and quieted." [2]

---

[1] Keene to Delafaye, July 4, 1732.   *R. O. S.,* 203.   [2] *Ibid.*

After some short operations in the open country the bulk of the troops and their general, Montemar, returned. Santa Cruz was left in command at Oran. News became scarce, and the situation was anxious. Brilliant successes were duly registered, but the intelligence was accompanied by demands for reinforcements. A great nobleman, the Duke of S. Blas, was surprised and killed in a sortie. The Moors blockaded not only Oran but Ceuta. Warlike levies from Algiers and trained troops from Constantinople appeared upon the field. At last the news arrived that Santa Cruz had gained a brilliant victory, but at the cost of his own life. The interest of the war died out as the truth became generally known. The pressure on the Spanish fortresses was indeed relieved, but it was due to dynastic differences in Morocco. The brilliancy of this campaign has been extolled by Spanish historians as by the governmental publications of the day. Bells were rung and cannon fired to rouse the king from his melancholy seclusion. But from private sources unpleasant facts gradually came to the surface. Bragadin in 1725 had reported that Spain lacked generals, and this deficiency had not yet been supplied. If the Moors had had as much sense as courage, the Spaniards would have fared badly. The commissariat was defective, and the troops perished of hunger and thirst. Montemar's partiality for native Spaniards nearly caused a mutiny among the foreign regiments. The generals quarrelled in his presence. The management was so poor that the Sardinian ambassador regained his nerve, and declared that he should not fear the whole Spanish army, let them attack when they would. In October Oran had been in great distress, and soldiers in large numbers deserted to the Moors. It transpired that on the occasion of the death of Santa Cruz the garrison was only saved by the accidental arrival of fresh troops from Spain. "Some of the regiments flung down their arms, and Santa Cruz got himself killed out of spite and courage when he could not rally them . . . their own officers tell me the greater part of the army is struck with a panic

whenever the Moors approach them." [1]   The loss in this so-
called victory amounted to four guns and three thousand
men.   Keene, overworked and underpaid, was apt at times
to take the darker side, but his reports are confirmed by
Villars, who had recommended that officers should be procured who had fought the Turks in Hungary, for these
nations frequently feigned flight, and were dangerous if in-
cautiously pursued.   To Elisabeth the loss of Santa Cruz
was irreparable.   He was probably the one Spaniard for
whom she had a genuine affection.   She had been attracted
from the first by his rough humour and kindly devotion.
Honest as he was in the expression of his feelings, he had
shown no dislike for the Italian stranger.   He shared with
her a strong aversion to all things French, and was thus
regarded as a staunch friend of England.   Both Keene and
the Duke of Newcastle considered his death to be a grave
political misfortune.   His bravery was conspicuous even
among Spaniards.   On his arrival at Oran Montemar had
forcibly confined him to his ship to save his life, for he
tried to go into action with a gangrened leg.   Of the
social trio which made what little life there was amid the
gloomy monotony of the Court, the Duke of Arco alone
remained.   Liria was never to return ; after leaving Vienna
for Paris he took part in the Neapolitan campaign, and
ended his butterfly existence in the more sunny society of
Naples. [2]

To Europe at large this African expedition was of no
little moment.   There is small doubt that it delayed the
Franco-Spanish alliance, and for this reason Fleury and
Villars had opposed it.   But for this the Family Compact
which was secretly formulated in the following year, and
found open expression at a later date, might have both been
framed and executed in 1732.   The war would have been
fought on its true issues, and not on the pretext of the

---

[1] Keene to Newcastle, Dec. 12, 1732. *R. O. S.*, 203.

[2] He died of consumption on June 2, 1738, at the age of forty-three. His
Russian mission had a curious issue. He went to induce the Czar to march
40,000 men to the assistance of the emperor, he stayed in order to detain them.

Polish succession, and in such a war England must have played a part.

The year had indeed passed in a diplomatic struggle between France and England, the result of which has left deep traces upon the history of the eighteenth century. The chief combatants were Keene and Rothembourg, but the former was fighting at a disadvantage, for it was rarely that he could obtain an audience, whereas Rothembourg as *ministre de famille* had peculiar privileges. By the end of the year the English minister was practically beaten, and it was long before he had his revenge.

The efforts of the French Government were directed fully as much against England as against the emperor. It hoped to tempt the queen by prospects of further acquisitions in Italy, and Patiño by the opportunity of withdrawing from the English their commercial privileges. The king's favour could always be secured by his love for France and his mania for military glory, which was thwarted by the English alliance, founded, as it was, on a policy of peace. In the early days of January Rothembourg sounded Patiño as to the further views of Don Carlos. Patiño replied coldly that his Highness thought of nothing but hunting, and that it was the interest of Spain that the cadet's establishment should be as independent of the monarchy as could be. He afterwards confided to Keene that, as the French minister could not set Spain at variance with England, he would endeavour to sow discord with the emperor.

Everything promised well for the maintenance of the Anglo-Spanish friendship. Castelar at Paris had become scrupulously civil to Lord Waldegrave. Patiño asseverated that there were no secret negotiations with the Court of Versailles. Rothembourg saw little of the royal family. His despatches for some months were understood to turn upon the caprices of the Court, the wretched condition of the administration, the unprofitableness of Spanish alliance, the contradictory composition of the king's character, the queen's prejudice against France, and the falseness of the ministers. The French Government felt so little hope of success in face of the opposition of the queen and Patiño, that it even considered the advisability of Philip's abdication and engaged in active intrigues with the malcontent party which was gathering round the heir. Villars is almost silent as to the early months of 1732, but Keene's despatch of February 23 portrays the possibilities of the present and the future.

"The hope that France may have of gaining a superiority at this Court if the king should abdicate seems to be as little founded as that abdication itself. . . . It is true they would remove the inveterate enemy to the present (French) ministry, the queen, out of the way, but would lose the king, who always has his country at heart, and a natural desire to live well with it, and I much doubt if they would find the same principles in the prince, he being entirely a Spaniard and of a temper to be easy himself and to let others be so too, without giving in to any projects of conquest, which I take it must always be the foundation of a strict alliance between France and this crown. He is very fond of the princess, who knows how to humour him, and will necessarily have a great influence whenever the government devolves upon him."[1] Rothembourg, with a view to the future influence of the princess, was extremely civil to the Portuguese ambassador, but Keene saw no probability of Philip's abdication, nor of his death, notwithstanding his irregular treatment of himself. It was certain, he said, that there was scarce a Spaniard who did not desire his abdication, but equally certain that not one would dare take a step towards it. "If I could give your Grace the character of the adherents of the prince (who is too submissive to his father ever to put himself at the head of a party) the bare knowledge of them would show that the queen has nothing to apprehend from that quarter, for either they are already gained into her interests, or are too inconsiderable to deserve her attention."[2]

The relations between the Bourbon Courts became to all

---

[1] Keene to Newcastle, Feb. 23, 1732. *R. O. S.*, 202.   [2] *Ibid.*

appearance unfriendly. The French ministry was no longer
on good terms with Castelar, and laid the blame of the mis-
understanding upon Patiño. Castelar rejoined that it was
Rothembourg's fault, for he held secret assemblies at his
house to revile the Spanish Government, and had not spared
the king and queen. It was thought that the French
ministry was trying to force a quarrel in order to gain an
opportunity for a full explanation, which might lead to a better
understanding. The association of Chauvelin with Fleury
at the head of the French Government increased mistrust.
The Spanish Court was reported to have so poor an opinion
of the talents of the Most Christian King that it believed
that no minister would be agreeable who did not indulge his
indolence, and such an one Chauvelin was very wrongly
suspected to be. He was, therefore, unfit to promote
an alliance which could only rest on conquest at the
emperor's expense. Patiño called Chauvelin's promotion
the Pragmatic Sanction of Fleury's ministry, and thought it
to be fully as unstable as the emperor's family arrangements.

Rothembourg meanwhile made desperate efforts to win
Patiño by representing the manifest ruin which the Assiento
Treaty inflicted upon Spanish trade, adding that, had he been
present, he would never have consented to the Treaty of
Seville. Patiño replied that he failed to understand French
policy ; before the treaty they had threatened Spain if she
would not confirm the privileges granted to England by
previous treaties ; now they were uneasy because Spain
continued these privileges when they themselves were
pledged to it, and were resolved to cultivate the friendship
of England. On July 9 Keene wrote that there was no
change in the relations of France and Spain, but that he
was not lulled into security, for his knowledge of Philip's
character made him believe that his success at Oran would
press him farther. In August he was more uneasy. News
came from Vienna that France was intriguing with the
prince, and the rumour was revived that Elisabeth designed
a partition of the monarchy in favour of her children. It
was stated that in one of Philip's fits of melancholia in 1727

she persuaded him to make a codicil granting to Carlos the succession to the crown of Aragon. This was in accordance with the will of Ferdinand the Catholic, which ordained such a division should any of his successors leave two sons. The queen had endeavoured, it was said, to obtain the Pope's sanction to this codicil. The old King of Sardinia got tidings of this design and informed the French Court, which then declared that it would never suffer the lawful heir of the Spanish Bourbons to be deprived of his inheritance. It is to a revival of this rumour that Keene's letter of August 19[1] refers. "As to the prince's faction, they seem at Vienna to give it too much honour and make it too considerable, for he gives himself but little trouble about public affairs, and those about him are but people of mean capacity but great timidity, and dare not enter into any engagements with a foreign power to prevent the queen's partiality in favour of her own family; neither do I think they have the least reason to apprehend her partiality so far as to attempt a splitting of the monarchy, for the king would never consent, nor the nation, brow-beaten as it is, submit to such a partition, so that there seems to be no actual union between this faction and France, nor any necessity for it to preserve the inheritance whole to the heir-presumptive." Keene believed that Ferdinand's popularity was due to the distaste which he showed to all foreigners alike, French as well as others; he could not think that a person of Elisabeth's temper would forget the usage which she had met from France, where she knew that she was hated for keeping Philip from giving a loose to his affections for his nation and family; she was unlikely, therefore, to trust her interests to French counsels. He was inclined to believe that her views and hopes were directed to Vienna, and that though she was endeavouring to vex the emperor into the best bargain she could get, it was neither her intention nor her interest to bring matters to an extremity unless she could flatter herself that England would take part in the

[1] *R. O. S.*, 203.

quarrel. Yet the ambassador felt bound to confess that, though Rothembourg still railed at the Court as much as ever, his audiences were becoming constant, and those who knew him privately reported that he had certainly some reason for content. The irritation of the Court against the emperor, which seemed without sufficient motive, increased Keene's suspicions, but Patiño assured him that he might be perfectly easy ; the alliance with England was the only one which they had, and his Court was resolved not to enter into any engagements without first communicating them to his Britannic Majesty.

The summary of Rothembourg's despatches, imbedded in the memoirs of Villars, give a very different aspect to the situation. On June 17 the French Government was informed that of the whole Court of Seville the queen alone was opposed to France. Two days later news arrived that the king and queen, feeling that the emperor would never allow Spain to set foot in Italy without a guarantee for the Pragmatic Sanction, were pressing for a secret treaty with France. Villars, representing the war party in the French Council, strongly advocated the alliance. His speech was an epitome of coming history. "If we unite with Spain it is clear that we ruin the commerce of England in two years, while our own will be more flourishing than ever. The German States and Sardinia, alarmed by the Treaty of Vienna, only want support to abandon the emperor. This support can only be France, but it is essential that she show some firmness. If all Europe is persuaded that France, in spite of her true interests, is opposed to any sort of war, she will be abandoned by all the world."

Chauvelin approved, and Fleury wavered. Castelar threw fuel on the flame ; he reported that the English were ridiculing Fleury, saying that they had deceived him all round, that the skill of their agents had prevented both the union of France and the emperor, and of France and Spain, that the Treaty of Seville had only been a trick to win the emperor ; Spain must now be induced to accede to the Treaty of Vienna ; France would then be isolated, and it mattered not whether she were friend or foe.

On July 1 the project of an alliance reached Castelar from the King of Spain. In August Spain was pressing the French Government to war against the emperor. On September 7 Chauvelin read to the Council the articles of an offensive treaty, containing a project for a double marriage between the two Bourbon houses. At the end of the month Rothembourg wrote that the king and queen, and all the country, eagerly desired the completion of the treaty. For this rapid change of policy there were some tolerably definite reasons apart from the constant tendency to drift towards a family alliance. Elisabeth, it is true, disliked France, and detested Fleury, but it was chiefly because the cardinal had dissuaded French support for her dynastic aims in Italy.

The hints let drop early in the year as to the possibility of further acquisitions had not fallen upon deaf ears. It appeared, moreover, that French assistance might be necessary even to secure Don Carlos in the rights conceded by treaty. Spain had accepted the article of the second Treaty of Vienna relating to the Italian Duchies, but had never acceded to the treaty in its entirety. Philip had refused to guarantee afresh the Pragmatic Sanction. It was believed, however, that this refusal was due to a wish to obtain a higher price. Negotiations were carried on between the Courts of Vienna and Seville throughout a great portion of the year. The English Government strove to facilitate a friendly understanding, and Robinson, its minister at Vienna, neglected no means of smoothing the way. Occasionally negotiations seem to have been carried on behind the back of the mediatory power. Patiño informed Keene that one Bolognesa, a banker, who had come to Madrid avowedly on a mere professional mission, had made diplomatic approaches much in the fashion of Ripperdá. These first suggestions had been supported by insinuations from the highest quarters at Vienna. English mediation was represented as a burden to both parties;

mutual interests could be better secured by a separate alliance. "Nothing," added Patiño, "can better prove how useful our alliance is to each other than to see the uneasiness which it causes both to Germany and France."[1] Both queen and emperor were possibly well disposed towards such a separate treaty. As late as September, Fleury told Villars of a rumoured offensive and defensive alliance between Spain and the emperor, and Villars replied that Castelar's expressions caused him to fear that it would be concluded, if the French were not. Patiño, no doubt, did his utmost to thwart the project, but the aggressive attitude of Don Carlos probably secured its failure.

In Italy, bickerings had never ceased. Don Carlos received the homage of the Florentines under the title of hereditary grand prince. He peremptorily demanded the curtailment of his minority in Parma; and his mother pressed his claims with all her usual warmth. The emperor disallowed the title, refused to enter into any engagements as to the minority, and declined to grant investiture of Parma until the fees were paid. Keene represented that Don Carlos' pretensions had the appearance of an attempt to shake off imperial suzerainty, and that the success of the great work which England had done for Spain was endangered. Patiño thought the infant's action foolish, and threw the blame upon De la Paz, who, to please the queen, compiled treatises to prove that the emperor had no right of interference until the Grand Duke's death. He represented that his Court had serious fears for the succession of Tuscany, that the king was full of glory, and that if the emperor would not let him live in peace, he should have none himself.[2]

The Spanish nation cared nothing for Don Carlos and his titles, but it, too, was approaching the same goal, though by a different track. Commercial disputes with England had again become acute. Patiño encouraged the formation of a Philippine Company with the object of increasing the

---

[1] Keene to Newcastle, Aug. 22, 1732. *R. O. S.*, 203.
[2] Keene to Newcastle, April 16, 1732. *Ibid.*, 202.

import and export duties at Cadiz, of which the great Acapulco ship, which sailed direct from Manilla, deprived the crown. The English and Dutch ministers complained that this company would, in contravention of treaties, pour into Europe the Indian and Chinese goods, of which the Maritime Powers enjoyed the monopoly. Patiño rejoined that his only object was to increase the duties at Cadiz, and that the king had a right to communication with his own colonies, and the passage to the Philippines by the South Seas could not be called such.

Keene and Vandermeer both seem to have thought their Governments ill-judged in pressing their objections. The company, they urged, would meet with strong opposition in the Philippines ; the promoters were men of straw ; no companies could succeed in Spain, for the natives were too extravagant to have capital to invest, and the Government was too arbitrary in its financial measures to allow foreigners to invest with any safety. It was, in fact, only out of pique at the interference of the Maritime Powers that the company was ultimately floated, and the charter granted.

With infinite patience, Keene had partly led and partly driven the Spaniards to open the commission for the consideration of claims. He was soon anxious that it should be closed again. What probability was there, he asked, of success in a commission where both parties were resolved to be always in the right ? . . . " all Europe stuck to its pretensions in the minutest affairs, and Spain more than any one ".[1] On the other hand, the English claims were frequently preposterous. " I am almost blind with poking into old autos ; one's understanding ought to suffer as well as one's eyesight in reading such stuff; besides the greatest part of them are imperfect, and I defy Doctors' Commons in the lump to comprehend and set them in a proper light. They are the sweepings of old escritoires and counting houses, which would never have seen the sunshine if his Majesty's goodness and desire to satisfy his subjects had not paid the expenses

---

[1] Keene to Delafaye, Sept. 23, 1732. *R. O. S.*, 205.

of the legalisation, as it is called. In short, never was there such a heap of mangled confusion. We shall be laughed at by our adversaries ; for example, no man in his senses can ask for reparation for a quarter-deck blown up in defence of his ship attacked by a Spanish privateer in open war. Yet one Mr. Chitty has done it in the most formal manner, and the support of this notable claim is an ill-spelled letter from the captain, who gives an account of his having beat the privateer and got away frem her. *Ex pede Herculem.* But we shall have this advantage, that merchants and Parliament men will see with their own eyes here how loud the drum has been beat in England by passion and malicious representation. I don't excuse Spain, but *Fiat Justitia et ruat mundus.* The Spaniards have been silent, but you will soon see that it is not for want of matter to produce against us." [1]

Irritation was increased precisely at the critical moment by the news that Admiral Stewart had taken a *guarda-costa*, and this was followed by intelligence that the " Solway " had, by way of reprisal, carried off a Spanish register ship from Campeachy Bay. [2] Keene regarded these violent measures as a great misfortune. Since he had known the country nothing had caused so great a spite. The governors of Spanish America were asking whether Spain were at war with England or no. The royal pride was stung to the quick. They had, said Keene, so little regard for their subjects' property that a hundred of their ships might be sunk without inquiry, as long as his Catholic Majesty's honour and protective licence were not meddled with : when English merchantmen were taken the Spaniards swore that the captors were pirates, but if these were captured they were *guarda-costas:* the French managed their trade better ; as long as it was profitable they stood by their accidents, and did not grumble about details. " Our demolishing *guarda-costas*

---

[1] Keene to Delafaye, April 11, 1732. *R. O. S.*, 202.

[2] The " Solway " was constantly *en evidence.* In the war of Jenkins' Ear she was captured by the Spaniards, and was then gallantly cut out by a small English privateer.

make a terrible stir here, for they are represented to be the king's ships that Admiral Stewart has taken, and not privateers. It is certainly high time to put a stop to that play, but take care of the 'Royal Carolina'[1] when you begin upon reprisals, for here we do what we think proper without consulting treaties till the work is over, and then we set about discussing to prove what we have done to be agreeable to treaties, and when we cannot make it out we content ourselves with swearing it is so. . . . But France, you see by Mr. Stewart's letter, can hold its tongue as long as she finds a trade that overbalances the ships she loses by the *guarda-costas*, while we cannot make up our accounts in the same way, though we are greater gainers."[2]

The South Sea directors also made a great mistake, in Keene's belief, in refusing to pay the duties owing to Spain from 1731, on pretence of an outstanding debt; payment would make a distasteful trade a little more palatable to the Spaniards, and if the trade were worth keeping, the sum demanded was not great. More reprehensible, however, was the English press, which, with an enterprise worthy of modern days, did its best to precipitate a rupture by representation and misrepresentation. At length, in the fulness of his heart, poor Keene broke out : "For God's sake, M. Delafaye, as long as we have a mind to be at peace with this country, let us avoid doing the business of France as much as we can. They are here *aux écoutes*, and are always ready with a *Vous avez raison, nous vous soutiendrons*."[3]

The business of France was already done, for on the day after Keene wrote this letter, Chauvelin read to the French Council the articles of the treaty with Spain.

Spanish irritation against England was yet further excited by the discovery of English cannon at Oran, and by the news that powder was conveyed from Gibraltar to the Moors besieging Ceuta. General Sabine engaged to do his uttermost to stop this nefarious traffic, but in Spain

---

[1] The South Sea ship.

[2] Keene to Delafaye, Aug. 19, 1732. *R. O. S.*, 203.

[3] Keene to Delafaye, Sept. 6, 1732. *Ibid.*

conclusions were drawn as to the demerits of a democratic Government that could not control its subjects. Thus it was not unnatural that the exasperation of the Spanish people against England was developing side by side with that of the queen against the emperor. An alliance with France under these circumstances must be both anti-English and anti-Austrian. Keene fully realised this; he had been outwitted, but not for long. Patiño, at the end of August, assured him that there was no alliance, but was silent when asked if France had not made proposals. France, the English envoy believed, engaged to assist Spain in the direct trade with the Philippines, and to guarantee the succession of Tuscany; she held out hopes of a future partition of Italy; in return, the Spaniards were expected to oppose the execution of the Pragmatic Sanction.

There is little doubt that by the end of September war was imminent. That it was deferred was due partly to reverses in Africa, partly to Patiño's resolution to cling to the English alliance, and so gain time to foster the Spanish marine. But the main cause for delay was unquestionably the sudden change in Philip's health. This had until lately been particularly good, notwithstanding that he had not been to bed for nearly three years, and that he never changed his clothes for at least nineteen months. He was excited by the African expedition, and was very jealous of his authority. It was impossible to see the queen alone, and she was obliged to avoid the slightest appearance of sharing her husband's power.

In August, however, Philip suddenly took to his bed, refusing to get up even to have it made. The queen was often found in tears, and a return to Madrid was discussed as the sole means of getting the king out of bed. Patiño tried to conceal his condition by the pretence of a sore upon his hip which hurt him when up and dressed. Throughout September Philip suffered from an acute attack of melancholia; he would speak to no one but menial servants. In October his digestion was dangerously deranged, and it was

feared that the feverish symptoms would attack his head
owing to the thickness of his hair, which had not been cut
for some years. The doctors thought that nothing but an
emetic could save him. But how to persuade him to such a
step? The Prince of Asturias was at last charged with the
commission, and left alone with the king for two hours.
In the most moving manner, after an abundance of tears on
both sides, he prevailed upon the king to let his hair be cut,
to change the linen which he had worn since his illness,
and obtained a promise that he would take an emetic. The
king allowed himself to be shaved, and the emetic was
attended with all the benefit that could be expected. The
influence of the prince was supposed to point to the decline
of that of the queen, but Keene thought the prince too
docile to oppose her. "I believe, indeed, she would
willingly have avoided this recourse to the prince, but the
king may be too long accustomed to the queen's tears to be
moved by them, and as those of the prince were new, they
could not well fail to make an impression. Besides, by the
precautions she had taken to keep any one from approaching
the apartment, there is no doubt but that she had a design
to do by force what the king at last consented to; and to
authorise her to proceed to such means, it was prudent to
try all softer ones, and convince the prince himself of the
necessity of obliging the king to take care of his health." [1]

Philip soon relapsed into his obstinate habits, and refused
to take even so innocent a remedy as a glass of whey. His
cries were heard from the *salle des gardes*, and they were so
surprising as uttered by a king who spoke so seldom and
so slowly that they were believed to be due to delirium.
Government was at a standstill. For nearly a month Philip
saw neither of his ministers, nor his confessor. Nothing
which required his signature could be despatched. Patiño
pretended to have talked with him, but when the queen
brought him to the bedside with some officers from Ceuta,
Philip fell into such a passion that the sentinels heard what

---

[1] Keene to Newcastle, Oct. 17, 1732. *R. O. S.*, 203.

passed. The French treaty made no advance. The blandishments of Rothembourg could only elicit a nod, or two or three words; he confessed that though he had tormented his imagination for two or three hours to make the king speak he could not get a single word out of his mouth.

These apparently trivial details were not only of supreme importance to Elisabeth's prospects, but were the subjects of intense interest to the European Courts. War and peace, the whole system of European alliances depended on the barber's scissors, or the effects of an emetic. Rothembourg instructed his Government that parties were already formed, one adhering to the prince as being already almost king, the other relying on the queen and her three sons, for the prince was delicate and unlikely to be a father. Villars advised that, if anything happened to the king, the prince should repair secretly to Madrid, taking Patiño and other counsellors of the queen, so that she should be unable to form a party. Keene, as usual, despatched detailed descriptions explaining the queen's difficult position. "It must end in an abdication, or in a change of ministry, or that silent frenzy may waste itself in a few weeks, and matters fall into their usual course. . . . The queen has shown no apprehension of the first. We are now further from the Council of Castile. No one can see the king without her privity or leave, and she has nothing to fear from the prince, who neither takes counsel, nor, if he would, has any one about him to give it. The princess is far from being satisfied with the queen, but whether it proceeds from her know-ledge of the prince, or from any other reason, she does not venture to interpose with him to take the advantage he might of present circumstances."[1] Nor did Keene think a change of ministry probable, for the king refused to see not only Patiño but all others, and the queen, who staved off abdication, could not fail to protect a minister so absolutely necessary to her service.

It was a sign of returning health when Philip reproached

[1] Keene to Newcastle, Oct. 24, 1732. *R. O. S.*, 203.

U

the queen because Patiño had not shown him a letter relating to Oran, which the prince presented.   Elisabeth
replied that she could not conceive how he could expect
any reports from his ministers when he would not give
himself the trouble to see them.   On the two last days of
October the king was better, and the French Government
earnestly pressed the conclusion of the treaty.   Peace
seemed to depend upon Patiño preserving his position; he
has often been called the Colbert of Spain, but he was also
her Walpole.   On October 31 Keene wrote to Delafaye:
" You will see that our enchantment is breaking, and that
we are again come into what we call order and despatch.
Here are thousands that wish for Patiño's fall, but, if he
does, the queen must follow, and new ministers will naturally bring new measures. . . . As for France, I cannot
think they will draw the sword, though they are tempting
their king to turn hero, as long as the emperor lives, and
should the King of Spain die before him, they can expect
little aid from this harassed country, in the want and confusion it will be in under a mere Spanish administration.
Their business then is only to separate Spain from us, and
do nothing for them afterwards, of which Patiño appears
as much assured as I.   I wish he was as much our friend
as he is their enemy, but commerce prevents it." [1]

Keene unduly depreciated the danger.   The queen, he
believed, would do nothing without Patiño's advice, but she
was beginning to break away from his counsels.   She
perhaps realised that the only chance of Philip's recovery
lay in war.   Moreover, the tension between the Courts of
Seville and Vienna was tightening.   France was in close
communication with the electors of Saxony and Bavaria,
and the Palatinate.   Above all, every effort was being
made to win the King of Sardinia, with whom, said Villars,
everything was easy, and without, everything perilous.
This was only to be done at a price.   The old king had
passed for the French ally, and he had lately died a

---

[1] Keene to Delafaye, Oct. 31, 1732. *R. O. S.*, 203.

prisoner. Prince Eugene, somewhat against his conscience, had approved the young king's action, and relied
on his attachment. But the clever Sardinian minister
Ormea hinted to the French envoy Vaulgrenant, that
if France gave Lombardy to the king, he would cede
Sardinia to France. Vaulgrenant thereupon received instructions to offer first a part of the Milanese, and then
the whole. Early in December Rothembourg wrote that
the Queen of Spain consented to the cession of the
Milanese.

The English Government meanwhile was unremitting in
its attempts to reconcile Philip with the emperor. It
suggested that the latter should preserve his rights by granting the title of Grand Prince to Don Carlos. But Spain
was as near war with England as with the emperor.

The arrival of a Spanish ambassador in England had
been ardently desired, and after many delays Montijo had
appeared. The Government had hoped for Castelar, and the
new ambassador was not calculated to further friendly relations, nor to become a successful social centre. His wife
could not speak a word of any language but pure Castilian,
and her appearance was scarce such as to tempt the English
beaux to learn Spanish for her sake. The husband sought
consolation away from home. Keene sent practical hints as
to his treatment: "He is the most amorous excellency I
have met with. Lay but a fair lass in his way, you may
mould him to what you please." [1] The French embassy
possibly offered this attraction, for the Duke of Newcastle
wrote that Montijo was not only holding conference with the
Jacobites, but was in close communication with the French;
he had told Chavigni, the French ambassador, that France
and Spain had the same end in view, and though they might
sometimes take different methods, must meet there at last;
nothing could be done with England while she stood well
with the emperor; the pains that France had taken to defeat
the Pragmatic Sanction and to disappoint the election of a

---

[1] Keene to Delafaye, May 16, 1732. *R. O. S.*, 202.

king of the Romans was an action worthy of the nation, and was restoring France to herself and to Spain.

In December both Lord Waldegrave and Keene reported that Spain was begging France to support the honour of Don Carlos, and this is confirmed by Villars. The emperor had given fresh offence by occupying an island in the Po, and by interference with the Neapolitan fiefs of the Farnesi. Spain insisted that France should speak strongly, and this would imply a rupture. The French proposed a commercial treaty for the exclusion of English and Dutch woollens from Spain, and even from the Levant; factories might be established at Smyrna, and French artisans would resuscitate the Spanish manufactures.

This project found no favour with Patiño; but on December 26 Keene wrote that the signature of the French treaty was confidently reported at Seville, and on the 30th that he had the best information of an intended marriage not only between the Dauphin and the Infanta Maria Theresa, but between Don Carlos and his cast-off *fiancée* Mlle. de Beaujolais. " Castelar must do something in his embassy, and nothing could be more glorious to him than such a double marriage. France offers the queen an honourable retreat in any city she chooses, and guarantees her dowry. She is irritated with the emperor and may let herself be imposed upon. This would for ever separate England and Spain, the French having a strong hold upon the queen; and if the prince has no children you will have a French queen on the throne of Spain, and the two houses will be more linked together, whereas if you can win the queen to some treaty with the emperor and England, the Prince of Asturias will never break it; you will be safe in your commerce, and the emperor not fear France for the Pragmatic Sanction." [1] Such a treaty, he added, Patiño was still suggesting: dispensation from minority for Don Carlos, an accommodation of the disputes in Tuscany, and the immediate investiture of Parma, might serve as the *sine quibus*

---

[1] Keene to Newcastle, Dec. 30, 1732. *R. O. S.*, 203.

non of Spain, for they that would have the Queen of Spain must humour her, and trifles would do it as well as realities ; she hated the family of Orleans, though both she and the Spaniards liked Mlle. de Beaujolais, and might therefore be induced to retard the French treaty.

This treaty, however, was thought to be concluded. Liria's recall from Vienna caused consternation throughout Europe. Elisabeth confided to Rothembourg that to make him sure that the treaty would soon be concluded she told him that Liria had orders to leave Vienna at once. Yet the English Government was simultaneously assured that this step had no political significance. Orendayn, with a hand upon his stately breast, swore that as sure as he was the Marquis de la Paz no convention with France existed. Patiño gave equally strong, if less dramatic, assurances. His actions were more truthful than his words. We know from Villars what Keene did not, that throughout November and December Patiño was struggling against war. Instead of powers for signature he sent to Castelar articles which France could not accept ;[1] he desired that all previous treaties, including those containing commercial privileges, should be annulled ; he would not let Rothembourg speak to the king and queen. "In so cruel a situation," cried Villars, "we must humour Patiño no more. If we cannot speak we must write to the king and queen. The queen wanting war and Patiño disliking it, this minister will bring his masters, in spite of their most vital interests, to a fresh alliance with England. This will infallibly happen. We must, therefore, expose this minister's character to the King of Spain."[2]

This was no empty threat ; Patiño was no longer master. Philip's health improved with the approach of war. He rose about 9 a.m., and waited in his apartments in his night-gown and slippers, without so much as his stockings on, retiring to bed however before dinner. The Duke of Arco had persuaded him to have pity upon his people, and

---

[1] Nov. 17, 1732. *Mémoires*, iv. 85.   [2] Dec. 14, 1732. *Ibid.*, 86.

admit his ministers to Council. But the duke was a professed enemy of Patiño, and no favourite of Elisabeth, though she thought it well to be polite to him, as he did not trouble himself with politics. On December 26 Philip dined, not in bed, but at table, and had his clothes on. He was to resume his ordinary life, and rejoicings were great. Mourning for the old King of Sardinia was suspended. The queen and the infants assumed the garb of a religious order as a sign of thankfulness. A hecatomb of deer and foxes was to be offered, for Arco had organised a grand *battue* for New Year's Day. But Elisabeth's piety ruined all. Philip's melancholia at times took the form of irreligious mania. On the night of the 26th the queen, "trusting too much upon his docility, pressed him with vivacity to perform the devotions of the season, which he absolutely refused to do, and neither caring to yield to the other, the king kept his custom of returning to bed before dinner, leaving little hopes of his going abroad, as it was thought he intended, and orders have been given to the Court to go into mourning again ".[1]

It was in this period of ill-temper, consequent upon returning health, that Philip confided to his valet that he could not bear his wife's four evangelists—her nurse, her confessor, Patiño, and another. His dislike for Patiño was unpleasantly palpable. "It is given out," wrote Keene in his last letter of the year, "that the king beat Patiño and bruised his head. The French say he is sore with chagrin, and are so glad at his illness that I cannot help being full as sorry."[2]

[1] Keene to Newcastle, Dec. 30, 1732. *R. O. S.*, 203.
[2] Keene to Delafaye, Dec. 30, 1732. *Ibid.*

THE POLISH SUCCESSION—IMPERIAL ADMINISTRATION IN
ITALY—ALLIANCE OF SPAIN AND FRANCE—TREATY OF
THE ESCURIAL—ALLIANCE OF FRANCE AND SARDINIA—
TREATY OF TURIN—ILL-FEELING BETWEEN SPAIN AND
SARDINIA—CONQUEST OF NAPLES AND SICILY BY DON
CARLOS—SIEGE OF MANTUA—THE PRELIMINARIES OF
VIENNA.

" Who could have thought," wrote Keene on October 10,
1733, " that the death of a King of Poland could have promoted matters into the state they are now in ? This reflection makes me pray for the life of the Doge of Venice, for
surely that object is not of much less importance than the
other."

The European powers had so long been playing with fire
that it was only a question of time when they should burn
their fingers. France and Spain had already determined on
war. France had hoped to find an occasion in the time-
honoured dispute as to the succession of Juliers-Beró.
Thus the Polish succession was, at least for Spain, the
flimsiest pretext. Some three years previously, indeed,
Liria, during his embassy at Vienna, had opened negotiations for the election of Don Philip as a compromise, but
neither the Spanish candidate, nor his rival from the Iberian
Peninsula, the Infant of Portugal, had found support.[1] The
emperor could not believe that the support given to the

---

[1] Campo Raso asserts that Elisabeth now instructed her agent Araceli to
press the claims of Carlos, but that Patiño induced her to withdraw by the prospect of the conquest of Naples.

Saxon claimant against the candidature of the father-in-law
of Louis XV. could be a cause for war. His troops
abstained from entering Poland. The Russian and Saxon
forces were sufficient to overawe the country, to procure the
election of Augustus, and the expulsion of Stanislas and his
French auxiliaries. Charles VI. had an unshaken belief in
the pacific intentions of Fleury. He thought that financial
and religious disorder would keep the French employed,
while the Spaniards had, he believed, shown themselves incapable of any great enterprise. The Catalonian exiles to the
end persuaded him that Spain did not mean war ; notwithstanding the entreaties of his generals, he ceaselessly drained
Italy of its resources. Don Carlos was absolutely exposed, he
might easily have been taken prisoner in his capital by a detachment of hussars. It was thought inconceivable that the
King of Sardinia should open the gate of Italy to the French.

Italy was thus left defended by but half of its normal
army of occupation. Nor were there any native sources of
resistance. The Italian nobility had been discouraged from
military enterprise. The Italian regiments, which had done
good service under the Hapsburg flag, whether Austrian or
Spanish, had been disbanded. Yet the Milanese troops could
have been relied upon against the Savoyards, whom they
hated. The German *régimé* had become among the people
heartily disliked. Naples had been disappointed in its hopes
of a royal viceroy in the person of the empress dowager.
Under Spanish rule the gravest judicial cases alone had been
referred to Madrid, and indeed the Italian nobility required
special licence to visit Spain. Now every trumpery case
was taken to Vienna. Italy was drained of her wealth, for
the nobility repaired to the Imperial Court to spend their
fortunes, while the German officers saved their pay, and the
soldiers' shoes and arms were bought in Germany. Trade
was thrown out of gear by the emperor's persistent attempts
to create a great commercial outlet on the Adriatic coast,
and by the introduction of new duties. Sheep-rearing in the
Abruzzi declined, and the Neapolitan wines no longer found
a market.

The worst features in the administration were, however, due to the emperor's chivalrous devotion for the Spanish refugees. It was mainly in their interest that Italy was exploited. Whereas previously most of the highest judicial and civil appointments were confined to Italians, they were now conferred upon Catalans, their numbers were augmented, and the salaries raised, while the judicial offices still open to Italians were practically put up to auction. For the benefit of the refugees also the impositions were enormously increased, and their produce withdrawn from the regular revenues and transferred to the privy purse. There was indeed little prospect of an actual rising, for the people wanted leaders. The nobles were fascinated by imperial grandeur, and captivated by the imperial titles which they could buy or beg. Yet it was certain that a Spanish force, on its first success, would meet with very general sympathy.

At the time of the King of Poland's death the health of Philip was extremely critical. His life was believed to be in danger, and perhaps was so, for the doctors having bled him in the foot would fain have repeated the experiment upon his head. War seemed little likely. The prince was known to be opposed to it, in Paris the queen was believed to be treating with England, and in Spain it was thought impossible that Fleury should make war. Yet the treaty was drafted, and Philip's signature alone was wanting. His health improved in March, he dressed daily though returning to bed for dinner. But he would not speak nor see his ministers. "Never," ejaculated Villars, "has a treaty so indispensable to two crowns taken so long to make." At length the king left Seville, and this was regarded as a certain sign of war. He travelled slowly northwards, he would not pass through any town. Streams were bridged in order that the high road might be avoided. He was escorted but by six squadrons of dragoons. The ambassadors were told that the royal *cortège* would leave at three, and to avoid observation it set off at one. Villars recognised that all this was the sign of an enfeebled intellect, but urged the necessity of satisfying the queen and preventing her reunion with the emperor.

This was no easy task. Vaulgrenant reported that Patiño had told the Sardinian Government that his master had no thought of a breach with the emperor, and that the differences relating to Don Carlos were on the point of adjustment. At the end of June the Court was at Aranjuez, and stormy scenes were reported between the king and queen. These probably arose with regard to the final conclusion of the treaty, for on June 28 a letter was received at Paris from the king affirming its conclusion. Such, however, was not the case, and this is perhaps the letter to which Patiño constantly referred as being the sole written agreement between the powers. The French were already preparing to attack Philipsburg, regardless of its being not an Austrian but an imperial fortress ; for the best way, urged Villars, to keep the empire at home was to frighten it.

Sardinia, however, was not yet won, and, in the words of Villars, with its king as an ally all was gold, and without him iron, though it was yet necessary to strike upon that iron. The price was constantly rising. The king would have nothing but Lombardy entire, and to that was ultimately added Mantua. He would brook no interference of the Spanish Bourbons in the north ; Spain must be confined to the Two Sicilies and the Presidi. To France was made a shadowy conditional promise of Sardinia or Savoy. Even Villars thought that the gold was bought too dear. Yet the League of Turin was concluded on September 23, 1733. No treaty as yet existed between France and Spain, and the queen showed the utmost reluctance to include Sardinia ; nevertheless, she clamoured for war. " The king and I are not timid children ; great enterprises do not frighten us." In September the emperor conceded the title of Grand Prince to Don Carlos, and granted the dispensation from the normal age at which majority should be declared and immediate investiture. This step was taken too late. On October 7 the French manifesto was read declaring war against the emperor in consequence of the aid given to the Elector of Saxony, although no imperial troops had entered Poland.

Spain could no longer withstand the excitement. Officers

were ordered to join their regiments, the fleet to sail to Barcelona. As Keene had prophesied, if France fought, nothing could keep the King of Spain from war, whatever the queen and Patiño might wish. Montemar, the destined commander-in-chief, was constantly closeted with Patiño. He was disliked in the army, but was more tractable than Spinola to orders from home. The king and the queen were never more easy nor in better humour. If they could not bear a long war, they hoped for advantages enough from a short one, and for freedom from the tyranny of the Quadruple Alliance. Yet still there was no treaty. Patiño assured Keene on October 16 that Spain was under no engagements to France, though she wished to hold her as a second string; he suspected that a treaty with Sardinia had been made and not communicated to his Court. On November 4 he told the English minister that he had done all he could to preserve the present system, that France had made proposals for some months which had been refused point blank, and that up to September 22 Rothembourg's conferences had been but "stuff and nonsense". A few days later he again insisted that Spain had not acceded to the Treaty of Turin. This was true; yet at this moment a treaty had been signed with France, and Patiño had the best of reasons for not confessing it to Keene.[1]

It had been thought hardly possible that England could remain neutral, and precautions were therefore taken in the event of her hostility. The Spanish-French alliance was directed as much against England as against the emperor. Spain, while striking at Italy with her left hand, was guarding her American colonies with her right. The Treaty of the Escurial professed to be the eternal, irrevocable family convention of the House of Bourbon. The two lines mutually guaranteed all the possessions that they possessed or claimed. France engaged to furnish 40,000 men wherever the common cause required; it was stipulated that operations should be decided by the generals of the two

[1] The treaty was signed on Nov. 7 at the Escurial. It may be read in " A. del Cantillo, Tratados, convenios y declaraciones de paz," etc.

powers.   France was pledged to the recovery of Gibraltar
by force if necessary.   Spain expressed the intention of
abrogating the exclusive privileges granted to English trade,
and in the consequent event of an attack by England upon
Spanish commerce it was provided that the squadrons of
Brest and Toulon would act in concert with the Spanish
fleet.

The English Government was not without a warning.
Information had reached it through Vandermeer that a
scheme was on foot for the recovery of Gibraltar and the
abolition of the Assiento.   Patiño had told him that there
could be no solid peace until the grievances against the
emperor had been redressed, and that even then the restitution of Gibraltar would be pressed.   Keene was soon able to
furnish convincing proof of the existence of the treaty.   A
clerk in the Venetian and Dutch Department of the Foreign
Office had proved serviceable to the English Government
during the Congress of Soissons.   He was now, under La
Quadra, at the head of his office, and was enabled to take
copies or abstracts of papers which passed through the
department.   He was on confidential terms with Keene, and
for fifty guineas handed him an abstract of the Family Compact.[1]   Its accuracy was confirmed by another spy, a servant
of the French ambassador, who believed it to have been
signed on November 8, and who was wrong only by one day
in the date and in the number of the articles.   " The whole
of the transaction," wrote Keene, " has been managed with
so much precaution that in all my acquaintance with foreign
ministers or the best informed of the Spaniards there is not
one that knows positively whether there is a treaty or not,

---

[1] This clerk was of permanent value to Keene.   He asked for a salary of
£50 per month, which Keene thought reasonable.   He had already given him
£500.   Keene, however, heard that suspicion had fallen upon one of the secretaries, and that he had been observed to meet people in disguise.   "Very
luckily for my friend the suspicion fell on one of his colleagues of the same
size."   It was thought advisable to let correspondence drop till they met
again at Madrid.   (Keene to Newcastle, Nov. 26, 1734.)   The clerk was
afterwards promoted to the important department of Vienna, and continued
to be serviceable.

neither do they as much as suspect the time of its being signed."[1] The British Government was, owing to advices from Paris, at first incredulous. Keene was requested to obtain a full copy, but this proved impossible, as the document had passed beyond his friend's reach into the archives.[2]

Further information arrived from the Sardinian Government. The Treaty of the Escurial had made substantial modifications in that of Turin without the consent of Charles Emanuel. Fleury had deceived him by promising the unconditional adhesion of Spain, whereas it depended on the cession of Mantua. Similarly he had deceived the King of Spain by concealing the fact that the King of Sardinia was not pledged to make conquests for his benefit. It was asked whether the 40,000 men offered by France were the same troops as those already pledged to Sardinia, and why the king was not named among the generals, as he was acting as commander-in-chief. Fleury replied that if difficulties had been raised Elisabeth would have taken the pretext to break off negotiations and to turn towards the emperor in whose name England offered *carte blanche;* he was given to understand that if he refused to sign Spain was infallibly lost. The King of Sardinia was not satisfied. Spain clearly wished to recover supremacy in Italy, while he would remain at the mercy of France and Spain, with the emperor hostile and England offended. "I cannot agree," he wrote, "that, by yielding, Spain can be rendered reasonable. If the great advantages which we have offered and obtained for her, almost in spite of herself, have had no other result but to inspire her with fresh pretensions, what must we not expect when she sees by this example that her caprices are always satisfied? On my side I shall always have reason to fear the most extraordinary moves conceivable from a neighbour of such a character, especially if rendered more powerful by a new principality."[3] Mantua must at all events be kept out of the hands of Elisabeth's sons. The king was not only

---

[1] Keene to Newcastle, March 13, 1734. *R. O. S.,* 217.

[2] Keene to Newcastle, May 12, 1734. *Ibid.*

[3] Dec. 25, 1733. Carutti, iv.

outraged by the share accorded to Spain in Italy, he was entirely indisposed to incur the hostility of England. Hence he endeavoured to regain touch with the Court of S. James. His minister, Ossorio, read the Treaty of Escurial to King George and to Lord Harrington.[1] He offered to delay the siege of Mantua and the accord with Spain. George thanked Charles Emanuel, saying that their interests were identical, and that provision must be taken for England's safety. Lord Harrington was in favour of immediate war, but Walpole declined to abandon his policy of neutrality unless the States-General would concur. On this occasion it was the boat that towed the ship. The Dutch oligarchy was fearful of the supremacy of the House of Orange, which, as on previous occasions, would be the inevitable result of war. They had no reason to gratify the emperor, and as he had stripped the Low Countries of troops, the weight of the French attack would fall upon the Dutch garrisons of the barrier towns. The French guaranteed the neutrality of the Austrian Netherlands, and the Spanish minister, S. Gil, was instructed to dangle before Dutch eyes a commercial treaty, which would relieve the jealousy of English maritime supremacy.

Meanwhile the war was in full progress. Military operations were conducted with more energy than might have been expected from the tedious incompleteness of the negotiations. Charles Emanuel opened the ball, received the keys of Milan, and advanced to the Adda. On October 25 Villars quitted Fontainebleau. The young queen pinned a cockade in his hat; at Lyons he found a second from Elisabeth Farnese; at Turin a third was pinned upon his hat by the fingers of the Queen of Sardinia. He was the hero of all three Courts, especially of that of the Escurial. The fiery old marshal was irresistible. By the middle of February, 1734, the Gallo-Sardinians had conquered the whole of the Milanese and part of the territory

---

[1] A French copy of the Family Compact was also forwarded from Turin by Lord Essex. It is to be found among his correspondence. Brit. Mus. MSS. Add. 27731.

of Mantua. Meanwhile the Spanish forces had been landed
on the Genoese and Tuscan coasts, and had occupied the
adjoining principalities of Mirandola, Massa and Piombino.
Carlos proclaimed himself of age, and leaving Parma
took command of the Spanish forces at Siena. The
utility of the trained Spanish garrisons now received its
proof. But the want of concert at once became apparent.
Villars urged that the armies of all three nations should
press eastwards, and after taking or masking Mantua,
block the passes of the Alps. The King of Sardinia, aware
of the Queen of Spain's determination as to Mantua, preferred to consolidate the conquest of his future dominions.
The Spaniards played a higher stake. Turning south-
wards, they marched through the Papal States to the
Garigliano, while their fleet preceded them and occupied
Ischia and Procida, and the headland of Miseno. In April
news arrived that Carlos was at Aquino with so little
prospect of opposition that he was quietly fishing in the
Garigliano. At S. Germano the people threw bread and
provisions to the soldiers from their windows. The march
to Naples was a military promenade. Carlos issued a proclamation restoring the privileges of the Neapolitan people,
relieving them of the taxes imposed since the German
occupation, and engaging to establish no new Court or
customs. Cowardly as Neapolitans were by reputation,
they had consistently kicked against the pricks of the
inquisition, and exorcised the spectre of the Alcabala. The
Capital surrendered, and Carlos read the act by which his
father ceded to him the kingdom of the Two Sicilies. The
delight of the inhabitants was unfeigned; Naples was again
a kingdom, and its capital again a Court. The whole of
Italy indeed had reason to hope that the days of foreign
occupation were at an end, and that the restoration of the
balance of the five Italian powers which had existed
previous to 1494 was imminent. Of these the Papacy and
Venice alone survived. Now a new Italo-Spanish dynasty
restored the Aragonese monarchy of Naples. The House
of Savoy would succeed to the possessions of the Visconti

and the Sforza, while the Queen of Spain's second son
would rule a Tuscany enlarged by the territories of Parma
and perhaps of Mantua.

No rest was given to the Austrians. Montemar marched
upon the Adriatic, stormed their entrenchments at Bitonto,
and dispersed the only army in the field. Capua and Gaeta
could offer no prolonged resistance. Before they fell the
Spanish forces had invaded Sicily. The Sicilians rose in
their favour as in 1718.[1] Three fortresses only offered any
opposition, and Trapani, the last of these, surrendered in
June, 1735. In July Carlos was crowned at Palermo,
where the enthusiasm reached its climax. Thus within
fifteen months the whole of the kingdom of the Two Sicilies
had changed its master. The success of the Spaniards was
far more striking than that of the marvellous expedition of
Charles of Anjou and of Charles VIII.; the familiar adage
was again confirmed that "the kingdom" was light to
win and light to lose.

In the north also the campaign had been in favour of
the attack, though the results were not decisive. Villars
again urged Charles Emanuel to undertake the siege of
Mantua. This the king was prepared to do if he might
retain it in return for concessions to France in Savoy, or
if it should be assigned to the Elector of Bavaria. Fleury
replied that Elisabeth made its possession a condition of
the Spanish alliance, whereupon Charles Emanuel declined
to advance. Villars threw up his command in disgust.
The old marshal never saw home again. Like many less
illustrious persons, he fell dangerously ill at Turin, and
died in June. The great names of the past generation
rapidly disappeared in this paltry war. While fiery Villars
died in retiring from the scene of action, the cautious
Berwick fell from the results of his foolhardiness. The
French had at the close of the preceding year occupied
Lorraine, and crossed the Rhine at Strassburg and taken
Kehl. The campaign of 1734 had opened with the siege of

---

[1] The troops from the smaller garrisons in attempting to concentrate were
destroyed or forced back by the natives.—Campo Raso, iv. 115.

Philipsburg. Prince Eugene was unable to do more than observe the siege. The German fortress fell, but not before a shot, either French or German, had carried off the head of the best and bravest of the Stuarts, five days after the death of his old companion (June 12). Within the same month the veteran Imperialist, Merci, fell in a desperate attack upon the Gallo-Sardinian lines at Parma. Even Prince Eugene hardly survived the war. Lesser men succeeded. Demoralisation and vice reached a pitch in the French army that had never been known before; all ordinary sins had lost their savour. The anger of Elisabeth was aroused by its depredations at Parma, which it was professedly guarding in deposit for her son. Berwick's successor, Coigni, met with no striking success in Germany. Königsegg, after a victory on the Secchia, in September, suffered a crushing defeat within a few days at Guastalla. Yet, when the fighting season ended, the Austrians still held the line of the Adda, and Mantua was untaken; the German reinforcements could still pour over the Brenner and the Semmering. In the following year the Spanish forces were at length induced to turn their faces northwards; they captured Orbitello and cleared the Presidi of Austrian troops. The arrogant attitude of the mediating powers produced a semblance of accord between the French, Sardinian and Spanish generals. The siege of Mantua was decided and undertaken. But the fortress of the marsh was destined to retain the hold of Germany on Italy for nigh a century and a half to come. The Sardinian king refused to lend his siege artillery for the capture of a town which was to be another's. A Spanish train was painfully dragged from Naples and Leghorn. The French blockade was so carelessly maintained that Venetian speculators threw in what stores they pleased.

Such was the military position, when the startling news arrived of the Preliminaries signed at Vienna, by the emperor and the French. Montemar was in momentary danger from his own allies; he fell back upon Bologna, where the German light horse nearly captured him, and

x

then with heavy loss upon Parma and Tuscany.   The proud
Spaniard was forced to accept an armistice through the
mediation of Noailles.   For the Spanish arms it was a
crushing disappointment.   They had amply retrieved the
reputation clouded by the African expedition.   The commissariat had been, as usual, wretched, and in the Neapolitan campaign there had been some desertion, chiefly
among the foreign Guards.[1]   But the activity of the Spanish
movements had been undeniable, and it was not without
reason that the officers openly expressed their contempt of
their French allies and Sardinian rivals.   While the French
were pulling rings from women's fingers, and robbing their
allies' vineyards, the Spaniards had conquered a great kingdom, and founded a dynasty which was to outlive a century.

---

[1] On the other hand, a large number of German prisoners entered Spanish
service.—Campo Raso, iv. 113.

DIPLOMACY DURING THE WAR—SEPARATE NEGOTIATIONS OF
SPAIN WITH THE EMPEROR—PRELIMINARIES OF VIENNA
BETWEEN THE EMPEROR AND FRANCE—INDIGNATION OF
THE SPANISH COURT — RUPTURE WITH THE POPE AND
WITH PORTUGAL—AUTOCRACY OF ELISABETH—ADMINIS-
TRATION OF PATIÑO.

IF the Spanish armies bore off the laurels of the war, the
palm of diplomacy must be awarded to the French ministry.
As through the last months of peace the sultry atmosphere
had betokened war, so since the first shot had brought down
the clouds peace had been in the air. Throughout the
foregoing campaign ambassadors had been as busy as were
generals, and every military movement was accompanied
by a diplomatic *tour de force*. To Englishmen, the chief
interests of the negotiations of this period lie in the Secret
Treaty or Family Compact of the Escurial. Yet it would
perhaps be wrong to exaggerate its importance; for it was
an episode rather than a new departure, and no dominating
fact in future history. The Queen of Spain had been reluctantly forced to accept French friendship as a *pis aller*.
The new treaty was of little more importance than the
family treaty of 1721, in the spirit of which it was conceived, and much of which it recapitulated.[1] [It is true

---

[1] Compare the important articles of the two treaties relating to Gibraltar.

TREATY OF MARCH 27, 1721.   TREATY OF NOVEMBER 7, 1733.
Secret Article 2. |Secret Article 6.

Continuará su Majestad Cristiani-   Empleará su Majestad Cristianisima
sima sin interrupcion sus officios los   sin interrupcion los oficios mas activos

that the Neapolitan Bourbons owed their kingdom to this fugitive alliance; but it was very generally believed that the emperor and not Don Carlos was the gainer by the exchange of the Southern Kingdom for the Central Duchies. It must be remembered also that the campaign which resulted in the conquest of the Two Sicilies was undertaken in direct defiance of the entreaties of the French ministry, and the original plan of operations, and that long before the Family Compact it was regarded in Italy as the necessary consequence of the establishment of Don Carlos in the Duchies.[1]

mas activos para empeñar al rey de la Gran Bretaña á restituir cuando antes fuere posible á su Majestad Catolica la plaza de Gibraltar y sus dependencias, y no desistirá de esta dimanda hasta que su dicha Majestad Catolica haya obtenido una entera satisfaccion sobre este punto, bien sea por la efectiva restitucion de la dicha plaza, ó bien por seguridades con que quede satisfecho de que se le restituirá en un termino fijo y determinado.—Cantillo, p. 196.

para empeñar al rey de la Gran Bretaña á restituir lo mas presto que sea posible á su Majestad Catolica la plaza de Gibraltar y sus dependencias, y no se desistirá de esta dimanda hasta que su Majestad Catolica haya obtenido una entera satisfaccion sobre este punto, sea por la entrega efectiva de dicha plaza á sus armas, sea por otros medios con los cuales esté asegurado de que se le entregará en un tiempo fijo y determinado; prometiendo tambien su Majestad Cristianisima usar de la fuerza para su logro se fuere necesario.—Cantillo, p. 277.

Keene's information was very accurate. "When Rothembourg and Patiño were treating of the 6th Article, my friend tells me Rothembourg proposed the same terms that were used in the private treaty of 1721, but the latter objected against the expression *continuaran*, because it supposed that they (the French) had once begun them (their efforts for recovery of Gibraltar), which he said was false in fact, and they substituted *emplearan*, and added the clause about using force if it should be necessary."—Keene to Newcastle, Jan. 7, 1734. *R. O. S.*, 217.

[1] Professor Seeley has fully discussed this treaty in the *English Historical Review*, January, 1886. The author feels obliged to differ from his conclusions as to its supreme importance. The term "Family Compact" has acquired in history an artificial notoriety from the important results of the treaty of 1761. The phrase itself may be regarded as accidental, as having no further connotation than the terms employed in the treaty of 1721. The dissimilarity of results in the treaties of 1733 and 1761 seems more noticeable than the identity of phraseology. D'Argenson, who, though not responsible for the Family Compact of 1743, had as Foreign Minister to execute its provisions, mentions that of 1733 perhaps only once, and then as a treaty

Keene proved perfectly correct in his estimate of the probable results of this treaty. " Having, as I hope, sufficiently proved the reality of the above-mentioned engagements, it remains to be proved with what views France and Spain may have contracted them, and how far they may be able to pursue them. The first point offers two considerations : either that there is an actual design to overthrow the balance of power, or that having a mutual occasion for each other in carrying on their private and separate interests, the French in mortifying the emperor, the Spaniards in gaining new acquisitions in Italy, they have reciprocally imposed upon themselves such engagements as neither of them intend to perform if they are happy enough to procure their particular ends without them." [1] Keene proceeded to show that, though the terms of the treaty, the idea of exalting the House of Bourbon, and humbling that of Hapsburg, the obligation to recover Gibraltar by negotiation or force, pointed to the former, yet the assurances of Fleury and Patiño, combined with the jealousy of France and Spain, and the readiness of Patiño to negotiate, apart from France, bore rather the appearance of the latter. He had already heard that negotiations had been renewed for the marriage of Don Carlos with an archduchess. Yet Keene's Civil Service friend supplied him with disquieting news : the King of France would move troops towards the channel : the Galician ports were being fortified : the map of Gibraltar was always on Patiño's table : three batteries were to be erected against the fortress. The French suggested a plan for the surprise of Port Mahon, and a Spanish engineer had secretly surveyed the works, whilst a considerable force was held in readiness at Barcelona for the purpose. Patiño informed the · Venetian ambassador

under restrictions. The Venetian ambassador, Venier, in his *Relazione* of 1735, discredits the existence of a formal treaty from the total want of concert between the Bourbon crowns, which he attributes partly to the queen and partly to Patiño, "averse to France from fear that the French ministry wished excessive predominance in Spain, to the peril perhaps of his own fortunes ".

[1] Keene to Newcastle, March 13, 1734. *R. O. S.*, 217.

that the despatch of a strong English squadron to the Mediterranean would be regarded as the signal for a rupture. On the other hand, the allies seemed more willing to propitiate England than to fight. Ormond was refused permission to visit either Dijon or Madrid. The Pretender's son, who joined the Neapolitan expedition in the Duke of Liria's suite, was ordered to withdraw. Patiño assured Keene that the story that Don Carlos threw his hat into the sea to accompany that of the young Pretender was a fable.[1] However inevitable war might be, every precaution was taken to avoid it. Fighting had hardly begun when the English Government was requested to negotiate a separate peace with the emperor. Patiño was scarcely within the limits of truth in assuring Keene that their agreement with France rested merely on a letter, but he was substantially accurate in describing the family convention as a treaty *in nubibus.*[2] The queen had never abandoned her ambition for an imperial marriage for her son. England alone could allay the anxiety of the German princes and the Northern powers, were such a proposal made or accepted by the emperor. In January the queen seemed willing to desert the French alliance on these terms. She hated the French as much as the king esteemed them. Keene professed himself to be the last of men to entertain so ill-founded a notion as to think that the queen or Patiño would have any regard to public faith or treaties whenever interest or opportunity

---

[1] " While the Chevalier de S. George was attending the embarkation (for Sicily) a blast of wind blew his hat into the sea ; immediately several officers endeavoured to take it up, but he called out : ' Let it alone, let it alone, I will go and get another in England,' whereupon the King of Naples, throwing his hat into the sea, said : ' And I will go along with you '. On which it was remarked that they might go bareheaded a long time if they got no hats until they came to England, and, besides, they would find none there that would fit their heads."—*Gentleman's Magazine,* vol. iv. 515.

[2] Is it possible that the Spanish ratification was never formal ? The vagueness of Cantillo's phrase increased the author's suspicions. These have been somewhat confirmed by Don E. Garcia. He kindly forwarded a copy of the only document relating to ratification which is to be found at Alcalá (Leg. 3365). It is merely a minute or draft of the act, with a blank space left for the date.

should tempt them to untie their hands. The dictating temper of the French and the conceited stubbornness of the Spaniards would, he believed, produce a rupture before the article for the recovery of Gibraltar could be executed. The emperor appears to have offered the hand of his second daughter for Don Carlos, with an increase of his Italian possessions. Patiño engaged not to communicate to France any proposals which the Governments of England and the States-General might wish to keep secret, and was offended at the separate negotiations of the latter at Paris. The Duke of Bournonville was at this time much in the confidence of the queen and her minister, and was also intimate with Keene. He assured the latter that the queen was free to treat with any power that she might choose; she had nothing to do with Stanislas or Lombardy; the former had been only named in the Spanish manifesto as a joke, *animi exhilarandi causa*, and she would sooner see the emperor master of Milan than the Sardinian king. On the proclamation of Don Carlos as King of Naples, Keene represented that his assumption of the regal title, and the establishment of a third Bourbon dynasty, would increase the difficulties of peace. Patiño, however, took a contrary view; it would prove that Spain had no ambition for herself in Italy, and that Europe therefore would cease to fear her. The French alliance, he argued, would never cause his king to abandon his interests, and his interests in Italy were distinct from those of France; if France entertained ideas of disturbing the balance of power, Spain, far from assisting, would think her own independence threatened. The queen, he added, must have a gratuity, some *fumée* for her son; he must be King of Naples and Sicily. He doubted whether the queen would surrender Tuscany, but it was possible that she would abandon Parma and Piacenza for an equivalent: but without an archduchess there could be no ease; if this marriage were effected, an eternal barrier would be raised between the two lines of Bourbon, and England could command the commerce of Spain for ages together; the Prince of Asturias, should he succeed, would let matters proceed on their previous footing, while Carlos was bound by gratitude to England. The Spanish demands were high. "I found," wrote Keene, "by Patiño's way of talking, that it was no difficult matter to know what would please their Catholic Majesties; it was only to imagine all that they could possibly wish for after a series of good successes on their side, and bad ones on the emperor's, and to grant them their full desires."[1]

The queen's influence over her husband was now so complete, and his neglect of business so entire, that she was freed from the attentions which she had been previously forced to lavish upon France. She was thought more likely to patch up a hasty and secret treaty with the emperor than continue an expensive war, now that she had almost satisfied her wishes. The emperor had indeed angrily rejected the mediation of the Maritime Powers, and attempted to detach Spain and Sardinia from France. Another secret treaty of Vienna might have taken place had not Maria Theresa declared that she would marry the Prince of Lorraine or no one. It was a trial of strength between the fidelity of a *fiancée* and the obstinacy of a mother. The queen was anxious to make her son independent of Spain in case she should be obliged to retire to Naples on the accession of her step-son. Patiño desired by an imperial marriage to win a solid guarantee for Naples and Sicily which Spain might not be able to defend.

It was essential that these tentative negotiations should be concealed from the king and from the French ambassador. A general arrangement, including the allies, would take too long, and a common war was, as Patiño said, easy, but a common peace was difficult, for the interests of the allies would clash. If Spain withdrew her troops and subsidies, the war would of itself collapse. Patiño was probably sincere; he dreaded the expenses of prolonged war, and despised the King of Sardinia. As the Spanish successes were more complete, their proposals were more

---

[1] Keene to Newcastle, May 4, 1734. *R. O. S.,* 217.

definite. Full possession, free of vassalage, of all that Don Carlos now possessed was demanded, and, as security, the hand of an archduchess. The king, however, was less easy to lead than had been expected. "The queen wants peace," said Patiño to Bournonville, "but the king likes battles, and we have to humour him." When Bournonville himself urged peace in the king's presence, the queen replied : " What ! Bournonville—you to give counsel to the king ! But, sire, he speaks as he thinks, and his thoughts are not so bad."[1] The king's recalcitrance gave little anxiety to Keene, who knew his nature. "As we may be sure of the queen and her minister, we may likewise be so of the king, for they never fail to bring him into their views, be it with more or less trouble, as the nature of affairs requires. . . . Custom and habit produce on him the same or a more regular condescendence to his queen's ideas than that which in the former part of his life was due to his complexion and passions."[2]

These negotiations were not entirely unsuspected by the French ambassador. He told Patiño that the Dutch were arranging a separate alliance between the emperor and Spain, that Spain was willing to leave Milan to the emperor, while the rest was regulated by the secret Treaty of Vienna. Patiño replied that this was impossible, as the Treaty of Vienna had never been beneath his eyes.[3]

At the beginning of 1735 the Maritime Powers were seriously negotiating a general peace. The States-General addressed themselves to France, but with the result that Patiño was offended. They had no idea, he said, of being bound by the answers and declarations of France ; they were allies indeed, but such as could speak for themselves ; nothing could be more disagreeable to his master than to be thought to be led by France. Simultaneously the

---

[1] Keene to Newcastle, Nov. 27, 1734. *R. O. S.*, 218.

[2] *Ibid.*

[3] Whether true or not, this assertion is a curious confirmation of the extraordinary secrecy which was preserved with regard to this mysterious treaty.

English Government received proposals which had satisfied the King and Queen of Spain, and professedly contained the suggestion made by Keene, though differing from his views as stated by himself. The ambassador's explanation was characteristic. The pacific arrangements made by Keene and Vandermeer, with the queen and Patiño, were, when ripe, submitted to the king, who read the instructions forwarded to Montijo in England. For this purpose the despatches were cooked in such a manner that Spain might not appear to be the first to desire peace or to mention an archduchess. Keene, of whose honesty the king had a high opinion, was represented as giving greater assurances than he had ever thought of. [1]

The English Government was perhaps not judicious. The speech with which George II. opened the Parliament of 1735 was regarded as a menace. The Maritime Powers, said Patiño, were acting, not as the mediators, but as the arbiters of Europe, and Spain would arm to the full extent of her power.[2] He freely criticised their project; the advantages were all upon the emperor's side ; he wanted a King of Poland, and he had it ; he wanted the guarantee of the Pragmatic Sanction, and it was promised ; by the possession of Tuscany and Parma, he would be so strong in north and central Italy that the King of Naples was at his mercy.

Each of the three powers felt itself aggrieved by the Anglo-Dutch proposals, and the result was a momentary unity, which resulted in the siege of Mantua. This was a critical moment, for Patiño had warned Keene that every pretext was being taken to delay the junction of the Spanish troops from Naples with the French and Sardinian force ; but this once effected, Spain would be loyal to her allies. The concert was, however, of short duration. The King of Sardinia preferred the emperor in Mantua to Don Carlos, and Patiño did not disguise his opinion that if the emperor would satisfy Spain he might keep

---

[1] Keene to Newcastle, Jan. 14, 1735. *R. O. S.*, 224.
[2] Keene to Newcastle, Feb. 21, 1735. *Ibid.*

Mantua and Milan also. Spain, he hinted, might still be separated, which, however, would be impossible if Mantua once fell, or if a treaty were signed between the three powers. Meanwhile he had formed a list of twenty articles in which the French had behaved disloyally to Spain, and this was intended as the justification for the withdrawal from the alliance. The arrival of the treasure ships made the minister somewhat "uppish" and less indisposed to war, though he affected the philosopher and said that it was always in their power to put the *siste gradum* to their operations. When he was twitted on the desirability of the Spaniards as allies because they always found the money, he replied that England could have them as allies at will.[1] Curious information came through Fuenclara, Castelar's son-in-law, from Venice. He had gathered from the Princess Leonora of Tuscany that the empress had expressed a wish for a double marriage between her daughters and the Spanish infants. At any moment Spain might be expected to break away from the allies of Turin and make a separate treaty with the emperor with or without the mediation of England.

It has been assumed, both in text-books and in substantial histories, that a triple alliance existed between Sardinia and the two Bourbon powers. But the whole gist of this strange war, and yet stranger negotiations, lies in the fact that such an alliance was found to be impossible. On April 15, 1734, Philip offered conditional adherence to the Treaty of Turin, but the Sardinian minister at Paris had not sufficient powers to accept the proposal; the matter was allowed to sleep, and Patiño finally declared that the lingering negotiation had better be suffered to drop. Spain and Sardinia therefore had no mutual obligations to each other. Sardinia was bound to France by the Treaty of Turin, and France to Spain by the secret and somewhat shadowy Treaty of the Escurial. The King of Sardinia had betrayed his ally by divulging this treaty to the English

---

[1] Keene to Newcastle, Sept. 5, 1735. *R. O. S.*, 225.

Government, while Spain had never ceased to negotiate a separate alliance with the common enemy behind the back of France. Fleury also was no mean adept at diplomatic hide and seek. He had little reason to be satisfied with his allies, and the first military successes had experienced a check. The league of Eastern Europe was beginning to bring its forces into the field. Reinforcements joined Königsegg in Italy, and for the first time a corps of 16,000 Russians made its appearance upon the Rhine. This was felt to denote an important change in European history, and it was doubtful how many more Russians there might be to follow. For some little time negotiations had been secretly proceeding, and on October 5 the Preliminaries of Vienna between France and the emperor were signed. The emperor agreed to cede to Don Carlos the Two Sicilies and the Presidi, and to Charles Emanuel Novara and Tortona, or Tortona and Vigevano ; Parma and Piacenza reverted to the emperor, and the Pragmatic Sanction received the guarantee of France. Stanislas resigned his claim to the kingdom of Poland, but should receive the Duchy of Bar, and that of Lorraine, as soon as by the death of the Grand Duke of Tuscany an equivalent could be found for the present duke.[1] On the death of Stanislas his possessions were to revert to the French crown.

It was by this last article that Fleury's proposal mainly differed from that of the Maritime Powers. By them nothing had been accorded to France. Fleury indeed had always professed that the action of France was disinterested from a territorial point of view, her aim being to break up the fresh growth of Hapsburg influence by establishing hostile forces in Poland and in Italy. Whatever views she had on Savoy were now surrendered in favour of the reversion of Lorraine. It is said that this acquisition was due, not to Fleury, but to Chauvelin, who, having vigorously opposed the treaty with the emperor, insisted that at least some advantage should accrue therefrom. It was, however, no new idea in French

---

[1] Gian Gaston, Grand Duke of Tuscany, died June 9, 1737.

diplomacy. In Spain the news of the perfidy of France was none the more liked for not being totally unsuspected. On October 8 Patiño heard from Italy of separate transactions of France with the emperor. To his letter of the 12th Fleury replied that his reasonings were so solid as to hinder France from entertaining the imperial proposals. The articles of the supposed treaty were laid before the French ambassador, who, probably with truth, professed his ignorance. But early in November the intelligence of the secret arrangement was confirmed. Fleury's apology was to the effect that the allies were freed from the importunities of the Maritime Powers, who were for thrusting themselves into everybody's business. From this unmannerly expression Patiño gathered, or affected to do so, that the English Government had no hand in the transaction, as had at first been suspected. The position was rendered the more critical by that of the Spanish army in Italy. It was necessary to assume a studied indifference and to avoid offensive expressions towards France until Montemar had placed his troops in safety. "I have never seen the king so gay," wrote Keene, "nor so talkative as he has been since he first heard of the transaction. They have found means to make him overact his part. The queen's behaviour requires a stronger word than affectation. Patiño keeps the best countenance he can, but it is not to be doubted that the first suffers extremely from the treatment he has met with from his own nation, the queen from being disappointed in her ambitions, and Patiño, among other motives, from finding himself a dupe, he who thought himself capable of duping the rest of mankind by the superiority of his genius over the genius of any other prince's Court in Europe."[1] Private utterances were less measured. The queen had always foretold the French perfidy since Rothembourg had pressed her to enter into the war; as long as she breathed she would have nothing to do with France. There were ideas of dissolving all old treaties and throwing Spain

---

[1] Keene to Newcastle, Nov. 14, 1735. *R. O. S.*, 225.

into the arms of England. Vaulgrenant was warned not to open his lips on the Preliminaries to the king, for the queen in his presence might be less mistress of herself. Spain, said Patiño, had from the first expressed her desire for pacification if France wished, but France had urged her to continue, had hardened and exasperated her against the emperor, the better to conclude her own bargain at Vienna. He dwelt on other cases in which France had deceived her ally, and it was understood that of these the non-execution of the article concerning Gibraltar was one; he had opposed the war to the utmost of his power; Spain had been dragged in to separate her eternally from the emperor, to put her on bad terms with England, to force her to grant commercial privileges to France and submit to her dictation. To the French advances for commercial favours, Patiño asserted that he had forthwith put a close; he knew the wretched condition of French finance, which could only be improved by trade, and the chief and only branch of this consisted in the flotas and the galleons, and was thus in the power of Spain, for the trade to the Levant was inconsiderable; if he knew the King of England's sentiments he would take such steps as would make France repent her perfidy for ages yet to come; this should be effected not by force but by imperceptibly undermining the French commerce, and by increasing English trade as they diminished that of France. This, said Patiño, would be the easiest and most effective revenge upon the cardinal; it would kill him with a *baton de coton.* He only regretted that his Eminence was now so old that there was no probability of his living long enough to feel the revenge that Spain would take.[1]

Curious information was elicited from the imprudent indignation of the queen's friends. Chauvelin had apparently differed from Fleury in the desire of the latter for a peace policy, and had regarded himself as the cardinal's successor. He was anxious to win the favour of the King and Queen of Spain. In September, 1735, he entrusted to

[1] Keene to Newcastle, Nov. 28, 1735. *R. O. S.,* 225.

Count Cucurani, son-in-law of Laura Pescatori, a series of proposals to the Spanish Court, of which Fleury was believed to have no knowledge. The king was requested to give his royal word that he would make no agreement with England or the emperor except through the agency of France ; secondly, to come to terms with the King of Sardinia, without whose aid the war could not be continued ; thirdly, to accept the Princess of Lorraine as the most suitable wife for Don Carlos ; fourthly, to consolidate the eternal friendship between the two houses by taking immediate steps for the marriage of the infanta to the dauphin. To the first two requests the king practically gave assent, the third elicited no reply, but to the fourth the queen cried out so loud that the French ambassador behind the door heard the words : " Yes, in sooth—when the infanta is forty, and not before ".[1] This story finds some little confirmation from information given to D'Argenson, that Fleury possessed a letter of Chauvelin's which, if published, would cost him his head. It referred directly not to Spain, however, but to the King of Sardinia, whom he informed that he had no hand in the separate treaty with the emperor.

The year ended amid general irritation. Patiño saved the honour of his penetration at the expense of that of his prudence. He professed to have foreseen for many months that which he took no steps to prevent. He declared that he would not trust the French with a glass of water. He was disposed to reject the French guarantee for Naples, and would prefer that of England alone. Montemar, forced to an armistice, believed that the French had formed a plot for his surprise. The King of Sardinia was as indignant as was the Queen of Spain. He categorically charged Fleury· with having negotiated behind his back, with having purposely prevented the adhesion of Spain to the Treaty of Turin, and with having made the acquisition of Lorraine the sole aim of French policy. The French point of view was admirably expressed in Fleury's reply of January 15,

[1] Keene to Newcastle, Nov. 28, 1735. *R. O. S.*, 225.

1736, a copy of which Lord Essex forwarded to his Government.[1] That the negotiations were secret he ascribed to
the immediate exigencies of the case: it had been discovered that Spain had treated with the emperor in the
hope of obtaining his daughter for Don Carlos, engaging to
assist in driving the King of Sardinia from Lombardy:
this being ineffectual, the Abbé Rumbello had been sent to
Rome to confer with Cardinals Acquaviva and Cienfuegos,
whence he was instructed to proceed to Vienna to offer
carte blanche to the emperor: meanwhile Patiño had told
the French Government that it must choose between Spain
and Sardinia: the French agent, La Baune, had been sent
to Vienna to watch the Spanish proceedings, but finding
the case to be urgent, he opened the negotiations which led
to the Preliminaries of Peace, and Rumbello fortunately
arrived at Vienna just too late to tempt the Imperial
Government.   Fleury continued that France had never
ceased to press Spain to accede to the Treaty of Turin, but
that he had not forwarded the replies of the king and
queen, because the impropriety of their language would only
have added to the existing irritation. Lorraine, he concluded, had never been thought of at the beginning of the
war; it was indeed an acquisition of great value, but its
reversion to France was still distant; the European powers
had urged that peace could not be effected without granting
some satisfaction to Stanislas, and Lorraine had appeared
to be the most natural equivalent.

Fleury's arguments were too convincing to be concilia-
ting, and did little to allay the King of Sardinia's wrath.
The French ambassador at Turin, a creature of Chauvelin, did not spare the treachery of Fleury, and the French
officers in Italy railed against Noailles even as they railed
and broke their swords after Villafranca in 1859.

Montijo meanwhile arrived from England and took a prominent position at Court.   During his progress through
France he had exchanged his Anglophobia for Gallophobia,

[1] Brit. Mus. MSS. Add. 27731, f. 48.

and added fuel to the flames. Keene hoped that England
would intervene in favour of Spain and win her gratitude at
so critical a moment. ·If she abandoned Spain, he believed
that she would give herself unreservedly to the emperor
and avenge her wrongs on English commerce. From the
Pope alone some satisfaction was obtained. Spanish re-
cruiting officers had been murdered in Rome and a Spanish
detachment forced to retire from Velletri. The Courts of
Madrid and Naples withdrew their ambassadors, dismissed
the *nuncios* and suspended payments to the Roman Court.
Their troops had returned in force, had hung or imprisoned
the leaders of the *émeute* at Velletri, and imposed contributions on the town, as upon Ostia and Palestrina. In
December the Pope offered full satisfaction, and conferred
the cardinal's hat upon Don Luis, then only eight years
old, confirming his nomination to the administratorship of
the Archbishopric of Toledo. This quarrel was followed by
a rupture with the Court of Portugal. Its ambassador at
Madrid, Don Cabral de Belmonte, made no secret of his
imperial sympathies, and was therefore far from popular.
His servants rescued an offender from the officers of justice,
and were in turn themselves imprisoned. The ambassadors
were dismissed from the Courts of Lisbon and Madrid, and
there was every probability of war. The situation was
aggravated by the alleged ill-treatment of the queen's daughter, the Princess of Brazil. She was forbidden to receive a
man midwife, sent expressly by the queen, on the ground
that it was contrary to ridiculous Portuguese notions of
delicacy and national etiquette. The queen disavowed any
intention of conquering Portugal, but Spanish troops were
massed upon the frontier, and opportunity was taken to
drive the Portuguese from their colony of Sacramento on
the River Plate. The Portuguese appealed to France and
to England, and Admiral Norris was sent to cover the
passage of the Brazilian merchant fleet to Lisbon. These
events, however, belong strictly to the ensuing year, and
peace with Portugal became a part of the general pacification.

Y

The return of the Court to Castile [1] had been followed by no diminution of Elisabeth's power. "She governs," says Venier in his *Relazione* of 1735, "both the king's will and the kingdom with despotic authority. It is true that she equally disposed of them in the past, but with greater skill and less freedom." She was filled at this time with belief in the power of her kingdom, and was still, the Venetian believed, Austrian at heart. Her affection to her own children was excessive, but she did not, could not, and did not pretend to love Don Ferdinand. Yet, in a serious illness, when Philip took no notice of his son, Elisabeth nursed him tenderly, visiting him twice a day, and consulting his doctors every hour.[2] This was believed, however, to be a pretence to propitiate the people who loved the prince as much as they disliked the queen ; they longed for his accession, believing that Government would be better, and that the grandees would have more power. The queen, to complete her monopoly, had since her return removed the prince from the Despacho, an affront which he suffered with resignation, the result perhaps of prudence, perhaps of a feeble understanding. The princess, if not pretty, had rare gifts, and was beloved by high and low. In her difficult position she gave proofs of consummate prudence and capacity, and she and the queen equally dissembled their mutual dislike.

If Elisabeth was the incarnate will, Patiño was the brain and the hand of the monarchy. "To turn the wheel of her vast designs, Elisabeth employs a single minister, capable beyond measure. Don Joseph Patiño is the man who has rendered himself necessary to the queen, to the aggrandisement of her sons, and to the kingdom. He is clear-sighted, ready in resource, untiring in labour, and

---

[1] There seemed a fate against residence in Madrid, where the Court had not resided since 1728. It intended to pass the winter of 1734-35 in the capital, but as the palace was being warmed it was burned. Jewels and tapestries were saved, but the fine pictures were destroyed, with the archives of the War, Marine and the Indies, and Finance Departments.—Keene, Dec. 27, 1734.

[2] Keene, Aug. 28, 1734. *R. O. S.*, 218.

disinterested. He gives a hearing easily, but with difficulty an answer, particularly when he has little or no interest in the subject. . . . He may now fitly be called first minister, though he has not been formally appointed; for he gives orders, and forms decisions on every class of business, with full authority, and only communicates to the queen what he thinks most necessary." [1]

De la Paz had died on October, 1734, and Castelar was also dead. Rumour, indeed, again spoke of the return of Alberoni, but Venier felt sure that Patiño would suffer no partner in his power: he won by compliments and promotion those who were brought into most intimate relations with the king and queen, and they in return daily extolled the honesty and good fortune of his ministry: the king's confessor, Clarke, was a man of more prudence than capacity, and he did not dare fulfil his function of recommending clergy for preferment without consulting the minister: of the queen's confessor, now Archbishop of Seville, it was needless to speak: Molina, President of the Council of Castile, Archbishop of Malaga, and Commissary of the Cruzada, was clever and daring, better fitted to trouble than to allay rough waters: yet he too, in all his most important civil and ecclesiastical duties, deferred entirely to Patiño, to whom he owed promotion, and whom it was thought possible that he might succeed. Meanwhile Patiño combined in his own person all four secretaryships, and served his mistress with fidelity, readiness, and affection. " The principle of this renowned and fortunate minister is one only, and that consists in force, which is in full accordance with the character of the queen. When this can work, there is neither end nor limit, and great conquests are of no avail as long as they can hope for greater." [2]

Very different indeed, continued Venier, was the power of Spain at present from its condition under Charles II. The nation realised the difference and the gain, and yet it chafed, and did not like the Government. The grandees

---

[1] Venier, *Relazione*, 1735. [2] *Ibid.*

especially resented the total neglect to which they saw themselves abandoned, and it was with ill-will that they brooked
that the glory and the gain won by Spanish arms all turned to
the profit of Don Carlos and to the prejudice of the crown.
The king was loved and revered, and all evil was imputed
to the queen and her minister. Yet little cared the one or
the other for those lords, whom they forced to suffer and be
still. The Government had become totally despotic; the
grandees lived betwixt subjection and suspicion, sunk in
idleness, with their empty titles only left to them. A king
ruled by his wife, a queen devoted beyond due bounds to
her son, a single minister of extreme cleverness, who, to
maintain his post, seconded and obliged the queen—such
were the authors of the strange events that had shaken
Europe. To the aggrandisement of Don Carlos the monarchy was sacrificed; the very hope of leaving it less strong
to the heir was a source of pleasure. Enormous sums were
extracted from the afflicted people, and sent to Italy for
Don Carlos; others were secretly exported, it was believed,
for the queen's private use. Armies had been despatched to
Italy, and placed at her son's disposal, which would hardly
see Spain again—such were to Spain the deplorable consequences of this rule. On the same principle depended
the policy towards foreign powers, which varied daily,
according to the shifting circumstances. One maxim alone
could be called most certain: the scant respect that was
felt for any other power, and the pretension of Spain to be,
if not superior, at least equal, to the greatest and the
strongest.

This highly coloured Venetian portraiture of the queen
and her minister is reproduced in the cooler tones of Keene.
The Sicilian abbots, Platania and Caraccioli, had descanted
on the growing opposition of the prince, the Spaniards and
the army, to the separation of Naples from the crown.

These suggestions the ambassador ridiculed. "I am
sure as long as his father lives the prince will not dare
lift up his eyes against any of his actions; and I much
doubt, after the king's death, he will give himself the

trouble to drive his brother out of the dominion settled on him by his father. As to the Spanish nation, it is as good as lost; they vent their displeasure in speculation, and long speeches in their private assemblies, but none that I know of have ability or courage enough to go any further; and as to the army, they generally serve those that pay them."[1] It was true, Keene added in another letter,[2] that great dissatisfaction was felt, but the people were too low-spirited, not only to resist, but even to express their thoughts; and the Councils, which by the ancient constitution might and ought to speak firmly on such occasions, were filled and governed by creatures of the Court. Sulky abstention was, as in the days of S. Simon, the only form of opposition. When the news of the proclamation of Don Carlos as King of Naples arrived but two grandees came to offer their congratulations at S. Ildefonso, and they were foreigners.[3]

There was, however, one great danger. A fresh attack of Philip's melancholia would matter little, but if any misfortune should happen to the queen or Patiño, even an illness of twenty days, confusion would be inexpressible. The queen indeed was heard to say that if Patiño were out of order she had Campo Florido to help her, but when this remark was conveyed to Patiño by La Pellegrina the Minister Apparent thought it prudent to retire to his Government of Valencia for his health.[4] Some alarm was indeed felt in May, for at Aranjuez one of the royal family fell ill every day, and Patiño was far from well. "It is true," wrote Keene, "he is charged with such a multiplicity of affairs that though he may be indisposed he has not time to be sick."[5] There was a difficulty as well as a danger. Absolute as Elisabeth was, she was

---

[1] Keene to Newcastle, May 12, 1734. *R. O. S.*, 217.

[2] June 7, 1734. *Ibid.*

[3] Keene to Delafaye, June 21, 1734. *Ibid.*

[4] Campo Florido was supported by the Italian party and by Laura Pescatori, and well liked by Elisabeth, but Keene thought him not the man to supplant Patiño or supply his place. May 12, 1724.

[5] Keene to Newcastle, May 24, 1734. *Ibid.*

not mistress of her time, and could not command her privacy. The king was hearty and gay, and went to mass and to hunt with equal regularity, but Keene doubted if he had the same use of his faculties as formerly; he took no notice of those who spoke to him or presented memorials. He passed his time in a very trivial manner with the queen and his five valets, who would read to him or amuse him with maps of Italy. But the queen could never be absent from his side except at the hour of toilet. Hence the importance of La Pellegrina, who, while dressing Elisabeth's hair, was the vehicle of secret instructions to or from the minister. But La Pellegrina was too pleasing a person to remain unmarried. She consequently lost the queen's favour, and was not yet replaced. Such are the inconveniences of personal government that Spain's great minister was seriously embarrassed and embroiled by the marriage of a lady's maid.

CHAPTER XVIII.

1736-37.

SPAIN ASSENTS TO THE PRELIMINARIES OF FRANCE—DEATH
OF PATIÑO—MINISTRY OF LA QUADRA—ADVANCES TO-
WARDS ENGLAND—THE COURT AT S. ILDEFONSO—
ARRIVAL OF FARINELLI—BETROTHAL OF DON CARLOS
TO MARIA AMELIA OF SAXONY.

THE year 1736 dragged on to the summer without any
essential change in the situation. The French wished to
keep the Spanish troops in Italy as a menace to the
emperor, and to make him more flexible on the subject of
Lorraine. The Spanish Court, on the other hand, believed
that if their army were withdrawn in safety, more weight
would be assigned to its representations. The French and
imperial generals in Italy were on bad terms. German
officers informed the Spaniards that in the arrangements for
an armistice the French took no precautions for the safety
of their allies. The Government of Madrid hoped that
France might yet come into collision with the emperor,
and that more might be made out of general confusion than
out of general peace. The king and queen were piqued by
the attempt of Fleury to treat separately with Don Carlos,
an unwarrantable interference in family affairs. Spain was
still attempting to regain touch with the Court of Vienna
independently of France. The injured powers were drawing
more closely to each other. Patiño confessed that he had
subsidised the Elector of Bavaria, and said that the elector
and the King of Sardinia had been most cavalierly treated,
as well as his own master. A treaty between Spain and
Sardinia was projected, and it was hoped that the Maritime

Powers might concur.[1]   Vaulgrenant professed to be jealous of the intimacy between Patiño and Keene.   He could not hinder a treaty with the English, but expressed a hope that it contained nothing to the prejudice of France.   Patiño replied that they were obliged to the French Court for leaving them at their liberty to make treaties ; and, as to their manner of doing it, France had only to reflect on the example which she herself had set for their imitation.   Yet, on May 18, Spain reluctantly signified her assent to the Preliminaries of Vienna.

The irritation produced by foreign war, and its disappointments, was always liable to vent itself on the minister who had been made responsible for its conduct.   It was to this that Alberoni and Ripperdá had succumbed.   It seemed not unlikely that Patiño might share their fate.   There were whispers that his relations with the queen were not so friendly as of yore ; that she complained that, not content with their joint manipulation of business for the king, he put matters in a false light even to her.   The appointment of Montijo to the Presidency of the Council of the Indies, without reference to himself, offended Patiño.   He wished to keep this important department under his own control, and to avoid the eyes of " so meddling a gentleman ".   A cabal was believed to be intriguing against the minister.   It consisted of Montijo, the Italian doctor Cervi, whom Keene describes as an odd sort of man, both in and out of his profession, Scotti, Laura Pescatori, and her *protégé* Campo Florido.   The queen's confessor had also turned against him, and was representing in an odious light the value of his plate and furniture, pretending also to discover that large sums were being conveyed abroad.   The minister's servants were secretly engaged to take an inventory of his plate.   Patiño was not popular.   He knew his vast superiority, and did not disguise the knowledge.   He realised to the full the absolute need which the queen had of his services ; she could not abandon him, for there was not a soul to

[1] This subject is discussed at length in Lord Essex's despatches.   Brit. Mus. MSS. Add. 27731.

succeed him. In this hour of irritation, with the burden of
the kingdom on his shoulders, and with failing health, he
perhaps trespassed on the queen's forbearance. At length
it was reported that she had publicly expressed herself
against her minister. This outbreak gave Patiño his opportunity. He insisted on replying at length to the charges
brought against him, and with triumphant result. He
furnished conclusive proofs of the great material progress
made by Spain in the course of his ministry, and then
passionately implored the king to guide him in the path of
further improvement. Full favour was restored to him, and
it was indeed doubted whether the queen's action had not
been concerted with her minister. It arose, said Keene,
perhaps from a fit of temper on the queen's part, or from
artifice to strengthen Patiño's credit with the king, and to
make him think that Patiño was his minister and not hers.
But the great minister's career was well-nigh over. In
September he was seriously ill with constant fever and a
cough. The doctors were blamed for not taking advantage
of a strong constitution unimpaired by excess, which would
have rendered bleeding and emetics safe. They timidly
administered oil of almonds and other ineffective palliatives.
The queen was at once in a violent state of agitation; she
realised the danger of the situation. "In a word," wrote
Keene, "there is no one man capable of succeeding him,
and if his employments are separated different views and
interests will clog the vivacity with which Spain has acted
of late years. Their marine must fall."[1] Imagination began
to wander to Alberoni as his successor. Every kindness was
lavished on Patiño by the king and queen. They ordered
the doctors to prevent his doing difficult business, and his
health improved. But early in October he caught a fresh
cold, and a relapse was the result. The doctors were unable
to give a name to his disease, but it apparently ended in
inflammation of the lungs. The faithful servant could not
put away his anxiety as to State affairs. He was heard to

---

[1] Keene to Newcastle, Sept. 29, 1736. *R. O. S.*, 230.

wish for but two hours' conversation with the king and queen, after which he should die happy. His last act was to send his secret papers to the king. He died on November 3. During his illness and on his death no sort of attention had been spared. The grandeeship was conferred upon himself and his heirs. He was buried with honours little less than royal. His brother Castelar had died before him, and a pension was granted to his niece, the Countess of Fuenclara.

The loss of Patiño was to the queen irreparable. She had from the first realised the worth of this right hand of Alberoni. He would at once enter into her plans and moderate her passions. He possessed the patient industry, the knowledge of detail which she lacked. If she struck out the line of policy which Spain should follow, Patiño built the road, and at times persuaded her to prudent deviations. He could overcome the obstinacy of the king, and the tendency of the queen to govern by pique rather than by reason. But for Patiño the Court would inevitably have made war with Portugal, for in this case the queen was as foolishly indignant and punctilious as the king. "Too much good usage has spoilt that Court," she cried; "if it were not for the little one the King of Portugal should have had his ears boxed." As a peace minister, Patiño may, considering his unequal opportunities, be ranked with Fleury and with Walpole, and had he lived to conduct the coming war, Spain might have boasted of a Chatham. He had not indeed the lively imagination of Alberoni, but possessed a sounder appreciation of the relation of means to ends. Keene realised that a great change had taken place, and utilised the opportunity to give a careful and lively picture of the condition and prospects of the Spanish Court. His despatches at this period present a portrait gallery hardly inferior to that of S. Simon, and his pictures are frescoes painted while the material was yet fresh. "The king," wrote the ambassador on November 6, "is not at all affected by Patiño's death; the queen extremely so, though she endeavours to hide it by a strained gaiety that discovers her concern. She allows in private that the loss is great, but she lets drop that it was the king and herself who formed him to foreign affairs, and if they have a loss in him, his Majesty and she are still alive both to direct their affairs themselves, and capable to form other ministers under their experience and instruction."[1] The nomination of Don Sebastian de la Quadra to the ministry of Foreign Affairs would, added Keene sarcastically, give their Majesties the opportunity of exercising both their faculties, for this gentleman was of very limited understanding. La Quadra, afterwards Marquis of Villarias, was destined to be the medium for the foreign policy of Spain during the remainder of the queen's reign. His ministry marks the third stage in the history of her personal influence. Alberoni had been the master, Patiño the *collaborateur*, La Quadra was the minister, the servant. For this his previous career had fitted him. He was the head clerk in the Secretary of State's office, and in this he had served for thirty years. Patiño, said Keene,[2] had founded his merits and preserved his reputation by employing and gratifying the natural dispositions of the king and queen, by flattering them with stories of their power, and by professing his readiness at short notice to set fire to the four corners of the earth, though sometimes not to discover his nakedness he was forced to find means to inspire them with a sort of moderation. La Quadra was one who would neither suggest violent measures nor prevent their execution; he would place his merit on his resignation to royal orders, neither prompting to any policy nor making himself responsible for the least accident imaginable; his fear of speaking more than he should would prevent his talking as much as he ought, and he would as soon disclose to a foreign minister the most important secret of the Court as tell him from whence he received his last despatch; he was honest, timid and indolent, and had no bias for any particular

---

[1] Keene to Newcastle, Nov. 6, 1736. *R. O. S.*, 230.   [2] *Ibid.*

power ; in foreign affairs he was seldom asked his opinion
on letters read to the king and queen, but if it were demanded
Keene felt convinced that like a novice he cast his eyes upon
the ground and professed to have but the bare capacity to
execute their orders, adding that he referred all matters of
policy to their high and sovereign intelligence. " This is
the foot upon which he entered into his ministry and the
reason why he will so long continue in it. He is therefore
more of a clerk of State than a minister, and his own indolence
and diffidence of himself will always keep him so, and that
by his own choice. As to the rest, he is faithful in reporting
all matters to their Catholic Majesties and as exact in returning their answers without modelling them to any particular views as his predecessor Patiño used to do."[1]   Montijo
was the ambitious spirit among the ministers ; he had hoped
to succeed Patiño, and offered to fill all the offices at once,
but it was intended to confine him to the Presidency of the
Indies. The Department of Finance and temporarily that of
Marine and the Indies were entrusted to the Marquis of
Torre Nueva, a weak, embarrassed, timid man, without any
good or bad intentions towards the English, but liable to be
led astray from his want of knowledge of the Indies. He
was a creature of Patiño, and ill-natured people said that
the minister had recommended his appointment to make his
own loss felt.

   The Government was now entirely in the hands of
Spaniards, and much upon the old Spanish footing, except
that there was no Council of State. D'Argenson has,
among others, said that under Philip's first wife the government was French, under his second Italian, and under his
son Spanish. Even if Patiño be reckoned as Italian this
statement passes over the last ten years of Elisabeth's
régime, during which the chief offices of State were more
completely in the hands of natives than during any other
decade of the century. It is true, however, that Italians
were found in the drawing-room and the bedroom if excluded

from the Council Chamber. Some of those who were in direct contact with the queen had caballed for Patiño's fall. But the queen probably utilised them for social rather than political purposes. The Parmesan doctor, Cervi, had made an enormous fortune by his doses of senna and rhubarb, and had justified Alberoni's belief that by patience and management he might outwit his French *confrères*. He was occasionally consulted on affairs of State, but as he was exclusively concerned with his own interests, did neither harm nor good to any foreign power. Scotti was still a personage of great weight, though in Keene's opinion a man of as bad morals as parts. His obvious function was to manage the queen's privy purse, to provide for her *menus plaisirs* and her wardrobe. But apart from this he maintained a correspondence with all the small fry of foreign spies and agents who did not write direct to the office of the Secretary of State. Consequently he sometimes took upon himself to converse on subjects which he did not understand, and was occasionally consulted by the king and queen, though not unaware of his capacity. Laura Pescatori had apparently lost her influence, and the queen's chief lady friend, since the departure of the Duchess of S. Pierre and the marriage of La Pellegrina, was the Marchioness Las Nieves. To her all who sought for appointments would pay their court. She had originally accompanied the infanta to France, and was now governess to the youngest infanta. It is hard to account for the attraction which she exercised on the queen. She is described as an ill-natured old Spanish woman who brought nothing good from Paris but an inveterate hatred of the French, to which she now added an equal dislike for the Portuguese. Her office was to collect the scandal of Madrid and of the kingdom, and as special hours were reserved for her report, she had many opportunities of recommending candidates for promotion.

It was clear that foreign policy would be affected by Patiño's death. Keene wrote that England had nothing to fear from the new ministers, but there was reason to apprehend the " vivacity and flirts " of the queen. " Now that she is let loose to her own imagination, without having any one about her that has weight enough to restrain it, Patiño's maxims of force and power will stick by her for a long time. This, with her own temper, will be capable of pushing her forward to any extremities ; and though in the execution she will find the want in the resources Patiño was master of, yet as this must be learnt from reflection and experience, it will not prevent her from beginning broils, and thus disturbing and distressing other powers whose interest is to preserve the tranquillity of Europe." [1] On the other hand, the resentment against France, which Patiño in his last months had fostered, was likely to subside, and this favoured the acceptance of the Preliminaries and the possibilities of a general peace, for the king and queen would soon weary of the details of an active diplomacy. The Court began to be sensible of its isolation. The King of Sardinia was drawn nearer to the emperor by his engagement to a Princess of Lorraine, whom the Queen of Spain regarded as a second string for her son Don Carlos. It was long, however, before the relations of Spain to France could be cordial, and the acquiescence in the Preliminaries of Vienna complete. It transpired that the emperor had made the cession of the Two Sicilies personal to Don Carlos without reference to his heirs. Hence the queen roughly handled Vaulgrenant.. All delays, she said, were due to the Court of France, which had hindered their sending their ambassador, Fuenclara, to Vienna ; a minister of her own would have settled matters in as many days as it had now cost months : he should now go to Vienna, let the French do what they could ; if the emperor did not think fit to grant her demands, Spain could do herself justice without the aid of France ; the 25,000 men who could be sent to Barcelona, at the shortest notice, joined to the troops in Italy, would rid her of any fear of the emperor's intentions against Spain or Don Carlos.

Yet the Spanish troops were returning from Tuscany ;

---

[1] Keene to Walpole, Dec. 4, 1736.   *R. O. S.*, 280.

and early in February their general, Montemar, arrived.
He fully expected to be placed at the head of the administration, but his influence had been undermined, and he met
with no extraordinary reception. The queen spoke much of
the conqueror in public, but connoisseurs regarded this as
not telling in his favour. She opposed his entry to the
ministry. La Quadra pleased her better every day, and he
was one who loved peace and quiet for its own sake. A
general peace appeared more probable. Fuenclara was sent
to Vienna, and was well received ; though his proposals for
the hand of an archduchess met with no definite response.
Keene was told by his usual informant that the queen had
resolved to write for an English princess, and to request
a description of beauty, qualifications, and health. The disgrace of Chauvelin was a sign of the decline of the war party
in France. Immediate hostilities were impossible, even if
desired. But thirty out of the fifty Spanish ships were sea-
worthy, and stores were short. The disappointments of the
past, and the financial condition of the present, contributed
to the desire for peace. An influential committee was appointed to suggest financial reforms, but its members were
quite unable to agree. The Pretender was out of favour,
and his pension in arrears. The credit of the Irish at Court
had dwindled. "They are despised and avoided," wrote
Keene, "by anybody who pretends to common-sense."
Spain seemed turning her face away from the Catholic
system sketched in the Pacification at Vienna, and looking
towards a Protestant alliance. The Spanish and Neapolitan
ministers at Florence, and the Spanish Consul at Leghorn,
were reprimanded for their attentions to the Pretender's
son. When Campo Florido took leave on his departure on
a mission to Venice, the queen told him privately not to
trust the French. He said that the spirit of his instructions
was different from what her Majesty's appeared to be.
"No matter," she replied, "I tell you this that you may be
upon your guard, and use your discretion." She was unwilling, however, to pledge herself. "A bear," said La
Quadra, "that is not bound can lick at ease." There was

a disposition to come to terms with Portugal, and both powers were inclined to arrange their difficulties without reference to France. At the close of the year Keene reported that there was still not the greatest harmony imaginable between the two Houses of Bourbon. On the other hand, the reverses of the Turkish war made the emperor more accessible. He was not so positive in his refusal of his second daughter's hand. He hoped by amusing the queen to keep the Spaniards out of Italy, perhaps even to get subsidies. The queen surprised all who knew her by not pressing for recognition of her claims to the allodial possessions of the House of Medici, for the Grand Duke of Tuscany was just dead. Yet when the emperor met with reverses she showed indecent joy, and said in public that, setting aside considerations of religion, she would sooner confide in the Grand Turk than the emperor.

There was now little likelihood that the relations of Spain and England in America would lead to serious trouble. The new minister was friendly and candid, if somewhat dilatory. Some little anxiety was felt as to a suspected attack from Havana upon the new colony of Georgia. An adventurer named Wall, *alias* Savery, made an extraordinary confession to the English Government as to information respecting the colony, which he had sold to Patiño, and of the means which had been taken to destroy the settlement. La Quadra, however, solemnly disavowed Wall, and Keene treated it merely as an instance of Patiño's system, who seldom or never refused to encourage projects, however impracticable, and then let their authors starve while waiting for supplies and further orders. The Vice-Admiral Mari showed his readiness to meet the English complaints by ordering a list to be made of all the shipowners in the Indies. He engaged that patents should be given only to people of good circumstances and reputation. In the last few years the complaints of depredations had almost ceased. In 1735 but two or three informations were laid ; in 1736 none ; in 1737, however, the number had risen to four or five. On the other hand, the rigour of the protective system at home was increasing. The *indulto* of 4 or 5 per cent. had been raised by Patiño to 9 ; it was now 16, and was shortly to be advanced to 20. The change of system in the Government was also not entirely advantageous. It was true that the English were freed from " such a turbulent enterprising genius as Patiño," but the redress of grievances was harder. La Quadra laid the papers before the king every Sunday night, but was often interrupted by the arrival of the French post. If they concerned the marine they were remitted to that department and thence to the admiralty. The admiralty report was " balloted about " until it came to the king. La Quadra then formed his answers from the words of the report and remitted it to the marine and thence again to the admiralty. Such delay might with so singularly impatient a nation as the English ultimately prove dangerous, but that danger was distant appeared from the concluding words of Keene's last despatch for the year 1737. " It is scarcely to be conceived that a country destitute as this is of foreign friends and allies, deranged in its finances, whose army is in a bad condition, its navy in a worse, if possible, without any minister of heat (unless Montijo should get the reins in his hand) to push their Catholic Majesties on to any extravagant enterprise, or of capacity to re-establish their affairs, can have any premeditated design to fall out with us at present, notwithstanding the blustering steps they have taken about our colony of Georgia ; and as to renewing depredations, I have as yet no reason to think they proceed from orders sent from here, but from the licence the governors of the Havannah and Puerto Rico have given themselves of late to give commissions chiefly for their own interest, though all allow that the American seas were never more filled with illicit traders than they are at present."

Within the Court circle there were signs of the approach of peace. The fire-eating Montemar returned from Italy expecting to take the leading part upon the royal stage. But the Spanish Bombastes was reduced to playing second

z

to the Neapolitan falsetto. Italy took her conquerors captive by the voice of Farinelli :

> Sounds, not arms, shall win the prize,
> Harmony the path to fame.

Nothing proves so conclusively the influence which the queen retained over her husband as her success in curing him of his rooted dislike for music. " The queen," wrote Keene on February 18, 1737, " is endeavouring to look out for diversion for the king, who has a natural aversion for music. If she can change his temper as far as to amuse him with it, it may keep them both from thinking of more turbulent matter." The queen's object, however, was not to soothe her husband's savage breast, nor to turn his thoughts from military glory. She had realised that her dancing and hunting days were well-nigh over. Her exquisite figure was falling a victim to the family *embonpoint*. She was apprehensive as to her health ; her legs were much swollen, and she could take no exercise. Were the king allowed to take his usual amusement out of doors he might fall under influences which she could not control. She no longer feared indeed his abdication, for she had carefully guarded all the avenues, but as the king and queen grew tired of field diversions something was absolutely necessary to amuse him at home, to keep his mind as much in motion as his natural melancholy would allow.[1] Hence the necessity of inspiring Philip with another passion and of making the interior of the palace more cheerful than of old. Private theatricals became the fashion. The cardinal infant and his sisters performed a play before their parents and a select party of guests. A ball was also given for the first time since the Treaty of Seville, and the courtiers were asked to dance before their Majesties. The infants' performance was regularly repeated. Every evening they rehearsed their little opera before the queen ; and on Sunday evening Philip attended at a full-dress performance, when the children wore magnificent

---

[1] Keene to Newcastle, Sept. 2, 1737. *R. O. S.*, 233.

habits suited to their parts. He appeared to be extremely pleased, as he had every reason to be. The least breath of air was now sufficient to keep the royal pair from stirring from their rooms ; no business was done, and, what Keene never expected to see, the king was hearing music with patience. In the summer the winning card was to be played. Nothing was discussed but the approaching arrival of Farinelli.

Carlo Broschi, surnamed Farinelli, was the finest singer of his time, perhaps of any time. He had already entranced the Courts of Vienna, S. James and Versailles. The queen tempted him from England, and pledged him never to return. The story is told that during a fit of the king's melancholia she arranged that Farinelli should sing in the adjoining room ; the king, startled from his depression by his notes, sent for him, and again and again ordered him to sing ; he offered any reward that the singer might demand, whereupon Farinelli, for his only guerdon, prayed that the king would rise, and wash and shave, and attend his Council. The anecdote is characteristic, but hardly bears the light of criticism. The singer's reward at all events was more substantial and more in accordance with the usual needs of distinguished vocalists. Farinelli was formally admitted to the royal household. In consideration for his singular talent for music, and on condition that he should never sing before the public, he received a salary of 1500 guineas, charged upon the post-office. He was allowed to ride in a two-mule coach, and to make his journeys in a coach and six. Near every royal palace was assigned to him a house.[1] The queen's triumph was complete, and her health improved. Every fine autumn day their Majesties would hunt, while every evening was whiled away by the sweet notes of Farinelli. Moreover, the troops from Italy had been collected for autumn manœuvres near Segovia, and the king and queen took much pleasure in reviewing them. Both were in excellent spirits ; neither their tem-

---

[1] A copy of this document may be read. *R. O. S.*, 233.

pers nor their countenances were altered by the news that
Fuenclara had lost all hopes of an imperial marriage.   The
queen, however, was not wholly bent on pleasure ; she was
much engaged with the advancement of her children.   Provision was first made for Don Philip.   He is described as
being of a most amiable character, but had already acquired
those French propensities which made him unpopular in
Spain, and were ridiculously exaggerated in after years.
"His Spanish governors have been and are such woeful
creatures that his French valets have got the better of
them, and disgusted him against them ; and, what is worse,
against the whole Spanish nation.   Everything must be
French to please him ; he does not even care to speak his
own language, except when entirely forced to it."[1]   This
creation of French valets was now appointed Grand Admiral of Spain.   No existing office could satisfy the needs
of the queen's second son.   The title was new, the jurisdiction extensive ; the salary, considering the condition of
Spanish finances, enormous.   With this post was combined
the command of the Spanish and Marine Guards.   Dissatisfaction was naturally great.   It was complained that one son
had Naples with Spanish money to support him in as much
state as its former possessors.   Men believed that the Prince
of Asturias had been compelled to renounce his claim to
this portion of his lawful heritage.   The great commands in
the military orders were divided among the queen's other
sons, one of whom had command of the fleet, and was
intended to unite to it the supreme authority over the land
forces.   Meanwhile the Prince of Asturias, idolised by the
Spaniards, was neglected, and not even summoned to the
Despacho.   Keene concluded his year's despatches with a
graphic account of the king and queen and their surroundings.   "The king is in perfect health, and most exceedingly
inactive, indifferent with respect to the general train of
affairs.   If I was to add that he was frequently incapable of
giving attention to them, I believe that I should not

[1] Keene, March 18, 1737. *R. O. S.*, 232.

advance a falsehood ; and as this prince's character consists of as many contradictions as qualities, it is impossible to give a true idea of him, which is the reason why your Grace must have heard so many different accounts of him, which are neither all false nor all true. An instance of what I am saying may be taken from his letting the queen manage almost everything at her will and pleasure, even with the emperor, whom he can never have any sort of liking for ; and yet, on some occasions, he wakens, as it were, at a despatch, and opposes her designs in matters of less moment. It is not in her power to get him to advance a person he has no opinion of, and it was with as much difficulty as *fourberie* that he was brought to consent to the higher Indulto. I could give several instances of the extreme remissness of this prince on the one side, and of his *opiniâtreté* on the other, but the foregoing will suffice. The queen's care and life, therefore, is divided between keeping him from an entire *abandon*, which she has successfully brought about by the diversions she has provided, and from his being really and truly informed of the state of affairs in any other light than she thinks proper, which she has effectually secured by not admitting any persons to approach him that are capable of furnishing him with any materials that may oppose her ideas, when he happens to be in a position to interest himself in what is transacting."[1] The king was now, as always, morbidly sensitive on any subject which reminded him of death. It was the etiquette to wear black in mourning, but the king steadily refused to do so except on the death of his son Luis. In January, 1738, the news arrived of the death of the English queen. The Court dared not appear in black, and covered their decent mourning with coloured surtouts. In holy week only was it permitted to wear black velvet, with red linings and gold buttons. The queen in public wore a dress of dark grey, with black ribbons. The king did not so much object to the sight of the ladies of the Court in mourning, and, consequently, they were dressed in black velvet as usual.

[1] Keene to Newcastle, Dec. 9, 1737. *R. O. S.*, 233.

Queen Caroline's death was soon forgotten in the engagement of Don Carlos to Maria Amalia of Saxony. The courtship was a profound secret. It was not so much, Keene thought, the marriage itself which pleased the king as the belief that no one knew of it, and that none of his courtiers could guess the princess; for " the queen repeated that the house of Saxony was a good one almost as often as the king talked of the secrecy of the negotiations, and she laid particular stress on her new daughter being the eldest daughter of the eldest daughter of the Emperor Joseph; and his Catholic Majesty, in public before the French ambassador, gave the preference to the house of Saxony before that of Bavaria; and at last, if I dare say it, he seemed to forget his own relation to the Duke of Bavaria's family, but likewise the French opinion that the house of Bourbon cannot receive any additional lustre from any other alliance whatsoever ".[1]

The secret, however, had nearly been divulged, for the queen had given the picture of the princess to the Court painter to copy, in order that the original might be sent to Don Carlos. The copyist saw on the back that it was painted by one " Sylvestre à Dresden ". It is true that he did not know where Dresden was, but the queen could not trust to his ignorance, and threatened him with the loss of his head if he mentioned the circumstance to any breathing man. The king was again subject to a slight return of his malady, though he was regular at his morning's mass and his evening's music. The queen was extremely fat, and the ailment in her legs and knees was becoming chronic. Both had taken a strong aversion to the French ambassador, Vaulgrenant, who was suspected of prying into the letters that lay upon the royal table; the king consoled himself with the reflection that he locked up all State papers, while the queen added, that all he could have seen were a few letters to her daughter in Portugal. The ambassador had perhaps a motive for his curiosity, for the queen had high hopes of the hand of an archduchess for Don Philip. The

[1] Keene to Newcastle, Jan. 13, 1738. *R. O. S.*, 240.

empress might well regard him as an eligible *parti*, for it
seemed certain that the Prince of Asturias would be childless, and the queen hoped for the crown of Naples for her
second son, on the translation of Carlos to that of Spain.
This was less open to the criticism of foreign powers, who
had feared the reunion of the Spanish and Austrian mon-
archies. Such a marriage, however, would have led to
another Treaty of Vienna. Spain would have made her
peace with Austria without the intervention of France,
and this Fleury was determined to prevent. A sudden
proposal was therefore made for a double marriage between
the two houses of Bourbon. Fleury was barely in time,
for the infanta was already sought by a Saxon prince. The
queen was flattered; she willingly consented to the marriage of Don Philip with Marie Louise Elisabeth of France,
but remembering the fiasco of the marriage of her eldest
daughter, she was resolved that no marriage should take
place between the dauphin and the younger infanta until
she was of marriageable age. All Europe was alarmed at the
news of these negotiations. Men always, said D'Argenson,
saw farther than facts and their just consequences, and thus
they imagined a complete reconciliation between France
and Spain, to be followed by a policy of perfect harmony.
The object of the Bourbon crowns, it was believed, was to
obtain Parma and Piacenza for Don Philip and his bride,
which, in D'Argenson's opinion, would be unreasonable,
and to make common cause in the commercial disputes
with England, which would be entirely reasonable. It was
necessary to persuade the emperor that the object of France
was to induce Spain to accede to the peace. Yet the queen
long held out, and the condition was that the guarantee of
the Pragmatic Sanction should be annulled. Spain in effect
gave the law which the emperor, owing to the war with
Turkey, was compelled to accept.

The slightest movement on the part of the Bourbon
crowns was enough to cause suspicion. The French,
incited by the Genoese to crush an insurrection in Corsica,
were believed to be actuated by the desire of manufacturing

a kingdom for Don Philip. But the king's health at this time was hardly such as to warrant an adventurous policy. He seemed outwardly well, but had fallen into such whimsical ways as to show that he was incapable of business, and, indeed, he troubled himself little about it. At mass he behaved as usual, and this was followed by a short conversation upon the Turkish war. The change which then came over him must be described in Keene's own words. "When he retires to dinner, he sets up such frightful howlings as astonished every one at the beginning, and have obliged the *confidants* to clear all the apartments as soon as he sat down to table; and as the queen cannot be sure of his behaviour for the rest of the day, she does not fail to keep him within doors, insomuch that they do not take the air in their favourite garden of S. Ildefonso as they used to do heretofore. His diversion at night is to hear Farinelli sing the same five Italian airs that he sung the first time that he performed before him, and has continued to sing every night for near twelve months together.[1] But your Grace will smile when I inform you that the king himself imitates Farinelli, sometimes air after air, and sometimes after the music is over, and throws himself into such freaks and howlings that all possible means are taken to prevent people from being witness to his follies. He had one of these fits this week, which lasted from twelve till past two in the morning. They have talked of bathing him, but fear they shall not persuade him to try that remedy."[2] Seldom have the bath and the razor proved such stubborn obstacles to such high ambitions. There must have been moments also when Elisabeth must have wished Farinelli back in England, or, what she would have thought synonymous, at Hanover.

---

[1] Farinelli in after years told Dr. Burney that he sang the same four songs every night till the king's death. Two of these were "Pallido il sole" and "Per questo dolce amplesso," by Hasse. Even Sir A. Sullivan might envy the composer for such a run, which is probably unexampled. Farinelli must have sung these songs 3600 nights in succession.

[2] Keene to Newcastle, August 2, 1738. *R. O. S.*, 241.

CHAPTER XIX.

1738-39.

COMMERCIAL RELATIONS WITH ENGLAND—COLONIAL AC-
TIVITY OF SPAIN—AGITATION IN ENGLAND—THE RIGHT
OF SEARCH—THE CONVENTION RESPECTING CLAIMS—
ITS REJECTION BY THE OPPOSITION IN ENGLAND—
DECLARATION OF WAR—THE SPANISH-FRENCH MAR-
RIAGES—AVERSION OF SPANIARDS TO THE RUPTURE
WITH ENGLAND—EVENTS OF THE WAR—THE POLICY
OF FLEURY AND THE OPINIONS OF D'ARGENSON.

FOR the year 1738 there was every prospect of peace, and yet before the summer it was clear that Spain and England were drifting into war. This was no heritage of the war of Polish succession. With England Spain had every reason to be content. She had resisted the entreaties of the Imperial Government to fulfil her alleged engagements. For a moment some predisposition had been shown in favour of Portugal, but England had scrupulously resisted the temptation of an attack upon the Spanish colonies. The Spanish Government had likewise behaved with caution and consideration; unusual attention was given to the English minister's remonstrances. It was the accident of peace which indeed directly led to war. Both Governments were now able to resume negotiations for a settlement of outstanding claims and for a more satisfactory understanding in future. A successful issue seemed probable. La Quadra had no warlike ambitions. The Spanish envoy, Sir Thomas Fitzgerald, generally known as Don Geraldino, was believed to be well disposed to England, and Keene had welcomed his appointment. No minister was more certain to act with judgment and impartiality than Keene. He thoroughly understood the Spanish character, he could make allowances for their dilatory and unbusinesslike habits and their national sensitiveness. He was well aware that the faults were not all on one side and that the English claims were frequently unreasonable.

The most unfortunate factor in the negotiations was perhaps the character of Quintana, who was successively Commissioner of Claims, Secretary for Marine and the Indies, and Plenipotentiary. He was particularly averse to foreigners; his head was full, said Keene, of Spanish smoke. " A more difficult, tenacious, disputable antagonist was never met with, starting and stumbling at the most trivial punctilios imaginable."   Keene foresaw that he would treat the interests of the South Sea Company with rigour, and to him is chiefly to be ascribed the authorship of the prolix replies which vexed the soul of the Duke of Newcastle throughout this year. Quintana was moreover not a practical man, but a most abstract and metaphysical negotiator upon matters of commerce. This was not quite an accident, for the English practical grievances were in a measure due to the growth of Spanish theory.

The English wondered that they could not enjoy the privileges of the reign of Charles II. But the situation in Spain had changed. Under Philip V. there was a distinct revival of colonial and commercial interest. The more enlightened statesmen definitely resolved to adopt the Mercantile System to which the fortunes of England and Holland were believed to be due. The colonies were intended to be the outlet for native industries, and the intrusion of other nations must be jealously watched. Much attention was paid to better means of communication with the colonies; monopolies and State bounties were granted to Colonial Companies. At the moment when Spain saw a prospect of deriving full advantage from her vast colonial empire she found herself perpetually thwarted by the territorial encroachments of English settlers and by the abnormal commercial enterprise which the peaceful administration of Walpole fostered. The nominal claims of Spain were denied precisely at the moment when it was intended to make them real. The recent Anglo-Portuguese dispute in Africa will illustrate the irritation naturally caused by the territorial and commercial pretensions of England within the professed limits of Spanish America.

Among the leading advocates of the Mercantile System was Ustariz, a pupil partly of Orri and Macanaz, partly of Alberoni and Patiño. He was acquainted with all the latest views of political economy, was a writer of no mean order, and resolved to put his theories in practice. His constant theme was the injury which the monarchy had received from foreigners and foreign commerce, and the deception which had been practised upon it in former treaties. He had gained a rapid ascendancy over La Quadra, who was in Keene's opinion more dull and stubborn than could be well conceived. Montijo, who from his embassy in England had some glimmering of the English character and claims, had been thrust aside by Ustariz. It was believed that if he could succeed to the Secretaryship of the War Office, of which he was head clerk, he would shoulder out La Quadra himself. Ustariz was popular at Court, and his success was greatly due to his ejection of Torre Nueva from the ministry of Finance. He had formed a syndicate to offer a loan for 2,000,000 ducats for the queen's present necessities, whereas the minister had represented the impossibility of raising such a sum. La Quadra's brain was filled by Ustariz with notions of the grandeur of the monarchy, and the Court became more intractable than Keene had ever known it.

It was clear that, with such a *personnel* in the Spanish Government, negotiations needed delicate handling. This was fully realised by Walpole ; and Keene was willing and able to second his endeavours. But Walpole's conciliatory policy was in itself one of the prime causes of the war. Agitation in England was from the first artificially fostered by the need of a popular programme for the purposes of Parliamentary opposition. The Spanish atrocities made a good party cry, the theme of speeches and pamphlets throughout the country. The mutilated Jenkins was the prototype of the impaled Bulgarian. The Bristol skipper had in 1731 lost his ear at the hands of an atrocious pirate named Fandino.[1] At the moment of the outrage he had, as he replied, when questioned before the bar of the House of Commons, commended his soul to God and his cause to his country. The country, after a delay of seven years, now took up his cause, though in the interval the Spanish Government had offered satisfaction, and sent stringent orders for the punishment of the offender. Walpole owed his fall, and Jenkins his fortune, to the frugal preservation of the severed ear. Letters, real or imaginary, from English sailors, languishing in Spanish prisons, found no lack of publishers. Outrages were aggravated by the fact that they were committed not only against peaceful traders by armed pirates, but by ferocious Catholics against God-fearing Protestants. There is no question that the introduction of the religious factor appreciably stimulated popular passion, and added to the danger of war. Of late there were symptoms of a fresh Catholic revival, and schemes for a reunion of the Catholic powers against Protestantism. The Blood Bath of Thorn and the persecution of Salzburg Protestants were merely extreme manifestations of a common tendency, the perversion of the Elector of Saxony only the most prominent result of extensive propaganda. It has been seen that hostility to heresy had played no slight part in the recent Pacification of Vienna. Protestantism was naturally in a nervous, irritable condition ; and though the religious question was not prominently put forward until the Seven Years' War, it is an accessory not to be overlooked in the War of Jenkins' Ear.   In the

---

[1] As early as 1761 the Tory Harvey spoke in debate of Jenkins' ear as a political fiction invented for purposes of opposition in 1738-39. Professor J. K. Laughton, in the *English Historical Review*, Oct., 1889, has proved from the Admiralty Records that Jenkins' tale was true, and this is confirmed by documents inspected by the author in the Record Office. Research, however, was hardly needed, for the outrage is categorically described, among others, in the *Gentleman's Magazine* for June, 1731 (vol. i. 265-288).

current political literature tho word Papist occurs almost as frequently as *guarda-costa*.

The English Government moreover was not united. Lord Harrington had long wished for war with Spain before the two lines of Bourbon could consolidate their power. The Duke of Newcastle, Secretary of State for the Southern Department, was already playing to the gallery, preparing for himself the favour or forgiveness of the opposition. In the most important emergencies he had often left his minister at Madrid for weeks without instructions. Keene would beseech his secretary for one of his Grace's *coups de plume*. But now despatch upon despatch was scribbled on every paltry claim, and added to the irritation and difficulties of the Spanish Court. Yet more unfortunate was the conduct of the opposition, unable to overthrow Walpole, but making government and negotiation alike impossible. Keene found his endeavours hampered at every turn by the licence of Parliament and Press. Every scurrilous speech and pamphlet was sent to Spain and translated. "They are but too well informed of all that passes, thanks to our patriots, who, by bawling for the honour of the nation, strip it of its weight and dignity." [1] At a decisive moment, when the tension between the Bourbon Courts was extreme, when Spain might easily have been attracted into an intimate alliance, the exigencies of the Parliamentary opposition and the avarice of a handful of speculative merchants drove Spain back into the arms of France, tempting the substantial renewal of the abortive Family Compact of 1733.

During the eighteen months before the rupture, there were moments when a peaceful termination seemed imminent, and others when war seemed certain. On the English as on the Spanish side, theoretical rather than practical grievances proved the chief obstacle to peace. It was at the opening of 1738 that there was an increasing tendency to dwell upon the general principle of the Right

---

[1] Keene, April 24, 1739. *R. O. S.*, 245.

of Search. Walpole was forced by public opinion to send
a squadron to the Mediterranean, to grant letters of reprisal to the American merchants, and to reinforce the
garrison of Georgia. These measures irritated Spain, and
before the end of April the French merchants feared immediate war. In June the Spanish ports were fortified,
officers ordered to rejoin their regiments, and sailors raised.
La Quadra stated that his master desired to live in perfect
friendship with George II., but that if pushed to extremities he should use all his power. The wish for conciliation seemed genuine. English sailors who had been
confessedly engaged in contraband trade were released, and
all plans for an attack on Georgia laid aside. The ministers
showed every civility to Keene, and made it generally known
that the differences would be adjusted. Don Geraldino had
caused trouble in England; he had intrigued with the
opposition, and had been encouraged to represent an accord
as being out of the question. He now received a hint from
his Government to be more conciliatory, and indeed exceeded his instructions in a sudden readiness for compromise. He had agreed that the claim against Spain
should be valued at £200,000, and that the losses inflicted
by Admiral Byng should be regarded as a set off to the
amount of £60,000, to which was added a further sum of
£45,000, representing the difference between a cash payment
in Europe and assignment on revenues in America. The
question of Right of Search and the limits of Georgia and
Carolina were referred to a commission of plenipotentiaries,
who were to conclude their conferences within eight months.
The Spanish Government resented the appearance of buying
a peace. Keene, however, waxed judiciously warm, and
told La Quadra that the Convention had been sent from
London to be signed but not whittled away. La Quadra
stated that the king was prepared to execute the promises
made in his name; if the South Sea Company declined to
liquidate its debt, he would, nevertheless, satisfy the claims
of the English nation in ready money; it would then be
no motive for a national quarrel if the assiento were an-

nulled for non-compliance with reason, equity, or treaties. It was fully admitted that the duties of *guarda-costas* required definition, but Spain naturally refused to abandon all safeguards for the protection of her colonial trade. Keene wrote that Spain had gone as far as she would go to avoid a war; the nation sacrificed not a little of its pride in accepting a Convention which contained much to its disadvantage, and which had been signed without sufficient knowledge and authority. A letter from the Consul General Castres, one of the plenipotentiaries appointed under the Convention, will illustrate the situation. "It is lucky that Don Geraldino was not here. For several days I would have given my plenipotentiaryship for a crown. It has risen in value considerably since."[1]

Keene's labours were being attended with satisfactory results. Spanish naval officers were ordered to behave well to Englishmen. A suspected ship was released on a mere application to the Admiralty. The chief difficulty lay in the obstinate and short-sighted policy of the South Sea Company. Keene does not conceal his opinion that successive Boards of Directors had been always in the wrong, and that the Spanish claims were justifiable. Other countries and companies, he wrote, would have given as large a sum as that demanded for the goodwill of the Court in so lucrative a trade, yet the directors would not bribe the Court of Spain with money which was really due to it; the Court was so disgusted with the *crambe repetita* which the directors ordered him to dish up that it was resolved not to lend an ear to further representations until it heard the money chink. Further complaints, Keene felt sure, would lead to the suspension of the contract. "You may remember," he wrote, "how long ago I foretold that this affair would bring us into an unlucky scrape, and therefore I took the liberty to write as much to the office, where I know everything has been done to prevent it; but, between ourselves, it looks as if the

---

[1] Oct. 18, 1738. *R. O. S.,* 241.

directors had been willing to shift the blow from their own shoulders to saddle those of their successors, and this it is what brought matters to extremities."[1]

It was for these reasons that the Spanish Government insisted on the exclusion of the South Sea Company dispute from the Convention, and Keene felt obliged to concede the point. The King of Spain had his own remedy to enforce the fulfilment of the contract : he refused to have his hands tied by such arrangements as the plenipotentiaries might make. On January 14, 1739, the Convention was signed by Keene and La Quadra and despatched to London for ratification. The Spanish Court was gratified at the conclusion of the dispute, and measures were taken for an early meeting of the plenipotentiaries. But these fair hopes of peace were dashed by the violence of the opposition in the session of February and March. It is not the only occasion on which an opposition has indulged in vulgar and unbridled epigram at the expense of a foreign power, but happily the results have rarely been so disastrous. The sensibility of the Spanish Court was stung beyond endurance, and the South Sea Company was encouraged to believe that it was an act of patriotism to fail to produce the accounts stipulated by their contract. Keene believed that even now peace was possible if only the English squadron were withdrawn that was menacing the coasts of Spain. In June, however, he warned English merchants that war was inevitable ; further meetings of the plenipotentiaries were useless, unless it were to give England time to mature her designs. News arrived of the order given by the English Government for general reprisals. On August 25 the King of Spain's Declaration of War was in print, and Keene was ordered to withdraw.[2]

[1] Keene to W. Cowrand, Jan., 1739. *R. O. S.*, 245.

[2] Keene was, owing to the part taken by him in the Convention, the best-abused man in England, next to Sir R. Walpole. Yet his merits were soon recognised, and after the peace of Aix-la-Chapelle he was sent to Spain to negotiate a fresh commercial treaty. "I hope and believe when you consider the whole you will be of opinion that my friend Keene has acted honestly

It was generally assumed in England that war with Spain implied war with France, and that the former power was encouraged in its obstinacy by the promises of French support. D'Argenson himself has stated that the Spanish Court was encouraged to break the Convention by the hopes which the French marriages had roused and by the direct engagements of Fleury. Yet it is extremely doubtful if such was the case. The French Government undoubtedly utilised the opportunity to recover the queen's favour. Disappointed at the failure of imperial marriages, she found compensation in fresh ties with the older line of Bourbon. Don Philip was married to a French princess, and the infanta was promised to the dauphin. Reconciliation was complete. " The queen has abandoned herself to France to such a degree that she has forgotten all former disgusts and almost fallen out with those who were for advising her to be contented with this reconciliation without throwing herself so absolutely into the arms of new friends. She says that France was the first that sought this reunion, and it was not she who made her court to France; that the former disgusts were the effects of the private motives, views, and interests that each of them might have then entertained, but that at present they are the true and solid maxims of national interest that operate between both Courts."[1] It is probable that the resistance to the Convention signed by Don Geraldino in July and August, 1738, was due to the hopes of a treaty with France. Keene believed that Spain was playing with England till she heard from France, and that Geraldino was but a cat's-paw, for his scheme, which caused such an outburst in the summer, was laid before the Court in April. The real source of irritation was the despatch of Haddock's squadron in June, 1738.

and bravely ; but, poor man, he is so sore with old bruises that he still feels the smart and fears another thrashing."—Pelham to Pitt, Oct. 12, 1750. " Stocks rise to high-water mark," wrote Horace Walpole, " and what is to me as clear is that the exploded Don Benjamin has repaired what the patriot Lord Sandwich had forgot or not known how to do at Aix-la-Chapelle."— Letters of H. Walpole, ii. 229.

[1] Keene to Newcastle, May 4, 1738. *R. O. S.*, 240.

France was probably by no means desirous of a rupture from which she would have difficulty in keeping aloof, but she naturally wished to separate Spain from England. Thus she endeavoured to procure a better understanding between the Court of Madrid and those of Lisbon and Turin. She went far towards pledging herself to secure Parma and Piacenza for Don Philip. Upon this the queen was still bent: it was her first object; the dispute with England was quite secondary, a disagreeable interruption. She longed for an able minister to settle this, and publicly wished that Patiño were alive. " I was very fond of him ; I should much like to have him back in these circumstances." [1] She now despised La Quadra, whose only merit it was to obey orders, and be sent back to his office with his papers, without complaint or representation, when not in a humour to discuss business. She said that she had fallen into the hands of a parcel of petty clerks, each of whom wished " to carve like a Patiño ".[2] The danger to England and Europe consisted in the fact that the weakness of her ministry forced the queen to rely on France. The cajolings and flatteries of France blinded her to her own interests and those of her nation. Fleury, Keene believed, wished to leave the two Courts united at his death, and he feared that an offensive and defensive alliance would follow—a prophecy that was most precisely fulfilled within a few months of the cardinal's decease. The queen never realised the importance of the American Question, to her it was an intolerable bore ; had she been interested, war would have come sooner, or not at all. Such was her infatuation, wrote Keene, that more serious moments were spent in patterns for lacing and embroidering the uniforms of the officers of the household than in thinking of English affairs.[3] La Quadra was reported never to take the trouble to read Don Geraldino's despatches about the Convention and the

---

[1] Keene to Newcastle, June 16, 1738. *R. O. S.*, 241.
[2] Keene to Newcastle, May 26, 1739. *Ibid.*, 245.
[3] Keene to Newcastle, Jan. 29, 1739. *Ibid.*

determination of the House of Lords, while letters from France were eagerly devoured.[1]

Nor again could the difficulties which were raised be ascribed to the king's sense of honour, of which much capital was made, nor even to his usual martial ardour. He was, to outward appearance, well and healthy, but was extremely nervous as to his condition, and could listen to no sort of business. After his short appearances in public he would applaud himself to his queen, and ask if he had not behaved himself like an image. The war, therefore, was not a queen's war nor a king's war. It has been often assumed that it was a national war : the sole national war, indeed, of this militant cycle. But on the side of Spain this seems extremely doubtful. The French, always unpopular, were, since the late war, in more evil odour than usual. There was among the nobility a strong feeling in favour of the English alliance ; and the people at large were indifferent to politics. The commercial classes were comparatively insignificant, and after all the Government rather than they was affected by the illicit commerce of the English traders. Keene had no ordinary knowledge of Spanish opinion. Immediately before war broke out he wrote that the public was averse to war and full of abuse for the ministry. It hated the expense of the French marriages and thought that France was tricking Spain, that instead of giving a dowry France coveted the Spanish portion of S. Domingo and untrammelled rights of navigation. It is noticeable that till within a month of the declaration of war no serious preparations were made in Spain, and even her defensive measures were solely due to the threatening attitude of Admiral Haddock's fleet. The new administration had taken stringent measures of economy. Pensions were suppressed, salaries suspended, the profits of army contractors curtailed. Pay was issued for the actual number of 60,000 men instead of for the 100,000 upon the rolls. Huraldi, the finance minister, even attacked the expenditure on the royal table. An annual

---

[1] Keene to Newcastle, March 30, 1739. *R. O. S.*, 245.

saving was effected which Keene places at 2,500,000 dollars
and the Venetian ambassador, Correr, at double.   Historians
have annually included these financial reforms in their account
of the war with England, but as yet its prospect was remote.
The Venetian ambassador states without hesitation that the
sum thus saved was intended for the purchase of Parma
and Piacenza from the emperor, who sorely needed money
for the Turkish war.   The Papacy facilitated the negotiation,
in which it had an interest, for it was believed that Don
Philip would recognise its suzerainty.   Keene also was disposed to take the same view of the destination of these
economies.   The main responsibility therefore of this needless war rested neither with Spain nor France, but with the
English opposition, determined to oust a minister who had
strayed too far from the militant principles of the Whig
party.   " They may ring their bells now," murmured
Walpole, as the city bells rang out in honour of the
declaration of war, " before long they will be wringing
their hands."

Spain had every reason to congratulate herself on the
war forced upon her by commercial greed and inconsiderate
jingoism.   In time of war, a nation with a seaboard and no
commerce enjoys great advantages over a power whose unprotected merchantmen are to be found on every sea.   The
commerce of Spain consisted solely in her galleons, which
might well escape the English cruisers, and were they
taken, the loss fell mainly on the foreign merchants to
whom their cargoes were consigned.   From the moment of
the declaration of war the Atlantic and the Channel
swarmed with privateers, many of them French ships
from Bayonne under Spanish colours, and the value of the
prizes swept into Santander amounted to an enormous sum.
The very depredations which had been carried on in America
by *guarda-costas*, real or false, were a proof of adventurous
energy, and a training school for seamanship.   The almost
complete independence of the Spanish governors, which was
a source of weakness in time of peace, and which indeed
had brought the rupture upon Spain, was perhaps an ad-

vantage when war broke out. They did not wait for orders from home, but took active measures to defend themselves. Untied by red tape, each province was practically autonomous and self-sufficing. Not only had Patiño introduced order into Spanish finances, but, unlike Walpole, he had trained a school of statesmen. Campillo and Somodevilla[1] were his pupils. When D'Argenson compared the English fleet of one hundred and ten sail with the thirty rotten ships of France and Spain, he exaggerated the weakness of the latter power. A respectable squadron under Pizarro reached American waters in safety. The quicksilver ships, with treasure on board, arrived just as the war broke out.

Yet there is little doubt that Spain, in declaring war, relied mainly on the engagements of France. It was universally believed in Europe that France could not refuse her aid, and this impression had been strengthened by the double marriage between the two lines of Bourbon. The indignation in England was stronger against France than against Spain. La Mina, the Spanish minister at Paris, was the hero of the day; no Spanish ambassador was ever in such high consideration; even the Parisian tradesmen shut their eyes to the increasing length of his account. The whole Court was working for Spain, and the union between the two crowns had never been so close. On the other hand, Lord Waldegrave found no one who would speak to him. His popularity was not increased by his joke on the French marine. "There goes the French fleet," he cried, as the pleasure boats passed under the Pont Neuf. He described his position as that of a bird upon a perch, and expressed his wonder that he had remained so long. Walpole, however, took every means to prevent a rupture, and among these was a proposal for a commercial treaty, providing for the free introduction of English woollens in return for that of French wines, a measure too far in advance of the age to be successful. Fleury felt that a closer alliance

---

[1] Better known as the Marquis Ensenada.

with Spain would entail his own overthrow. Spain would
gladly have repaid France for the expulsion of Alberoni
by the overthrow of Fleury. He knew that La Mina
was the instrument of the opposition for this purpose, and
probably was the cause of his recall. He objected to Montijo
and then to Campo Florido as successor to La Mina; but
the Queen of Spain stood firm, and said that he must choose
between the two, that an old priest had no right to veto
all her kingdom at his pleasure. Fleury's choice fell upon
Campo Florido, who bore no good reputation among French
diplomats; he was reported to be small at soldiering, and
great at plundering. Had Patiño lived, it was said that he
would have lost his head. La Mina was preparing to
make a sudden exit with his debts unpaid, and Campo
Florido was expected to follow in his steps. He was an
extravagant swindler, wrote D'Argenson, worthy to be an
Italian.

Fleury's strength lay in the weakness of the French
marine. The opposition realised that war in its present
condition was impossible. The future foreign minister, the
Marquis d'Argenson, was of opinion that France should
help Spain in America, but not in Italy; yet he felt that
France should have forced Spain to execute the Convention,
and should even have paid the balance due to England.
She should have postponed the Spanish marriages,
or made them conditional on peace, but Fleury had
cajoled Spain, meaning to close his ministry with all the
éclat of a reconciliation of the house of Bourbon; meantime the nation should prepare for war, and enforce
peace by armed mediation : French trade in America and
the Mediterranean was threatened : at least two-thirds of the
cargoes of the galleons belonged to French subjects : their
seizure would produce universal bankruptcy : the English
colonists in Florida and Jamaica were likely to expand at
the expense of the French possessions : Portugal might be
induced, by promises of Montevideo and by threats of the
bombardment of Lisbon, to invade Spain, whose frontiers
were unprotected : there was no hope of a successful diver-

sion in favour of the Pretender during a war so popular in England; the only danger for George II. lay in the popularity of his own son : Spain should be treated as a child, and forced to peace ; a tender heart and a cold exterior should be the policy of the elder Bourbon line towards the younger. Above all, it was feared that there would be a second volume to the Treaty of Vienna of 1725 ; that the Queen of Spain, tired of the shuffling policy of France, would turn another sudden somersault, and patch up a peace of despair with England, giving another thirty years' lease of the assiento, and drawing the line of demarcation for free navigation such as the English Court proposed. This was the meaning attributed to the phrase of the Queen of Spain that she had found the means to blow the priestling Fleury into the air. The feeling at Paris was intensified by the news of the early English success at Portobello. This important place had been captured with ease, but at the wrong time of the year, for Portobello was the *Nijni Novgorod* of the Indies, and was wealthy only during the season of the fair, when barrels of gold and precious stones were rolled along the quays like common merchandise. It was believed that the English would take all the Spanish American ports, and flood America with cheap goods. " A good thing, too ! " broke out D'Argenson, in the midst of his jeremiad, " why cannot the King of Spain content himself with his customs and his mines, and let other nations supply his Americans cheaply ? " This expression, in fact, pointed to one of the dangers to which Spain was exposed. Everything was in favour of English contraband : the avarice of the Spanish officers, who wished by corruption in the colonies to return and make a show in the mother country, and the convenience both of colonists and Indians, who did not indeed desire the English as masters, but wished to be free of Spanish commercial tyranny.

Fleury had warned the English Government that any occupation of Spanish territory would be regarded as a *casus belli.* He was now induced to threaten, but in a feeble manner ; he represented that France would become annoyed if matters went much farther. But the tide of success was turning. Anson indeed had passed Cape Horn, threatened the coasts of Chili and Peru, and plundered Panama ; the Acapulco ship, the " Hermione," had fallen into his hands, the richest prize on record. But this was more than compensated by the disastrous failure of the English forces at Carthagena and by the discreditable reverse in Cuba. The English force in American waters was in fact annihilated. Exultation was equally great at Paris and Madrid. Depression gave place to exaggerated joy; it was believed that this disaster would be the ruin of a nation hated by all the world. Carthagena would be to England what Syracuse had been to Athens. What a pity, wrote D'Argenson, that our fleets do not unite to invade England and replace some Stuart who will be tolerant. Two French squadrons were now in American waters, and their doubtful attitude increased the difficulties of the English admirals. From henceforth communication with Spain was scarcely interrupted. No impression was made upon the colonies of Spain ; the future conquests of England were to be made at the expense of her French allies. This alliance could not much longer be delayed, for the American war gave place to, or rather was merged in, a great European conflict, the War of Austrian Succession.

DEATH OF THE EMPEROR CHARLES VI.—CLAIMS OF PHILIP AND ELISABETH—WAR OF AUSTRIAN SUCCESSION—THE SPANIARDS IN ITALY—EFFECTS OF FLEURY'S DEATH UPON THE WAR—TREATY OF WORMS—FAMILY COMPACT OF FONTAINEBLEAU—GALLO-SPANISH CAMPAIGNS IN ITALY— DISACCORD BETWEEN FRENCH AND SPANISH COURTS— VAURÉAL'S EMBASSY TO MADRID—HIS CHARACTER OF ELISABETH—D'ARGENSON'S POLICY IN ITALY—SEPARATE CONVENTION BETWEEN FRANCE AND SARDINIA—INDIGNATION IN SPAIN—MISSION OF NOAILLES—DEATH OF PHILIP V.

THE death of the Emperor Charles VI. without male issue had long been looked forward to as the opportunity for the Spanish monarchy to reassert its claims. The king and queen had never concealed their dislike to the Pragmatic Sanction, which secured the succession of Maria Theresa to the possessions of the house of Hapsburg. They had indeed given their guarantee in 1725, when they had expected that the young heiress would marry Elisabeth Farnese's son, but they professed that this was rendered void by the emperor's failure to fulfil the conditions. In the Second Treaty of Vienna the guarantee was by implication involved, but the terms were not clear, and Philip had for some time attempted to obtain the abrogation of the article.[1] He had

---

[1] D'Argenson states that he could not see how the Spanish Court was pledged by the treaty of 1731. Yet this treaty confirmed, with stated exceptions, the Quadruple Alliance and the treaty of 1725, the latter of which included the guarantee of the Pragmatic Sanction.

made this a condition of his accession to the treaty between
France and the emperor in 1739. It was to be expected
therefore that on the death of Charles VI. on October 31,
1740, Philip would press any claims that he might have to
the dominions of the house of Hapsburg. These claims
were sufficiently far-reaching. By virtue of an understanding between Charles V. and his brother, Ferdinand, it was
alleged that the whole of the possessions of the younger
Hapsburg line reverted to the elder on failure of issue male.
A distinct claim was also raised to the kingdoms of Hungary
and Bohemia on the ground that on Rudolph's abdication
the rights of his sister, the queen of Philip III., were
reserved in the event of failure of issue male in the Styrian
line. Such claims, however, could be little more than a
pretext for the attack upon the Austrian possessions in
Italy, which the queen had been urging even before the
emperor's death. The defenceless position of Maria Theresa
made the success of such an attack possible, the sudden
invasion of Silesia by the young King of Prussia seemed to
make it certain.

An immediate landing in Italy was prevented by the
presence of an English squadron, but Neapolitan troops
were pushed up to the Papal States, and a large force was
concentrated along the eastern seaboard of Spain. Early in
December, 1741, Montemar with the first army corps landed
at Orbitello. He had wished to make Sestri his base of operations for an immediate attack on Parma, but was overruled
by Campillo. Valuable time was thus lost, and Charles
Emanuel enabled to complete his preparations. The queen
cared little for the maritime war, and much for the prospect
of an establishment for Don Philip in Italy. She ruffled
the tranquillity of Fleury by crying aloud for the conquest
of Italy, or at least of Parma and Tuscany. She placed
before the cardinal a painful alternative. Either he must
give passage to the Spanish troops, and so abandon his
neutrality, or Spain would make peace with England, and
English ships would convey the Spanish troops to Italy.
Fleury, as usual, adopted half measures, and allowed

Spanish detachments to pass secretly through Southern France. There were frequent rumours of peace between Spain and England, which, indeed, but for the confident hopes of the capture of Carthagena, might have taken place. After the news of the English disaster, Fleury waxed bolder. A Spanish squadron sailed from Cadiz, and formed a junction with a French fleet from Toulon. Admiral Haddock, on preparing to attack the Spaniards, was warned that the French admiral was ordered to protect them. He retired to Port Mahon, and 14,000 Spanish troops were landed on Genoese territory.

Much as heretofore depended upon the attitude of the King of Sardinia. The danger of Maria Theresa placed him in a position of unusual importance, but either system of alliance offered so much that it was difficult to make a choice. Upon the emperor's death, the English Government communicated with the king, calling upon him to help Maria Theresa, in return for a substantial accession of territory in the Milanese. He pointed out that he was not under the obligation of any guarantee, and that the terms offered were not sufficiently high.

France was still at peace with the Court of Vienna, but Fleury was pursuing his policy of dismemberment of the Hapsburg monarchy without declaring war. In the autumn of 1741 he proposed to Charles Emanuel a partition of the Austrian States in Italy between the king and Don Philip.[1] His reticence as to the principle on which the partition was to be made alarmed the prudent Sardinian minister, Ormea, who replied that the pretensions of Spain in Italy were boundless, and might well upset the balance of Italian powers; Tuscany for instance could not resist her, if the Austrian dominions fell to pieces, and there was a danger of Spanish occupation of Corsica; at all events, before entering upon joint action, it was necessary to agree upon a scheme of partition. The king submitted two alternative

[1] In December, 1740, Algarotti had been sent to Turin with similar proposals by the King of Prussia. For an account of this mission see *Arch. Stor. It.*, series iv. vol. xviii.

proposals. To Don Philip were assigned Parma and
Piacenza, Mantua and Cremona, the two latter to revert
to Sardinia if he became King of Naples; the rest of Lombardy would fall to himself. Or Philip might prefer Mantua,
Parma, the territory of Piacenza and Sardinia, with the
royal title, retaining Parma and Sardinia if he succeeded
to Naples. In this case the share of Charles Emanuel would
be the Milanese with the town of Piacenza, and the title of
King of Lombardy. If the Spanish troops moved before the
convention was concluded he threatened to oppose.

It was clear that the expectations of Elisabeth Farnese
for a kingdom of Lombardy were incompatible with those
of Charles Emanuel. He was actuated now rather by his
fears than by his hopes. The Spaniard was becoming a
more dangerous neighbour than the Austrian. The Spanish
troops were ordered to move upon the Milanese. Charles
Emanuel did not oppose them, for his treaty with the Queen
of Hungary was not yet concluded, but he entered a protest
at Versailles and at Madrid. No time was to be lost, and
the king accepted terms which were to all appearance not
too favourable. The Austrian Government consented to
send a sufficient force to protect the Milanese, Modena and
Parma, and Piacenza; while the Sardinian forces acted in
support. This treaty was without prejudice to such claims
as the king might afterwards raise to territorial aggrandisement; they were dormant, but did not lapse.

Meanwhile the Spanish forces, under the Duke of Montemar, effected a junction with the Neapolitans in the Papal
territories, and marched towards the Po. The Duke of
Modena abandoned his capital, and took refuge with the
Spaniards, of whom he assumed the command, much to the
disgust of their general. Charles Emanuel and the Austrians
took Modena and Mirandola, and drove the Spaniards back
on Rimini. The queen was now to realise how difficult of
execution were her Italian projects in the teeth of English
opposition. Success in Italy was the corollary of peace in
the Indies. The English fleet had almost lost importance
in American waters, but the war in Italy gave it new value

in the Mediterranean. Montemar could not move, because he was ordered to wait for the co-operation of Don Philip, who was to attack from Provence with 15,000 Spanish and an equal number of French auxiliaries. Admiral Matthews commanded the Mediterranean, blockaded the French and Spanish ships in Toulon, threatened Naples and Brindisi, and burnt six Spanish galleys in the French port of S. Tropez. Commodore Martin with five ships appeared in the Bay of Naples, and with watch in hand gave the king's ministers an hour in which to sign a convention withdrawing the Neapolitan troops from the Spanish army. The threatened bombardment of Naples was the complement of the action off Cape Passaro. The one lost to Spain the certainty of the Kingdom of Sicily, the other the possibility of a Kingdom of Lombardy. The Neapolitan troops withdrew, and but for the cautious inactivity of the Austro-Sardinian forces it would have gone hard with the Spanish army.

The Spanish prospects in Italy were indeed seriously affected by the Treaty of Breslau.[1] The Kings of Prussia and Poland withdrew from the coalition against Maria Theresa, and the Austrian forces were likely to be largely reinforced for the campaign of 1743. Fleury realised the danger, and entreated the Queen of Spain to win Charles Emanuel. He refused to accede to her terms, and she vowed vengeance against "that brute of Italy," though it should cost all Spain. But could Spain, asked D'Argenson, flatter herself by· the *fanfaronade* of a Montemar to make a conquest in the face of all Europe, which she had failed to make with only the King of Sardinia to resist her? Spain should, he added, be forced to treat ; were he minister, the Austrian possessions in Italy should be offered to Sardinia and the other Italian powers, and Italy cleared of Germans ; the Bourbon powers should turn against England ; the imminent ruin of France and Spain was due to Fleury's cowardice, his want of genius and good faith. The speculations of

---

[1] July 28, 1742. Augustus III. signed at end of September.

D'Argenson were important, for they were soon to become a factor in practical politics. On January 30, 1743, Fleury died, and in the following year D'Argenson became Minister for Foreign Affairs.

Fleury's death or dismissal or resignation had been so long an object of hope and expectation that it took Spain, if not Europe, by surprise. No one was probably more cordially hated by the Queen of Spain than the old fox, the wretched little priest. She would fain have driven a coach-and-four through the treaties and conventions of all Europe, but Fleury had unfailingly applied the drag. He had neutralised the family alliance at the moment of formation by antagonistic ties. He had professed devotion to the legitimate succession and yet was felt to be Philip's most dangerous opponent in the event of his nephew's death. None knew better the strength of the legitimist party in Spain, and no French statesman knew so well the storm which the realisation of its policy would conjure up in Europe. Throughout his ministry he held down the old war party of militant Bourbonism, which would willingly have obeyed the trumpet from whichever of the two Courts it sounded. Pacific as his policy was, his methods were different from those of Walpole. The English minister relied upon abstention, the French upon intricate negotiation. As to the effects of his administration upon France the widest difference of opinion existed, but that of posterity has been far more favourable than that of the cardinal's contemporaries. To Spain he was probably no good friend ; he held the nation in a state of restless suspense, not offering a firm alliance, yet not content with consistent abstention. He infinitely complicated her relations with England, hampering her friendship and yet not supporting her in hostilities. This was doubtless partly due to policy ; he wished to tow Spain in the wake of France, even as Frederick the Great described England as towing the States-General. Yet his half promises and half measures were perhaps in a great degree due to his being constitutionally half hearted. Prime ministers have the same difficulty as ordinary men in making up their minds, and greater opportunities of changing them.

It was certain that Fleury's death would be the signal for a more active policy. The French king was believed to have been fascinated by the wider views of Chauvelin. He was weary of his old tutor, who had grown into a Mayor of the Palace. " Here I am first minister at last " was his exclamation on hearing of Fleury's death.

The Queen of Spain had taken the direction of military operations into her own hands. She superseded Montemar by the younger and more active Gages, whom at the opening of the year 1743 she ordered to attack the enemy within three days. He moved rapidly from Bologna, and attempted to surprise the Austrians in their winter quarters on the Panaro, but was forced back upon Bologna and Rimini. Don Philip, who since Fleury's death had been joined by a contingent of 10,000 French troops, attempted in vain to penetrate into Piedmont, and had to content himself with the occupation of Savoy. The future again depended upon the King of Sardinia. He had felt justified in demanding for his services a price which Maria Theresa, in the intoxication of her success in Germany, was unwilling to give. The French Government renewed its efforts to win him, though seriously hampered by the resistance of the Queen of Spain to cede her son's claims on Lombardy. It is doubtful if Charles Emanuel did more than amuse his enemies by these negotiations, and utilise them for the purpose of putting pressure upon the Court of Vienna. Their whole course was confided to the English Government. In September, 1743, the Sardinian envoy, Ossorio, at the allies' headquarters at Worms, received a despatch from Turin informing him that the French Government had conceded all the king's demands, and that unless England and Austria at once signed the long-delayed treaty, the bearer had instructions to proceed to Paris with full powers to the Sardinian ambassador at the French Court. This ultimatum brought the Court of Vienna to reason ; and on September 13 the Treaty of Worms was signed. Maria

Theresa ceded Vigevano, part of the territories of Pavia and Piacenza and Anghiara. She agreed that Finale should be redeemed from Genoa, for which purpose England was prepared to find the money. The Austrian contingent in Italy, of 30,000 men, was placed under the king's command, while England engaged to furnish subsidies during the continuance of the war. In consideration of these concessions Charles Emanuel withdrew his claims upon the Duchy of Milan. The Spanish Government was more directly affected by the Secret Articles which were attached to the treaty. It was provided that the king's renunciation of Milan should not take effect if an archduke, with right of succession, married a Bourbon. The allies agreed, after the repulse of the Bourbon forces in North Italy, to attack the dominions of Don Carlos, of which Naples and the Presidi should fall to Maria Theresa, and Sicily to Charles Emanuel, who should likewise receive any conquests that might be made in France.

This treaty was followed by the declaration of war by France on Charles Emanuel, on September 30, and on October 25 was signed the Treaty of Fontainebleau between the Courts of France and Spain. Its provisions were of no ordinary kind and calculated to meet no merely temporary crisis. It contained all and more than all that had been comprised in the abortive family treaties of 1721 and 1733. It professed to permanently weld together for defensive or offensive purposes the two branches of the house of Bourbon. The two crowns mutually guaranteed their possessions present or future, they engaged not to lay down their arms nor to enter into negotiations but by common consent. The King of Spain transferred his rights on Milan to Don Philip. To the queen were conceded the Duchies of Parma and Piacenza for her life, with reversion to Don Philip. The contracting powers engaged to force the Pope to place the Queen of Spain in possession of Castro and Ronciglione or to pay compensation. The war should be prosecuted until Charles Emanuel ceded to France the territory annexed to Savoy by the Treaty of Utrecht, and until Gibraltar and Port Mahon had been wrested from England. The formal declaration of war by France against England was the necessary consequence.

Whatever might be the permanent worth of this family compact it appeared to act as an immediate stimulus upon the Bourbon powers. Only a month before the King of Spain had been anxious for peace with England ; he had even thought of resignation in order that his son Ferdinand might effect it with less shame. A fresh impulse was now given to the war. Orders were sent to the French and Spanish squadrons which had been for a year blockaded in Toulon to force their way to sea. In February the combined fleet attacked Admiral Matthews off Hyères. The battle was indecisive ; the English admiral was ill-supported by Lestock, while the French admiral De Court was believed to have robbed his Spanish colleague of a decisive victory. The Spanish fleet bore the brunt of the action and carried off the honours of the day. Stormy weather blew the French into Alicante and the Spaniards into Carthagena, while Admiral Matthews was forced to repair to Minorca to refit. The advantage was with the allies ; they had gained the open sea, and could now convey stores and troops to Italy in comparative safety. There was no chance of reinforcements for the English admiral, for the squadrons from Rochfort and Brest were preparing to convoy the Pretender's son to the English coasts. The utmost vigour characterised the operations in Italy throughout the year. Traun had been superseded by the more adventurous Lobkowitz, who drove the Spaniards back along the Adriatic to the boundary of Naples. Don Carlos abandoned his neutrality and marched to join the Spaniards. Lobkowitz retaliated by rapidly marching across Italy to Rome with the intention of heading the Spanish and Neapolitan forces and gaining Naples. Don Carlos, however, effected his junction with the Spaniards at San Germano and met the Austrians at Velletri. The King of Naples nearly fell a victim to the impetuous attack of Lobkowitz and to his own stolidity. But he saved his kingdom. Throughout the summer the armies lay opposite each other on the hills above the Pontine Marshes, and in November Lobkowitz was forced to retire upon Viterbo and Perugia. Here he was in danger of being cut off by the rapid movements of Gages, but succeeded in making good his retreat into his winter quarters on the Adriatic.

The fighting in the north had been yet more desperate, but had ended to the disadvantage of the Bourbon forces. Don Philip, in the hopes that Genoa would declare against the Austrians, had originally attempted to force his way over the Col di Tenda into Piedmont. But Genoese co-operation was prevented by the English fleet, and after taking Nice and Villefranche the allies found themselves unable to attack the Sardinian positions at Cuneo. Don Philip then changed his plan of campaign, and attempted to turn the Sardinian position by the Val di Stura. With the greatest difficulty he drove the Sardinians back over the mountain passes, and was finally able to form the siege of Cuneo, which alone barred the entrance into the plain of Piedmont. Here, however, the Sardinians stood firm, and at the approach of winter the allies were forced to effect a disastrous retreat into Dauphiné with the loss of half their forces. Meanwhile the threatened invasion of England, from which much was expected, had come to naught, for a storm had scattered the French transports at the moment of execution. Yet the result of the year was by no means wholly unfavourable to the Bourbon cause, for Frederick of Prussia had again declared against the Austrians, and this entailed the weakening of their forces in Italy.

General Gages had fully justified his selection by the Queen of Spain. With the beginning of spring he threatened to take the Modenese from the Austrians, and then by a brilliant series of marches transferred his army across the Apennines to the territory of Genoa, which had now entered into alliance with the Bourbons. General Gages and the Gallo-Spanish army under the infant and Maillebois were thus able to follow a combined plan of operations, with the Genoese seaboard from Genoa to Savona for their basis. General Gages, descending the Scrivia, took Novi and Gavi, while Don Philip, following the Bormida, occupied Acqui, and effected a junction with his ally before Alessandria. The combined armies then fell upon the King of Sardinia's position at Bassignano on the Tanaro, and drove him head-long towards Turin, capturing Valenza, Casale, and Asti, while the Austrians retreated to Novara, unable to make the least show of resistance. It appeared as though the object of the Queen of Spain's ambition were within her grasp. Previously to the battle of Bassignano Spanish detachments had crossed the Apennines and occupied her birthright, Parma and Piacenza, and had secured the passage of the Ticino by the capture of Pavia. The citadels of Alessandria and Asti were blockaded by the allies, and could hardly hold out through the winter. Turin could offer no resistance, and Mantua could alone remain to complete the conquest of Lombardy and Piedmont.

The success already obtained was, however, destined to be the climax of the glory of the Queen of Spain. The situation was more favourable than in the memorable campaign of 1734, for Don Carlos was now firmly established at Naples, and the hated Sardinian rival who had then demanded so large a share of the spoils was now in danger of being made a prisoner in his capital. Maria Theresa was fully occupied. She had indeed recovered Bohemia from the King of Prussia, but Flanders had fallen a prey to the French forces under Marshal Saxe. The death of the emperor, Charles VII., and the election of the Duke of Lorraine, was but a sentimental consolation. There was now little fear of the English fleet, for while Philip was marching on Milan, Charles Edward was on his road to London. Above all, the French and Spanish forces had fought through a year's campaign shoulder to shoulder, and had established a tradition of common victory.

It was, however, in the relations of France and Spain that was again secreted the germ of future failure. The Family Compact of Fontainebleau was meant in sober earnest; it was the work of Louis XV. in person; he had drafted all its details. Intercourse between the two Courts was frequent and affectionate ; it was stimulated by Noailles and by Campo Florido, by the letters of the Spanish dauphine, and of the French infanta. To make assurance doubly sure, Campo Florido was sowing his Spanish dollars broadcast. Madame de Chateauroux, the Duke of Richelieu, perhaps the ministers themselves were among his pensioners. It was said of him that he always stole to bribe, and bribed that he might steal. He had bribed, it was asserted, the Queen of Spain herself, when he was about to be expelled from his viceroyalty of Catalonia for malversation.

The choice of the ambassador to succeed La Marck at Madrid had not been fortunate. Vauréal, Bishop of Rennes, was an ecclesiastic of loose life, but of engaging manners. His lavish display, his eloquence, and his flattery made him a favourite in Court society at Madrid. Yet it is hardly likely that his undercurrent of satire was altogether unobserved. No member of the Court was spared except Montijo. Villarias was worthless, but was the least bad man in the country. Scotti, who was now again much in the queen's confidence, was described as a visionary lunatic, geographer, mathematician, politician, all in one, belonging to all arts and all professions, beginning his conversation with every variety of topic, and ending in dirty anecdotes of his *bonnes fortunes.* Well might D'Argenson reply that Vauréal's portraits were after Rembrandt. No one has painted so dark a picture of the Queen of Spain. The libertine bishop was proof against the charm of voice which had fascinated the Prince of Monaco, and the elegance of figure which had captivated the Duke of S. Simon. Both had perhaps deteriorated. The Italian female voice does not gain in softness with advancing years, and the *embonpoint* of the Farnesi developed readily into corpulence. Yet, allowing for exaggeration, the bishop's correspondence is the most valuable representation of the queen and the surroundings that exists for the last few years of her reign. A balance may perhaps be struck between this and the equally partial but less detailed portrait drawn of Elisabeth by the Duke of Noailles. There could be no question now as to the reality or completeness of the queen's influence. There was but one mind that reigned supreme, and that was hers—there was none that dared make a proposition against her wish. The whole monarchy reduced itself to her single personality, as far as foreign affairs and her personal interests were concerned. Other matters she left to the caprice or ignorance of her ministers, and they were consequently in the greatest disorder. The king had no will apart from his wife. The sole thing she could not persuade him to do would be to declare against France. The queen had always been Austrian at heart and opposed to France. Since the emperor's death her interests had made her change upon the first point, but France she loved none the better. She hated and despised the Spaniards, by whom she knew that she was not loved, but as she hated the French yet more, she affected to extol the Spaniards at their cost. Her character was a compound of ambition, jealousy, and mistrust. It was a common saying that she only loved her children as the objects of her ambition. Never was any one so suspicious; she thought that all men's object was to deceive her. She was to an extraordinary extent, even in the merest trifles, incapable of examination and discussion. If she willed, the object of her will must be taken as passed. This quality was accentuated by an incredibly high opinion of herself. It was in this that her strength consisted; she applied to politics an absolute and inflexible will. It was not enough to wish what she wished, it must be wished when and how she pleased. A curious contradiction was her timidity; fear had a softening influence upon her, she seemed then to be quite another person, she became pliant and insinuating. She had the talent of making her wrongs pathetic, of persuading those who spoke to her that she gave them her complete confidence, and genuine gratitude. In her character all extremes appeared to meet. She would pass from the greatest violence of manner to the most extreme indifference without a moment's interval: anger, prayers, tears, and fits of fury would rapidly succeed each other. With her ambition was mingled a strangely reckless disregard of self. "I have seen the queen in every kind of situation, in her moments of desire, of hope, of fear, yet I have never seen her occupied with her own future. I doubt if she has anywhere in the world 100,000 crowns in cash."[1] Elisabeth's ambition for the future of her children was boundless; for herself she only cared to be absolute in the present.

The king, heavy and dull, sensuous and devout, still adored his wife. He cared for nothing, and would make what use of his senses the queen pleased. His one amusement was to pore over military maps, to follow the movements of his armies, to make imaginary marches, and fight impossible battles. By his side always stood the queen, knowing nothing of diplomacy or war, but giving the decisive word in each. Yet she had still the habit of affecting reference to the king, of submitting her judgment absolutely to his will. On being contradicted by the French minister, she would cry: "I am only a fool, of course; I understand nothing, and it is not my business; there is the king; speak to him". Then, turning to the king, she said: "But speak then, sire, for you put me out of patience. It is always I who have to talk for you; everything falls on me, though I do nothing but repeat what you have determined."[2] At times these little farces would drive the ambassador to distraction, and he would break into savage diatribe: "Apart from her having always hated France, I cannot see that she has a single virtue, except her dull, untempted chastity, of which she has often bragged to me". "But what a number of failings all united in one person;—no sense, no judgment, vanity without dignity, avarice without economy, extravagance without liberality, falseness without finesse, lying without secrecy, violence without courage, weakness without good nature, fear without foresight, no talent but that of mimicry, and no grace; her laugh is excruciating,

¹ Vauréal to D'Argenson, Aug. 20, 1745.   Zevort, 457.
² Vauréal to D'Argenson, Nov. 19, 1745.   Zevort, 458.

her stories enough to knock one down, and her jokes enough to kill one."

In this picture, which is doubtless overdrawn, it is interesting to trace many of the characteristics which Alberoni noticed in the young girl, faults upon which he gravely commented in his intimate correspondence with her father.

The queen's chief associate, if not her first favourite, was Scotti. He knew that the surest way to please the queen was to abuse the French ; yet to the French he was superficially civil, because he knew that Spain could not do without them. The French Government tried to win his favour by conferring upon him the *cordon bleu.* This, however, not only offended the jealous Spanish courtiers, but wounded the dignity of the queen. "No, he is one of my servants," she said, "he does my commissions ; he is not the man for a thing like that." A greater favourite was the Duke of Atri, a determined enemy of the French. He had lately died, and was succeeded in his office of Grand Master by Montijo, an honest man even in Vauréal's opinion ; his only fault was that he was a Spaniard, and could not, therefore, like the French. The queen had given him his office because she could not help herself, and graciously allowed him a half-hour's conversation between 1 and 2 a.m. This was a severe trial to Montijo, who was in the habit of going early to bed, but from the days of Alberoni the queen had not been considerate in this respect.

Between the queen and the French ambassador relations were likely to be strained. The situation was aggravated when in November, 1744, the Marquis d'Argenson became Minister for Foreign Affairs. For the continued alliance of France and Spain no choice could have been more unfortunate. He, as Vauréal, detested Elisabeth Farnese, some of whose qualities he possessed. He was as impatient as she, could see the obstacles to his desires as little. But while her aims were practical, if not always practicable, D'Argenson was eminently an idealist. He was a political prophet rather than a statesman, and hence the extreme interest of his memoirs to posterity. A minister, who was at once free-trader and Republican, and who believed in doctrines of nationality and federative union, flew over the heads of the careful work-a-day diplomats and ministers of the first half of the eighteenth century. Such a man necessarily regarded Spain with some contempt. " I take it that Spain, governed as she is at present, is a child to whom it is necessary to give salutary doses, but great care must be taken not to tell it of what the medicine is composed, for it is a child that cries and howls until it is cured, and then, no doubt, it will be quiet." This metaphor is constantly repeated with variations. Spain must be dosed, or whipped, or led by the hand like a younger sister. D'Argenson had disliked the family alliance, which had seemed to pledge France to the ambitious schemes of Elisabeth Farnese ;[1] he had disliked the Treaty of Fontainebleau, which drew the nations closer together. He had an instinctive feeling that Spain was destined to ruin France. To this effect he would quote the Abbé Regnier :—

> Nos maux ne finiront jamais,
> Le destin de l'Espagne est toujours de nous ruiner,
> Et le sèicle à venir aura peine à juger,
> S'il nous a plus coûté de la vouloir détruire,
> Ou de la vouloir protéger.

He seemed to see in the future the disasters of the Peninsular War, and the quarrel over Spain which led to that of 1870. But above all D'Argenson was opposed to Spanish ambitions in Italy. They ran directly counter to his ideal of European policy and of French interests. There were four monsters he believed to combat whom was the mission of France. These were England, Austria, Spain, and Russia. France was not by interest an ambitious power ; it was her duty to protect rather than to absorb or partition the lesser States, and above all to be the champion of the principle of nationality. Thus he would wish the Austrians and the Spaniards entirely

[1] " We were violently plunged into a close union with Spain, a union which, under the sway of the step-mother, who now rules there, will never be real except at the price of wars, unjust ambitions, and, the most ruinous of all, wars in Italy."—II. 194.

excluded from Italy. For Italy he conceived a federation of native princes and republics, of which the hegemony should rest with the King of Sardinia, who was to be to France in Italy what the King of Prussia was being made to France in Germany. Italy would recover its courage under the banner of Piedmont, where it still survived. France had no interest in making as many crowned heads as Elisabeth Farnese had children. She had insisted on a great establishment for Carlos, now it was the turn of Philip, that of Luis was to come. Yet another principality must form her widow's portion. It was said that she meant to conquer Portugal when she had carved out compensation for the Prince of Brazil in Italy. France had made a great mistake in establishing Don Carlos, let her not repeat it with Don Philip. "Would to God," he wrote, "that we had only worked to leave Italy to the Italians. . . . If the Spaniards had been confined to Spain, France would have done that country better service."

To such a minister the pretensions of Elisabeth were intolerable. Since the Treaty of Fontainebleau she had been ever striving to bind France more closely. The conquest of the Milanese seemed to her the sole object of the alliance. She looked with a jealous eye upon French successes in Germany and French conquests in Flanders. It became necessary to persuade her that the object of the latter was to obtain more favourable terms for Don Philip in Italy. " Avarice, jealousy, ingratitude," wrote Vauréal on April 8, 1745, " are all that we must expect from Spain while governed as she is . . . our king has declared war against all the enemies of Spain, there is no mark of friendship and confidence that he has not given. What is the result? Pretensions have increased with the favours received, want of sympathy for all the interests of France has been unblushingly displayed. The successes of the king in Flanders and Germany have caused the bitterest annoyance ; mistrust and suspicion have increased."[1] Such suspicion was not altogether unjustified.

---

[1] *Rev. des Deux Mondes*, Dec. 15, 1889, p. 725.

D'Argenson was disloyal to the engagements of Fontainebleau. He wished Vauréal to tempt Spain into separate negotiations with England, in order to have an excuse for breaking the tie between France and Spain. Above all Elisabeth feared and suspected his partiality for the house of Savoy. She, as D'Argenson, conceived a federation of Italian princes, to be as far as possible independent of both Spain and France, but she meant the hegemony to rest with the kingdom of the south and not with the petty principality on the Alpine slopes. She hated the King of Sardinia as a rival, but even apart from this she had all the prejudices of her birth, and, as all the petty princes of Italy, had an instinctive dread of the power which was ultimately to absorb them. She early suspected D'Argenson of negotiations with the King of Sardinia, and could even give the date and articles of a Treaty of Turin at a time when, as D'Argenson complained, the French Government was not even on speaking terms with the king, when it did not know him from Adam and Eve. The queen not unnaturally believed that all obstacles were due to D'Argenson; she heard through Campo Florido of his unpopularity in France and strove to overthrow him. Under such circumstances military affairs necessarily suffered. The Spanish forces in Italy were more numerous than the French, and the queen claimed therefore the control of operations. In this she was encouraged by Scotti, who was said to invent false news for her benefit. In the campaign of 1744 Scotti with map in hand had urged the practicability of the passage of the Maritime Alps for horse, foot, and artillery, the mountains were of no height at all. The queen chimed in; she had traversed those same mountains thirty years ago in a *chaise à porteur*; she had recognised that they were perfectly easy for an army and all its train to cross. The events of 1745 produced a dangerous elation. The queen could not realise that the successes of the allies might be but temporary. She could not conceive the possibility of a turn of fortune. "An ambitious woman," writes D'Argenson, "and empty hot-heads had the absolute disposal of operations." She refused to know the weak spots in her naval and military administration, and to recognise the difficulties which stood in the way of her designs.

The plan of operations advised by the veteran Maillebois was to concentrate the troops of both nations on the upper waters of the Po, in the course of the winter to ensure the capture of Alessandria, which would entail the surrender of Charles Emanuel in the early spring. In this plan General Gages and Don Philip himself had fully concurred. But the king's territories were not a portion of the future monarchy of Philip. The queen was impatient, and looked for immediate results. Even before the battle of Bassignano she had insisted on weakening the allied army for the purpose of conquering Parma and Piacenza. "Parma is my country," she urged, "the infant there will be quite at home, the inhabitants remember their old mistress, you will see how we shall be received." [1] The complete success of Philip and the warm reception with which his troops had met justified her prediction, and stimulated her ambitions. It was thus that after Bassignano she insisted that the allies should descend the Po, and occupy Milan itself. This led to an almost open breach. Maillebois, D'Argenson, and his brother, the Minister for War, stoutly resisted. Vauréal expostulated vainly. "I found the queen in such a state of excitement that it was impossible to say two consecutive words, the queen would not let me speak; in her own conversation there was no sequence at all, nothing but phrases begun and never finished, such as: 'We know our own business,' 'They want to lead us like children,' 'Every one must think of himself'. She got out of bed half-an-hour before the usual time, and when the king said that it was too early, she replied: 'I want to get up, you can stay there if you like'. The king seemed to feel awkward, and I thought it better to retire." [2] The queen persisted in her resolution. Gages was ordered to march on Milan, whether he was beaten or not. A feeble contingent was left to Maillebois for the blockade of Alessandria. The advantage which concentration had

---

[1] *Rev. des Deux Mondes*, Dec. 15, 1890, p. 735. [2] *Ibid.*

given to the allies was lost; the French forces were frittered
away in keeping clear their communications with Genoa
and Provence, and in watching the passes of the Alps.

It was this moment that D'Argenson chose for the
realisation of his darling project, a federation of Italian
powers. The outline of the scheme was due to Chauvelin,
who had been willing to give Naples to Don Carlos, but
wished to exclude the French, the Spaniards, and the
Imperialists from Italy. The obstacle to success had been
the greed of Elisabeth Farnese. Would it not be possible
to leave Spain out of the question? The French and
Sardinians would always suffice to drive the Austrians from
Italy. The scheme of D'Argenson contained detailed provisions for a federal Republic on the model of Germany,
Switzerland, and the United Provinces. These comprised
an assembly in the form of the diet to regulate common
interests, the protection of the frontiers at the common
expense, and a federal army of 80,000 men formed from the
contingents of the several States. The command of this
force was intended for the King of Sardinia, as the most
powerful of Italian princes. Such a scheme necessitated a
revision of the map of Italy. The Duchy of Milan was
ceded in imagination to the King of Sardinia. To Don
Philip were assigned Parma and Piacenza, with a strip of
Piedmont along the right bank of the Tanaro. Venice
should receive Mantua, and the State of Genoa should
embrace the coast up to the frontiers of Provence.
Carlos was left in possession of Naples and Sicily, while
Charles of Lorraine should succeed his brother in Tuscany.
This plan was, asserts D'Argenson, sketched by the hand
of the French king, who entered eagerly into his minister's
scheme, which was not only kept entirely secret from the
Court of Madrid, but from the other members of the French
ministry. It was divulged to Charles Emanuel in October,
1745. Charles Emanuel was no idealist. For him general
principles and national enthusiasm had no value. " L'Italia
farà da se" was to him an unmeaning phrase. He had,
complains D'Argenson, the same maxims as Victor Amadeus,

but he lacked his width of view; he preferred a small gain won by rascality to a great prize which might be the result of frankness. He set great store by the *petite finesse Italienne.* At all events the king had no difficulty in pointing out objections to the project. The whole German Empire would resent such an outrage on its traditions; the titles of the Dukes of Savoy rested on imperial grant; such an act of treason would render the house liable to the perpetual fear of confiscation; the essential point was not to contest the right, but to diminish the power of the emperor in Italy; his authority reduced to a mere form would hurt no one, certainly not those who had been long accustomed to it.

Yet time was pressing, and both parties had gone too far to easily withdraw. On the night of December 25-26, with the French agent's post-chaise at the door, a convention was drawn by virtue of which the king agreed to desert the Anglo-Austrian Alliance, on condition of receiving equivalent subsidies from France and Spain. The natural result of this convention was the immediate publication of an armistice. But this produced difficulties which might have been fore-seen. Alessandria was besieged by Spaniards and French alike; and, indeed, the Spanish general, Lasci, was no-minally in command. Moreover, the Spanish forces were marching upon Milan. It was accordingly suggested by the king that the French Government should recommend its generals to suspend hostilities; and D'Argenson, without the knowledge of the Minister of War, ordered Maillebois to abstain from attacking the Sardinians, or even the Austrians, for fear that it should produce a suspicion of bad faith. The agent Champeaux was instructed to inform Charles Emanuel, by word of mouth, that if Spain refused its adhesion to the treaty, Maillebois would withdraw to France, and leave the infant to his fate.

It now became necessary to inform the Spanish Court of the steps which had been taken without its knowledge. D'Argenson proposed that a period of four days should be given to enable it to make up its mind. "Two will be

enough," replied Louis XV. The King of France wrote a
letter to his uncle, explaining the situation; whilst upon
Vauréal devolved the unpleasant duty of unfolding the project
vivâ voce. It was in vain that D'Argenson instructed him
to avoid all that might rouse the temper of the queen, and to
mingle with decision all necessary unction. At the first
mention of the new territorial arrangement, the queen broke
out : "And what of the Treaty of Fontainebleau ? Is there, ·
then, nothing sacred in this world ? What did I tell you ?"
she cried, turning to her husband. "I then saw," wrote
Vauréal, "a sight quite the reverse of what usually happens.
The queen generally takes upon herself to explain the king's
sentiments, while he talks little and unconnectedly. Yesterday the queen, absorbed in grief, did not utter a word, while
the king, as though in a moment transformed into another
man, and as though the news had revived in him all the
feeling of which he is capable, spoke to me in the liveliest
and strongest terms. I dare not repeat his expressions."[1]
The king was even more irritated at the manner than at the
matter of the treaty. He was ordered to sign a treaty,
affecting the fortunes of his son, before he had had time to
read it. His blood mounted to his face ; he was treated, he
said, like a child without sense, who was led along, whip in
hand. "The king, my nephew, takes from me the Milanese
without a word of warning, and if I do not agree he
threatens me. Never has such a thing happened to a King
of Spain. The demand is against my honour, and I cannot
consent." The king spoke loud ; the news passed rapidly
into the street ; Castilian pride was outraged. "As soon as
the news spread all was sackcloth and ashes, and the storm
against the French was terrible." Philip's dignified and
indignant reply to his nephew was followed by an envoy
extraordinary, the Duke of Huescar, whose journey to Paris
attracted the eyes of Europe. On his first interview with
the King of France the envoy was as absolute in his refusal
as had been his master. In the second and third he hinted

---

[1] Vauréal to D'Argenson, Jan. 27, 1746. *Rev. des Deux Mondes*, Jan. 1,
1890, p. 56.

that an arrangement might be possible if the share assigned to Don Philip were larger. So, too, at Madrid, it was becoming clear that resistance was useless, and would but prejudice the infant's cause. The queen had said to Vauréal : " I have had many masses said for the souls in purgatory, they are my good friends ; but I made it a condition that they should inspire my husband with a good resolution ".[1] On March 8 she again sent for the ambassador : " The king and I have not slept all night ; we have done nothing but talk about the treaty, which the most Christian king has signed with the King of Sardinia, and the firmness with which he is resolved to execute it ; we yield at last, and are willing to execute it ".[2]

Consent was now too late. On that very day Asti had opened its gates to the Sardinian troops, and the road was clear to Alessandria. The coincidences were indeed curious. On the day following the night on which the convention between France and Sardinia was signed, the Treaty of Dresden was concluded. This in itself changed the prospects of the King of Sardinia, if only he could gain a little time. The peace with Prussia would enable the emperor to send troops to Italy. Charles Emanuel reflected that he had been too hasty, and began to hedge. He confided the step which he had been forced to take to the British ambassador, who swore to secrecy, and indeed the Court of Vienna was kept in the dark by its ally as to the intentions of the Sardinian king. The further negotiations with France were all explained to the British envoy. The Minister of War pressed for an immediate armistice, and for the permission to revictual Alessandria. The King of Sardinia had gained time, a relieving army was ready, and, owing to the abstention of Maillebois, was within striking distance. The whole negotiation was now disclosed to the imperial ambassador. Forgiveness was readily accorded, and while the Sardinian troops were preparing to attack in front, the Austrian reinforcements were marching on the

---

[1] *Rev. des Deux Mondes*, Jan. 1, 1890, p. 82.   [2] *Ibid.*

rear of the Gallo-Spaniards.   Asti fell, the Spaniards before
Alessandria at once broke up, they believed that they were
betrayed, and that the capture of Asti was a sham.   Both
Gages and the infant expressed their belief to Maillebois
that his astounding want of precaution could only be due to
arrangement.   The breach was open ; it was feared that when
the Imperialists came the Spaniards would throw themselves
into their arms, and join in the extermination of the French.
There was indeed some reason for such suspicion.   England
and Austria were willing enough to tempt Spain to desert
the Family Compact.   It is said that at this very time a
Spanish agent, the Abbé Armandi, was proposing an alliance
between Spain and Austria, by the terms of which Spain
should assist the emperor to recover Silesia, and to wrest
Alsace and Lorraine from France.   It is certain that a little
later negotiations were opened through the medium of the
Genoese ambassador at Madrid, Grimaldi ; but D'Argenson
asserts that this was with the knowledge and consent of
Marshal Noailles.   France was clearly in danger of complete
isolation, and her peril was increased by the final discom-
fiture of the Pretender at Culloden.   It became absolutely
necessary to heal the wounded feelings of the King and
Queen of Spain.   The latter was triumphing in the truth of
her own predictions of French perfidy, and showing ill-
disguised delight in French reverses.

It must be confessed that the *amende honorable* of the
French king was complete.   Orders were sent to Maillebois to
place himself entirely at the disposal of the infant, which obliged
him to abandon his strong position at Novi and expose his
communications to grave risk.   Though D'Argenson was still
nominally minister his personal views were completely neglected, and his despised rival, the Duke of Noailles, was
selected for the special embassy to Spain.   He did not
indeed supersede Vauréal, but took the place of the family
ambassadors of the early years of Philip V.   Noailles was
well received.   Philip saw in him not the envoy of a power
with which he had every reason to be discontent, but an old
friend and comrade.   Noailles in turn was flattered by the

intimacy into which he was admitted, and repaid it by correcting the unflattering portraits which Vauréal had drawn of the king and queen. These are worth reproducing as being the last picture of the family group before it was broken up. " I found the king so changed that I should not have known him if I had not met him in his palace. He is considerably fatter and seems shorter than he was, having great difficulty in standing upright and walking, which is only the result of his total want of exercise. As to his intelligence, it seems much the same ; he has plenty of sense, answers with propriety and precision when one talks on business and when he cares to give himself the trouble. He has forgotten nothing of all that he has done, seen, and read, and speaks of it with the greatest pleasure. There is not a meet in the Forest of Fontainebleau which he does not remember. He is devoted to you, sire, and never speaks of you but with affection and the keenest interest. Every one says that he is more touched at your successes in Flanders than at those of the infant in Italy, and one can truly say that his heart is wholly French. . . . As for the queen, she appears to be intelligent and lively, her replies are *à propos*, and her politeness has an air of distinction. I have not yet had sufficient intercourse to be able to sound her character, but speaking generally I think that the portraits of her have been overdrawn. She is a woman, an ambitious woman, and she fears to be deceived—deceived she has been, and this gives her an air of distrust which she perhaps pushes too far, but I believe a sensible and disinterested man who knew how to gain her confidence could lead her with patience to be quite reasonable in her measures." Noailles and his son well knew how to gain the queen's favour. They were scathing in their sarcasm of the Franco-Sardinian convention. Madman and brute were the mildest terms that they applied to D'Argenson. Noailles in his letters to Louis XV. reprobated the impudence of D'Argenson, whose indecent invectives had all been reported at Madrid, and the injustice of threatening the queen with a rupture if she did not accept a treaty made without her participation and contrary to previous engagements. The fundamental error of all French ambassadors, he wrote, had been the same : they had never taken the trouble to know the country.

The queen, feeling herself to be understood, gladly dwelt upon the grievances of the past and won the heart of the old nobleman. " After all she is a good creature, she has been slandered, look how she honours me with her little confidences."[1] Negotiations went comfortably forward. It was clear that the infant had little chance of Lombardy, but he might find compensation in Piedmont. But at this moment the Spanish Court was subjected to a fresh shock from French perfidy. For some time past the Dutch minister Wassenaer had been discussing with D'Argenson a project for a general pacification. It was likely indeed to prove abortive, for it was kept completely secret from the parties interested, from Spain, from England, and from the emperor. When the proposals became known they were summarily rejected by the two latter powers. Meanwhile the intentions of Wassenaer and D'Argenson had come to the knowledge of the queen, and Noailles had to bear the brunt. " Well," she said on meeting him, " what share do the Dutch give to the infant? It is not considerable from what I hear." Noailles appeared astonished and vowed, not entirely without truth, that he did not know of what she was talking. " Well," the queen replied, " since you are so badly informed, we are glad to tell you that a new proposal for a general peace has been presented by M. de Wassenaer, and that a very slender portion is allotted to the infant."

Shortly after this, Noailles left Spain, hardly knowing whether he had succeeded or failed. But the queen overwhelmed him with politeness, and the parting took place amid mutual expressions of warm affection. His son received the *toison d'or*, and his relation the Duke of Bournonville obtained the command of the Flemish guard, which he had

[1] *Rev. des Deux Mondes*, Feb., 1890, p. 780.

long coveted in vain. The queen fondly hoped that Noailles would be her apologist and supporter at the Court of Versailles. She little thought that she was to cease to be a factor in the political world. Noailles had promised that further negotiations with Sardinia and Holland should not be concealed, and apparently convinced the queen of the necessity of abandoning all hope of Milan or Mantua, on condition that they should not be transferred to the King of Sardinia. Military events contributed to the growing moderation. The infant had narrowly escaped capture in Milan. Castelar was surrounded at Parma, and though rescued by Gages the place fell to the Austrians. Gages was forced after a victory at Codogno to fortify himself at Piacenza. Here at length he was reunited to Maillebois, and the Bourbon armies, taking the offensive, made a spirited attack on the Austrian lines, but without result. This was the last great action of Elisabeth's stormy reign. On the night of July 9, at 1·45, Philip was stricken with apoplexy. He never spoke again and died almost immediately in his wife's arms. Within a few days the dauphine with her newborn baby were likewise dead. Elisabeth had within a week lost the government of Spain and her hopes of future influence in France.[1]

---

[1] "Philip," wrote D'Argenson, v. 16, " died of chagrin and corpulence, which he had contracted by excessive indulgence to his appetite, which was more regular than moderate. He was laborious without doing anything useful. No man has ever given such an example of the misuse of marriage, allowing himself to be ruled by his wife, who ruled him badly. He sometimes groaned under the yoke, but his conscience and his temperament bound him thereto by force. His queen had compelled him to sacrifice the honour and the wealth of Spain to conquer domains in Italy, and God has decreed that she should never enjoy them. The Treaty of Turin excited the king's wrath, but when he witnessed the disasters of his arms regret at not having accepted the treaty in time brought him to his grave."

CHAPTER XXI.

1746-66.

ACCESSION OF FERDINAND VI.—TREATY OF AIX-LA-CHAPELLE
—PARMA AND PIACENZA ARE AWARDED TO DON PHILIP—
ELISABETH'S RETIREMENT AT S. ILDEFONSO—HER IN-
TRIGUES AT THE FRENCH AND SPANISH COURTS—DEATH
OF FERDINAND VI.—ELISABETH'S REGENCY—ARRIVAL OF
CHARLES III. IN SPAIN—FINAL WITHDRAWAL OF ELISA-
BETH FROM COURT—HER DEATH.

THE day of widowhood had been dreaded by the queen,
even before she was a bride. For long years she had lived
in constant terror of the king's death or retirement. Yet
now she was taken by surprise. She was under fifty-five,
was still active in mind, and sound in body, but her life was
ended by the night of July 9. The blow fell at a critical
moment, when the fortunes of her favourite son Philip were
as yet undecided. She hoped against hope to retain his
influence in the Government. The people could hardly
restrain their joy at Philip's death within the bounds of
decency and respect. "It is not easy," said Morosini, "to
describe the inward joy felt by every class of person."[1]
The widow could not mistake the outward manifestations of
dislike which the people had hitherto been forced to conceal.
Yet her step-son treated her with a consideration which was
regarded as evangelical. Contrary to established precedent,
she was allowed to remain in Madrid. Philip's ministers,
Villarias and Ensenada, continued in office.

Elisabeth, however, had to reckon not only with Ferdinand, but with his wife; for it was commonly said that

---

[1] *Relazione*, Nov., 1747.

it was not Ferdinand who had succeeded to Philip, but Barbara to Elisabeth. Italian influence was at an end. "There is only room here for Portuguese and musicians," was the forecast for the present reign. Farinelli could be no longer denied to the new queen; the singer became indeed a power not only in the *salon* but the State.[1] It was certain that Philip's death would influence the continuance of the war. Elisabeth's favourite, General Gages, was recalled, and La Mina, who was opposed to the French alliance, was ordered to withdraw the troops from Italy. Though Ferdinand treated his brother Philip with all kindness, he was relieved of military command. The Austrian Government wished to push its success by re-conquering Naples and Sicily. England, anxious to recover the friendship of Spain under the new *régime*, interposed her offices. Keene was sent to Lisbon, and the Portuguese Court offered its mediation between Spain and the empress. This the queen-dowager did her best to thwart. She prevailed upon Villarias to reject the mediation, and exercised her influence in Portugal to obtain its withdrawal. She was in close communication with France, which, in order to recover the assistance of the Spanish forces, offered to conquer Tuscany for her son. To some extent the desires of the new Government and Elisabeth were at accord. The latter wished her son to be magnificently settled in Italy, the former desired that he should, at all events, be settled out of Spain. His ambitious temper, his French sympathies and French connections, were likely to prove a source of constant irritation were he suffered to return.

Thus opposition to Elisabeth's son led directly to the fulfilment of her desires. The Gallo-Spanish forces re-entered Italy and relieved Genoa, which had revolted from the Austrians, and was now undergoing a protracted siege. Further successes were prevented by the usual want of accord between the generals. The empress, notwithstanding the French successes in the Netherlands, was unwilling

[1] Elisabeth had held the singer strictly to his contract, and had forbidden him to sing before the Prince and Princess of Asturias.

to make further concessions in Italy. But the English and
French Governments concurred in a project for peace which
was embodied in the Treaty of Aix-la-Chapelle; and to this
Maria Theresa and Ferdinand acceded in October, 1748.
Yet Spain was so far wedded to the old system that peace
was accepted with great reluctance. The negotiations had
been delayed by "that old fool Macanaz," as D'Argenson
called the veteran. The peace was regarded as a fresh instance of French desertion; its communication to Carvajal
by Vauréal nearly killed him. But it was the commercial
privileges accorded to England, and not the abandonment
of Italian conquests, that caused dismay, for the face of Spain
was once more turned westwards. Provision was made for
Philip in the Duchies of Parma and Piacenza, and Guastalla.
A second independent Bourbon Court was established in
Italy. Elisabeth's home and heritage were restored to a
descendant of the Farnesi. The object in which her ambition and her sentiment were alike concerned was accom-
plished even after her fall from power. Her success,
however, was not without its cost. Her intrigues in
Portugal had been discovered. Villarias was superseded by
Carvajal, who was Portuguese by origin, and whose sympathies, as befitted a descendant of the house of Lancaster,
were strongly English; in July, 1747, Elisabeth was ordered
to leave Madrid. She was offered the choice of Segovia,
Burgos, and Valladolid as a place of retirement. She preferred, however, the solitude of S. Ildefonso, which was
left to her under her husband's will, and where he himself
was buried. She paid so much respect to his memory,
wrote the English traveller Clarke, as to cry once every year
on the day he died.[1] Yet there seems no reason to doubt
her real attachment. The dullest husband may cause the
liveliest regret.

It did not seem quite certain that Elisabeth's retirement
would be final. The Venetian ambassador, Morosini, informed his Government that her indomitable spirit and the

---

[1] Clarke's *Travels*, p. 327.

personal fascination which she could still exercise when it pleased her were beginning to diminish the effects of her former unpopularity, and he attributed her withdrawal to the jealousy of her step-son and his queen. " This princess, gifted with extraordinary ability, full of life and spirit, extremely prudent in the concealment of her feelings, had the skill in her widowed estate so to behave herself as to convert the unpopularity of former days, not only into a general feeling of compassion, but even into universal affection. This was due to unceasing liberality, and the pleasant welcome which she gave to every sort of visitor. To the charm of her personality was added the consideration that was naturally given to the mother of the heir-apparent, with the result that her receptions were crowded sometimes to the obvious disadvantage of the gathering in the royal palace. The court thus paid to her was disagreeable, especially to the queen, and this was the real cause of her removal, though it was thought desirable to veil it under the decent garb of the laws which do not allow the queen-dowager to reside in the capital. Yet the real reason was founded on jealousy."[1] The outer world was not entirely excluded from the solitude of S. Ildefonso. Noailles kept up his correspondence with Elisabeth, and took care that she should not be forgotten in the French Court. The grandees, he said, regarded her as the mother of their future king. . The old system and the new were represented in the ministry by Ensenada and Carvajal. The latter, writes D'Argenson, was the most learned man in Spain, but for purposes of Court and social life the most stupid in the world. Ensenada had never read a book, but he was quick-witted, not too scrupulous, a man of the world, ruling by his brilliant qualities. He was one of Elisabeth's creatures and Patiño's disciples, full of schemes for the material development of Spain, determined to utilise European complications for expansion in America. It was no light matter that such a minister was loyal to his late mistress, and his position at the head of the Depart-

---

[1] *Relazione*, Nov., 1747.

ments of War, Finance, Marine and the Indies gave him
many opportunities of doing her service.

Yet on only one occasion during Ferdinand's reign did
Elisabeth's name become prominent in affairs of State.
Ruzini, Morosini's successor, in his *Relation* of February,
1754, described her as confining herself to the Château of
S. Ildefonso, which she had chosen among all the cities of
Spain as a most noble voluntary prison-house for the rest of
her life. For eight whole years she had never moved beyond
her rooms. "Though she has no share in the business of
the Court, yet by her magnificent mode of life, her kindly
and agreeable manners, and by certain singular proofs of
intellectual ability, it can be readily seen what she once was,
and what she might still be, but for the chances of fortune."
It was within a few months of this report that Elisabeth's
name came once again before the world.

In 1754 there was, as there had often been before, a
struggle at the Court of Madrid between French and
English influence. On the one side were Keene and the
Spanish minister, Wall, an Irishman, curiously enough,
favourable to British interests ; and on the other the French
ambassador, Duras, and Ensenada. Any Spanish minister,
whose chief interest was colonial development, was necessarily the foe of England, and, consequently, the friend
of France. Ensenada regarded with dislike the English
monopoly of trade with the Spanish colonies. He had tried
to remedy this, but by means which were reasonable and
legitimate. He had supplemented the galleon system, which
was mainly dependent on foreign shippers, by register ships
which, under royal licence, could sail at any time, and thus
gave greater facilities to the smaller native firms. Not content
with this, he encouraged the rivalry of French commerce.
It appears tolerably certain that he made unauthorised
contracts with the French West India Company, and that,
at Brancas' instigation, he planned a joint attack from
Campeachy and Havana upon the English settlement on
the river Walis. Wall had been present in the action off
Cape Passaro, and said that it had never been proved

whether English or Spaniards fired the first shot, and that so too Ensenada hoped to bring the two nations within shot in American waters, and then war would be inevitable. It seems undoubted that Elisabeth had a share in these intrigues. Duras was in the habit of performing the extremely uncomfortable journey to S. Ildefonso on insufficient motives, and on Ensenada's fall papers were found which were said to compromise the queen-dowager. She may have been prompted by the mere excitement of the old diplomatic see-saw that she had so often played, or the clue may be found in her ambition for her children. Luis had been an infant archbishop and a baby cardinal, but he had never become accustomed to the crozier, and his instincts were strictly secular. He resigned the sees of Toledo and Seville, reserving, however, a revenue of £12,400. He had neither his father's military tastes nor his mother's ambitions, but was a keen sportsman and a good mechanic, making watches and mechanical instruments, and spending much time in his splendid aviary at S. Ildefonso. His mother was building a palace for him at Rio Frio, and cardinal as he was he was inclined to give it a mistress. The confessor was persuaded that celibacy was dangerous to a youth of his lively temperament.[1] Marriage implied the renunciation of much pecuniary advantage, and this could only be compensated by a connection with some royal house. Hence Elisabeth entered eagerly into intrigues with the Courts of France and Portugal. She hoped to renew the project of a Franco-Portuguese alliance, and the marriage of Don Luis to the Princess of Brazil was to be the reward, and the conquest of Tuscany the result of the alliance. The King of Naples, it was expected, would acquiesce in her designs. The arrest of Ensenada, however, entailed a second period of forced abstention from politics. Ferdinand after his wife's death went hopelessly out of his mind and died on

---

[1] Don Luis in later years, while chasing a butterfly, fell himself into the meshes of a lovely country maid. The possibility of such a *mésalliance* had never occurred to the Spanish royal mind, and it entailed an alteration of the royal marriage laws.

August 10, 1759.   Under his will Elisabeth was nominated
regent, while her son made his arrangements for the crown
of the Two Sicilies.   She arrived at Madrid on August 17
amid loud and frequent acclamations from the crowd.[1]   The
novelty of her return, the uncertainty of the extent of her
influence over her son, and the expectation of her filling
vacancies in the Church, the army, and the Civil Service,
gave her Court an appearance of splendour and herself an
air of popularity.   During the last reign to slight the queen-
dowager was a passport to favour, and the courtiers who had
done so were now at a loss how to act.   The regency, however, was a disappointment; Elisabeth was placed under
restrictions which were none the less keenly felt for being
disguised.   She professed that she would remove no one
from his post, nor fill vacancies.   She complained that Wall
did not despatch business with her, pretending to attribute
it to his indolence and not to his orders from Naples.   Wall
and his colleague, Prince Yaci, perpetually strove to convince
her that it was impossible to gain additional glory by suggesting even the best of counsels to her son; she had justly,
they said, obtained by the advice given to King Philip that
renown which had stamped immortal fame upon her reputation.   They were aware that her interference in business
could not fail to put her on bad terms with the queen-con-
sort, whose influence over Carlos was such that she
would infallibly carry her own point.   Elisabeth understood
the drift of this advice, which she was little inclined to
follow, and regarded the ministers with consequent dislike.
The courtiers began to fall away, they believed that the
young queen would hasten her husband's voyage, that there
would be a struggle between the regent and the consort, but
that the weight would fall into the scale of the wife.

Elisabeth set workmen to repair Ensenada's palace, which
she intended for her residence, but Amalia wrote to beg that
she would live with them at the Buen Retiro.   This was
regarded as ill-judged.   " It is apprehended," wrote Lord

---

[1] The following account of Elisabeth's last residence at Madrid is mainly
derived from the despatches of Lord Bristol.

Bristol, " that sooner or later some great *éclat* will break out between the two queens, and then the mother will move out of the palace with a bad grace, a step which she might now take with a good and a natural one, for it is scarcely possible for a royal family to be worse lodged than in the Buen Retiro." [1]

On October 17 the new king and queen arrived at Barcelona, and Elisabeth's last lease of power was at an end. It soon became clear that the queen-mother had no share in politics, and her son carefully avoided seeing her alone ; to her great disgust he would not admit her to the Despacho. The young queen showed all filial duty and respect, but she herself had an unreliable temper, and Elisabeth had never learnt to control her tongue. Family jars were constant, and of these Lord Bristol gives a characteristic instance. Queen Amalia had the not uncommon taste for diamonds, which the French Court thought it judicious to turn to good account. The daughter-in-law gleefully showed to Elisabeth the brilliant gift which she received. The queen-dowager coldly admired the setting of the stones, and added that the French Court never made such presents without a further motive. " The king," concluded the ambassador, " is very uneasy, and knowing the character of his mother and his wife, apprehends some unpleasant consequences from the sneers of the parent and the promptness of his consort." [2] The dual control became, as had been anticipated, impossible, and Elisabeth again retired to S. Ildefonso. Her ambition, however, it was believed, had not burnt itself out, for on the disgrace of Wall in 1764, when Grimaldi came into office, Lord Rochford wrote that the queen-dowager would probably intrigue to win the favour of the new minister. Two years after this, on July 20, 1766, she died.

Elisabeth's life was wanting in dramatic completeness, for its climax came too early. For twenty long years it is devoid of political interests, and the materials for her per-

---

[1] Bristol to Pitt, Oct. 8, 1759.   [2] Bristol to Pitt, June 9, 1760.

sonal history are scanty. Occasional references are to be found to her in ambassadors' despatches, or in the works of travellers who visited S. Ildefonso, which was now one of the sights of Spain. The Milanese Kaimo describes her charity to the poor, her liberality to religious foundations, her vain attempt to introduce the products of Italian civilisation into Spanish life. More interesting is a passage in the *Travels* of Dr. Clarke, who visited Spain in 1760-2. He describes Elisabeth as being of middle stature and dark complexion, with great spirit in her countenance. "Though she is now seventy she keeps the same hours that Philip V. did, and turns night into day. When she gives audience she is held up by two supporters, being unable to stand long; and though almost blind, still retains her ancient spirit and vivacity. Her ambition probably will never expire but with her breath, and whenever she dies, I am persuaded that her last words will be : 'Remember Tuscany for Don Luis'." As an old lady, nothing annoyed Elisabeth more than to be told of the last resting-place assigned to her at the Escurial. She would reply that she much preferred not to die at all, but if die she must, she would be buried by her husband at S. Ildefonso, and nowhere else. The termagant found obedience even after death. Any traveller who has seen the pigeon-holes in the Escurial vaults where the Kings and Queens of Spain are laid will enter into the bright Italian's feelings, and will rejoice that, as she was never to return to Italy, she should at least rest in the spot which she had converted into one of the loveliest nooks of Spain.

CONCLUSION.

ESTIMATE OF THE HISTORICAL IMPORTANCE OF ELISABETH'S CAREER.

GALUZZI, the historian of the Grand Duchy of Tuscany, after lamenting the inglorious extinction of the house of Medici in the person of the electress palatine, thus concludes his work : " The Farnese, on the contrary, blessed by heaven with a numerous offspring, and becoming a partner in the government of the kingdom, was able to make herself admired and feared by other powers, was able to repair by her talents the injuries which the crown had been forced to endure in the Treaty of Utrecht ; and, in short, to alter the political system of Europe ". This summary of Elisabeth's career is hardly an exaggeration. It is, indeed, difficult to estimate her influence upon Spain, for it was indirect. The nation never assimilated her, nor she the nation. Her obvious interests were often antagonistic to those of Spain. It was often said that she sacrificed Spain for Italy, the heir for the cadet, that she drained away in alien enterprises the manhood and resources which should have been devoted to the Peninsula and the Indies. Yet if the Spain of 1714 be compared with that of 1746, the nation may look with pride upon the intervening years. It is not every country that needs a Walpole. Spain was, and perhaps is, emphatically a military nation, which decays in peace. Elisabeth found for it adventure, stirred its energies, broke into, not the industrious development of peace, but a profitless *siesta*. The people had been momentarily braced by its war for national existence ; Elisabeth kept alive its flagging energies by artificial stimulants. She did not, as her restored successor, after the War of Independence, allow it to fall asleep

(397)

again on its bare hillside. Whatever her place in Spanish history, her influence upon Europe is beyond question. In European history Italy is often, if not always, in vulgar phrase, the tail that wags the dog. The War of Succession had its American as well as its European issues; but within Europe the possession of Italy was the vital question, and it was the fate of Italy that the Treaty of Utrecht decided. That decision Elisabeth reversed. Italy was by her un-Germanised. That German rule was not for ever expelled was due to her French ally and her Savoyard rival. That the independent dynasties, which she established, ultimately looked to Milan, and beyond it to Vienna, was no fault of hers, but of the French Republic and the French Empire. Elisabeth's selfish schemes were more in consonance with contemporary Italian feeling than were the generous dreams of D'Argenson. Scarce an Italian from Milan to Palermo would have tolerated the military hegemony of Savoy. The Italy of the early part of the eighteenth century was not self-sufficient, and it had no wish to be united. The Spaniard was preferable to the Frenchman, the German, and, above all, to the Savoyard. The Spanish arms were welcomed in Sicily, in Naples, and in Milan; their departure was, on Galuzzi's testimony, bitterly regretted in Tuscany. Moreover, it was no Spanish domination that Elisabeth introduced. She, for her own interests, wished that the cadet branches should be as independent as possible of the Spanish monarchy. Liberation is not synonymous with unity; there are still Germans and Italians who believe it to be antithetical. At all events, Italy must needs be nationalised before it could be united. In destroying the monarchy of Naples and the principality of Parma, Garibaldi and Cavour kicked down the steps by which the heir of Victor Amadeus and Charles Emanuel mounted to the Quirinal. Italy, as well as England, has reason to honour the name Elisabeth.

It is not altogether fanciful to connect the Spanish with the English queen, for in personal character they had something in common. If the halo of virginity hovers round the one head, on the other rests the crown of conjugal fidelity. Both had a somewhat masculine temperament, leading them to prefer men to women. Both were characterised in a high degree by the quality which ambassadors term vivacity and laymen a violent temper. Yet in each case passionate outbreaks had an element of art, or were at least under the control of reason. Both queens finally were shifty in their means, but resolute in their ends.

The life of Elisabeth Farnese as a woman was undramatically dull, in her royal capacity it was a sensational success. The moral to crowned heads is not a good one. It is unnecessary to be educated or even industrious. Unselfishness is disadvantageous. A reputation for bad temper furthers the fulfilment of desire. The end desired must be constantly in sight ; inconsistency has its place only in the choice of means. In the cricket field there was once a maxim that the successful bowler keeps on the wicket, but varies pace and pitch. This in the game of politics is the lesson learnt from the successes of Elisabeth.

APPENDIX.

THE TREATY OF THE ESCURIAL.

CHAPTER XVII., P. 310 NOTE.

By the kindness of Mr. H. W. G. Markheim and Monsieur Louis Farge I have been able to trace the history of the ratification of this Treaty.

The Treaty was signed on Nov. 7, 1733, and upon Nov. 23 Philip V. addressed a letter to Louis XV., with his seal attached, expressing concurrence (Paris, *Arch. Nat. Espagne*, 1733, Nov. et Dec., 408, p. 120). On Dec. 4 the ratifications were despatched from the French Foreign Ministry to Rothembourg (*Ibid.*, p. 140). After their arrival at Madrid there appears to have been some difficulty in procuring the exchange of the ratifications. On Dec. 17 Du Theil, who was acting for Rothembourg, wrote to the French Minister : "En conséquence de l'arrivée des ratifications du Roy que j'annoncay à M. Patiño (interview of Dec. 12) il a fait travailler à celles du Roy Catholique. Elles estoient expediées et signées hier et elles doivent estre échangées ce soir" (*Ibid.*, p. 227 verso). The French Foreign Ministry was, however, becoming anxious ; for the following memorandum was written on the above letter of Du Theil's : "On demande quand M. Patiño voudra qu'elles (les ratifications) s'échangent, le terme étant plein" (*Ibid.*, p. 240). Spanish scruple or indolence was at length overcome, and on Dec. 17 Rothembourg wrote : "M. de Patiño m'a fait dire par mon secrétaire qui vient dans le moment d'échanger les ratifications . . . (p. 247). Je luy (Du Theil) remettray les ratifications pour éviter la dépense inutile d'un courier jusqu'à Paris" (p. 251). Philip in fact signed at Buen Retiro on Dec. 16.

It was within the above dates that the tension between the Courts of Versailles, Madrid, and Turin was becoming marked, and on Nov. 26 Fleury wrote in answer to the remonstrances of the King of Sardinia : "Si notre ambassadeur eut fait quelques difficultés elle (Elisabeth) en eut pris prétexte de rompre et de se tourner du côté de l'Empereur au nom duquel l'Angleterre luy offrait la carte blanche". The Treaty of the Escurial was, indeed, favourable to Elisabeth, but, in view of the repeated English offers and the hated Treaty of Turin, not quite favourable enough ; and this is probably the explanation of the draft for a fresh Treaty, which exists in the Archives (*Espagne*, 408, p. 350), and which more explicitly safeguards the interests of Don Carlos.

SKELETON GENEALOGY SHOWING THE DESCENT OF ELISABETH FROM THE POPE PAUL III. AND THE EMPEROR CHARLES V., AND HER CLAIMS TO THE POSSESSIONS OF THE FARNESI AND THE MEDICI.

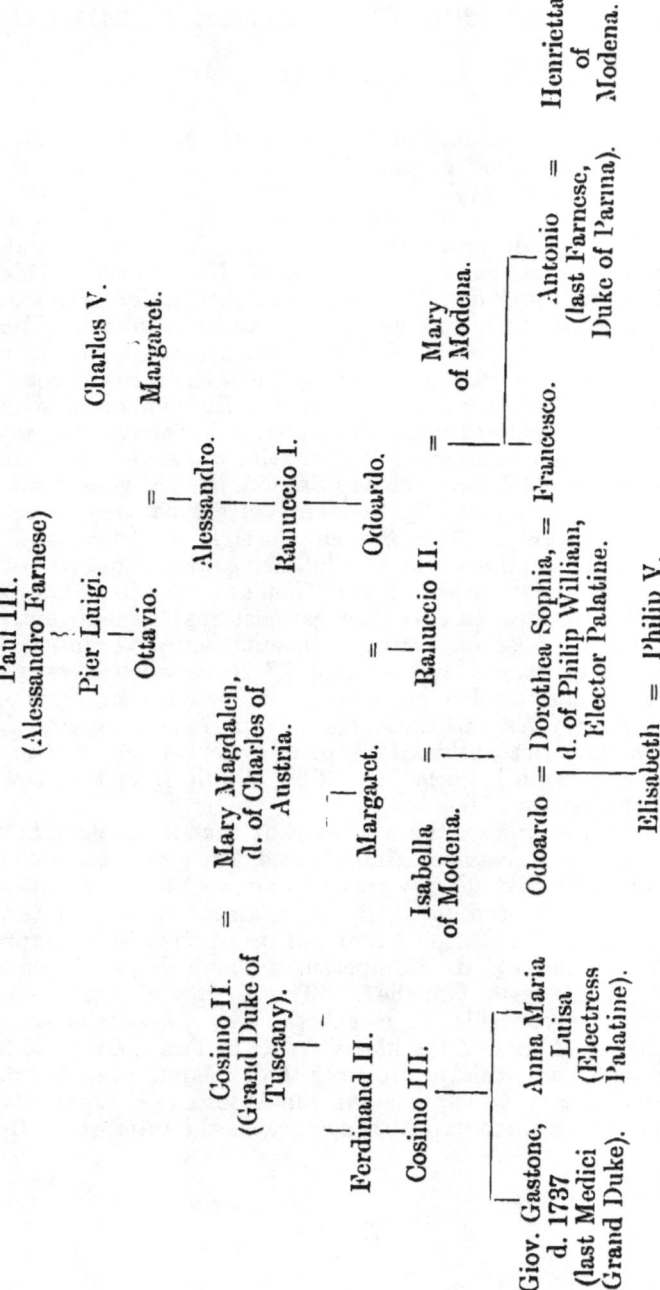

THE CHILDREN OF PHILIP V.

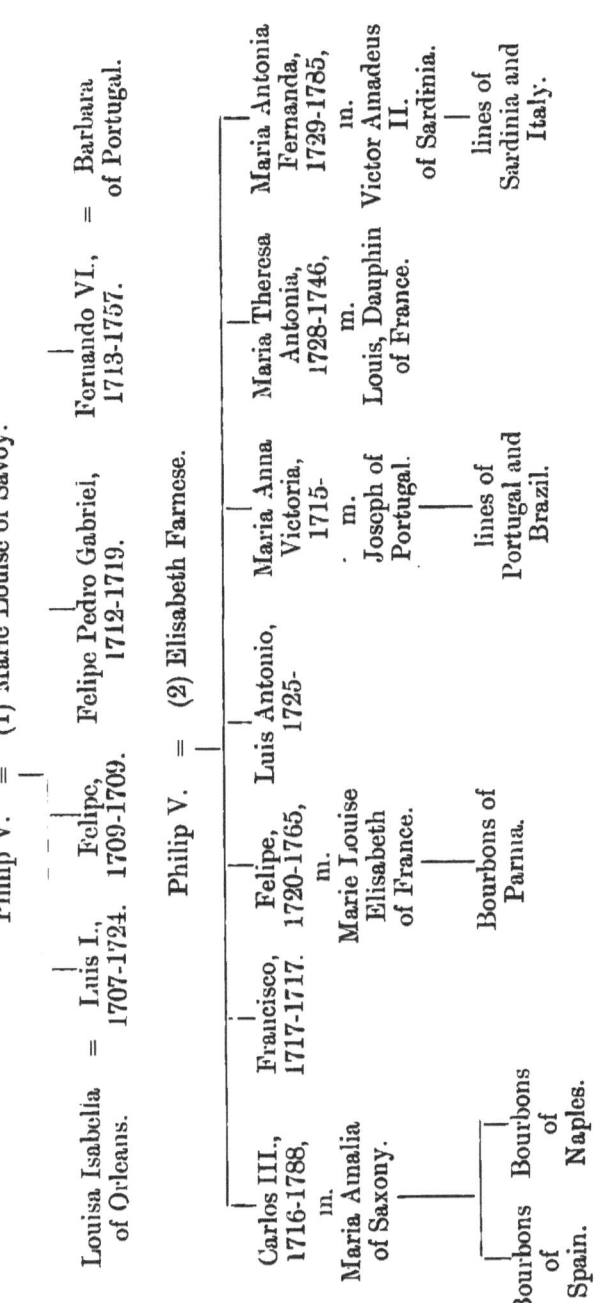

INDEX

INDEX.

A.

Academy of History, 37.

Acquaviva, Cardinal, 15, 21, 320.

Aix-la-Chapelle peace, 352 note, 353 note, 390.

Alberoni, Cardinal, 3 to 183 passim, 188, 193, 200, 201, 214, 263, 273, 323, 328, 329, 330, 331, 333, 358, 375.

Alcabala, Tax of, 82-303.

Alcalá de Henares, 32.

Aldrovandi, Cardinal, 81, 84, 117, 167.

Algarotti, 363 note.

Altamira, Duchess of, 143.

Alva, Duchess of, 157.

Amalia, Queen, see Maria Amalia.

Amelot, 38.

Anne, Princess of England, 133.

Anson, Commodore, 360.

Aranjuez, Palace of, 48, 150, 155 note, 263, 298, 325.

Arco, Duke of, 142, 145, 147, 158, 276, 293, 294.

Armandi, Abbé, 384.

Amida, Bishop of, 196.

Arueth, von, 176, 187 note.

Arriaza, 204.

Assiento, 77, 79, 197, 223, 239, 279, 300.

Asti, 371, 383, 384.

Asturias, Prince of (Luis), see Luis.

Asturias, Prince of (Ferdinand), see Ferdinand VI.

Asturias, Princess of, see Montpensier, Mlle. de.

Asturias, Princess of, see Barbara, Princess of Portugal.

Atri, Duke of, 375.

Avanzini, Pier Antonio, 5.

B.

Badajoz, 264.

Baden Treaty, 50, 95, 99, 132, 180.

Balbazes, de los, Marquis, 22, 24.

Balsain, Palace of, 150, 155 note.

Barbara of Portugal, Princess of Asturias and Queen of Spain, 181, 265, 267, 322, 389.

Barcelona, Siege of, 10, 56 note, 72, 103.

Barrenechea, 223.

Bassignano, Battle of, 371, 379.

Bavaria, Elector of, 12, 227, 290, 304, 327, 342.

Beaujolais, Mlle. de, 135, 178, 292, 293.

Bedmar, Marquis of, 12.

Bolando, 137 note, 141 note, 181, 195.

Belgrad, Capture of, 93, 99, 105.

Bellardi, Filippo, 32 note.

Belmonte, Don Cabral de, 321.

Bermudez, 167, 172, 203, 205.

Berri, Duke of, 55.

Berwick, Duke of, 38, 57, 119, 120, 142, 190, 304.

Bineham, 270 note.

Biscay, Rising in, 115.

Bitonto, Battle of, 304.

Blondel, 239.

Bolingbroke, Viscount, 89, 90.

Bolognesa, 282.

Borgia, Cardinal, 145, 146, 149.

Bourbon, Duke of, 12, 177, 183, 184, 192, 193, 210-214, 261.

Bournonville, Duke of, 167, 216, 223, 245, 246, 311, 313, 386.

Bragadin, 35, 39 note, 103 note, 166, 173, 183 note, 275.

Brancas, Marquis of, 226, 231-238, 244, 245, 251, 267, 392.
Brazil, Princess of, see Maria Auna.
Brazil, Prince of, 377.
Breslau, Treaty of, 365.
Bristol, Earl of, 395.
Bruninx, 132.
Bubb, afterwards Bubb-Dodington, 58, 72-80, 86, 87, 89, 93.
Buen Retiro, Palace of, 61, 120, 148, 394.
Buol, Count, 176 note.
Burke, Chevalier, 61, 152.
Bussy, 250.
Byng, Admiral, 112, 189 note, 350.

C.

Cadiz, Elisabeth's Visit to, 265.
Cagliari, Capture of, 88.
Cambrai, Congress of, 132, 219, 222.
Camilla, 25, 124.
Cammock, Admiral, 136, 159, 189.
Campeachy Bay, 249, 285.
Campillo, 357, 362.
Campo Florido, 325, 328, 335, 358, 372, 378.
Campo Raso, 295 note.
Cantillo, 310 note.
Capua, Siege of, 304.
Caraccioli, Abbé, 216, 324.
Carlos, Don (Prince of Parma, King of Naples, King of Spain), 122, 132, 135, 136, 166, 171, 176, 178 note, 179, 180, 186, 187 note, 206 note, 226-258, 271, 272, 273, 277, 280, 282, 283, 291, 292, 295 note, 296, 298, 303-327, 334, 342, 343, 368, 369, 371, 377, 380, 393, 394.
Caroline, England, Queen of, 342.
Carthagena, 360, 363.
Carvajal, Marquis, 390, 391.
Casale, 371.
Castelar, Marquis of, 38, 103, 163, 196, 204, 208, 226, 243, 250, 251, 254, 256, 262, 277, 279, 281, 283, 291, 292, 315, 323, 330.
Castel, Vetrano, 121.
Castres, Consul General, 351.

Castro, 132.
Catalonia, Disaffection in, 36, 60, 102, 207.
Catherine I., Czarina.
Cayley, Consul, 249, 267, 268.
Cazalla, Visit to, 268.
Cellamare, Prince of, 46, 56, 59, 74, 94, 103, 105, 115, 116, 157.
Cerdagne, 187, 206 note.
Cervi, 108, 328, 333.
Ceuta, 275, 286.
Chalais, Prince of, 15.
Champeaux, 381.
Charles II., King of Spain, 2, 22, 72, 75, 249, 323, 346.
Charles VI., Emperor, 2, 90, 227, 228, 232, 240, 296, 361, 362.
Charles VII., Emperor, 371.
Charles XII., King of Sweden, 106, 107, 114, 118.
Charles Edward, Chevalier S. George, 310, 371.
Charles Emanuel, King of Sardinia, 290, 296, 301, 302, 304, 313, 314, 315, 316, 319, 320, 327, 334, 362-387, 398.
Chateauroux, Madame de, 372.
Chauvelin, 224, 244, 256, 279, 281, 282, 286, 316, 318, 319, 320, 335, 367, 380.
Chavigni, 291.
Chesterfield, Earl of, 232.
Chitty, Mr., 285.
Cienfuegos, Cardinal, 320.
Clarke, Dr., 390, 396.
Clarke, Father, 203, 207, 216, 323.
Clement XI., Pope, 117, 123.
Clermont, Mlle. de, 12.
Cobham, Lord, 121.
Codogno, 387.
Coigny, 305.
Colmero, 84.
Cologne, Elector of, 173.
Commercial Treaty with England, 75, 175.
Conti, Prince of, 119.
Cordero, 99, 100.
Corfu, Siege of, 68.

Correr, 356.
Council of Castile, 35.
Council of Finance, 36.
Council of the Indies, 36.
Council of Marine, 36.
Council of Orders, 35.
Coxe, 206 *note*.
Cruzada, Bull of, 83.
Cuba, 360.
Cucurani, Count, 146, 319.
Culloden, Battle of, 384.
Czar, see Peter the Great.
Czar, see Peter II.
Czarina, see Catherine I.

D.

D'Aitona, Marquis, 18.
D'Albert, Count, 30.
D'Argenson, Marquis, 308 *note*, 319, 332, 343, 353, 357-361 *note*, 365, 366, 372, 375, 376, 378, 379, 380, 381, 384, 385, 386, 387 *note*, 390, 391, 398.
Dataria, Tribunal of, 83.
Daubenton, 52, 60, 69, 81, 113, 121, 122, 130, 133, 135 *note*, 136, 137, 169, 175, 213.
D'Aubigné, 14, 18.
Daun, Marshal, 6, 114, 272, 273.
Dauphin, see Louis XV. and Louis.
Dauphine, see Maria Theresa.
De Court, Admiral, 369.
Delafaye, 218 *note*, 251, 286, 290.
Departmental System, 36.
De Pez, 135.
Despacho, 35.
Donativo, The, 72.
Donaudi, 95, 98.
Dresden, Treaty of, 383.
Dubois, Cardinal, 80, 114, 115, 116, 120, 121, 132, 134, 136, 193.
Duclos, 217.
Duran, 123.
Duras, 392, 393.
De Buys, 192.

E.

Elector Palatine, see Frederick William.

Electress Palatine, 255, 397.
Elisabeth Farnese, *passim*.
Empress, 179, 230, 315, 343.
Ensenada, Marquis, 194, 357, 388, 391-394.
Erizzo, 158 *note*.
Escalona, Duke of, 122.
Escurial, Palace of, 150, 155 *note*, 396.
Escurial, Treaty of, see Family Compact.
Essex, Earl of, 320.
Eugene, Prince, 93, 99, 105, 175, 177, 186, 187 *note*, 198, 202, 206, 209, 216, 225, 226, 228, 229, 237, 238, 240, 250, 255, 261, 263, 291, 305.

F.

Falari, Madame de, 137.
Family, Compact of the Escurial, 276, 299, 300, 301, 302, 307, 308, 315.
Faudino, 348.
Farinelli, Carlo Broschi, 338, 339, 344, 389.
Farnese, Antonio, Duke of Parma, 7, 18, 50, 230, 237, 250.
Farnese, Francesco, see Parma, Duke of, 3, 5, 11, 15, 16, 22, 23, 27, 41, 42, 45, 47, 50, 53, 54, 56, 59, 60, 64-68, 74, 77, 84, 85, 86, 93, 94, 98, 105, 107, 108, 117, 122, 123, 127, 132, 170, 230.
Farnese, Odoardo, 2.
Farnese, Ranuccio II., Duke of Parma, 2.
Farnese, Dorothea Sophia, Duchess of Parma, 2, 3, 252, 255.
Farnese, Henrietta, of Modena, Duchess of Parma, 230, 253, 256.
Farnesi, The, 1-7.
Ferdinand VI., King of Spain, 132, 166, 167, 169, 176, 181, 204, 213, 254, 260, 263, 265, 267, 270, 280, 288, 292, 311, 322, 340, 343, 369, 388, 389, 390, 392, 393.
Ferrol, 194.

Fleury, Cardinal, 122, 157, 193, 203, 210-245, 250, 253, 256, 261, 281, 282, 283, 296, 297, 301, 304, 309, 316, 317, 318, 319, 320, 327, 343, 353, 354, 357, 358, 359, 362, 363, 365, 366, 367.
Florence, Treaty of, 255.
Florida, Blanca, 194.
Fontainebleau, Treaty of, 368, 371, 276, 377, 378, 382, 384.
Franca Villa, 121.
Frederick Augustus I., Elector of Saxony, King of Poland, 295, 297, 348.
Frederick Augustus II., Elector of Saxony, King of Poland, 6, 365 note.
Frederick William I., King of Prussia, 186, 191, 205, 210.
Frederick II., King of Prussia, 362, 363 note, 365, 366, 370, 371, 377.
Frederickshall, 114.
Fuenclara, Count of, 315, 334, 335, 340.
Fuenclara, Countess of, 330.
Fuenterrabia, Siege of, 118, 119, 120.

G.
Gaeta, 304.
Gages, General, 367, 370, 379, 384, 387, 389.
Galuzzi, 258, 397, 398.
Gavi, 370.
Gastañeta, Admiral, 112.
Genoa, Relief of, 389.
George I. of England, 71, 75, 77, 78, 88, 97, 104, 129, 132, 173, 178, 180, 182, 204, 205, 216, 219.
George II. of England, 251, 302, 314, 318, 350, 359.
Georgia, Colony of, 337, 350.
Geraldino, Don (alias Sir Thos. Fitzgerald), 345, 350, 351, 353, 354.
Gerona, 123.
Gibraltar, 72, 92, 97, 114, 121, 128, 129, 136, 171, 174, 180, 182, 183-187, 193, 195, 198, 206, 208, 209, 215 note, 216, 218, 219, 220, 223, 225, 226, 234, 239, 249, 250, 252, 259, 263, 273, 274, 286, 300, 307 note, 308 note, 309, 311, 318, 368.

Girgenti, 112.
Giron, Don Gaspar, 143.
Giudice, Cardinal, 10, 12, 27, 51, 52, 55, 56, 59, 69, 72, 75, 77, 81, 84, 122.
Goertz, 106, 114.
Gozzadini, Cardinal, 15.
Grammont, Duke of, 54.
Granada, Elisabeth's Visit to, 268.
Grimaldi, 384, 395.
Grimaldo, 28, 60, 93, 130, 134, 135, 136, 138, 145, 149, 159, 162, 163, 172, 175, 176, 181, 183, 184, 188, 196, 203.
Guadalajara, 28, 30, 39, 175.
Guastalla, 305.
Guerra, De, 163.
Guevara, 113.
Guipuscoa, 115-119.
Gyllenborg, 106.

H.
Haddock, Admiral, 353, 355, 363.
Hanover, Elector of, see George 1.
Hanover, Treaty of, 186, 188, 192.
Harrington, Earl of, 302, 349.
Hasfeld, Marshal, 119.
Hasse, 344 note.
Havana, 337.
Havrech, Prince of, 102.
Heinsius, Pensionary, 74.
Hercules, The, 265.
Hermione, The, 360.
Higgins, Dr., 245 note.
Holstein, Duke of, 191.
Holzendorf, 161, 189, 192.
Hosier, Admiral, 195, 206.
Huesca, Duke of, 382.
Hulin, 245.
Huraldi, 355.
Huxelles, De Marshal, 119, 210.
Hyères, Battle of, 369.

I.
Incendio, Mutiny on the, 268.
Indies, President of, 163.
Infanta, see Maria Anna and Maria Theresa.
Influenza, The, 268.
Ischia, 303.

J.

Jadraque, 25, 27, 28, 30, 31, 32 *note*.
Jamaica, 183, 147.
Jenkins, 247, 348.
Joseph I., Emperor, 2, 132, 342.
Juros, The, 38 *note*.

K.

Kaimo, 396.
Keene, Sir Benjamin, 3, 163, 185, 189, 199 *note*, 206 *note*, 217-352, 353, 354, 355, 366, 389, 392.
Königsegg, Marshal, 87, 197, 198, 201-240, 259, 261, 263, 305, 316.

L.

La Baume, 320.
La Fare, 135.
La Mancha, 142.
La Marck, 372.
La Mina, 357, 358, 389.
La Quadra, 300, 331, 335, 336, 337, 345, 347, 350, 352, 354.
Landi, Beretti, 103, 114, 127.
Lascaris, 99.
Lasci, General, 381.
Las Nieves, Marchioness, 333.
Law, John, 131.
Lawless, 178.
Lede, Marquis of, 88, 103, 121, 157, 163.
Lerida, 123.
Lestock, 369.
Lezze, Da, 267.
Liria, Duke of, 119, 143, 190, 204, 206, 250, 255, 256, 268 *note*, 276, 293, 295.
Livry, Abbé, 177, 178.
Lobkowitz, 369, 370.
London, Treaty of, 132, 180.
Lorraine, Prince of, Charles, 380.
Lorraine, Prince of, Francis, 180, 312, 371.
Lorraine, Princess of, 319.
Louis XIV., 71, 73, 174.
Louis XV., 134, 160, 177, 206 *note*, 209, 211, 213, 214, 216, 260, 269, 371, 382.

Louis, Dauphin, 292, 319, 343.
Louisa Isabella, Mlle. de Montpensier, Queen of Spain, 134, 164, 168, 178 *note*.
Louville, Marquis of, 69, 70, 80.
Luis Ferdinand I., King of Spain, 17, 32, 49, 51, 58, 108, 131 *note*, 133, 134, 146, 148, 162, 164, 165 *note*, 166, 169, 172.
Luis Antonio, Don, 216, 321, 393, 396.

M.

Macanaz, 20, 36, 51, 60, 81, 124, 137 *note*, 223, 347, 390.
Madame, see Orleans, Duchess of, 54, 168 *note*.
Madrid, Palace of, 322 *note*.
Maffei, 87, 89, 110, 111.
Maggiali, Abbé, 24, 43, 44, 45, 46, 52, 107, 150.
Maillebois, Marshal, 370, 372, 381, 383, 384, 387.
Maine, Duke and Duchess of, 116.
Maintenon, Madame de, 10, 21, 42, 47, 174.
Majorca, Conquest of, 56, 60, 86.
Mantua, Siege of, 305.
Mari, Marquis, 66, 103, 113, 336.
Maria Amalia of Saxony, Queen of Naples, Queen of Spain, 342, 394, 395.
Maria Anna of Neuburg, Dowager Queen of Spain, 2, 22, 23 *note*.
Maria Anna, Infanta of Spain, Princess of Brazil, 134, 177, 178 *note*, 179, 210, 264, 321.
Maria Theresa, Infanta of Spain, Dauphine of France, 319, 343, 372, 387.
Maria Theresa, Archduchess, 176, 179, 181, 186, 187 *note*, 226, 227, 229, 254, 292, 312, 361, 362, 363, 365, 367, 368, 371, 390.
Marie Louise Elizabeth of France, Princess of Parma, 343.
Marischal, Lord, 120, 130, 136.
Maro, Del, 99, 152 *note*.
Martin, Commodore, 365.

Matthews, Admiral, 365, 369.

Massa, Occupation of, 303.

Maulevrier, 135.

Medici, Cardinal, 18.

Medina Celi, Palace of, 9.

Melarede, 98.

Melazzo, 114, 121.

Merci, 121, 305.

Messina, Capture of, 114.

Methuen, 38, 56, 72, 73.

Minorca, 132, 174, 186.

Mirandola, Duke of, 156.

Mirandola, Occupation of, 303, 364.

Miseno, Occupation of, 303.

Modena, Capture of, 364.

Modena, Duke of, 7, 364.

Modena, Henrietta, Princess of, see
Parma, Duchess of.

Molina, Archbishop, 323.

Molines, Cardinal, 84, 85.

Monaco, Prince of, 372.

Monteleone, 78, 183, 203, 272.

Montemar, Duke of, 121, 275, 276,
299, 304, 305, 317, 319, 335, 337,
362, 364, 365, 367.

Montgon, Abbé, 196, 206 *note*, 211-
216, 224, 227, 250 *note*, 260.

Monti, Marquis, 96.

Montijo, Count of, 158, 291, 314, 320,
328, 337, 347, 358, 372, 375.

Montpensier, Mlle. de, see Louisa
Isabella.

Morgan, Capt., 189.

Morosini, 388, 390, 392.

Morville, 192, 212, 213, 224.

Muley, Abdelah, 199 *note*.

N.

Nancré, Marquis of, 96, 97, 113, 114.

Naples, Occupation of, 303, 304.

Navarre, Lower, 187, 206 *note*.

Newcastle, Duke of, 205 *note*, 243,
276, 291, 349.

Newfoundland, Fisheries of, 132.

Noailles, Duke of, 306, 320, 372, 373,
384-387, 391.

Norris, Admiral, 321.

Novi, 370.

Nunciatura, Tribunal of, 83.

O.

Oran, 272-277, 386, 290.

Orbitello, Landing at, 362.

Orendayn, 163, 183, 187 *note*, 188,
191, 192, 197, 202, 203, 207, 216, 262,
293.

Orleans, Duchess of, 10, 54, 168 *note*.

Orleans, Duke of, Regent, 54, 56, 59,
65, 68, 71, 91, 94, 96, 97, 98, 99, 104,
108, 115, 116, 128, 129, 133, 134,
137, 147, 171, 174.

Orleans, Duke of, 177, 192, 193, 242.

Orméa, 291, 363.

Ormond, Duke of, 120, 121, 130, 136,
157, 189, 190, 191, 208, 210.

Orri, 20, 32, 38, 40, 41, 50, 52, 53, 60,
347.

Ossorio, 302, 367.

Ossuna, Duke of, 98, 99.

Ostend Company, 172, 173, 177, 180,
186, 195, 209, 216, 226, 239.

P.

Palermo, Capture of, 110-112, 121.

Palm, Count, 187 *note*, 205.

Panama, 360.

Pardo, The, 13, 48, 155 *note*, 259.

Pardo, Convention of, 221.

Parma, Duchess of, see Farnese,
Dorothea.

Parma, Duchess of, see Farnese,
Henrietta.

Parma, Duke of, see Farnese, Antonio.

Parma, Duke of, see Farnese,
Francesco.

Parma, Duke of, see Farnese, Ranuccio II.

Parma, Occupation of, 257.

Parma, Palace of, 5.

Pasajes, 118.

Passaro, Cape, Battle of, 112, 113, 132.

Passarowitz, Peace of, 105, 114.

Patiño, Don José, 103, 113, 136, 174, 187 *note*, 194, 196, 204, 205, 208, 215, 221, 223, 226, 228, 233, 234, 235-330, 331, 332, 333, 334, 336, 337, 354, 357, 358, 391.

Paul III., Pope, 1.

Paz, Marquis de la, 202, 220, 226, 229, 230, 234, 235, 236, 239, 283, 293, 323.

Pellegrina, La, 266, 325, 326, 333.

Pensacola, 128.

Percival, Lord, 168 *note*.

Perlas, 177.

Pescatori, Laura, 45, 46, 101, 107, 121, 135, 146, 319, 328, 333.

Peter the Great, Czar, 106, 107, 114, 169.

Peter II., Czar, 206, 264, 276 *note*.

Peterborough, Lord, 122.

Peterwardein, 68.

Phastenburg, 176 *note*.

Philip III., 362.

Philip V., *passim*.

Philip, Don, Prince of Parma, 181, 186, 226, 295, 340, 342, 343, 344, 353, 354, 361-371, 377, 379, 380, 382, 389.

Philippines, The, 195, 284, 287.

Philip, William, Elector Palatine, 2.

Piacenza, Palace of, 5.

Piedmont, Prince of, 7.

Pio della Mirandola, Prince, 7, 120.

Piombino, Occupation of, 303.

Piombino, Princess of, 21, 24, 28, 33 *note*.

Pizarro, 357.

Platania, Abbé, 216, 324.

Poggiali, 2, 4, 6, 11.

Poland, ex-King of, see Stanislaus I.

Poland, King of, see Frederick I. and Augustus II.

Polignac, Cardinal, 116.

Pompadour, Marquis of, 116.

Popoli, Duke of, 156.

Port Mahon, 72, 87, 92, 121, 128, 185, 187, 274, 309, 368.

Porto Bello, 195, 206, 359.

Porto-Carrero, Abbé, 116.

Porto Longone, 88, 98.

Portugal, King of, 330.

Portugal, Princess of, see Barbara.

Poyntz, 225, 239.

Pragmatic Sanction, 186, 242, 251, 254, 255, 281, 282, 287, 291, 292, 314, 316, 343, 361.

Pretender, The, 57, 71, 72, 74, 76, 78, 90, 106, 107, 120, 130, 136, 170, 183, 187 *note*, 188, 189, 190, 191, 192, 204, 205 *note*, 206 *note*, 210, 216, 335.

Prie, Mde. de, 193.

Prince Frederick, The, 216, 218, 219, 220.

Procida, Occupation of, 303.

Prussia, King of, see Frederick William I. and Frederick II.

Puerto Rico, 337.

Puntal, Arsenal of, 265.

Q.

Quadruple Alliance, 91, 96, 113, 115, 119, 130, 224, 233, 237, 241, 255, 299, 361 *note*.

Quintana, 346.

R.

Ragotsky, Prince, 105.

Rastadt, Treaty of, 25.

Rebecca, The, 247.

Regnier, Abbé, 376.

Regent, see Orleans.

Resolution, The, 136.

Rialp, 62.

Richelieu, Duke of, 116, 177 *note*, 178 *note*, 195, 196, 198 *note*, 207, 216, 238 *note*, 372.

Ripperdá, 60, 73, 74, 75, 78, 139, 169, 170, 174, 176, 177, 179-204, 210, 216, 238, 259, 263, 282, 328.

Robin, 135.

Robinet, 51.

Robinson, 250, 282.

Rochford, Earl of, 395.

Ronciglione, 132, 368.

Rothembourg, Count, 217-220, 226, 251, 254, 256, 277, 278, 279, 281, 289, 291, 293, 299, 308 *note*, 317.

Roussillon, 187, 206 *note.*
Royal Caroline, The, 286.
Rubi, Viceroy of Sardinia, 88.
Rumbello, Abbé, 320.
Ruzini, 392.

S.

S. Aignan, Duke of, 22, 52, 54, 55, 68, 75, 115.
S. Blas, Duke of, 275.
Santo Buono, Prince of, 157.
Santa Cruz, Marquis of, 142, 145, 158, 179, 223, 275, 276.
San Felipe, Marquis, 84, 88, 104, 124.
S. George, Chevalier, see Charles Edward.
S. Gil, 302.
S. Jean, Pied de Port, 179.
S. Ildefonso, 161-164, 263, 266, 390-396.
S. Pierre, Duke of, 157.
S. Pierre, Duchess of, 27, 157, 165, 266, 333.
S. Saphorin, 91, 176 *note,* 182, 206.
S. Simon, Duke of, 2, 5, 8, 23 *note,* 26, 27, 59, 127, 134, 135, 139, 141, 143, 144, 145 *note,* 148, 150-155, 162, 164, 168 *note,* 178, 179, 236, 325, 372.
Sabine, General, 208 *note,* 249, 286.
Sacramento, 321.
Salazar, 156.
Sandwich, Earl of, 353 *note.*
Santoña, 121.
Sardinia, Conquest of, 86-89, 93, 94.
Sardinia, King of, see Charles Emanuel.
Sardinia, King of, see Vittorio Amadeo.
Sartine, Intendant, 52.
Savoy, Duke of, see Vittorio Amadeo.
Saxe, Marshal, 371.
Saxony, Elector of, see Frederick Augustus I. and II.
Schaub, Sir Luke, 91, 127, 128, 129, 130, 131, 133.
Scotti, Marquis, 21, 25, 121, 122, 123, 127, 128, 129, 130, 131, 135, 138, 159, 160, 163, 166. 169, 170, 186, 266, 328, 333, 372, 375, 378.

Seaforth, Lord, 120.
Sestri Levante, 21, 123.
Seville, 265, 269, 297.
Seville, Treaty of, 224, 239, 240, 241, 242, 244, 246, 249, 250, 251, 279, 281.
Sicily, Invasion of, 110.
Sicily, King of, see Vittorio Amadeo.
Sicily, Occupation of, 304.
Sinzendorf, 176 *note,* 182, 186, 216.
Soissons, Congress of, 222, 223, 300, 245.
Solferino, Duke of, 157.
Solway, The, 285.
Somaglia, Countess, 24, 43, 46.
Somodevilla, see Ensenada.
South Sea Company, 76, 217, 247, 286, 346, 350, 351, 352.
Spinola, 243.
Stair, Earl of, 114.
Stalpart, 192.
Stampa, Count, 272.
Stanhope, Colonel, Earl of Harrington, 93, 96, 104, 118. 120, 131, 134, 135, 136, 161, 178-210, 238, 239.
Stanhope, Earl of, 60, 73, 74, 75, 79, 80, 91, 92, 113, 114, 121, 225.
Stanislaus, King of Poland, 209.
Stewart, Admiral, 248, 285, 286.
Sweden, King of, see Charles XII.
Syracuse, 114.

T.

Tallard, 210.
Tessé, Marquis de, 159, 162, 165, 166, 177.
Theodore, King of Corsica, 199 *note.*
Tinachero, Duke of, 53.
Toledo, Archbishop of, 163.
Torcy, Marquis of, 21, 31, 53, 54, 55, 57, 61, 157.
Torres, Count de las, 208, 209.
Torrenueva, Marquis of, 332, 347.
Tortugas, The, 75.
Townshend, Lord, 181, 185, 188, 190, 225, 241, 242.
Trapani, 114, 304.
Traun, 369.

Triple Alliance, 80, 89, 90, 99.

Tullibardine, Lord, 120.

Turin, Treaty of, 299, 301, 315, 319, 320.

Tuscany, Cosimo III., Grand Duke of, 62, 67, 136.

Tuscany, John Gaston, Grand Duke of, 237, 240, 253, 255, 271, 272, 273, 283, 316, 336.

Tuscany, Leonora, Princess of, 315.

U.

Urgel, Siege of, 120, 126.

Ursins, Mme. des, 8-33, 35, 37, 39, 41, 43, 47, 48, 49, 51, 54, 59, 139, 144, 155, 158.

Ustariz, 347.

Utrecht, Treaty of, 25, 71, 79, 88, 92, 99, 131, 132, 180, 258, 368, 397, 398.

V.

Valenza, 371.

Vandermeer, 191, 197, 209, 231, 241, 284, 300, 314.

Vaulgrenant, 291, 298, 318, 328, 334, 342.

Vauréal, Bishop, 372, 375, 377, 378, 379, 382, 383, 384, 385, 390.

Vienna, Treaty of, 180, 181, 186, 187, 192, 205, 206 *note*, 213, 226, 239, 359.

Vienna, Second Treaty of, 246, 254, 255, 256, 259, 281, 282, 313, 359, 361.

Vienna, Preliminaries of, 216, 221.

Velletri, 321, 369.

Vendôme, Duke of, 10 *note*, 18, 53, 54, 59.

Venier, 309 *note*, 322, 323.

Veraguas, Duke of, 53, 115.

Villarias, 372, 388, 389, 390.

Villars, Duke of, 116, 119, 134, 209, 210, 211, 213, 214, 216, 220, 231, 235, 242, 266, 276, 278, 281, 283, 289, 290, 292, 293, 297, 298, 302, 303, 304.

Vigo, 121.

Vittorio Amadeo, 64, 67, 68, 87, 89, 90, 91, 94, 95, 96, 98, 99, 100, 101, 111, 114, 135, 237, 239, 240, 269, 280, 290, 294, 398.

W.

Wager, Sir Charles, 206, 256.

Waldegrave, Earl of, 277, 292, 357.

Waleff, Baron, 120.

Wales, Princess of, 132.

Walker, Consul, 131.

Wall, Don Ricardo, 392, 395.

Wall, *alias* Savery, 336.

Walpole, Horace, afterwards Lord Walpole, 205 *note*, 206 *note*.

Walpole, Horace, 353 *note*.

Walpole, Sir Robert, 191, 211, 225, 302, 330, 347, 350, 352 *note*, 356, 357, 366.

Wassenaer, 386.

Weber, Dr., 89.

Westminster, Treaty of, 88, 90, 99.

Wharton, Duke of, 189, 190, 208 *note*.

Wightman, General, 120.

Windischgratz, 180.

Worms, Treaty of, 367.

Wüsterhausen, Treaty of, 191 *note*.

Y.

Yaci, Prince, 394.

Z.

Zuminghen, 121.

ABERDEEN UNIVERSITY PRESS.